Praise for *Shattered*

"Dani Pettrey is a name to look for in romantic suspense, and *Shattered* will keep you turning pages until the very end. It should be on your keeper shelf."

—Dee Henderson, best-selling author of *Full Disclosure* and the upcoming *Jennifer: An O'Malley Love Story*

"In *Shattered*, Dani Pettrey rocks it once again with indomitable characters, fierce courage, and cutthroat danger. Sit down, buckle up, and hang on for an avalanche of a story!"

—Ronie Kendig, award-winning author of *Wolfsbane* and *Trinity: Military War Dog*

"*Shattered* is a masterful story that blends suspense and distinct characters into a what-if tale that keeps the reader turning pages and begging for more. Watch Pettrey rise!"

—DiAnn Mills, author of The Chase; www.diannmills.com

"With plenty of action, snappy dialogue, an intriguing mystery, an engaging cast of characters, and enough twists and turns to keep even the most astute suspense lover guessing, *Shattered* is an entertaining read that's sure to please Dani Pettrey's many fans."

—Irene Hannon, bestselling author of the GUARDIANS OF JUSTICE series

"Dani has an uncanny ability to create characters that reach out to grab your heart. It was a pleasure to catch up with them again. I look forward to the next book in the series."

—Lynette Eason, award-winning, bestselling author of *When the Smoke Clears*, Book 1 in the DEADLY REUNIONS series.

Books by Dani Pettrey

Submerged

Shattered

ALASKAN COURAGE
· BOOK TWO ·

SHATTERED

DANI PETTREY

BETHANY HOUSE PUBLISHERS
a division of Baker Publishing Group
Minneapolis, Minnesota

Published by Bethany House Publishers
11400 Hampshire Avenue South
Bloomington, Minnesota 55438
www.bethanyhouse.com

Bethany House Publishers is a division of
Baker Publishing Group, Grand Rapids, Michigan

Printed in the United States of America

Library of Congress Cataloging-in-Publication Data
Pettrey, Dani.
    Shattered / Dani Pettrey.
        p.   cm. — (Alaskan courage ; bk. Two)
    Summary: "Piper McKenna would be overjoyed at the sight of her estranged brother, except that he's covered in blood. She knows he's innocent, but can they prove it?"—Provided by publisher.
    ISBN 978-0-7642-0983-3 (pbk.)
    1. Brothers and sisters—Fiction. 2. Serial murder investigation—Fiction. 3. Alaska—Fiction. 4. Canada—Fiction. I. Title.
PS3616.E89S53 2013
813'.6—dc23   2012035226

Cover design by Koechel Peterson & Associates, Inc., Minneapolis, Minnesota/Gregory Rohm

Author represented by MacGregor Literary, Inc.

13 14 15 16 17 18 19   7 6 5 4 3 2 1

1

Piper bolted upright, sweat dampening her pj's despite December's chill.

What was that?

Her bleary gaze flashed to the clock—1:30—then to Aurora standing like a sentinel at her bedroom door. The husky's white fur rippled down her back, her ears alert.

Piper shifted the tangle of snowflake flannel sheets binding her legs, listening.

There it was again. Creaks echoed along the floorboards below. Heavy steps. Not Kayden's.

Aurora lunged at the door, pawing the battered wood frame. A low growl rumbled through the dog's throat.

Piper got to her feet, ignoring the cold shock of the floor as she crossed the room.

She cracked her door ever so slightly and peered into the darkness.

Another creak echoed from the downstairs hall. The footsteps paused at the base of the stairs.

Aurora whimpered, nudging at the opening with her muzzle.

Piper reached down to grab Aurora's collar but wasn't quick enough. Aurora charged into the hallway.

Piper shot out after her, but her sister pulled her up short— with a rifle in her hand. Kayden released her grasp on Piper and raised her finger to her lips.

They moved down the hall as Aurora barreled down the stairs, growling.

A male grunt sounded below them. Something hit the ground hard.

Kayden aimed her rifle at the chaos below. "Get the lights," she whispered.

Piper flipped the switch.

Aurora stood at attention a foot away from the man on the floor. He pulled his arm away from his face and looked up.

"Reef?" Piper gaped at her brother in horror. "Is that blood?"

∞

Landon Grainger slammed back the shot of rum and let the warm fire crinkle through his chest.

"Looks like you've got some sorrows to drown, Officer." Becky Malone shifted on her stool, leaning in until the spicy scent of her perfume tickled his nose.

He set the empty glass on the bar and signaled the bartender for another. "You have no idea."

She trailed her finger along the rim of her glass. "Oh, I think you'd be surprised how much I know."

Her confident tone startled him. Was he that transparent?

"Heartbreak is no stranger to me."

Landon grimaced. Apparently he *was* that transparent.

"Another shot?" the bartender asked, the bottle poised over Landon's empty glass.

He hesitated, wanting the oblivion, needing it. . . . But it was the needing it that had him wary enough to try to stop his slide. "Better make it a beer." He needed to walk out. Needed to drive home. One beer and he'd call it a night. He shouldn't have entered the bar in the first place, definitely shouldn't linger.

"You know"—Becky scooted closer, her thigh nestling against his—"I find company is a surefire cure for heartbreak."

He'd have asked why she was so certain it was heartache fueling his need to forget but knew the question would only expose him further. If Becky mentioned Piper's name . . .

Piper. Landon gripped the neck of the beer bottle with two fingers and tilted it to his lips. Funny how quickly old habits returned. If he wasn't careful, he'd find himself at the bottom of the slippery slope he was skirting. He'd walked the straight and narrow for too long to let the pain knock him back that far.

"What do ya say?" Becky trailed her fingers down his chest, creating no less burning than the rum had. "I'm real good company."

"I'm sure you are, but . . ."

"Those buts . . ." She shook her head. "They're half your problem."

He took a quick draught of his beer, tossed a ten on the bar, and stood.

Becky cocked her head with a smile. "Is that an invitation?" She swiveled to face him. Her long legs were bare between the fringe of her black jean miniskirt and the tops of her red alligator boots.

"Aren't you a little underdressed for our Alaskan weather?" Thanksgiving was barely past and it was already ten below and snowing. She was a Yancey local. She should have known better.

"Oh, sugar." She got to her feet and smoothed her skirt. "I know how to keep warm."

Warmth sounded good. He'd been cold and alone for far too long, and it was painfully clear that nothing would ever happen with Piper—at least not as far as he was concerned. He bit back the memories of the night's events.

Becky's fingers intertwined with his. "Why don't we take this party somewhere more private?"

" . . . *it would seem like wisdom but for the warning of my heart.*"

Why had he read *The Lord of the Rings* so many times growing up? So many lines were ingrained in his mind.

"Just a few drinks between friends," she said, leading him toward the door.

"And then?" He knew exactly what she anticipated then.

"And then . . ." She grabbed her coat off the rack, pushed

9

open the door lined with tacky red tinsel, and led him into the parking lot.

Tariuk's frigid coastal air slapped the harsh sting of reality across his weathered cheeks.

Becky slipped her arms into her jacket and wrapped them around his waist. "And then . . . we'll see what feels right."

Nothing about this feels right. "I appreciate the offer—"

"But?"

"But . . ." He sighed, glancing at the loosened strand of Christmas lights lifting in the wind, then lashing back against the battered gutter of Hawkings Pub. It wasn't one of Yancey's finer establishments, but on an island as small as Tariuk, it was about as out of the way as he could manage.

She smiled. "I told you those buts are only holding you back."

His cell rang and her eyes shifted to his pocket.

"I've got to take this."

She didn't bothering loosening her hold.

"Grainger."

"It's Tom."

Becky nuzzled against him.

He tried to extricate himself from her hold. "This isn't a good time."

"You can say that again."

"What's going on?"

"There's been a murder."

⬥

Landon downed a couple Tylenol to ward off the headache he knew would be coming and drove with one hand on the wheel while he guzzled what remained of an energy drink. He'd attempted to erase, or at least drown out, the earlier evening's memories, but after a few drinks and a close call with Becky, they only gouged deeper. What had once been an effective form of escape now imprisoned him, cementing in his mind everything he was trying to forget.

He crushed the empty can in his fist.

What was it going to take to forget Piper? To stop the agonizing pain slowly eating away at his insides?

He tossed the crumbled can on the floorboard and accelerated.

The road was empty except for him—a long, dark abyss stretching ahead. He'd been teetering on the brink for a while, but tonight . . . He clamped the wheel, pain spreading through his limbs, his heart. Tonight had pushed him over the edge. Reality had struck like a bolt of lightning.

Watching Piper with Denny Foster at Cole and Bailey's engagement party had made it all so painfully clear. One day it would be Piper's engagement party, Piper's wedding, and he'd be standing on the sidelines forced to watch the woman he loved pledge her life to another.

Ahead, faint whispers of red danced in the overpowering glare of floodlights. Squinting against the assaulting brightness, Landon pulled to a stop beside the patrol car with its lights still swirling. Taking a steadying breath, he stepped from his truck, bracing himself for what lay ahead.

The frozen ground crunched beneath his boots as he made his way past the Midnight Sun Extreme Freeride Competition's temporary headquarters—a series of modular trailers and tents, and on to Trailside Lodge, where the athletes were housed. The normally quaint and sedate wooden-beam lodge was a flurry of activity, and the floodlights only seemed to be heightening the confusion and further fueling the frenzy. A crowd stood outside, gawking at the sheriff and his deputies as they cordoned off the front area with caution tape, effectively corralling the fifty-some guests, probably mostly event competitors—snowboarders and skiers—into a partition along the lodge's main stone entryway.

Deputy Tom Murphy spotted him through the crowd and advanced toward him.

"Whose bright idea was the floodlights?"

Tom cleared his throat and inclined his head toward Sheriff Slidell.

Landon sighed. *Of course.* An elected official with no previous police training, Landon's boss waffled between near noninvolvement on one case to dramatic oversight on the next.

Despite his position, Bill Slidell didn't know the first thing about running a proper crime scene, and it showed, painfully.

"Let's see if we can't cut these lights once we are certain the area's been secured. No need to go scaring folks any more than they already are."

Tom tipped his hat. "You got it."

Landon entered the lobby, surprised at finding a fire still roaring in the large stone hearth and the still-lit Christmas tree. Easily twelve feet high, the giant spruce almost touched the vaulted wood ceiling. The flames reflecting off the decorative silver balls magnified the fire's glow amidst an otherwise empty lobby.

Andy Miner, the owner and manager of the nineteenth-century establishment, stepped from the back room. "Landon, I'm glad you're here. Slidell made all my guests get up and stand out in the cold. It's nearly two in the morning, for goodness' sake."

Landon glanced at Tom.

Tom shrugged. "Boss's orders."

He grimaced. "Let Slidell know once the perimeter's secure there's no harm in letting folks back inside. Tell him they'll be more cooperative and easier to question if they're not freezing to death." *Not to mention easier to keep track of.*

"You got it. Do you want to wait for me or head up on your own?"

"Where's she at?"

"Ladies' restroom, top floor."

"Who's stationed up there?"

Tom cleared his throat. "Slidell wanted us down here, searching."

"So you left the murder scene unmanned?"

"We taped the entrance, and with all the guests out here . . ."

Landon headed for the stairwell, taking the steps two at a time to the seventh floor. His heart pounded in rhythm with the pounding of his boots against the concrete stairs. He preferred to get his blood pumping, his adrenaline going, before entering a crime scene, sort of revving the organ before experiencing the shock of what awaited. He figured that way it wasn't such a jolt to his system—at least not physically.

He exited the stairwell as Tom exited the elevator. "I thought you were going to talk to Slidell about killing the floodlights." Slidell would react far better to Tom's suggestion of bringing the guests inside than his. After the last murder case they'd worked, Landon thought he and his boss were finally finding common ground, but now, with Slidell's reelection campaign in full swing, his boss was becoming more a politician and less a cop with each passing day.

"I am, but there's something you need to know first."

"What's that?"

"I didn't want to say anything in front of Andy, though I'm sure he knows. By now everyone probably knows."

"Everyone knows what?"

Tom rubbed the back of his neck. "The witnesses . . . they say . . ."

"Witnesses?" Could they be that lucky? "They witnessed the murder?"

"Close enough. Walked in on the killer finishing up. Her blood all over him."

It wasn't often that a case caught such a big break. "Run me through what happened."

"One of the athletes said she left something up here earlier in the evening."

"You get her name?" *Please tell me you got her name.*

"Just a sec." Tom fished a small notepad out of his shirt pocket. He flipped it open and scanned the page. "Ashley Clark."

Landon made note of the name. "Go on."

"So she and her friend came back up to retrieve it."

"The friend's name?"

"Tug Williams, also a competitor."

"Okay." Landon jotted down the name.

"They get off the elevator, start down the hall. They hear some commotion coming from the ladies' changing room, so

Ashley pokes her head in. Sees the victim dead in the killer's arms, the murder weapon still in his hands."

"We have the killer in custody?" Why hadn't Tom said so?

"Afraid not. He argued with Tug before ramming past him and Ashley and fleeing the scene."

Argued? "The witnesses knew the suspect?"

"That's correct."

"So who is it?" Why was Tom hedging?

"You aren't going to like it . . ."

A sick feeling roiled through Landon's gut. "A woman's been murdered. I don't like any part of it."

"The killer's Reef McKenna."

Darkness flashed before Landon's eyes. "Reef?" It couldn't be.

"Both witnesses ID'd him."

This will kill Piper. "Has Slidell already put out an APB?"

"Nope. Just set us to work securing the guests and the perimeter."

He doubted Reef had remained on the premises. "Any sign of him?"

"Not a glimmer. You want us to send someone out to his family's place?"

"I'll go." If anyone was going to break it to them, it would be him.

2

Shock reverberated through Piper as she watched her brother scrub blood from his hands.

"I'm going to get Cole," Kayden said, disappearing through the back door before Piper could argue.

"He won't understand." Reef shut off the water and turned to face Piper, blood still smeared across his shirt.

"Of course he will, when you explain." Cole would understand, just as everyone else would. Reef had found the poor woman after she'd already been killed. "Let's get you into a clean shirt. Cole and Gage are always leaving stuff here." She rummaged through the hall cabinet and yanked out a sweatshirt—Landon's UAF sweatshirt that she'd borrowed months ago. Back when they were still . . .

She shut the closet door. She didn't know what they had been then *or* what they were now. Everything seemed inside out between them.

"Here." She tossed it to Reef, despite the strange longing to hold it tight.

"Thanks." He pulled the bloody shirt over his head and tossed it on top of the washer.

Piper hopped up on the dryer, careful to keep her distance from the shirt. There was so much blood soaked into it. She winced at the loss of life, at the pain the poor woman must have suffered. "Tell me again why you didn't call the police," she said as Reef washed the blood that stained his chest. Landon would harp on the fact that Reef hadn't called the police, she just knew it—surely as she knew Landon, or *had* known Landon. Things seemed so different now. *He* seemed so different now. Distant. Edgy. Withdrawn.

"Because I panicked." Reef swiped his chest with a dry rag. "Tug and Ash thought I did it. They wouldn't listen." He pulled on Landon's sweatshirt and stalked back to the kitchen.

Piper hopped down to follow him. "But didn't you explain?"

"I tried, but . . . Wait a minute . . ." His blue eyes narrowed. "You believe me, don't you?" He shook his head. "Of all people, I thought . . ."

Guilt seared her conscience. How could she even for a second believe her brother capable of murder? "Of course I believe you. I'm just trying to understand, so when Landon comes, I can explain it to him." Landon would assume the worst, given the circumstances. If only her brother had called the police.

∞

Verifying the crime scene was indeed secure and that the medical examiner, Booth Powell, was taking charge of the victim's body, Landon headed for the McKennas' property. He figured Reef would run to Piper. She was the one person in the world who'd believe him no matter what.

With a heavy heart, he climbed from his truck and walked the familiar path to her door. No festive occasion would greet him—not even a casual weekly meal. For the first time, he was approaching the McKennas as a law official, and it gave him pause.

Just as he lifted his hand to knock, the front door swung open, the evergreen wreath clanging against the glass.

"Thank goodness you're here." Piper yanked him inside.

Not the welcome he'd been expecting.

She wore a bright-pink set of flannel pajamas with some sort of design he couldn't quite make out in the dim hall light. Her lush amber hair, still mussed from slumber, fell well past her shoulders.

"There's been a terrible misunderstanding," she said as they passed through the front room, where bunches of white and silver balloons still bobbed against the ceiling beside the swags of sparkling streamers. Four hours ago this home had been filled with laughter; now it'd been replaced by heartache.

"I need to speak with Reef."

"He's in the kitchen." She stopped outside the swinging door. "The poor thing is so shaken."

He'd just taken a woman's life—he'd better be shaken up.

Piper laid her hand against his chest, her lithe fingers resting over his heart. *Fitting*, he thought dryly. *It belongs to her.*

"I'm so glad it's you. That you are the one who came to talk to him."

He wasn't there to talk. He was there to arrest. He stepped past her into the kitchen, where the scent of her buttercream frosting still lingered in the air.

Reef sat at the kitchen table. His hands, clasped together on the table's surface, were clean—as was the shirt he'd clearly just slipped on.

Landon looked back at Piper with disappointment. She'd actually helped him clean up evidence?

"What?" She frowned.

"Reef's shirt."

"It's on the washer." She pointed to the laundry room door.

"I need it."

"Why? I told you it's all a big misunderstanding."

"It's evidence, Piper." He strode into the laundry room, exceedingly thankful to find Reef's shirt balled on top of the washer rather than in it.

Snagging a plastic Ziploc bag from the cupboard overhead, he shoved the shirt inside and sealed it before further contamination could occur.

"You're not listening to me, Landon." Piper trailed him back to the kitchen, not an inch from his heels—just as she'd done as a kid. Back then he'd sworn she'd done it just to annoy him. Now she was dead set on getting his attention.

"Reef." Landon stopped at the table's edge. "We need to talk."

Reef lifted his head, his dark-rimmed eyes bloodshot, his expression indicating shock.

Shock at what he'd done, or shock at getting caught?

This wasn't Reef's first run-in with the law, but Landon hoped it was his first taste of death, and hoped even harder that it tasted foul.

"I know that look. I know what you're thinking." Piper positioned herself between Landon and her brother.

He was thinking how badly he wished he could spare her from the pain Reef was going to bring on them all.

"You think Reef had something to do with tonight's accident."

"Accident? Is that what he told you? That there's been an accident?"

"No. I mean the mix-up."

"Mix-up? Piper, a woman's been murdered."

Reef's head lowered, and a guttural moan rumbled in his throat.

Landon stepped around Piper. "Reef, I need you to come with me."

"You're taking him in?"

"Yes."

"But he can explain."

"Great. He can explain at the station."

"Is that necessary?"

"He *fled* the scene of the crime."

"Because—"

Landon held up his hand to silence her. "I need to hear it from Reef."

She turned to her brother. "Tell him."

Landon shook his head. "Hold it. Before you say anything, I need to advise you of your rights. Protocol has to be followed." Landon indicated for Reef to stand, and he did so, his movements tremulous. Landon pulled out the handcuffs. As upset as he was with Reef, the painful fact remained that he was arresting his best friend's baby brother, and it stung.

Reef nodded and turned to accept them.

"You have the right to remain silent. Anything you say can and will be used against you in a court of law."

"What's going on?" The lingering gravel of sleep clung to Cole's voice. He stood in the doorway, his hair tousled, his gaze suddenly shocked wide awake. He stepped inside, and Kayden followed.

"I've got to take Reef in for questioning. He fled the scene of a crime."

"Kayden said a woman's been murdered?"

"That's correct. One of the Freeride competitors. Karli Davis."

"And, Reef"—Cole's eyes darted to his brother—"what happened?"

"I didn't do it," Reef said.

Cole gaped at Landon, confusion marring his brow.

The despair radiating in his friend's eyes cut straight through him. He hated being the one to compound the McKennas' pain. They were family. Maybe not biologically, but they were his family all the same. "I'm taking him to the station. We need to talk."

"Does he need a lawyer?"

"I'd highly recommend it."

3

Landon placed the tape recorder on the interrogation room table and slid into the metal chair opposite Reef.

He cleared his throat, and Reef looked up, a pale shadow of the exuberant hothead he'd been at the engagement party mere hours ago. He sat hunched forward, much as he had at Piper's, his hands clasped on top of the Formica table, his thumbs twitching back and forth.

Slidell remained behind the two-way glass, no doubt keeping a critical eye over the proceedings.

"Let's get started." Landon pressed the Record button and slid the tape player forward. "You've been advised of your rights, Mr. McKenna?"

"Yes."

"And you're waiving your right to an attorney at this time?"

"I am. I didn't do this."

"Why don't you start by telling me what happened?"

"Karli texted and asked if I wanted to have some fun."

"What time was this?"

"Maybe an hour after I left the party."

"Cole and Bailey's engagement party?" It was important to be precise.

"Yeah."

"She texted your cell?"

"Yeah."

"And what was your response?"

"I said why not. Not much else to do around here."

Landon ignored the hometown jab. "Go on."

"I went to her room. We grabbed some beers and headed for the hot tub."

"At the lodge?"

"Yeah. They've got one of those rooftop Jacuzzis. We drank some and hung out in the tub."

"Anyone else up there?"

"Ash and Tug were in the tub when we got there, but then they headed in after maybe fifteen minutes."

"About what time was this?"

"I don't know. . . ."

Landon lifted his chin. "Take your best guess."

"Eleven . . . ?"

"All right, and then what?"

Reef looked down, his hands shifting to his lap. "We decided to call it a night."

"Why?"

Reef cleared his throat. "I was tired of playing her games, so I left."

Games? He'd come back to that. "And went where?"

"Back to my room."

"Can your roommate verify that?"

"Dillon? Nah, he was out for the night before I even got back from Cole's."

"So you go back to your room, and then what?"

"I turned on the TV."

"But that wasn't the end of your night?"

Reef shook his head. "No." The word came out raw.

Landon reclined in his seat. "Why don't you tell me about it?"

Reef stared at the door, then down at his feet. "I went back to see her."

"Why?"

"I felt bad."

Now they were getting somewhere. "About what?"

"Storming off."

Landon straightened. "You stormed off? Had you two fought?"

"We had a disagreement."

"Over what?"

"Her choices."

"Choices that affected you?"

Reef shrugged.

Landon followed a hunch. "You and the lady have a prior relationship?"

"Wouldn't call it a relationship. We hung out."

"How long ago was this?"

"Off and on the past couple seasons."

"So what ended it? Why the split?"

"No split. It wasn't like that."

Landon leaned forward, resting his arm on the table. "So what was it like?"

"I told you. We hung out."

"Sexually?"

Reef nodded once.

Landon followed another hunch. "She hang out sexually with anyone else that you know of?"

Reef looked away, a quick burst of color flaring in his cheeks.

"I'll take that as a yes. You know the names of these other guys?"

"Guy." Reef bit out. "Far as I know."

"And his name?"

"Rick Masterson."

Landon kept his voice even, despite the shock reeling through him. "Rick Masterson, the Freeride circuit promoter?"

Reef sank back. "Yeah."

"Isn't he married? And about a dozen years older?"

"Last I heard."

"So you and Karli fought about her relationship with Rick?"

"Again, *not* a relationship."

"But you fought about him?"

"We didn't fight. We disagreed."

"About her affair with Rick?"

"About the fact that I wasn't interested in being used."

"What did she say to that?"

"I didn't give her a chance to say anything, just left."

"But you went back?"

"Yeah."

"Because you felt bad?"

Reef exhaled, rubbing his hands along his thighs. "Karli never was one to show emotion, but she'd actually teared up. I felt I should go back and . . ."

"And?"

"Make sure she was okay."

"What time was this?"

"I don't know, maybe fifteen minutes later."

"Walk me through what happened."

"I stepped off the elevator and heard her scream."

Landon cocked his head. "You heard Karli scream?"

"Yeah."

"How'd you know it was Karli?"

"Trust me. I've heard her yell enough in competition. Besides, she was the only one up there when I left."

"What did you do?"

"I called her name."

"She answer?"

"No, and I couldn't tell where she was. I called her name again. She didn't answer, but I heard something in the ladies' changing room."

"Define *something*. What specifically did you hear?"

"A thump and some—I don't know—sounds of movement."

Landon nodded, prompting him to continue.

"I announced I was coming in, just in case someone else was in there. . . ."

"And was there?"

"Not that I saw."

"What did you see?"

"Karli." Reef squeezed his eyes shut, his face contorting. "She was lying on the floor, facedown. Blood was . . ." He swallowed. "I thought maybe she fell, slammed her head on something. I bent down and rolled her over, and that's when I saw . . ."

"Saw what?"

Reef swallowed. "That she was dead."

"How'd you know she was dead?"

"Her eyes were wide open. I could just tell. I saw the blood and tried wiping it up."

"Why?"

"I don't know. I was just trying to stop it."

"Stop what?"

"The blood."

"But you said you knew she was already dead?"

"Yeah."

"So why worry about stopping the blood?"

"I don't know, man. I just needed to stop it, but I couldn't. I couldn't help her. I slumped to the floor and pulled her in my arms, and that's when . . ."

"When?" Landon prodded.

"Ash and Tug came in. Ash screamed, and Tug asked what I'd done. I told him. I tried explaining I'd found her like that, but he was freaking out." Reef raked a shaky hand through his hair. "I know I shouldn't have left, but Tug kept yelling 'What'd you do?' I panicked, pushed past him and ran."

"To Piper's?"

"Yeah."

"What did you do when you got there?"

"I scrubbed Karli's blood off my hands while I explained what happened to my sisters. And then you showed up."

"I want to make sure I've got this perfectly clear. You're claiming that you did not kill Karli Davis?"

"No. I told you I found her that way."

"With blood on her chest?"

"Yes."

"What about the weapon?"

Reef blinked, staring off somewhere in the distance. "Weapon?"

24

"The eyewitnesses said you had a weapon in your hand."

His eyes darted back to Landon as if he'd been awakened from a dream. "The knife."

"Yeah. What can you tell me about the knife?"

"I saw it lying there and I picked it up."

"Why?"

"I don't know. It just seemed out of place. I saw it on the floor beside her body, and I picked it up. I dropped it when Ash screamed. Sounded just like Karli's had, all high-pitched and squeaky."

"Before Ash and Tug showed up, did you see anyone else? Anywhere on the floor?"

"No."

"So you heard Karli scream, you heard scuffling, but when you entered the changing rooms you saw no one but Karli?"

"Right."

"You saw no one enter or leave through the changing room door other than you, and then Ash and Tug."

"Right."

Landon leaned forward. "Reef, it's vital to the investigation and best for you if you're completely honest with me."

"I was. You can't honestly think I hurt Karli. Come on, Landon. You know me. You lived with us."

A long time ago. "That may be, but evidence doesn't lie. You can make this a lot easier on yourself and your family if you tell the truth. Lies are only going to hurt those you love." He knew that firsthand.

"I'm not lying. I didn't hurt Karli."

"Karli wasn't hurt, Reef. She was *killed.*"

"I didn't do it. I didn't kill Karli."

Landon glanced back at the two-way glass behind him. He knew what had to be done. Time to rake Reef over the coals, even if he was his best friend's little brother, even if it was the last thing he wanted to do.

"Reef, two witnesses place you at the scene of the crime,

holding the murder weapon, with the victim's blood all over you. Once confronted, you ran and tried to cover up evidence."

"I didn't try to cover up anything."

"You washed critical evidence off your hands."

Reef looked at his hands, fingers splayed. "I was just trying to get her blood off. My friend's blood."

"Your friend? A minute ago you said you were sick of playing her games. That doesn't sound much like a friend."

"We were going through a rough spot, but I cared for her."

"You cared about a girl that was two-timing you with a married man?"

"I told you our relationship wasn't like that."

"I thought you said it wasn't a relationship. That the two of you were just hanging out."

"You know what I mean."

"No, Reef, I don't. Did you and Karli have a relationship or not?"

"I guess, if you want to get technical, yes. We were friends."

"Friends that were sexually involved?"

"Yes."

"So your friend, sleeping with another guy while she's bedding you, didn't bother you?"

"I didn't say that."

"So it did bother you?"

"I wasn't happy about it."

"I imagine not. Did you tell her you weren't happy about it? Was that what caused the breakup?"

"I told you. We didn't *break up*."

"Okay, is that why you hadn't *hung out* for a while?"

"Yes."

"When she texted you tonight, did you think she wanted to start hanging out again?"

"Maybe." Reef scuffed the toe of his boot against the tile floor.

"But Karli wasn't serious about it, at least not serious enough to end her liaison with Rick Masterson. That's what you fought over—right?"

Reef remained silent.

Landon stood, striding as he spoke. "You probably said some things you regretted, you went back to talk with her, it didn't go well, you argued, one thing led to another, and . . ."

Reef slammed his palms on the table. "I didn't kill her!"

4

Landon left the interrogation room and moved into the viewing stall where Slidell and the rest of the deputies on duty had been watching.

Slidell cocked a brow.

Landon sighed. "The evidence points overwhelmingly to Reef, but , . ." A few things nagged at him.

"But nothing," Slidell said. "The evidence points to him. All of it. Two eyewitnesses put him there with the murder weapon in hand. He admitted he and Karli fought earlier. He had means, motive, and opportunity. Reef's our guy."

"But that's just it. He admitted they fought. If he were guilty, why would he incriminate himself like that?" It didn't make sense.

"Guilty conscience."

"Then why not admit to the crime?"

"Penalty would be too steep."

"Perhaps, but . . ."

"Enough buts. It's as clear as day. Karli said something that pushed Reef over the edge, and he killed her. Heat of the moment. It happens."

"It couldn't have been heat of the moment."

"Why not?"

"He had the knife. That shows premeditation."

"So he got mad, went for the knife, came back and killed her.

28

It's happened a thousand times before. Come on, Grainger; get your head in the game. If this is going to be a conflict of interest, I need to know now."

"It won't be." He was simply being thorough. Examining every aspect of what they currently knew—weighing it against the evidence.

"All right, then—let's get this wrapped up."

"I don't think we can expect to have anything wrapped up so soon." There was still a lot of work to be done.

"We've got the killer, and the evidence to prove it. Let's move forward. After last summer's rash of murders, townsfolk need to see swift action, and I intend to give it to them."

He studied his boss. "This rush wouldn't have anything to do with your upcoming election?" An open-and-shut case would certainly boost his chances.

"This *rush*, as you call it," Slidell said, his face threateningly close to Landon's, "is to see a murdered woman's killer behind bars. To let the people of Yancey know they're safe. So book him."

"Without looking at any other suspects?"

"There aren't any other suspects. He did it. Witnesses saw him."

"They didn't actually see him kill her."

"No they didn't see him slit her throat, but we know he did. Based on the overwhelming evidence, it would be irresponsible to hold off on charging him. We can't put a killer back on the streets."

"Of course not."

"Glad you finally see it my way." Slidell stalked from the room.

"Where are you going?"

"To book Reef McKenna for the murder of Karli Davis."

"But there's still work to be done, trace evidence to analyze, people to interview. . . ."

"You go right along working it, but I guarantee all you're going to find are more nails to seal that boy's coffin."

Landon stood in the doorway as Slidell informed Reef he was being charged with Karli's murder.

Reef's eyes filled with tears and disbelief as he struggled to his feet. He gaped at Landon. "I didn't do this. You know I'm not capable of something like this."

"Then the evidence will show it, Reef."

Deputy David Thoreau grasped Reef by the arm at Slidell's bidding. "Let's go, McKenna."

"You know me." Reef hollered at Landon as Thoreau hauled him from the room and down the hall toward the cells. "I didn't do this! I didn't do it!"

Landon stood there, his heart hammering in his throat. How would he tell Cole—and worse yet, Piper?

He entered the station lobby and found the McKenna siblings waiting with expectant eyes, a mixture of hope and fear clouding their vision.

Piper was first to her feet. She took one look at Landon and sucked in a sharp intake of breath.

"I'm sorry." He swallowed—the reflex feeling like shards of glass scraping along his raw throat. "Reef has been charged with the murder of Karli Davis."

"He couldn't have done this. I mean, he's the kid who bawled his eyes out when Old Man Cleary's dog got run over. He couldn't hurt someone like that. He doesn't have it in him."

"The evidence against him is strong."

She stepped toward him, so close her fingertips brushed his. "Evidence can be wrong."

This was going to break her heart, and it pained him to have any part in it. This was Piper. The woman he loved. The woman he wanted to protect above all others. But if Reef was guilty—if he'd murdered Karli Davis—helping Piper see the truth *was* protecting her. "Evidence is impartial."

Her brow creased, and she stared up at him. "You actually believe he's capable of murder?"

"As I said, the evidence against him . . . it's overwhelming." He involuntarily reached for her, aching to comfort her, to somehow fix this, but there was nothing he could do. Emotion had no role in an investigation. It couldn't. He had to work solely by the evidence and not by what he wanted to be true. "I know this is difficult." Boy, how he knew.

"Difficult?" Disbelief filled her beautiful eyes.

It was clear—she expected him to take Reef at his word, but he couldn't. The evidence would prove Reef's guilt or innocence, and right now it unfortunately pointed strikingly to his guilt, as much as Landon wished otherwise.

"What happens now?" Kayden asked.

"Since Reef's been formally charged, there will be an arraignment. Possibly tomorrow, more likely the day after. Give people time to get here." Being situated along the southern tip of the Kodiak archipelago, Tariuk Island and its only town, Yancey, took time to reach. The D.A. or one of his assistants would need to fly down from Anchorage to Kodiak Island and then grab the ferry to Yancey.

"Arraignment," Cole said, raking a hand through his hair. "I can't believe this is happening."

His fiancée, Bailey, wrapped her arm around his waist, and he clutched her to him.

"That's it?" Piper asked. "No looking for other suspects? The investigation is over?"

"I'll continue to pursue the case, of course. There's still work to be done." Just as he'd explained to Slidell, though he feared his boss was right—that all he'd find were more reasons to put Reef away.

"If there's still work to be done, then why did you arrest him?" Kayden asked.

"The evidence was strong enough to warrant the arrest, and Slidell—"

"Of course," Piper said on an exhale. "Slidell's bid for re-election is right around the corner, He wants an open-and-shut case."

Landon sighed. Her discernment was impeccable. "I'm not Slidell. I'll work the case to completion."

"Good." She linked her arms across her chest. "Then you'll find Reef's innocent."

"I hope so." He truly did, but it sure didn't look good.

Landon exited the station shortly after the McKennas left. Or as it turned out, all had left but Cole.

He stood leaning against the grille of Landon's truck, his breath a white vapor in the streetlight-lit night air. He straightened at Landon's approach.

"I thought you were heading home?"

"I wanted to speak with you, alone."

Landon's step hitched. "All right."

"I know you said there's still work to be done, but . . ." Cole swiped a shaky hand over his head. "You spoke with Reef." He looked Landon dead in the eye. "You think he did it, don't you?"

"I never said that."

Cole slumped against the truck bed. "You didn't have to."

"What I *think* doesn't matter. The evidence does, and you have my word that I'll work this case to completion." He wouldn't presume and rest on initial evidence like Slidell. He'd dig deeper. But in the end, he feared the result would be the same. If Reef killed Karli, what he found would only confirm the preliminary evidence.

Cole shook his head. "Things haven't always been good between me and Reef. Actually, things have never been good, but I never thought . . . never imagined . . ." He put a hand to his forehead. "I'm a terrible brother for even entertaining the idea, however remotely, that Reef could be guilty. For not jumping to his adamant defense, like Piper."

"You're a great brother. You're just being realistic and protective."

"Am I?"

"Yes. As head of the family it's your job to protect them."

"So I should be protecting Reef, not doubting him."

"What if you are protecting the rest of your siblings *from* Reef?"

32

5

Landon climbed from his truck and headed for the Trailside Lodge entrance, the brisk December wind biting his cheeks. The lodge was wrapped in an eerie silence, and other than the deputy posted at the front entrance, there was nothing to suggest a murder had occurred. Clear twinkling lights adorned the handful of trees lining the front of the property. Against a still-dark sky that held the promise of snow, they glistened like tiny stars.

Taking a steadying breath, he stepped past Deputy Earl Hansen into the lodge and headed directly for the stairwell and up to the murder scene.

Deputy Jim Vaughn sat on a folding chair posted outside the changing-room door.

"Anyone been in here since Booth removed the body?" he asked.

"No, sir. Everyone followed your orders."

"Thanks, Jim."

"Let me know if you need any assistance."

He liked Jim. Always willing to help. Exactly the kind of man he liked to have serving beside him. "Will do."

Slipping his booties on, Landon stepped through the door. He pulled on his gloves and carefully surveyed the room. Four toilet stalls, three showers. A handful of sinks and a row of lockers with a long wooden bench stretched in front. Tile covered the area from the showers to the sinks with thick rubber matting covering the rest. Tape outlined the exact position of Karli's body on the tile—smack in the center of the showers and sinks, just beyond the lockers.

Landon stared back at the door, the only door in and out, replaying Reef's version of events in his mind. *If* Reef was telling the truth, there was no way the person who killed her could have exited without him seeing.

Even with the shock of finding Karli's body, even if trying to tend to her distracted him, surely he would have seen movement, heard someone exiting the room. The only way Reef's story could be true was if the killer had hidden until Reef and the witnesses left the room.

Landon walked the periphery, studying the possible options—the maintenance closet was small, but there was room enough for a person to hide. The showers, toilet stalls, and even a few of the larger ceiling-to-floor lockers were all possibilities, so to be thorough, Landon would see that full fingerprint and trace evidence analysis were run on each and every one of them, despite Slidell's opposition. *"Waste of taxpayers' money."* He could practically hear the rant now. But none of that mattered. Finding the truth did.

Since they were dealing with a public facility, only evidence of a male's presence would raise any suspicion, and even then explanations existed. Crazy things were known to happen in a room mere steps from a rooftop Jacuzzi. The chances of finding anything of use or significance was a long shot, but the victim and the McKennas deserved no less. In the search for truth, even the improbable deserved attention.

Precision, adherence to rule, and lack of emotional entanglement were the keys to an effective investigation. He couldn't allow his feelings for the McKennas to interfere with the investigation. Otherwise he'd be doing Karli Davis a horrid disservice, not to mention Reef's own family. He hated the pain Reef's actions, if guilty, would cause the McKennas, but it was far better for them to know the truth than to continue believing a lie. And if Reef was a killer, he truly belonged behind bars.

Landon sank down on his haunches beside the tape outline. Karli had been found in her swimsuit, a terry towel bunched on the ground a few feet away.

Had she been in the process of changing when the killer surprised her? During interrogation, Reef had specifically said he tried to wipe up the blood. Had he used the towel to do so? What had his plan been? How had he thought he'd get away with it?

Landon tried to envision a potential sequence of events.

Reef and Karli fought. Reef left in anger. Perhaps rather than returning to his room as he'd claimed, he'd gone in search of a weapon, something to scare Karli with, something with which to finally exert some control over her. Knife in hand, he'd caught her off guard in the changing room. They fought some more, things turned from bad to worse, and he'd killed her.

Landon shook his head with an exhale. Reef had had past run-ins with the law, but so did a lot of angry teens. Did a reckless youth equate with a criminal adult?

Sadly, it often did—but murder? Despite Reef's disrespectful treatment of his family at times, and his irresponsible lifestyle in general, Landon would never have pegged him for a potential killer. But he'd been deceived before. *By his own father.* That trial taught him a hard-and-fast rule—people lie; evidence doesn't. And that was precisely how he had to work the case—by the evidence.

He stood, mentally working back through the timeline.

Reef had left Cole and Bailey's engagement party shortly after 10:00.

Reef's cell showed receipt of a text from Karli at 10:26.

Reef replied at 10:28 that he'd be right up.

Ashley Clark and Tug Williams told Thoreau that they'd been in the hot tub with Reef and Karli from approximately 10:45 to shortly after 11:00.

Reef claimed to have left after he and Karli "disagreed" but that he returned approximately fifteen minutes later, immediately heard Karli's shout, and rushing in, found her dead in the locker room.

Ashley and Tug then discovered Reef with Karli's body shortly after midnight.

Ashley's call to 9-1-1 at 12:05 corresponded perfectly with the timeline. As did the medical examiner's initial estimated time of death being placed between 11:00 and midnight.

Reef was found with the victim, covered in her blood, and as of yet, there was nothing to suggest anyone else had been present. For somebody else to have killed Karli, they would've had to have done it during the fifteen or so minutes Reef was gone. Then the killer would have had to escape before Reef arrived—but that was unlikely since Reef claimed to have heard Karli's scream and sounds of movement—or while Reef, who'd been less than fifteen feet from the only door in and out, was in the changing room.

If Reef hadn't killed Karli, he'd played right into the killer's hands, because Landon had never seen such overwhelming evidence in a murder case, other than when someone was caught in the act of the actual murder.

Deputy Vaughn cleared his throat from the doorway. "We've got a situation."

Landon arched his brows.

"Seems someone broke into Reef's room."

"What?"

Landon followed Vaughn down a flight and along the corridor to where he found Piper wedged between Deputy Thoreau and the door to Reef's room.

"Caught her red-handed," Thoreau said.

"Yeah, you got me. Came for my brother's things. Cuff me now." She held out her hands.

"That won't be necessary." Landon stepped forward and signaled Thoreau to ease off.

"I tried explaining nothing could leave the room, but she won't listen."

Amazing how vexing a five-foot-four woman could be.

"Thanks, David. I'll take it from here."

Thoreau held up his hands. "She's all yours."

Piper planted her hands on her hips as Thoreau stalked down the hall. "And I suppose you're going to tell me the same thing?"

Landon looked up and down the hall to be sure all the other doors were shut tight, that they hadn't gained an audience. He pulled her inside Reef's room and shut the door behind them. "What are you doing here?"

"I came for Reef's stuff."

"That's thoughtful of you, but he can't wear street clothes in jail."

Her eyes narrowed. "You're going to make him wear one of those awful orange jumpsuits?"

"I'm not making him—those are the rules."

"Okay. Fine. Then I'll take his things and keep them at the house for when he comes home."

He lightly grabbed her arm as she started to walk over to Reef's belongings.

She froze at his touch and looked up at him. How was it possible for her to look so amazingly strong yet so vulnerable at the same time? He ached for nothing more than to tug her into his arms, to comfort and protect her in his embrace. She looked exhausted. "Why aren't you home in bed?" The day ahead would prove one of the most difficult she'd faced.

"How could I sleep knowing Reef's in that cell?"

"You can't do anything for him right now. Go home and sleep."

She cocked her head and leaned into him, the scent of her honeysuckle shampoo tickling his nose.

"Why do you smell like"—she took a sniff and stiffened—"women's perfume?"

Becky Malone. He grimaced. "Long story."

"And . . ." She took another sniff, gazing up at him with quizzical eyes. "Smoke?"

Twenty minutes in Hawkings, even as far as possible from the smoking section, and the vapor of smoke still clung to his clothes. A reminder of where he'd been and how easily he'd fallen back into old patterns. "Really long story. You need some sleep. Let me get Jim to drive you home."

"I have my Jeep."

"I'd feel better if someone drove you."

"I'm fine. I'll just grab Reef's belongings and be on my way."

"You can't, Piper. Everything needs to be catalogued."

"Why? What do you think you'll find?"

He opened his mouth.

"Never mind. Don't answer that. I know you won't find anything incriminating, because Reef didn't do anything."

"I hope that's the case."

"But you don't think it is." She took a step closer, and he yearned, physically *ached*, to pull her into his arms, but once again he stifled the urge.

"You *really* think he's capable of murder," she said.

It didn't matter what he thought. All that mattered was the evidence. "If Reef's innocent, the evidence will prove it."

"You know," she said, rising on her tiptoes to look him straight in the eye, "some of us don't need evidence to trust the people we love."

He swallowed, hard. He did. He'd discovered the painful truth that those closest to you had the power to deceive you the most.

∞

After seeing Piper safely on her way, hopefully for what would be the last time that night, Landon sat down with Ashley Clark and Tug Williams in the seating area at the end of the hall, a mere thirty feet from the changing rooms where Karli died. He wanted them situated close to the crime scene, to keep what happened fresh in their minds without directly exposing them to the lingering gore.

"We already told the other cop everything we know," Tug said, slumping down on the couch.

"And we appreciate it. I just need you to go back through it with me."

"Fine." Tug exhaled, rubbing sleep from his eyes. He wore sweats, a thermal Henley, and a pair of sheepskin slippers.

"Why don't we start with you two telling me how you spent your evening?"

"The whole thing or just when everything happened?" Ashley asked. At least she seemed cooperative.

"Let's start at the beginning."

"Well, we finished our runs."

Landon lifted a brow.

"Our practice runs," Tug explained, irritation lacing his voice at having to go back through the information all over again.

"Every competitor is assigned practice times when they can use the runs," Ashley explained. "Tug and I have from four to six."

"And you practiced the whole two hours?"

"Yeah. The competition start isn't far away."

"Will they still hold it . . . considering . . . ?"

"Are you kidding?" Tug laughed. "Rick doesn't stop for any-thing. There could be an avalanche and the event would still go on."

"Rick Masterson?" Landon asked.

"Mmm-hmm." Ashley nodded.

"What can you tell me about him?"

The elevator beeped, and Landon's attention shifted as the doors slid open. Bev Miner, Andy's wife and co-owner of the lodge, stepped off with a tray in hand.

"I thought you could use something warm to drink." She set the tray on the table and lifted the ceramic kettle. "I've got tea or cocoa."

"Bev, that's kind of you," Landon said, "but not necessary. The night's almost gone. You should be in bed."

"Sleep after a woman's been murdered in my home? I'll be lucky if I ever sleep again. Poor dear." She shook her head, her bony fingers wrapped tight around the kettle handle.

He smiled, understanding her uneasiness. "A cup of tea would be great." Coffee would have been better, but any amount of caffeine would help keep him alert through this all-nighter.

"None for me," Tug said, waving Bev off.

"I'll take some cocoa." Ashley leaned forward with a smile.

Bev emptied the contents of the cocoa packet in a mug, filled it with steaming water, and gave it a stir before handing it to Ashley.

"Here you go. You poor dear, having to witness . . ." Bev shook her head. "All I can say is I'm glad he's behind bars. Guess it shouldn't have come as a shock. Reef McKenna has always chased trouble."

Landon sighed. He feared that's precisely what everyone else in town would think, and he hated the pain that gossip would cause Piper. Reef's past troubles had been the actions of an angry and reckless youth—it wouldn't take much for folks in town to believe his rash acts could lead to murder.

"Let me know if you folks need anything else," Bev said, stifling a yawn.

Landon nodded and lifted his cup. "Will do."

Anxious to get the interview back on track, he looked at his notes. He decided to hold off on the questions about Masterson and review some details about the timeline. "So, let's get back to the night's events. Can you think of anything that seemed out of the ordinary?"

They looked at each other, shook their heads, and Ashley answered, "Not really. . . . I just can't believe Reef actually killed her."

"What do you mean *actually*?"

"I don't know." She shrugged. "It's just that the two of them . . . They could really get into some heated arguments."

"Over?"

"Anything. Karli was an opinionated girl. Quite honestly, I'm not surprised she finally ticked off one person too many."

Landon shifted in his chair and studied Tug, considered his earlier flippant, offhanded remarks and his abrasive demeanor. "Did you have a prior relationship with Karli Davis?"

"Me?" Tug straightened, distancing himself from Ashley. "No."

Ashley stared at Tug, her questioning gaze raking over him.

"Are you two involved?" Landon asked, realizing the nerve he'd hit.

Ashley's lips pursed. "Tell him, Tug."

Tug cleared his throat, straightening like a chastised child. "We're involved."

"It'll be a year next month," Ashley added proudly.

"Congratulations." No wonder Tug was so uncomfortable being questioned about another woman. Landon would have to find a time to speak with Tug in private, but for now he just needed the facts pertinent to Karli's murder. Unless Tug had spent one-on-one time with Karli immediately prior to her death, any past relationship or dalliance the two had shared could wait to be revealed at a more discreet time. "Look, I won't keep you two much longer. I just need the facts about last night."

Some of the apprehension faded from Tug's face, but none of the irritation. "Whatever, let's just get this over with."

Landon was liking Tug less and less by the second. "Very well. We were at you two finishing up your practice runs."

"Right," Ashley said. "So we finished practice, put our equipment away, went up to our rooms to shower, and then headed out to grab some dinner."

"Around what time would you say?"

"Sevenish."

Tug pinched the bridge of his nose. "Seriously, it's four in the morning. We train with our coach at seven. We need to get some sleep."

"I understand, and I apologize for keeping you."

"Then don't." Tug perched forward, preparing for flight.

"I understand my questions may seem tedious or appear unwarranted, but I need the whole picture. I'll go as quickly as I can."

"Whatever, dude." Tug sank back.

Ashley quickly continued, knowing her gem of a boyfriend was losing patience. "We ate, then headed up to my room maybe an hour later and watched a movie on pay-per-view."

"Let me guess," Tug said, "you want to know what movie?"

"It'll help confirm the timeline."

"*Invictus*, with Matt Damon."

"You watch the whole thing?"

"Yep." Tug kicked his feet up on the coffee table.

"Then we went to the hot tub," Ashley said, resting her hand on Tug's knee.

"Was anyone else up there?"

"Nope. Just us until Reef and Karli showed."

"When was that? How long do you think you'd been there before they showed?"

Ashley looked at Tug and shrugged. "Maybe a half hour."

"I'd say that's about right."

"What kind of mood would you say Karli and Reef were in?"

Ashley's brows pinched together.

"Happy, tense . . . ?"

"Happy. Karli was sparked."

"Sparked?" That was a new one.

"Tipsy," Ashley clarified.

"Was she drunk?"

"Don't know that I'd go that far, but they brought alcohol with them, so I imagine that's where she was headed."

"Was it unusual for Karli to be drinking?"

Tug laughed, and then quickly attempted to cover it with a cough at Ashley's displeasure. "Sorry, I didn't mean it like that. It's just Karli liked to drink."

"Whenever she wasn't racing," Ashley said.

"Really?"

"Let's just say, Karli liked to push the limits."

"How else?"

"I don't know . . ." Ashley hedged. "I mean she liked to party, moved around a lot, did her own thing."

"She have many friends?"

Ashley looked at Tug, clearly uncomfortable. "She hung around a lot of different people."

"But wasn't close with any?"

"Depends on your definition of close." Tug snorted.

Ashley rolled her eyes.

"You're saying Karli slept around?"

"Oh yeah."

Ashley swatted Tug—this time garnering a slight grunt of pain.

"What?" He rubbed his side with annoyance. "It's the truth."

"I know . . . It's just . . ." Ashley bit her bottom lip. "She's dead."

"I understand you don't want to speak ill of Karli considering the circumstances. But the kindest thing you can do for Karli is to tell it to me straight. Keeping secrets only slows the process. Trust me—in the end the truth always comes out." Painful as it may be. "Best to just get it all out in the open from the start."

Ashley sighed. "All right. Yes. Karli slept around."

"I'm going to need names." Landon pulled his notepad from his shirt pocket.

Tug chuckled. "You're going to need a longer sheet of paper."

✼

Piper stilled in the silent entryway of her house. So much had happened in the past eight hours, it made her head spin. The joy and celebration of Cole and Bailey's engagement party, the excitement of Reef's surprise arrival, the tension between him and Cole when Cole realized Reef had come home for a competition and not for his family, being woken by Reef covered in blood, seeing her brother arrested . . . by *Landon*.

A wave of nausea rumbled over her, and she tossed her keys on the front table. *That's odd.* She thought she'd remembered leaving the letter from Elma on the table beside the key bowl, but now it sat with the rest in the mail basket. Seemed like an odd time for Kayden to be cleaning up. Seemed odd for Kayden to be cleaning, period. For someone so health conscious, her sister was a borderline slob.

Even odder, Rori hadn't come to greet her. It was late, but Rori *always* came.

Stretching the kinks from her neck, she moved toward the

kitchen. Something in the living room caught her eye. She squinted and stepped forward. Rori was sacked out in front of the garland-draped hearth.

She bent down and patted her. Other than the snores raising Rori's chest rhythmically, the husky didn't stir. *Bizarre.* Then again, it was the middle of the night.

Getting to her feet, she left Rori deep in sleep and continued on toward the kitchen. She passed the laundry room, splotches of blood still marring the pearly white of the washer. Landon had confiscated Reef's clothing and collected samples, but the stain of blood remained. The cupboard door was open overhead, and she wondered if Landon had forgotten to close it when he grabbed the Ziploc bag.

She moved into the kitchen, got a glass of water, and sank against the countertop, her eyes scanning the room. The back door was cracked open. Had Kayden really gone to bed without checking the door? Fear tickled her spine. *Something isn't right.*

She went back into the living room, knelt once again by Rori, and tried harder to rouse the dog. Rori moaned but remained deep in slumber.

Piper climbed the stairs two at a time, flipped on the hall switch, and cracked Kayden's bedroom door.

"What?" Kayden shielded her eyes with her hand against the bright hall light.

"Did you leave the back door unlocked?"

"What? No. I made sure it was locked before we headed to the station."

"It's unlocked now."

"Okay."

"So who unlocked it, and why is Rori so out of it?"

"What's going on?"

"I'm trying to figure out why the back door's unlocked and our dog's knocked out."

"What do you mean knocked out?"

"I mean Rori's sacked out in the living room. She didn't wake when I came home, didn't even budge when I patted her."

Kayden glanced at the clock. "Why are you just getting home? Where have you been?"

"That's beside the point. What matters is I think someone's been in our house."

"If someone had been in our house, I highly doubt Rori would be sleeping so peacefully."

"Unless they drugged her."

Kayden sat up. "Why would someone drug our dog?"

"To be in our house without Rori tearing them apart."

"Seriously, Piper, you're upset. It's late. You need some rest. We both do." She lay back down.

"Kayden." She flung the door open, switched on the ceiling light, and moved to sit at her sister's side.

"Are you kidding me?" Kayden covered her face with the pillow.

"Aren't you the least bit concerned that someone has been in our home?"

"I think you're in overdrive. It's understandable, but you're overreacting."

"Overreacting?"

"Is anything missing from the house?"

"Not that I can tell so far."

"TV still there, the stereo?"

"Yes." She'd seen both in the living room.

"In all the years we've lived here, in all the years our parents lived here, has our house been broken into once?"

"No, but I—"

"Need sleep. We both do. Morning is going to come before either of us is ready."

∽∞∾

The time in the house had been cut short. Par for the course tonight. Little had gone right from the beginning. The stubborn girl wouldn't talk, and his time of prying it out of her had been interrupted by Reef McKenna. That interruption, however, would keep his involvement masked, so he couldn't complain too much. No one would trace anything back to him or *them*—not after fortune had smiled upon him with a scape-goat. At the end of the tumble he'd landed on his feet—except for one thing. And if he didn't find it, everything might come crashing down around them.

What had the stupid broad done with it? Just like her mother—taking information that didn't belong to her. The kid should have learned when doing so got her mother killed. Did she really think she'd be any different?

He'd tossed her room again, tossed Reef's room, and ended up here. When things quieted down, he'd walk away, just as he had at the lodge. The small-town sheriff had actually left the crime scene unmanned long enough for him to escape. For him to blend right back in with the crowd.

He shifted in the cramped quarters of the closet, waiting. Perhaps he should drug the inquisitive one too, shut her up for a bit. No. That would draw far too much attention. He'd just slip out and return in the light of day.

They'd be at the station in the morning, no doubt, and he could take all the time he needed, meticulously searching the house room by room, drawer by drawer. Meticulous was the only way to get things done. That and a lot of patience—his had slipped tonight. He wouldn't make that mistake again.

6

Landon downed another cup of coffee at the station, knowing there was no time to rest. Not when so much was on the line. He needed to devote every minute until Reef's arraignment looking for anything that might suggest they had the wrong man. After a day and a half of investigation, all he'd found were more reasons to lock Reef away.

"How'd it go?" Slidell asked from the doorway. "Got everything you need?"

Landon looked up from his paper work. "It's a start."

"It's a start?" Slidell took the seat opposite Landon and tipped the metal-frame chair onto its back two pegs. "I spoke with the D.A., and he's planning to bypass the grand jury. He's on board with telling the judge there is overwhelming evidence for Reef to stand trial. You know what that means?"

Yeah—if Reef was innocent he'd just lost valuable time to prove it.

"It means no red tape," Slidell said with a satisfied smile.

"And if he's innocent?"

"Not this baloney again." Slidell dropped the front legs of his chair to the floor with a clang. "He did it. The sooner you come to terms with the truth, the better."

"Don't you think that's a bit premature?" Given the evidence thus far, it wasn't. But they still needed the autopsy results, trace evidence, fingerprints off the murder weapon.

"Premature? He was caught in the act."

"They didn't actually witness him slit her throat."

"Close enough."

"I'm not willing to put someone behind bars for the rest of his life for 'close enough.'" While it didn't appear that Reef was innocent, Landon could legitimately fight for time—time to conduct a thorough investigation. Unfortunately, Slidell was fighting equally as hard to take that time away. Hungry for a conviction, he was trying to push Reef's case through the express lane.

While Landon couldn't in good conscience argue Reef's innocence, he could argue the importance of a methodical investigation.

"I thought we agreed that this wasn't going to be a problem. That you're a professional and would not allow your friendship with Reef's family to cloud your judgment."

"It won't cloud my judgment. Just as I hope your desire for reelection won't cloud yours."

Slidell rocked forward. "That's the second time you've insinuated that I'd put an innocent man behind bars to better my chances in the election."

"I'm simply stating that a thorough murder investigation cannot be rushed. It's barely been twenty-four hours."

"Don't worry. I'm sure you will have plenty of time to conduct your investigation while Reef's awaiting trial, but in the end I'm confident your efforts will show nothing but evidence of that boy's guilt. The D.A.'s moving quickly on this. Arraignment's only a couple hours away." Slidell got to his feet. "I'm going to grab some breakfast. You want me to bring you anything?"

"No thanks." He had no appetite.

Slidell studied him a moment, then tapped the doorway on his way out.

Landon sighed. Only a couple more hours to find something, *anything*, that might suggest Reef's innocence.

Of course, Piper expected him to simply take Reef at his word, but he couldn't. It would be one thing if it was Cole or Piper or any of the rest of them he'd spent nearly every day with, but Reef was different. He'd barely seen Reef in close to a decade, and prior to that, they'd hardly been close. He couldn't overlook hard evidence for the word of a man he hardly knew, let alone a man he didn't trust.

∾

Gage shook his head as the cameras flashed and reporters chattered. "Could this get any worse?"

"I don't think so," Cole said, coming to stand beside him.

Bailey clasped Cole's hand in hers. "I'm worried about Piper."

Gage followed Bailey's gaze across the crowd to his sisters— Kayden, strong and stalwart; Piper, a mixture of fiery sadness. If Reef was found guilty, if he *was*—heaven forbid—guilty, Piper would never be the same. None of them would.

Reef had always been irresponsible; a risk taker with no concern for his bodily safety or, at times, the needs of others—but a killer . . . ? It'd been years since Reef left home, but Gage still knew his brother. Didn't he?

"Thank you for coming," Slidell said, cutting through the din of reporters.

With the Freeride Competition being in Yancey, the media exposure in town had grown from Jason with the *Tribune* to nearly a dozen reporters from across the country, and a handful from around the world. Now his brother's name and picture would be broadcast to the world as the lead suspect in a murder investigation.

"I want, on behalf of all of us in Yancey, to express our deep sorrow over the malicious death of a young athlete with a bright and promising future ahead of her. I am pleased to announce that we have the suspect in custody and he will be arraigned shortly."

A bevy of hands rose in the air as questions spewed from the reporters.

"What was his motive?"

"Did he know the victim?"

Slidell lifted his hand. "I am not able to comment on the specifics of the case at this time."

"Rumor has it that it was a lovers' spat. A revenge killing."

"Rest assured we are conducting a thorough investigation. That is all for now." Slidell stepped from the spotlight without a glance in the McKennas' direction and retreated down the hall.

The reporters dispersed, moving into the courtroom to await Reef's arrival. His arraignment hadn't even taken place and they were already pronouncing him guilty. *Vultures.*

"Do you want to go in?" Cole asked.

"And be surrounded by reporters? I'd rather wait out here. At least until it's time for Reef to come in."

"I have a feeling it'll be a while yet," Cole said, taking a seat with Bailey on one of the wooden benches lining the courthouse foyer. "The D.A. isn't even here."

"Or the defense attorney," Piper said, pacing by.

"He'll be here," Gage assured her.

"He better be."

"Sit down while we wait. You look exhausted."

"Because she stays up at night playing Nancy Drew." Kayden yawned, slumping down beside Cole on the bench.

"What?" Gage narrowed his eyes.

"Yeah," Cole said, stretching out. "Landon told me about that."

"Landon?" Kayden looked up at Piper. "You didn't go to him with your break-in theory, did you?"

"Break-in?" Gage and Cole said in unison.

"There was no break-in," Kayden assured them.

"How can you be certain?"

Kayden sighed. "Because nothing was stolen."

"What if they couldn't find what they were looking for?"

"What *who* was looking for?" Gage asked.

Cole leaned forward. "Landon didn't say anything about a break-in."

"Then what *did* he say?"

"Instead of heading home when we left the station after visiting Reef, Piper went to the lodge to get his things."

"That's where you were?" Kayden asked.

Piper shrugged. "I just wanted to get Reef's stuff."

"Okay, but what's this about a break-in?" Gage asked. "You think someone broke into Reef's room?"

"Reef's room?" Piper cocked her head. "Hmm. I hadn't considered that."

"Great." Kayden sighed. "Fuel her nonsense."

"Why do you assume it's nonsense?"

Gage clamped a hand on her slender shoulder. "Why don't you start at the beginning. . . ."

Piper relayed her theory that something wasn't right in the house, that numerous things appeared disturbed, and that she feared Rori had been drugged.

Gage rubbed his brow. It did sound like Piper was overreacting, but then again, Piper's gut reactions had an alarming accuracy. *But why?* Why would someone break into the girls' house and not take anything? "How was Rori the next morning?" he asked.

"Perfectly fine," Kayden said.

"Actually, she was super thirsty," Piper added.

"Because she'd slept in front of the fire all night," Kayden countered.

"Look, I know it sounds a little out-there, but I have a really strong feeling about this."

"Understood," Gage said. "Let's just try to figure out if there are any other plausible explanations."

She linked her arms across her chest. "I'm all ears."

Still unsatisfied with her family's supposedly plausible explanations, Piper strode to Cole. "Where's Reef's lawyer? The arraignment was supposed to start five minutes ago."

"He'll be here. Besides, I wouldn't worry too much—the D.A. isn't even here yet."

"What if he missed the ferry or doesn't make it?"

"God will get him here," Cole said, his steadfast gaze calming her.

What would she do without her big brother always there to protect her? Just as Landon had always been, until . . .

She exhaled.

Things hadn't been right between them in months. Instead of drawing them closer, as tragedy often did, the events of last summer had pulled her and Landon apart. At first she'd attributed Landon's distance to some kind of punishment for continuing to date Denny against his wishes, or even foolishly considered the possibility that maybe, just maybe, he'd finally realized she was an adult and the distance was his awkward attempt to show her he wouldn't be meddling anymore. But he'd only grown more distant, and while she thought she'd be thrilled to not always have him in her business, the truth was she missed him. Missed his twisted, dry sense of humor . . . missed his annoying manner . . . missed *him*, period. Didn't he realize how much she needed him now? Needed him to listen, to trust her enough to look beyond the obvious. Reef didn't murder Karli. Someone else had. If Landon could only get beyond his black-and-white mentality, he'd see that.

She grimaced. Why did he have to be so muleheaded? So by the book?

The front door swung open, and a gust of frigid wind swirled in, ruffling the hem of her skirt. The cold bit at her cheeks, her fingers.

All heat was gone—dissipated in an instant by the stark reality of winter. The hope of the new arrival being Harland Reeves, the defense attorney they had hired, vanished, and shock stole its place as quickly as the wind had swallowed the warmth. *Meredith Blake.*

"Mer?" Gage said, his voice cracking.

7

"Hello, Gage." Meredith's tone held no trace of shock, no real emotion of any kind. She pulled the leather gloves from her hands one finger at a time.

Piper watched Gage take a tentative step toward Meredith, so many emotions battling for purchase. "What are you doing here?" he asked.

It was too much to hope that Meredith had heard what was happening to Reef and rushed back to Yancey after so many years just to lend legal and moral support. With Meredith there was always an ulterior motive, and when it came down to it, she simply wasn't that nice.

"Prosecuting a case," she said matter-of-factly.

Gage's face paled. "Not my brother's?"

Meredith tried to slip an errant strand of blond hair back into her tightly woven bun. Despite the rigid do, she was still strikingly beautiful. Distinct almond-shaped eyes the color of warm mocha, high cheekbones, and full lips. It was no wonder Gage had fallen for her and her exotic beauty. They all had. But that was before they realized the truth of who she was and the pain she was capable of inflicting. "Yes," she said, finally getting the wayward hair to comply. "That's correct."

"You haven't set foot in Yancey in nine years and you chose prosecuting my brother for murder as the time to come back?"

"Your brother made the choice for me when he killed Karli Davis."

"Why this case? You could have passed. You had to know it was him."

"I'm a professional. I prosecute the cases I'm given, but I don't expect you to understand that."

"Is it even ethical?" Piper asked, her ire fully riled. "You know the defendant."

"Correction. I *knew* the defendant. It's been close to a decade, and he was just a kid the last time I saw him. So, yes, I can ethically prosecute him, and I intend to do so to the fullest extent of the law."

"But you knew Reef," Gage said, agony weighing down his words.

Piper's heart ached. Meredith was about to destroy their family all over again. Set aside caring, didn't she possess a single ounce of human compassion? Had she no mercy? No sense of decency? How could she stand there, emotionless, and threaten to destroy another member of their family? A family that had once loved her so dearly.

"Mer?" Gage said, breaking through the haze of Piper's thoughts. "You *knew* Reef. He hasn't changed."

Meredith draped her wool dress coat over her arm. "Does anybody ever truly know anyone?"

Gage's jaw tightened, the tiny muscle in his right cheek quivering. "I guess not."

Piper rested a hand on Gage's back as Meredith left them standing there and entered the courtroom.

"She's not worth it," Kayden said. "She never was."

Gage's hands balled into fists at his sides.

The front door blew open, ushering in another gust of arctic chill as Reef's lawyer, Harland Reeves, entered.

❧

Piper sat on the courtroom's wooden bench, not so unlike the pews they'd grown up sitting on at church. Her mind flashed back to Reef—curly blond hair, bright blue eyes, and full of mischief—crawling under said pews during the service, much to their parents' amused consternation. But they could never stay stern with him for long. He'd say sorry, smile, and all would be forgiven.

Now . . . ? She shook off the thought. Her brother wasn't trying to get away with something. He was innocent. He'd given his word, and she *knew* his heart. Mischievous, reckless, and even rebellious, Reef was also tender and gentle and hated to see anyone or anything suffer. He couldn't have killed Karli.

Her gaze darted to the growing crowd gathering inside the courtroom. In a town Yancey's size it took no time for news to spread. Surely by now just about everyone had heard. She wondered if those present came to offer their support or to gawk. Sadly, she imagined it'd be a mix of the two.

Meredith sat at the prosecutor's table, her legal pad and pen before her. She didn't bother looking back. How could she prosecute Reef?

So many emotions tumbled through Piper, but the nagging feeling that someone had been in their house wouldn't let go. While it was odd that nothing had been stolen, it didn't ease her suspicions. The back door had been locked. Kayden said so, and her sister was meticulous about stuff like that. Rori hadn't been herself. That all of it would simply be a coincidence—as her siblings believed—on the night her brother was falsely accused of murder seemed even more far-fetched than her theory of someone breaking in. But why had nothing been taken, and how could the break-in possibly link to Reef being falsely accused of a crime? She sighed. Maybe Kayden was right and her imagination was running amuck. She was tired and scared and sad. It was like being stuck in a nightmare she couldn't escape.

Landon glanced back at her from his position in the first row.

Unreasonable as it was given the circumstances, she wanted him at *her* side. Wanted his strong, protective arm draped across her shoulders. Wanted his cedar aftershave to soothe her the way it always had in the past.

She wanted . . . She bit her bottom lip with a grimace. This was not the time to be thinking about what she wanted and certainly not the time to be thinking about Landon. All her energy needed to be fixed on Reef and on proving his innocence.

The side door opened, and her breath caught as her brother emerged handcuffed and being led in by Deputy David Thoreau.

Dark splotches rimmed Reef's eyes and an air of disbelief marked his steps. His bloodshot eyes held Piper's gaze. He trusted her to sort out the mess he was in, and she would. One way or another, she'd prove his innocence.

Reef's attorney conversed with Thoreau, and after a brief and somewhat heated discussion, Reef's cuffs were removed.

Reef rubbed his wrists and took a seat. Piper studied the attorney Landon had recommended from his years in Fairbanks. Harland Reeves was tall, lean, and athletic. Probably early fifties, though it was hard to tell for sure. He wore a decent suit but nothing too fancy. He leaned in to speak with Reef, his focus fixed on his client. She prayed he was as good as Landon claimed, that he could protect her brother from a crime he didn't commit.

The court clerk cleared his throat. "All rise for the honorable Judge Morrell."

Piper rose. Cole rested a hand on her back, letting her know he was right there. He was always there. She prayed he'd be there for Reef too, despite their differences over the years. While Cole was probably the last person Reef wanted on his side, he was going to need Cole's strength to get through this ordeal. More importantly, he needed Jesus. Maybe this would be what it took for Reef to be willing to talk about Him.

Judge Maureen Morrell entered. Her dark hair, streaked with silver, was pulled back in her trademark French twist. In her late fifties, she had aged remarkably well. Her pale skin contrasted her dark hair and eyes in a striking manner.

Piper and she passed each other on the street almost daily—Piper on her way to their family shop, Last Frontier Adventures, and Judge Morrell on her way to the Polar Espresso for her morning mocha. Piper never thought they'd be meeting like this. It seemed unfathomable that Maureen Morrell held her brother's life in her hands.

"Please be seated," Judge Morrell instructed. "Mr. McKenna, the purpose of this proceeding is to advise you of your rights, advise you of the charges against you, and to set conditions for bond, if that is appropriate in your case. I see you have counsel present."

Harland stood. "Harland Reeves for the defense, Your Honor."

Meredith stood. "Assistant District Attorney Meredith Blake, on behalf of the people, Your Honor."

"All right, Ms. Blake, are you ready to proceed in this arraignment matter?"

"Yes, Your Honor. At this time the people would file, with this court, a complaint against the defendant Reef McKenna, date of birth, July 20, 1987. The people are filing one count of first-degree murder."

"And, Mr. Reeves, have you advised the defendant of his constitutional rights?"

"Yes, Your Honor."

"Good, then let's proceed. Will the defendant please rise."

Reef got to his feet.

"Do you understand the charges against you?"

"Yes, Your Honor."

"And how do you plead, Mr. McKenna?"

"Not guilty, Your Honor." His voice trembled.

Piper's gaze shifted to Landon. How could he think her brother guilty of murder?

"So noted." Judge Morrell shifted paper work. "I see the D.A. has cited special circumstances due to the overwhelming evidence against Mr. McKenna."

Meredith stood. "Yes, Your Honor. I think you will see the evidence against Mr. McKenna is extensive. The D.A. believes it is in the people's best interest that a grand jury trial be waived and we move straight to setting the trial date."

"Your Honor." Harland rose. "I hardly think we need to be so drastic."

"I'm sorry, Mr. Reeves, but the D.A. does have the right to move straight to trial. And I concur that is the prudent course of action given the overwhelming evidence."

Hot tears beaded in Piper's eyes.

"Let's see . . ." Judge Morrell scanned a document in front of her. "With the holidays so near, why don't we schedule opening arguments for January second. Mr. Reeves, does that provide enough time for you to build your case?"

"I'd like a few more weeks."

"All right. Does January fifteenth suit?"

"That would be fine. Thank you, Your Honor."

"And now to the matter of bail."

"Your Honor," Meredith began. "Taking into consideration the overwhelming evidence against Mr. McKenna, and his high risk of flight, the State requests that bail be denied."

"Denied?" Piper gaped at Cole in horror. "They can't do that. Not with Christmas only a few weeks away."

"Your Honor," Harland said, "the State is seriously over-reaching. No evidence is foolproof—especially after such a short investigation period. The McKennas are well respected in the community and lifelong residents. Surely their involvement and longevity—"

"Your Honor," Meredith interrupted. "That may be true for most of the McKennas, but not Reef. Let the record show that the defendant hasn't permanently resided in Yancey for nearly seven years. And he has spent those years living a transient life-style—traveling from place to place, never setting down roots."

"Mr. McKenna is not a hobo, Your Honor," Harland said. "Nor is he a transient. He travels for his job."

"His job?" Meredith scoffed. "Try hobby."

Harland kept his focus pinned on Judge Morrell. "Your Honor, my client is a professional athlete. His profession re-quires him to travel."

"All right, Mr. Reeves, then where does Mr. McKenna main-tain his permanent residence?"

"With the circuit."

"Surely the circuit doesn't run year-round. Where is his home?"

"Yancey, Your Honor."

"Where he hasn't been in seven years," Meredith added.

"Because of his livelihood," Harland countered.

"That may be, but what I'm trying to ascertain is his attachment to one place. Let's try this another way," Judge Morrell said, pushing the sleeves of her robe above her elbows. "Does Mr. McKenna own a home?"

"No, Your Honor."

"Does he draw a regular paycheck?"

Harland looked at Reef.

He leaned over and murmured something.

Harland nodded and cleared his throat. "His income comes from his wins and any endorsements he procures."

"Has he lived in any one place for a year or more?"

Reef shook his head.

"No, Your Honor."

"Six months?"

Reef shook his head again.

"Three?"

Reef nodded.

"And where was that?"

After a brief exchange, Harlan Reeves answered, "In Brazil."

"A foreign country. That's hardly reassuring," Maureen pointed out.

"Mr. Reeves, I hate to tell you this, but your client perfectly fits the definition of a transient lifestyle."

"A requirement of his profession."

"That may be, but he's still a flight risk."

"His family will vouch for him."

"I imagine they would, but that doesn't make him any less of a flight risk. It just makes them liable." Judge Morrell shifted and addressed Landon. "Deputy Grainger, you're the lead officer on this case. You know the McKennas. Do you believe the defendant is a flight risk?"

He looked at Piper.

Her chest tightened. *Don't do it. Don't make him spend Christmas in a jail cell.*

He looked down, his jaw tightening.

"Deputy Grainger?" Judge Morrell asked impatiently.

"Yes, Your Honor," he said, his voice cracking. "I believe Reef is a high-flight risk."

A torrent of frustration crashed over Piper. She'd never allow Reef to jump bail. Landon had to know that. If he couldn't trust Reef, couldn't he at least trust *her*?

"Taking all of that into consideration," Judge Morrell continued, "it is the court's decision that bail be denied."

"But, Your Honor . . ." Harland protested.

"Mr. Reeves, I appreciate the fervor you display on behalf of your client, but my decision has been made. Mr. McKenna will remain in custody until his trial."

"Your Honor, if we could just—"

"We are finished here," Judge Morrell said. "Thank you."

Piper rushed to Reef's side before the deputy could escort him out and hugged him. "I won't let this happen. I'll find a way to prove your innocence. I promise."

8

Gage waited until everyone left the courtroom—everyone except him and Meredith.

She stood at the prosecutor's table, stuffing files into her briefcase.

He strolled up behind her, catching a whiff of her perfume. *Lilacs.* The scent brought back memories of happier times—summers lying with her on the hammock beside the large lilac bush in her backyard. How had they gotten from there to here?

"You're really going through with this," he asked.

She stiffened. "If by *this* you mean prosecuting Reef's case . . . then yes, I'm really going through with this."

"And you feel nothing?"

"On the contrary, I feel a great deal for the victim and her family."

He stepped closer, resting his hand on the table mere inches from hers. It'd been so long since he'd touched her, since their lives had been so closely intertwined. "And for my family?" He gazed at her. "For me?"

She held his gaze, no emotion registering in her eyes. "I've closed that chapter of my life."

"Just like that?" He bit back the pain. "We lose our son, and the next day you're gone. You didn't even bother to come to Tucker's funeral."

"People don't have funerals for premature fetuses."

"He wasn't a fetus; he was our *child*, our *son*."

"Unlike you, I see no need to dwell in the past."

He could barely breathe for the pain that seeing her brought back. "Mer . . ."

"I don't have time for this." She lifted her briefcase. "If you'll excuse me." She pushed past him, and he did nothing to stop her. He'd tried once and it had done no good.

He heard a swish of the main courtroom door behind him while Meredith exited out the side door. Had one of his siblings ducked back in to witness his encounter with her?

Remaining at the table, he followed the curve of the wood with his long, lean finger—tracing the place where she'd doodled. She'd always doodled when she was nervous.

Was she nervous about the case or possibly its connection to him? Maybe she didn't have a heart of stone after all. He shook his head. Now who was being foolish?

He exited the courtroom to a flurry of reporters. Just Reef's dumb luck the town would be crammed with reporters covering the Freeride Championships. Sports reporters covering a murder case? They had to be champing at the bit.

"Miss McKenna"—a reporter shoved the microphone in Piper's face—"did you have any clues your brother was a murderer?"

"My brother is no such thing."

Gage stepped forward to intervene, but Cole wrapped a guarded arm around Piper and addressed the reporter through clenched teeth. "I suggest you walk away."

"Is that a threat? Does this murderous tendency run through the entire McKenna clan?"

"That's enough." Landon stepped between the McKennas and the swarm of reporters.

A dizzying haze of flashes rent the air.

Meredith appeared at the opposite end of the hall, and all the reporters clamored over each other to reach the fresh prey.

"How do you know the prosecutor?" A bold voice ventured.

All but one, apparently.

Gage turned to find a pixie—no more than five foot four, her blond hair pulled back into a ponytail with wispy bangs framing her beautifully sculpted face. *Enchanting.* "What?"

"Meredith Blake. How do you know her?"

Gage grimaced. He was wrong. Not a pixie, more like a gnat.

"The assistant D.A. . . . You obviously know her." Impatience skirted her tone.

He glanced down the hall at Meredith fielding questions like a pro, the glow of ego and ambition radiant upon her. "I did, once." Or at least he thought he had.

"When was that?" The pixie shoved a recorder in his face.

He swatted it away. "Who are you?"

"Darcy St. James," she said proudly. "I'm a reporter."

"With which paper?" he asked, oddly curious which blood-sucking paper she leeched for.

"*Ski Times,*" she said, with a bit less enthusiasm.

Was she serious? "*Ski Times?*" He tried not to chuckle. "I can't imagine them covering *this* type of trial."

"Trial. Ski trial . . . criminal trial . . . witty. But I assure you, *Ski Times* is always after stories that affect athletes. I'm sure they'd be interested in your brother's trial—and if not, there are plenty of hard-hitting periodicals that will be."

So . . . she was looking to make a name for herself. "I've got news for you, honey." He stooped to meet her five-foot-four gaze head on. "Exploiting my family is not going to be the hard-hitting news story that gets you there. So shoo off," he said with a flick of his hand.

"Shoo off?" She huffed. "And who are you to call me *honey?*" With each word she poked his chest—her delicate finger inflicting surprising force. "If you don't want to answer my questions, I'll just go ask Meredith. I'm sure she'll be more than happy to offer a response."

"Then you obviously don't know Meredith," he said dryly. She wouldn't give an aspiring reporter the time of day. That was the thing with climbers—they only had use for the people on the rungs above, never the ones below.

Darcy St. James stalked away from the brutish McKenna brother. He was gorgeous, but he certainly wasn't charming. What was his problem, anyway? She'd asked a valid question, and he'd belittled her—his brisk nature, a neon confirmation that she'd hit the mark. There was definitely a connection between him and the assistant D.A. The color had drained from his face the instant Meredith Blake entered the courthouse—a mixture of love and anguish swimming in his heather-gray eyes.

Irritation churned inside as she stalked across the courthouse lobby, the heels of her boots thumping. How dare he insinuate she was trying to exploit his family? He hadn't even given her a chance to explain. If he hadn't been so bullheaded and confrontational, she could have explained that she was trying to help.

She'd interviewed Reef McKenna numerous times in the past, and the news of his arrest for Karli Davis's murder had flat out shocked her. While the evidence looked bad, she was not one to jump on the party wagon. Especially when that party wagon was gunning for reelection. She wanted to dig deeper. To make sure they actually had the right man behind bars. If not, the real killer was still out there. And if so, what had happened? How had Reef McKenna gone from the charming, playful athlete she'd known to a killer?

There were so many questions to be answered. It seemed only right to begin with those who knew Reef best, with his family. Perhaps she should have approached it differently, not jumped on her curiosity about the McKenna brother and the assistant D.A. But there was definitely a connection there, and it had shifted her focus.

She studied Meredith Blake in the limelight—her flawless complexion radiant in the glow of camera flashes, her shoulders squared and her brow high. What had gone on with the pair?

Landon guided the McKennas into the break room. "Okay, I managed to get you a group visitation. You can meet with him here, but Slidell insists a deputy remain with you at all times."

"Why?" Piper asked. As the rest settled around the room, she dropped her purse and a package she had brought for Reef onto the table next to the sad excuse for a tabletop Christmas tree.

"So Reef doesn't try anything stupid."

"I'd say you killed any chance of that with your little flight-risk speech." She still couldn't believe he'd done that. Killed any chance of Reef being able to stay at home until the whole mess got sorted out. If her brother had to spend Christmas in this cold place . . . Heat flared in her again, despite the chilly temperature of the room.

"What are you saying?" Landon sat on the edge of the table, hardly an inch from where she stood.

She tried to ignore how his presence made her heart race. *Frustration. It's all out of frustration.*

"Please don't tell me you were hoping he would run, Piper."

"Of course not, you big buffoon. Reef would never do that to us." She glanced again at the Christmas tree atop the table by Landon's elbow. Its drooping branches suggested underwatering, and the lack of light in the windowless room didn't help matters. If someone didn't show it a little love, it'd end up looking like the Charlie Brown Christmas tree before the week was out.

"Piper, I couldn't lie."

"I wouldn't want you to. I just can't believe you really think he'd run. . . ." Reef wouldn't do that to them.

"He's done it before."

"Leaving Yancey, yes. Not running from the law. There's a distinction."

"I was trying to protect your family."

"Protect us? How?"

Cole leaned forward from his seat across the table. "Piper, I—"

Landon put up his hand. "It's okay, Cole. I can handle this. Piper, if you vouched for Reef and he ran, you'd lose everything."

"I keep telling you, he wouldn't do that to us, wouldn't take off and leave us holding the bag."

"Are you sure?"

"Of course."

"You sound sure, but your jaw just tightened." His finger brushed her skin, and she tried to ignore how good his touch felt.

"So?"

"So, that's what you do when you're conflicted."

"You think you know me so well . . ." she said, diverting the subject. She wouldn't admit for even one instant that she'd hesitated. Reef had been irresponsible in the past but not with something this significant. Not with something that could cost them everything if he took off.

"I do." Landon stood, his face now a breath from hers. "*Know* you."

She swallowed, waiting for a retort to form, but the door opened, and Thoreau led Reef in handcuffed.

"Remove the cuffs," Landon instructed Thoreau.

"But Slidell said—"

"You can tell him to blame me if anything goes wrong."

Thoreau shrugged. "Suit yourself. I'll be right outside the door."

Landon nodded.

Piper wrapped her arms around Reef. "We'll get this straightened out. I won't let you go to jail for a crime you didn't commit."

Reef smiled, but it was tight, forced. "It's not looking so good."

She braced her hands on his shoulders, looking him square in the eye. "We're going to get you out of here. You didn't do anything wrong."

"The judge obviously doesn't see it that way. What if the jurors don't either?"

"They will." *They have to.* "What did Harland say?"

"That it doesn't look good."

"But he believes you?"

Reef rubbed his hands together. "I guess so. We didn't have much time before the arraignment. He said to visit with my family and then he and I will have a long talk."

She looked at Cole. "I don't want someone who thinks my brother is capable of murder representing him."

"You don't know what Harland thinks, Piper." Cole stepped over to rub her shoulders. "Let him and Reef chat, and I'll talk with him afterward, see exactly where he stands."

Thoreau tapped on the glass. "Slidell said five minutes."

"That's all we get?" Kayden asked.

"I'll push it as long as I can." Landon opened the door to confer with Thoreau.

"I brought you some things." Piper handed the package to Reef. The package Landon had searched. He'd claimed it was protocol, and she understood his needing to follow the rules, but seriously, what'd he think—that she'd slipped a shiv in there? How absurd. She wasn't a criminal, and neither was her brother.

Reef pulled out the red-and-white snowflake-patterned quilt that always adorned the family room couch at Christmas. If he couldn't spend Christmas at home, she'd bring as much of it as she could to him.

Next he pulled out the tin of cookies. She'd been sending them to him every Christmas since he'd left Yancey. Praying one year he'd finally make it home. And now that he had, he was spending it behind bars.

"Thanks, Piper." He cracked the lid. "Butterscotch." A real smile curled softly on his face. "My favorite."

"I know." She ran her hand through his hair. "Just like I *know* you're innocent."

Deputy Thoreau opened the door a crack. "Time's up."

Landon stepped inside. "Sorry, guys."

Reef stood, trying to put on a brave front, but she knew he was scared. She could see it in his eyes. Just like when he was a little boy terrified of thunder—every storm she'd find him cowering in the coat closet. She'd crawl in with a flashlight, a handful of books, and a warm blanket; and the two of them would huddle under the blanket, reading by flashlight until long after the storm passed.

Often their mother would find them there the next morning, still asleep. The first time, she'd nearly had a heart attack, thinking they were missing, but after subsequent storms, she knew exactly where to look. How Piper wished this storm would pass.

She embraced Reef tightly as Thoreau stepped into the room to haul him away. "I won't stop fighting until I get you out of here, Reef. You have my word."

9

Landon found Cole and Bailey waiting in his office when he returned from escorting Reef back to his cell. Bailey stood as he entered. "I'll wait in the lobby." She planted a kiss on Cole's cheek and gave Landon a hug before leaving.

"How's Piper?" He was so worried about her.

"She's a lot stronger than she appears."

A family member's guilt would test even the strongest of faith—it had flat out crushed his fledgling one.

"But . . ." Cole sighed.

"But?" Landon leaned forward.

"It's probably nothing." Cole shook his head. "We're all under a lot of strain, and so much has happened. . . ."

"What's going on?"

Cole rubbed his hands along his thighs. "Piper thinks someone may have broken into the house the night of Reef's arrest." He relayed everything. The unlocked back door, the opened cupboard, and the deep-sleeping husky.

"Anything missing?"

"Not that we can tell."

"How's Rori now?"

"Fine. Look, I know Piper's imagination can get going, but . . ."

"Her gut instinct is usually right." It was impressive, really, though he'd never admit it to her. It'd only fuel her antics.

"What about yours? You think someone broke in and drugged the dog?"

Cole sighed. "I don't know what to think anymore. I've asked the girls to be extra diligent, but I'd say there's nothing to be done for now."

"I'm sorry, man. Let me know if I can do anything."

Cole nodded. "Harland's coming by the house tonight. I'd like you to be there."

Would that prove to be too much a conflict of interest? Would he have to pull back when the McKennas needed him most?

"It's cool if you don't—"

"No, I'd love to be there. It's just I don't think it's ethical if I sit in on that discussion."

"Right." Cole slid his hands in his pockets. "I hadn't thought of that. Well, at least drop by for dinner afterward. Bailey's making her Irish stew."

"I'll be there." He just couldn't be a part of anything that could, no matter how innocently, corrupt the case.

"Grainger," Slidell hollered.

Landon lifted his chin. "I better . . ."

"See you at dinner."

"Yeah."

Landon entered Slidell's office, his muscles tightening. "You wanted me?"

"Booth just called. The preliminary autopsy on Karli Davis is done."

∞

Landon entered the autopsy room. The stench of death enveloped the stale air. Karli Davis lay on the cold steel table, her chest covered with a series of stitched zigzags that formed a very dark Y.

Landon popped a menthol cough drop in his mouth before stepping closer, finding the trick more helpful in masking the odor than smearing Noxzema beneath his nose, as some of the other cops did.

"Landon." Booth slipped on a fresh pair of gloves. "Perfect timing."

His thoughts exactly. He'd observed one autopsy in its entirety, and it was something he'd never forget. Being present for the initial external exam and then briefed after the completion of the internal suited him just fine.

"Cause of death," Booth said, bypassing the pleasantries, "was a lateral cut to the carotid artery." Booth pointed to the incision on Karli's neck. "She died fairly quick once the lethal cut was made."

Landon pointed to several gouges beneath Karli's right knee. "And what about those?"

"I'm unable to be certain which came first, the leg or the neck injury."

"So the killer was going for either torture or postmortem mutilation?" For the victim's sake, he prayed it was the latter.

Booth nodded.

Landon shook his head. Reef killing in the heat of anger was one thing, but torture or postmortem mutilation? Was there any way Reef could be that sick, or did they have the wrong man?

"It does look like the killer got interrupted before he could finish whatever he was attempting to do." Booth indicated the jagged end of the three-inch gash on her leg. "Looks like he jerked away quickly."

Most likely when Ashley and Tug arrived. "What do you think he was attempting?"

"Perhaps he enjoyed the kill but it went too quick for his tastes, so he decided to continue cutting. Or"—Booth exhaled—"he could have been carving some sort of mark or insignia into her."

Either reason demonstrated the killer's need to exert power over his victim.

Landon bent for a closer examination. "It looks like there's scarring in the area."

"Yes. My guess is from a recent injury or surgery."

"How recent are we talking?"

"Under a year, probably less."

"What about her blood alcohol?" Ash, Tug, and Reef all said Karli had been drinking. The alcohol in her system could have slowed her reactions and reduced her ability to struggle with the killer.

"Analysis strip showed the presence of alcohol in her system. We'll have to wait for the full tox screen results to know how much."

"Good work, Booth. As usual."

The lanky Louisiana native smiled. "Just hope it results in the clear-cut evidence you need to put the killer away."

Landon appreciated Booth not naming Reef as the killer—not until all the evidence was in. Though he knew most in town would not give Reef the same benefit of the doubt.

"Let me know as soon as you hear something." He was particularly interested in the trace-evidence results from the changing room. If they could prove another man had been in the women's changing room, maybe, just maybe they'd have a new direction to head.

"Will do, but you know they are short staffed at the lab. Could be weeks, and that's if we're lucky."

Lucky was the last thing Landon felt.

10

Following the family's visit with Reef, Gage headed to the Polar Espresso. The rich, roasted smell he loved brought little soothing to his troubled soul. But the more he adhered to routine, the better he believed he'd cope.

He took his place in line, debating his beverage choice. The sweet scent of caramel-laced sticky buns filled the air, and the heat emanating from the kitchen contrasted sharply with the brisk winter draft sweeping in every time the shop door opened. He turned and glanced at the line forming behind him and stopped short. Darcy St. James.

"You again," he groaned.

She rolled her eyes. "I was about to say the same."

"Right."

"What? You don't honestly think I followed you here?"

"Of course not. That would be totally beneath a reporter."

"What can I get you, Gage?" Mack asked from behind the counter.

"Large Moose Madness, with an extra shot, and one of Pam's sticky buns." He could practically taste the warm, gooey bread melting in his mouth.

"You got it."

He paid and waited as Mack filled his order, willing the man to be quick. The less time spent around Darcy St. James, the better.

Her fingers moved rapidly across her Blackberry, no doubt sending texts regarding her intended story to her boss.

Women like her got under his skin, and try as he might, he couldn't help himself. "Saw you lost your nerve," he said smugly.

She paused and looked up at him. "I beg your pardon?"

"You didn't question Meredith." He leaned in and, ignoring the intoxicating scent of her perfume, dropped his voice an octave. "Too intimidating, was she?"

"Hardly." Darcy stiffened.

"Well, just so we're clear, you're not making a story out of my family." Best to drill that into that pretty head of hers before she made her next move.

"Actually, I'm trying to—"

"Prey on a family when they're suffering?" he supplied before she could finish, before she could lie.

Taking a deep breath, she seemed to rise in stature. "I'll have you know that I'm—"

"One Moose Madness Extreme and sticky bun," Mack called.

Gage held up a finger. "Hold that thought." She could hold it for all of eternity, as far as he cared. He turned, retrieved his order, and thanked Mack.

"See you tomorrow." Mack smiled.

Without so much as a glance in Darcy's direction, he strode straight past her and headed for the door.

"What can I get for you?" Mack's voice echoed behind him.

Darcy prattled something, and then Landon heard the distinct sound of her three-inch bootheels clipping across the hardwood floor after him.

"We weren't finished," she said, before he could make his escape.

"No?" he asked, slipping the piping-hot pastry from the bag and stealing a bite. Warm caramel slicked his tongue.

"No, and I most certainly am not preying on your family. I'm trying to help."

"Uh-huh." He licked the extra caramel from his sticky fingers. "Sure you are, lady. Whatever helps you sleep at night." He slid

74

out the door as a couple entered, the brisk winter air refreshing against his heated skin.

Stepping to the curb, he waited as the plow rolled past, and Darcy stepped in front of him. "Just who do you think you are?"

He grimaced. Didn't the lady know the meaning of quit?

"You," she said pointedly, "know nothing about me. And if you'd stop being so boorish for just a second and let me explain—"

"There's no need. Trust me; I know everything I need to about women like you." He took a sip of his drink, the heat of it matching the fire coursing through his veins. The woman had some nerve.

"Women like *me*?"

"That's right." He stalked across the street.

"Please enlighten me," she said, hurrying to keep up with his long strides. "Exactly what kind of woman am I?"

Reaching the other side, he stopped, giving her a once-over.

She maintained a defiant stance—shoulders stiff, head cocked—but an unmistakable blush crept over her cheeks at his raking gaze.

Taking a breath, he leaned in. "You're the kind of woman that harasses a family while their brother is on trial for murder." His voice deepened as his anger rose. "The kind of woman whose only concern in life is getting ahead. And the kind of woman who doesn't care who she hurts in the process."

"Boy . . ." Darcy whistled, shaking her head. "Some woman must have really done a number on you."

His jaw clamped tight.

"Wait a minute." Her eyes widened. "Meredith Blake?"

How had the woman put that together so quickly? His muscles coiled tight. It didn't matter. It was clear it would be only a matter of time before the gnat resurrected the whole painful matter. Without a word, he turned and stalked away.

❧

Darcy trudged back to the coffeehouse, realizing stiletto heels and ice didn't make the best combination. Wouldn't Gage

McKenna have loved it if she'd fallen on her bum chasing after him? His disdain for her was clear, as was his pain. She'd hit a nerve, a very raw and exposed nerve. Meredith Blake had crushed his heart, and now he was lumping all career women into the same category.

While Darcy was ambitious, it wasn't for a story or a career boost, as he so adamantly claimed—she was after the truth. After taking off from hard-hitting news the past two years to cover the sport she loved and the adventure athletes she'd grown up with, a deeper story had finally tugged at her heart and filled her with hope that she could do some good. Her instincts said there was more to the case, more to the victim's life than met the eye. If Gage McKenna couldn't see past his preconceived notions to let her help, she'd find another way to get the information she needed. *Boorish man.*

11

Piper paced the length of the front porch, waiting for Reef's defense attorney to arrive. The air smelled of snow, and the dark clouds thickening overhead confirmed another storm was on its way.

Why is this happening, Lord? Reef couldn't have murdered that poor woman. He needs to turn back to you, and I pray this ordeal helps him to do just that, but he isn't a killer. Under all that recklessness and rebellion lies a tender heart that couldn't harm anyone. Please let Landon see that. Help him to move beyond his need for facts and procedure and let him see with his heart for a change. I pray the real killer will be found and that Karli Davis knew you, Lord. I pray she's in heaven with—

The front door opened and Bailey stepped out wearing a dark green cashmere sweater. She was lovely inside and out. It was no wonder Cole loved her so. It was obvious to even the greatest of skeptics—the way he looked at her, so full of love. Piper wished someone would look at her like that. Denny Foster was nice, but what they shared was comfortable. She didn't want comfortable, she wanted the powerful love her brother and Bailey shared.

"I thought you could use something warm to drink." She offered Piper the mug.

Nutmeg and cinnamon swirled in the brisk early December air.

"Cider?"

Bailey nodded. "Just like you like it—extra cinnamon and a dollop of caramel."

"Thanks." Piper wrapped her hands around the ceramic moose mug, the heat of the liquid easing the chill in her fingers.

Careful to position the giant moose antlers just right, she tipped the mug for a sip. While it wasn't the easiest of mugs to drink from, it depicted her favorite animal and always made her laugh. A gift from Reef, of course. As absent as he'd been the past seven years, he'd always remembered her. Sending little care packages that never ceased to make her smile, and occasionally made her break out into a full-blown belly laugh. There were only two men in her life that could fill her with such exuberant emotion—Reef and Landon.

One was behind bars and the other . . .

"Piper?" Bailey rubbed her arm. "You okay?"

"Yeah, I'm fine."

A soft smile graced Bailey's lips. "You know what Gage says about fine."

"I know. I almost wish he'd never seen *The Italian Job*."

Bailey chuckled. "You and me both. He's still on the whole Handsome Gage kick. How long has it been now?"

Piper smiled, actually smiled, and it filled her with pain. *Please don't let this tear our family apart.*

"You should come inside. Temperature's dropping." Bailey indicated the thermometer mounted to the porch wall. The red hovered at zero degrees Fahrenheit.

"I'll be in soon. I just need some fresh air."

Bailey nodded and slipped back inside.

Piper took another sip of cider, letting the warmth slither down her throat. What she needed was for Harland Reeves to arrive. She wanted a minute alone with the man to discern if she truly believed in her brother's innocence. If he didn't, it didn't matter how good of a lawyer he was, he wouldn't be representing her brother.

Harland's rental car rounded the bend, his tires crunching the packed snow.

She stepped off the porch and strode to Harland as he climbed from his car. "How did it go with Reef?"

"We had a good talk."

"And . . . ?"

The front door opened and Cole poked his head out. "Piper, let the poor man come inside before you start your barrage of questions."

With a sigh she followed Harland up across the porch. There went her chance to speak with him alone.

Harland paused to wipe his boots on the mat before stepping inside.

"Thanks for coming." Cole shook the man's hand. "Everyone is in the family room."

Almost everyone. It was the first family meeting in years that Landon hadn't been present for. While she understood his absence, it felt strange without him there. But everything between them felt strange lately.

The scent of evergreen wafted down the hall as they approached. The fresh spruce they'd cut last weekend was now adorned with strings of popcorn and their family ornaments.

Gage had a nice fire crackling in the hearth, and everyone stood to greet Harland.

Cole moved to Bailey's side and wrapped an arm around her waist. She smiled up at him as they took a seat on the sofa beside Kayden.

Gage remained at the hearth, and Jake stood on the periphery, as usual, hovering by the tree he'd helped decorate. It'd taken her two Christmases, but she'd finally gotten him to participate. When would Jake realize he wasn't just a Last Frontier Adventures employee, that he'd become part of their family?

She sat beside Harland on the smaller of the two sofas. "You spoke with Reef?"

"Yes. I just came from—"

"And?"

"Piper, let the man speak," Kayden admonished.

"It's perfectly all right." Harland smiled. "I understand what

79

an anxious time this is for all concerned. Reef and I had a good long talk."

"And?"

"And we've got our work cut out for us." He pulled a legal pad and pen from his briefcase.

"I believe what my sister is so impatiently trying to ascertain," Kayden said before Piper could pounce again, "is whether or not you believe our brother is innocent?"

"Yes," Harland said confidently, "I believe Reef is innocent."

"Really?" Piper let out the breath she hadn't known she'd been holding.

"When my clients tell me they're innocent, I take them at their word, but—"

"Mr. Reeves"—Piper held his gaze—"the person representing my brother must *know* he's innocent."

"I understand, and I *do* believe him. If I didn't, I wouldn't be taking this case."

"Good." At least that was a positive.

"Where do we go from here?" Kayden asked.

"I will speak with Deputy Grainger and take a look at the police report," Harland said. "We need to know exactly what they think they have on your brother."

Bailey quietly excused herself and slipped from the room.

"Is there anything we can do?" Piper asked.

"Normally I have a team to do the legwork, but taking into account the distance from my firm and our current workload . . ."

He sat forward on the sofa. "To be completely frank, I came here as a favor to Landon. Our firm is overloaded right now, but when I heard you were close friends of his, I couldn't say no. And now that I am convinced Reef is innocent, I can't in good conscience walk away. But since it is *just* me, it limits the amount of time I can spend on the investigation. In this type of case, I feel it's vital to learn all we can about the victim. Who she was involved with, what other potential suspects there might be, how—"

"I can do that." He'd just handed her a place to start.

"Actually," Harland said as Bailey reentered the room with a mug of cider, "what I was going to suggest is that we need to find somebody with the time and resources to do some digging."

Piper's eyes narrowed. "Why can't we just look into it ourselves?"

"For one, most people don't like to speak with family members of the lead suspect. For another, you really need someone with the expertise to get the investigation done right."

"Like a private eye?" Cole asked.

"Or a reporter," Jake said as Bailey handed Harland the steaming mug of cider.

"Thank you, dear." Harland took a sip before responding. "Precisely."

Kayden's brows pinched together. "How can a reporter help? Aren't they to be avoided?"

Gage sighed. "Like the plague."

"Reporters are paid to track down information," Harland said.

"So are private investigators," Gage countered.

"Yes, but reporters are paid by their bosses. With an investigator you have to fork out the money. And people are more likely to spill dirt to a reporter. They feel as if they are giving an inside scoop, whereas PIs can come across as . . ."

"Intimidating," Jake supplied.

"Right." Harland nodded.

Kayden's frown deepened as she turned her stern gaze on Jake. "How do you know so much about reporters?"

He shrugged. "Just offering suggestions." When would Kayden stop grilling the poor man? Just his showing up in Yancey with a duffel bag and no history didn't make him a criminal. It simply made him ripe for adoption into their family. He was hurting. From what, Piper didn't know, but if they could provide any healing, she was more than happy to do her part.

"Excellent suggestions," Harland said. "The choice is yours. There are a couple investigators I can suggest. The one I am most inclined to recommend is currently out of the country;

the other is working a case for us up in Fairbanks. I may be able to persuade him to come down for a day or two, but he won't be cheap, and—"

"This is our brother's life," Kayden interrupted. "We have the money."

"I'll contact the investigator, see when and if he has an opening. But I can't guarantee he'll have the time, and quite honestly, I think it best to have someone who can work on this full-time."

"So a reporter?" Gage said with a groan.

"That's my recommendation. Reporters have access to a lot of things the general public doesn't, and like I said, people are far more likely to confide in them."

"Why would a reporter help us?" Kayden asked.

"Reporters are always up for a big story, the chance to track down an angle currently unexplored."

Gage snorted. "You can say that again."

Cole's gaze shifted to him. "You know somebody?"

Gage groaned. "I'm afraid I might."

Piper didn't like it. Not one bit. A reporter might have resources she didn't, but nobody knew her brother like she did. If Harland and her siblings wanted a reporter involved, fine, but she would be digging on her own. It was the only way she could assure the job got done right.

12

Drawing in a steadying breath, Gage entered Gus's Diner. It had only taken a few inquiries around town to track down Darcy St. James.

Brenda waved as he entered, and he returned the gesture, pausing to wipe his boots on the mat. He quickly appraised the diner patrons. A hearty mix of locals and event folks crowded the tiny space. The scent of vanilla and fresh batter decided his meal of choice.

Darcy hadn't arrived yet, which was perfect. That way it would appear their meeting was completely by chance, just as she'd tried to pass off their "coincidental" run-in at the Polar Espresso yesterday.

He hopped onto the stool at the far end of the counter and shifted to his left so he could keep an eye on the door.

"What can I get for you?" Brenda asked, tugging the pencil from behind her ear.

"Stack of flapjacks."

"Want a side of meat?"

"Gus got any chorizo sausage?"

"Yep. Got a fresh supply in last night."

"I'll take a double side of that."

"You got it." She poured him his usual glass of milk before pinning his order slip on the metal roundabout.

Gus yanked the ticket, read it, and leaned his upper body out of the kitchen. "Sausage has an extra kick to it today," he said with a gleam in his aging eyes.

Gage rubbed his hands together. "Just how I like it." He wasn't sure which of them enjoyed spicy food more. Over the years it had turned into a playful competition, each always trying to *out heat* the other with their latest find.

Last fall Gus had gotten Gage good with some concoction called Killer Red. While it hadn't ended his urge to try new things, it had certainly taught him to take a smaller first bite.

The whistle of the wind drew his attention back to the door. Darcy St. James, today more appropriately dressed in a full-length down jacket and mukluks, entered and struggled to shut the door against the howling wind. He took two quick strides to her side and lent a hand.

The door shut to the elements, and she sighed with a slight laugh of relief. "Thanks." She looked up and her smile deviated into a frown. "You!"

"We meet again."

She pulled the gloves from her delicate hands. "And I suppose you're going to blame me for this encounter as well?"

"No, actually I was—"

"Going to tell me what a horrible person I am?"

"No," he said, ignoring the irritation she sparked in him. This was for Reef. He had to remember that, no matter how frustrating the woman proved to be. "I wanted to say I'm sorry if I was rude yesterday."

"Brutish is more like it." She took an open stool, and he sat on the one beside her.

Brutish? Where does this lady get her vocabulary? "Fine, perhaps I was a bit gruff."

"And judgmental and arrogant and—"

"Hey, I call it like I see it."

"So do I."

"Look," he said between gritted teeth. "I'm trying to apologize."

"You should."

"I am!"

"Good." She lifted the menu, scanning it.

The woman was downright impossible, and this was an absurd idea.

Brenda slid his plate of steaming pancakes in front of him. They smelled fresh and buttery and delicious. "Double order of sausage." She set the second plate down. "And another milk." She handed him a fresh glass.

Darcy's lips twitched on a smirk.

"What?" He slathered butter along the golden cakes.

"Milk?"

"What about it?" He poured syrup on top.

"Just not something I often see adults drink, but I suppose that explains it."

"Explains what?"

She fought back a smile. "Never mind."

"What can I get for you?" Brenda asked.

"I'll have wheat toast and half a grapefruit."

"No grapefruit this time of year."

"Okay, whatever seasonal fruit you have will be fine."

"Wow. You really live on the edge," he mocked.

"And you eat like a four-year-old."

Spearing a forkful of pancakes, he popped it into his mouth with gusto.

"With manners to match."

"Enjoying my food isn't proper?" He stabbed another forkful.

"It's just the rough enthusiasm you display while eating it."

He downed a swig of milk and grinned. "You should see me when I really love something. *Enthusiasm* doesn't come close to describing it." He laughed at the meager plate of toast and canned peaches Brenda placed before Darcy.

"I'm sorry, but these"—Darcy prodded the slippery fruit with her fork—"aren't fresh."

"This is Alaska, honey. It's the dead of winter. That's as fresh as you're going to get."

"I see. Very well." She laid her napkin across her lap and bent her head in prayer.

Gage snorted. *Figures.* Of course she'd be a Christian, just as Meredith had been. Apparently being a Christian and acting like one didn't necessarily go together—which was precisely why he wanted no part of the religion.

"Why are you still here?" she asked, not bothering to hide her irritation.

"I'm eating." He winced as she took a bite of dry toast. "Aren't you going to put something on that?"

"I like it like this."

"Sure you do." He glanced down the length of her. "In case you haven't noticed, you don't need to be dieting."

"I'm not dieting; I'm eating healthy."

"And jelly is full of poison?"

"No, but I prefer to be sensible."

"How's that working out for you so far? Must be a wild ride." He shook his head. He knew women like her. So controlling they couldn't let themselves experience anything that might jolt their daily regimented routine.

"Why am I explaining myself to you again? And why are you still here?"

"I'm eat . . . ing." He knew precisely what she was getting at, but he was simply having too much fun vexing her to let the cat out of the bag yet.

"Since it appears I'm going to have to spell it out for you . . . Why are you *eat . . . ing* with *me*? I thought you wanted nothing to do with a vulture like me." She studied him a moment and her eyes narrowed. "Wait a minute. . . . You want something from me."

Fun time was over. "What could I possibly want from you?"

She pondered a moment—he could practically see the wheels spinning. "You need a reporter, need someone to dig up dirt."

She was good. He'd give her that much. "And why would I come to you when there's a ton of more experienced reporters all over town?"

She mulled that over, her shoulders dipping slightly.

Gage smothered a smile. He had her right where he wanted her.

She snapped her fingers. "Because for some reason you've decided I'm curious enough or desperate enough to go on some wild-goose chase."

"It's not a wild-goose chase. It's the chance to prove a wrongly accused man's innocence."

"You think your brother is innocent?"

"Of course I do."

"Despite the fact he was caught in the act?"

"He wasn't caught in the act. He found her that way. You know, for a reporter you really have a problem getting your facts straight."

"I have my facts straight."

"You only have the facts they want to share. There's a whole other side to the story."

"Such as?"

"I'm not willing to share private details with someone who isn't at least interested in finding the truth."

She shifted to face him, her shoulders squaring. "I assure you, I *am* after the truth."

"Even if it contradicts the facts being presented?"

"I stand by the truth, not the party line."

He smiled. "Well then, there may be hope for you yet."

∞

Reluctantly, Darcy rode with Gage to the McKenna family home, and after brief introductions and everyone joining in to explain the plan, Kayden said, "So you see . . . we need somebody to track down the other leads."

Darcy shifted in the oversized armchair in the McKennas' family room. They had ideas, perhaps, but not leads. Not yet.

"We need somebody who knows how to dig for information, somebody who has access to sources we don't," Cole said.

"So you want me to find out if there's anything the police are overlooking? You want me to poke around and see if anyone else had cause to kill Karli Davis?" Precisely what she had already planned to do, but now she'd have the McKennas' cooperation and backing behind her.

"We know our brother is innocent," Piper said.

"We just need help proving it," Kayden added.

"We can always go the private investigator route if you're not interested." Gage was trying to play it cool, but she knew they needed her help—*he* needed her help.

"I'll do it, but on one condition."

Gage smiled as if he knew what was coming. "Which is?"

"You don't mislead me, don't keep any secrets from me. I can't do my job if you're hiding stuff from me." She was after the truth.

Gage stood. He was much taller than she when they were both standing, but with her seated, his six-foot-three frame flat out loomed over her, leaving her surprisingly more impressed than intimidated. Despite his poor eating habits, he was in great shape—long, lean, and sculpted.

"Did you hear me?" He waved a hand in front of her face.

Embarrassment rushed her cheeks. She'd been too busy staring at the man to listen to him. "I'm sorry—could you say that again?"

"Gladly." He linked his arms across his chest. "We will be honest with you, but this isn't a free license to dig into our personal lives. This is about Reef and Karli—*period*."

He didn't want her digging into his past with Meredith. While the relationship had piqued her curiosity, it wasn't why she was considering joining them. "Agreed, but you need to understand that you can't try and protect Reef by keeping things from me. I need the truth."

"Fair enough," Cole said.

"I have one condition," Piper said, standing. "You talk to Reef." She quickly continued, "Not for a story. The entire conversation needs to be off the record. I want you to talk with him and decide for yourself if you believe he is innocent or not. If you believe he's guilty, there's no sense moving forward."

Astute. "Okay." She needed to do that for herself, anyway.

If she believed him guilty, she'd be upfront with them. She was an ethical reporter, unlike some she knew.

"There's one more thing," Jake said. He'd been silent until then—appraising her, assessing the direction of the conversation. He'd been introduced as a close family friend, but there seemed to be a weird dynamic between him and the older sister, Kayden. To be honest, Jake intrigued her. She was usually a quick judge of character, but he did elusive well.

"Yes?"

Jake addressed the McKennas. "You should seriously consider having her sign a nondisclosure agreement for anything she might learn that is not pertinent to the case."

Kayden's eyes narrowed. "How did you come up with that?"

Jake shrugged. "*Law and Order.*"

"Right," Kayden said slowly, clearly not buying it.

"Sounds like a good idea," Cole said. "I don't think we need to bother Harland with it, though. I'll see what Gus can draw up."

Darcy had seen a flyer posted in the diner regarding the owner providing the town with general legal assistance—par for the course in this wacky but somehow charming town. She nodded. "Fine with me."

If she believed Reef innocent and was going to move forward working with the McKennas, she had no qualms with signing a nondisclosure agreement. It was only right. "In the meantime," she continued, "I'll speak with Reef."

Cole gave a nod of agreement. "I'll let Landon know you are coming."

"Landon? As in Deputy Grainger?" she asked.

"Yes."

Hmm. So there were more connections than she'd realized. She stood and collected her bag. "I'll speak with your brother and be in touch."

"Thanks for coming." Cole shook her hand. "And for considering our proposition."

"I'll take her back to the hotel," Gage offered.

"Thanks." She'd ridden from the diner with him and had no way of getting back on her own.

She followed him to his Land Rover, completely decked out with roof-rack, roll bar, and snorkel. She could only imagine the adventures he'd had in it.

"I appreciate you hearing us out," he said, starting the ignition.

"Wow. So you can be sincere," she said half playfully and half as a barb for his earlier treatment of her.

He winked and chuckled with an edge of bitterness. "Don't get used to it."

13

Slidell stopped Landon as he headed for the station parking lot. "Would you like to explain why a reporter is interviewing Reef?"

"She asked permission to see him, and he obviously consented. There's no law against him having visitors." He didn't feel the need to share the fact that the McKennas had sent her over. That was their business, not Slidell's.

Slidell's eyes narrowed. "Where are you off to?"

"Got someone I need to see."

"This better not be some wild-goose chase."

"All part of a thorough investigation," Landon said, stepping out of the station into the falling snow. Large flakes stuck to the brim of his hat as he walked to his truck, and he tried not to think about how much Piper loved snow. Tried not to think of Piper, *period*.

∞

Darcy walked straight from the sheriff's station to Last Frontier Adventures, the shop the McKenna family owned and ran. Gage told her he'd be working the rest of the day and she could contact him there if she decided she was in.

"Wipe Out!" greeted her arrival, and she took in her surroundings. Hawaiian leis topped the displays, lit palm trees stood in the corners, and the scent of coconut swirled in the air.

"Darcy," Jake said, stepping out from behind the counter. "Good to see you again."

"Thanks—you too." She looked past him. "Is Gage around?"

"Yeah, he's in the garage finishing up with the boards." He jabbed a thumb over his shoulder toward the rear of the building. "You want me to grab him?"

"No, I'll just head back." It would give her a chance to look around. See what Gage did for a living.

"Just head down the back hall, make a right at the end and out through the door."

"Got it. Thanks." She followed Jake's instructions, passing a gallery of photos running the length of the hall—pictures of the McKennas with families, couples, and individuals enjoying the outdoors. Gage was in nearly all the white-water rafting pics, an enormous grin on his face. The bigger the rapids, the wider his smile. It seemed the love of adventure ran through all the McKennas' hearts.

Dragging herself away from the snapshots, she stepped through the rear door into the garage, though *warehouse* would have been more fitting. Sixty by eighty feet, the steel-frame structure held an enormous variety of adventure equipment—kayaks, rafts, paddles, climbing ropes, skis, snowboards. The McKennas had quite an operation. "Back in Black" blared over the speakers, the entire building practically vibrating with the bass.

Gage was bent over a snowboard, carefully applying wax. He stroked it—caressing the wax smoothly and evenly onto the board. Just as her dad had done with his beloved surfboard so many years ago.

She watched Gage's long, lean fingers glide along the plane of the board a moment before interrupting.

"Hello," she hollered, hoping to be heard over the music.

He looked up at her and cupped a hand to his ear. "What?"

"Sorry to interrupt," she yelled as loudly as she could manage.

He lifted a remote and pressed a button. The music ceased.

"How'd it go?" he asked, not wasting any time.

"It went well."

The sleeves of his Henley were rolled up, and her gaze dipped to his bare forearms. His sculpted muscles were a sight to behold.

"And?"

"I definitely want in."

He arched a brow. "You believe him?"

"I do." She'd asked him point-blank and truly believed him innocent, despite the evidence against him.

Gage set down the jar of wax and strode to her. "And you're not just saying that to get some inside scoop?"

"I wouldn't do that." She wouldn't lie to get ahead. It was a fixed line she'd vowed never to cross.

"Why? Because it's beneath a reporter to lie?" He chuckled, his face dangerously close to hers.

"No—because it's beneath *me*," she said, holding his gaze.

He held her stare, and continued to hold it.

Her breath hitched, her heart throbbing.

"So we have a deal," he said finally.

"We sure do." She just prayed it wouldn't be her undoing.

Landon knocked on the trailer door, amazed at the size of the thing. It could probably swallow his cabin whole.

The door swung open, and a woman in her early twenties greeted him. Clad in her tight ski pants and Under Armour cold gear top, her attire left little to the imagination.

Landon diverted his eyes.

"Can I help you?"

"I need to speak with Mr. Masterson."

"It's someone for you," she called over her shoulder.

"Who is it?" a male voice asked.

She turned back to Landon. "Who are you?"

He flashed his badge. "Deputy Grainger."

The door opened wider, and a middle-aged man stepped out. He had dark, thinning hair and a tall, lean physique. So this was Rick Masterson, a legend on the slopes and off.

"What's this about?"

"I need to ask you a few questions about Karli Davis."

Rick glanced at the lady. "Why don't you give us some privacy, Brittany."

"Sure thing." She sashayed past Landon and down the metal steps.

"Come on in." Rick held the door open.

The inside of the RV was even more elaborate than the outside. Leather couches lined the living area, all situated to face the enormous plasma TV mounted on the wall. Custom mahogany cabinetry and a lot of beveled glass finished the room. This guy liked the good life.

"Nice place you got here."

"Well, it's home nine months out of the year." Rick picked up the remote and muted the game. "Have a seat. I can't say I'm surprised you're here."

"Why's that?"

"I know how rumors go around here."

"Here?" Landon played dumb.

"Within the circuit." Rick sat, draping his left arm across the sofa's back. "All kinds of nonsense gets circulated."

"Are you saying the relationship you and Karli had was nonsense?"

"Relationship?" Rick laughed. "Is that what you heard?"

"What I heard was that you two had been intimate."

Rick swiped a finger across the bottom of his nose. "Where'd you hear that?"

"I'm not at liberty to say. Is it true?"

Rick lifted his glass and jiggled the ice against the crystal.

"Mr. Masterson?"

"I'm a married man, Deputy Grainger. I'm sure you can appreciate my delicate position." He drained the remaining amber liquid from his glass.

"And I'm sure you can appreciate the fact that a woman has been brutally murdered."

"Of course. But Karli's death has nothing to do with me."

"How can you be certain?"

"Hold on a minute, there. You're not suggesting I had anything to do with her death, are you?"

"Not at all. I'm just trying to get the full picture."

"There was no Karli and me in the picture."

"Ever?"

Rick rubbed the back of his neck.

"Mr. Masterson, it'd be best if you simply told me what I need to know, and then we can both move on."

Rick cleared his throat. "You'll keep this conversation between us?"

"As long as it isn't pertinent to the investigation."

"Fine." Rick stood and moved to the bar. He lifted the brandy decanter, offering to pour Landon a glass.

"No thanks." He didn't drink on duty, period.

"Suit yourself." Rick refilled his glass.

"You were defining what sort of relationship you and Karli shared," he said, trying to keep Masterson on track.

"We had sex. That clear enough for you?"

"Once, multiple times?"

"Off and on last season, until she got hurt."

"Hurt?"

"Karli took a bad fall near the end of last season. Tore her ACL."

That explained the scar tissue he and Booth saw on her knee. "And she was already back to competing?" *Impressive.*

"Karli was tough."

"People must have admired that."

Rick laughed. "Admiration and Karli rarely went together in folks' minds."

"Oh yeah—what did?"

"Having a good time or a really lousy one," he said, taking a sip of his brandy.

Landon liked the guy less and less with each passing comment. "Meaning?"

"Karli was either the life of the party or she was ruining it for everyone else."

"Could you give me an example?"

"Sure. No one expected Karli to be back on the slopes so soon. An ACL tear usually puts an athlete out for a full season, sometimes longer. But Karli hardly missed a beat. Her first event back, she competed fiercely. When she won, the gal in second place congratulated her on the podium, and Karli remarked something like 'Why would I want congratulations from the first loser?' That was Karli. Tongue of an asp."

"She ever threaten to tell your wife about you two?"

Rick flinched.

"I'll take that as a yes."

"Look, Karli spouted a lot of junk. It didn't mean she'd go through with it."

"Guess you no longer have to worry about that."

Rick jiggled his glass. "I see what you are doing."

Landon sat back. "And what is that?"

"You're trying to find a scapegoat for that McKenna kid."

"Why would I want to do that?"

"Because this is his hometown. What do you have, all of three hundred people in this place?"

"Six hundred and nine, last count."

"Whatever. My kid's school has more students than your town."

"And your point is?" Landon loathed men like Masterson, men who thought money and power dictated the rules.

"I know how you small-town folks are. You protect your own." His face reddened—an ugly mix of alcohol and anger. "Well, I've got news for you, Barney Fife; I'm not going to be the patsy that gets railroaded so the stupid kid can walk."

"It's Deputy Grainger, and I suggest you calm down."

"And I suggest you get out of here before I call my lawyer."

"I'm not done with my questions."

"Well, I'm done answering."

$$\infty$$

The theme from *Top Gun* played as Gage fished his phone out of his pocket. "'Ello?"

"It's Piper." Country music blared in the background.

"Where are you?"

"Never mind that. I think I'm on to something."

Of course she was. "Piper, Cole said to let Darcy handle it."

"Which is why I'm calling you. I need you to find Darcy and tell her to check out Rick Masterson."

"As in the guy in charge of the Freeride Circuit?"

"One and the same."

"What's he got to do with Reef?"

"Not Reef—Karli." Noise heightened in the background. "Look, I can't talk right now. Tell Darcy." She hung up.

Gage looked at his phone. What was Piper up to now?

∞

Having to see Darcy St. James for the third time in one day wasn't Gage's idea of fun, but a strange enthusiasm coursed through him as he climbed the Caribou Inn's front steps.

A quick call to Ida at the front desk had confirmed that Darcy was in for the evening, apparently enjoying complimentary tea and dessert in the dining area of the inn.

Wiping his boots on the mat, Gage pulled the hat from his head and ran a hand through his hair.

"Thanks, Ida." He winked at the owner behind the counter as he entered. She blushed, her wrinkles bunching in the delightful way his grandmother's always had when she smiled.

He stepped through the lobby and into the dining room and scanned the full tables looking for Darcy's expressive face. She was seated at the table in front of the stone fireplace, opposite another blonde. He stepped toward the pair.

With a chuckle, Darcy lifted her teacup. "You're kidding?"

The woman laughed, the sound prickling icicles along his spine. "Dead serious," she said.

Meredith. He stopped less than a foot from their table.

"There he was, covered in poison ivy from head to toe, but he'd rescued the dumb turtle."

"That's hilarious, and—" Darcy's gaze met his, and she stopped midsentence. "Gage." Color rushed her cheeks.

Meredith's laughter settled, and she turned with a smile. "Your ears must have been burning. We were just talking about you."

"I'll bet you were."

Meredith added a spoonful of sugar to her tea. "What are you doing here?"

He glared at Darcy. "I have no idea."

∽

Excusing herself as gracefully as possible, Darcy forced herself to maintain an unhurried manner as she strolled from the room. As soon as she was out of Meredith's line of sight, she booked it toward the front door.

Not bothering to waste time grabbing her coat, she bolted outside and down the steps after Gage. With his long legs, a single step in his easy gait took her several hurried ones to keep up.

She knew exactly what he was thinking. She could read his anger from the back of his head—his neck stiff, tension marring his usually relaxed shoulders.

"Gage," she called.

He ignored her.

"Gage." The cold stung her hands. She balled her fingers into a fist, hoping to warm them.

He stopped at the street's edge, his passage blocked by vehicles.

She caught up to him. "Hey." She tugged his arm.

He turned, his dark eyes fierce and yet somehow sorrowful. "I suppose you got what you wanted."

"What . . . I?"

"She tell you the whole tragic tale?"

"I don't . . ." She frowned. *What tragic tale?*

Gage shook his head. "You know, you're good. You actually had me going. Your whole 'I'm only after the truth and it's beneath me to lie' speech. I actually started to think there was more to you, but my first instinct was right. You're nothing but a leech."

The heat of his words clashed with the frigid wind slashing against her legs.

"It's not what you think. There weren't any empty tables, so she asked if she could share mine. I didn't bring you up."

"Right. You really expect me to believe that?"

"It's the truth."

"You were clearly talking about me."

"She started sharing about life in Yancey and . . ."

"I'm sure you just ate that up."

"I am trying to discover the truth about what happened to Karli Davis—not what occurred between you and Meredith Blake." While she was insanely curious—she simply couldn't picture the snobby assistant D.A. and the intense McKenna brother together—she'd promised to keep her focus on Karli and not dig into Gage's past.

"Then try to remember that."

14

"Grainger," Slidell hollered the minute Landon stepped foot in the station.

Landon bent his head, knowing exactly what his boss's tone meant. Bracing for a tirade, he stepped into Slidell's office.

Mayor Cox leaned against the file cabinets, his sleeves rolled up, his face a pulsating shade of red.

Great. The day just kept getting better and better.

Slidell rocked back in his chair. "I just got off the phone with Mr. Masterson's lawyer. He says you questioned his client without notifying him of his rights and without counsel present."

"I wasn't interrogating the man; I was simply asking him a few questions." He glanced at the thermostat. What did they have it set on, eighty?

"Masterson says you threatened him."

"I did no such thing."

"Well, his lawyer believes otherwise. We'll be lucky if he doesn't sue us."

"You've got to be kidding."

"This is no joke, Deputy Grainger. Mr. Masterson is threatening to pull the entire Freeride event from our town. Do you have any idea how much income will be lost if he does?" Cox dabbed his head with a handkerchief—the motion odd in the dead of winter.

"I asked the man a few questions. Which is well within my jurisdiction."

Slidell leaned forward, sweat pooling in the crease of his chin. "I'm your jurisdiction, and I'm telling you to stay away from Masterson."

"You're telling me not to do my job?"

"On the contrary, I'm telling you exactly what your job is. Stop harassing upstanding businessmen like Rick Masterson and get this case closed."

"Masterson? Upstanding?" Landon suppressed a chuckle.

"Precisely." Mayor Cox fumed. "I'll be lucky if I can convince Mr. Masterson not to pull the championship."

Thoreau tapped on the door.

"What?" Slidell snapped.

"Craig says he'll be by in an hour to fix the radiator."

"An hour?" Slidell roared.

Landon's cell rang. "I've got to take this." He didn't give Slidell or Cox time to argue, just stepped into the hall. "Grainger."

"Deputy Grainger, it's Ashley Clark."

"Hi, Ashley. How are you doing?"

"Not well. Look, I don't know what kind of outfit you're running here, but it is completely unprofessional. How could you send her here?"

Landon pressed his hand to his ear in an attempt to mute out the clamor of the station behind him. "Send who? I don't know what you're talking about."

"Reef's sister."

"What?" A horrid feeling settled into the pit of his gut. *Piper.*

"She showed up at qualifying today, said she needed to follow up on the questions you asked."

"She did *what*?"

"Sending the killer's sister to interrogate me. I've never—"

"Let me stop you right there. I did not send Piper."

"But she said . . ."

"I can only imagine what she said, but I give you my word—I didn't send her."

"You're saying she just came on her own?"

"I'm afraid so. She's convinced her brother is innocent."

"Look, I know what I saw."

"And I appreciate you telling me."

"But I shouldn't have to explain it personally to Reef's family."

"I agree, and believe me, I'll take care of this."

"She won't come around again?"

"Not unless she wants to end up in jail for interfering with an ongoing murder investigation."

"I don't want to get her in trouble. I just want her to stop coming around. She's too sweet. Having to see the hurt in her eyes. Having her question what I say. It makes me feel like a heel—or worse yet, dishonest. Which I am not."

"You have my word. She won't bother you again. I guarantee it."

"Thank you, Deputy Grainger. It's hard enough being considered a stool pigeon by the team. Everyone likes Reef. Well . . . most everyone."

"Who doesn't?"

After a brief pause, she continued. "I don't know. I'm just saying not everyone on the team is buddy-buddy with everyone else. It's a competition, after all."

"It would really help if I had a list of who you think liked Karli and who didn't. Same with Reef."

"Look, I've said enough. This is a small community. I don't want to be known as the team snitch. I've already taken enough flack for telling you what I did."

"I understand, but I assure you anything you say is strictly between us."

"Obviously not. Reef's sister proved that. I'm done talking."

The line went dead.

"Hello? Ashley, hello?" With a grunt, Landon slammed his phone shut. He was going to kill Piper.

∞

Piper opened her front door. "Denny." She smiled. "What are you doing here?"

"Picking you up for our date." He handed her a bouquet of red poinsettias and white roses.

"Our date?" With everything going on, she'd totally forgotten.

His shoulders slumped. "You forgot?"

"I'm sorry, but with everything happening with Reef, I really don't feel much like going on a date."

"It'll cheer you up. Come on." When she hesitated, he said, "I've been planning this for weeks, and it's all ready."

She bit her bottom lip, not wanting to hurt his feelings. "Okay. Give me five minutes." Maybe a few hours out would be a nice distraction. Maybe it would even clear her mind so she could think of a better way to help Reef.

"Dress warm," he called.

She paused, about to ask why but decided she'd rather be surprised.

A half hour later, she stepped from Denny's Subaru at the end of Knotchcliff Road—all that lay before them was wilderness. "Okay. I'm curious."

He squeezed her shoulder as he headed for the trunk. "When aren't you?"

A full moon graced the thick black sky, its radiance bouncing off the freshly fallen snow.

"Do you mind holding this?" He held out the battery-operated lantern.

"All right." She turned it on, watching its glow spread across the snow in front of her.

Denny slipped a pack over his shoulder and tucked a blanket beneath his arm. "Ready?"

She nodded, though she felt anything but. Being with Denny, having fun while her brother sat in a cell, didn't feel right, and she had a strange feeling they were being watched. She scanned the ridgeline.

Denny nudged her arm. "Let's go." He led her along what many would consider a long-neglected trail. Narrow and winding, it wove through the thick of the forest. The closely clustered spruce sheltered them from the elements, the ground growing bare and brown beneath their feet.

The scampering of tiny feet rustled through the tree limbs above and in the undergrowth below. The trees began to thin, and soon snow covered the path again. Fresh hoofprints larger than her hand indicated a moose's recent departure. She studied the woods surrounding them, hoping for a glimpse of her favorite animal, but saw nothing.

"Just a little farther," he said.

The unsettling feeling they were being watched intensified with each step she took. She turned and looked behind her. *Nothing.* Maybe her mind really was playing tricks on her, after all.

A few more steps and they entered a clearing—flat and broad at the edge of the rise overlooking the sea below. Stars, in the thousands, twinkled before her.

"Well?" he asked.

"It's breathtaking."

"Just like you," he said smoothly.

A little too smoothly—almost as if it'd been rehearsed. *Stupid, Landon.* He wasn't even there and he was ruining her date, making her overanalyze Denny's remarks. Landon had never liked Denny; he'd always been quick to point out the type of player he pegged Denny as. While it was probably true, Denny treated her well, and in all honesty, she enjoyed the attention. She enjoyed his company, but she knew now it would never turn into anything substantial. She didn't love Denny, and so it was only right for her to end things. Not tonight, after he'd put so much effort into the date, but soon.

Denny shook out the gray wool blanket and spread it atop the glistening blanket of snow. On top of that he placed two glasses, two plates, a thermos, and a series of containers.

A winter picnic beneath a canopy of stars. How thoughtful.

"My lady." Denny knelt and patted the blanket.

She joined him as he sat, and he spread a second throw across their laps.

The sky draped like a gigantic fishbowl before them, making her feel like a kid at a drive-in, only this time the screen was the sky and the show was God's amazing handiwork.

Denny opened the thermos, and the rich scent of chocolate swirled into the air.

"Hot cocoa?"

"Homemade just for you." He winked. "Whipped cream or marshmallows?"

"Whipped cream. Thanks."

He obliged, and then shifted beside her. "You okay?"

"Sorry. Just a lot on my mind."

He sighed. "Landon again?"

"What?" She frowned. Landon was in her thoughts, but he wasn't the full cause of her distraction—it was the case, her brother, the sense they were being watched . . . It was everything. Why had Denny keyed in on Landon?

Denny propped his arm across his bent knee. "He's always with us."

Landon had been so distant lately, almost absent from her life, even in regards to Denny. She'd thought his absence would make her happy, but in all honesty, it made her sad . . . lonely even. Crazy as it was, she missed him. "I know he can be in our business, but . . ."

Denny clasped her hands in his. "No, Piper. What I mean is we can't go on a single date without you bringing up Landon or getting lost in your thoughts about him."

She hadn't seen that coming. "Are you sure?"

"Positive. You're always talking about Landon or being distracted by him."

"He's just so . . . frustrating at times." Denny expressed how he felt. Why couldn't Landon? He said he was sorry about what was happening with Reef, but there was more there. When he looked into her eyes, there was emotion brimming, but he always pulled back. It drove her nuts.

Denny stroked her hand; the fleece of his gloves against the wool of her mittens created a warm friction. "You know, sometimes I think you talk so much about him because you like him."

"Of course I like him. He's like my older brother, for all intents and purposes. We have that whole sibling love-hate thing going on." Or at least they had since last summer when something she still didn't fully understand shifted.

"I'm afraid that's true, just minus the sibling part."

"What do you mean?"

"That you have feelings for Landon."

"Romantic feelings . . . for *Landon?*" Something inside her heart sparked. "No," she said with an assurance she didn't feel. In truth, her feelings for Landon were changing—growing and deepening in a way she couldn't explain. But he was pulling away, and it left her frustrated and restless.

Denny trailed a finger along her jaw. "Are you sure?"

"Uh-huh." She released a nervous laugh, entirely *unsure.*

"I'm glad to hear you say that, especially because I'd hate you to get hurt by who I saw him with the other night."

"Who'd you see him with?" She took a sip of cocoa.

"Becky Malone."

She nearly sprayed him with cocoa. "Becky Malone?"

"Yeah."

"You saw *Landon* with Becky Malone?"

"Yeah, they were leaving Hawkings Pub together."

"Whoa. Back up. Landon was at a bar?" *Mr. Straight and Narrow. No way.*

"Yeah."

"He must have been there on business." It was the only thing that made sense.

"Sure didn't look like business to me," Denny said, pulling some cookies from a container and arranging them on one of the plates.

"What are you saying?"

"That Landon and Becky stumbled out of Hawkings looking real friendly, if you know what I mean." He popped a chocolate chip cookie in his mouth.

"Landon and Becky Malone? No way." *Wait* . . . Her stomach lurched. Was that why he'd smelled like perfume and smoke the other night? *Landon*—she swallowed—*and Becky Malone?*

"I know you don't believe me."

"No, it's not that. It's just . . ." It made no sense.

"You think it's contrary to his character."

"Well, yes."

"Maybe there are things about Landon's character you don't know. Have you ever considered that maybe Landon has a dark side too?"

"Landon . . . a dark side?" Laughter erupted from her lips. The notion was absurd.

15

Landon parked behind Denny Foster's Subaru Forester at the end of Knotchcliff Road, adrenaline pulsating through his veins.

Piper never listened. Never learned. First poking her nose into his investigation and ticking off the eyewitness, and now this—out in the middle of nowhere with Denny, again.

He cut through the forest, headed for the clearing they'd all used back in high school as a summer make-out spot. Knowing Denny, that's where they'd be. Visiting it in winter didn't make Denny any less predictable. Seriously, what did Piper see in the guy? Sure, he had good looks and money, but she was more than that.

Laughter reached his ears—Piper's. She was probably touching Denny's arm the way she did when he said something she found amusing. Just as she had the night of Cole and Bailey's engagement party.

It had nearly brought him to his knees. He couldn't shake the image from his mind, couldn't breathe, so he'd ended up at Hawkings trying unsuccessfully to drown the memories from his mind.

It'd been wrong. He never should have let it get to him. Never should have turned to alcohol to numb the pain. He knew better. Seeking solace in a bottle never brought anyone any good.

Stepping clear of the forest, he found them. Piper's hand was resting on Denny's arm, just as he'd imagined, and the two of them were huddled beneath a blanket with a picnic of sorts spread out before them. How cheesy could Denny be?

The urge to hurl gnawed at his gut.

"But what if you're wrong?" Denny said, stroking her chin with his gloved thumb.

"But Landon's—"

"Ready to throttle you?" he said, stepping forward.

Piper sprang to her feet. The blanket that had been covering her pooled at her feet. "What are you—?"

"Doing here?" His jaw tightened, his heart whirring in his ears. "I could ask you the same. Surely, you're not out in the middle of nowhere with a man again."

Denny scrambled to his feet. "We were just having a picnic. And I don't see how it's any of your business."

"Not my business? Well, it seems Piper and I are both lacking in the ability to determine what is and isn't our business."

Her brows pinched together. "What are you talking about?"

"Not here." He grasped her by the arm. "We'll talk in the truck."

"Truck?" She tugged against his hold. "I can't leave."

"Wrong." He pulled her with him.

Denny hurried after them. "You can't just haul her away."

Landon tightened his grip. "Watch me." When Denny continued his pursuit, Landon turned and growled, "Denny, stay out of this."

Piper trudged alongside him, tugging against his hold. "Landon, you're being rude . . . and ridiculous."

"I'm being ridiculous? You're the one who acts without thinking. First with Ashley, now with Denny in the middle of nowhere?"

"And you are the one who acts without feeling."

"What the blazes is that supposed to mean?" That he didn't care, didn't feel? She couldn't be further from the truth. He'd been drowning in his feelings for her.

"Why can't it ever be the other way around? Why can't you express what you are feeling? Or is it simply that you don't feel?"

Don't feel? He wanted nothing more than to press her up against his truck and show her exactly how he felt about her— kissing her until she was weak in the knees. But the last time he'd followed his heart, it got shattered. This time, it looked like it was going to get shattered no matter what he chose to do, and there wasn't a thing he could do to stop it. As long as he had breath in his lungs, his heart belonged to her.

He opened the passenger side door of his truck and hefted Piper in. "Trust me, I feel plenty."

Her eyes widened, and he knew he'd said too much. He slammed the door and stomped around to the driver's side.

Climbing in his truck, he started the engine. "Feelings," he said, shifting the gear into drive, "put you in the middle of nowhere with a man, and that's dangerous."

She linked her arms across her chest as he sped down the road. "I'm in the middle of nowhere with you."

"That's different." And she knew it.

"How exactly? You are a man, aren't you?" She cocked her chin up a defiant notch. "Or is it just that you're not dangerous?"

"More dangerous than you know." His mind flashed back to that night in the cabin. Pressing Piper up against the wall. Every fiber of his being yearning to kiss her.

She huffed. "Please."

"I'm serious, Piper. Next time you pull a stunt like that . . ."

"What? Going on a date?"

"Putting yourself in harm's way or interrogating a key witness in an ongoing murder investigation."

"Oh, so that's what this is all about."

"I mean it, Piper—next time I'll . . ."

"What? Spank me?"

His fingers tightened on the wheel as he pulled onto the main road. "Don't think I haven't thought about it."

She expelled a disgusted huff of air. "You're being utterly ridiculous."

"Do you have any idea what you've done?"

"Tried to get the truth."

"You've shut down a key witness."

"Tug changed his story?" Hope laced her voice.

"Tug?" He frowned. "I was talking about Ashley."

"Oh." She stared out the window.

"You talked to Tug too? Wow. This keeps getting better and better."

"Why? Because your witnesses changed their story?"

"No. Ashley didn't change her story, and as far as I know Tug hasn't either. They aren't going to lie just because you welled up your big brown eyes."

"I don't want them to lie."

"Then what did you want to happen?"

"I wanted to make sure they were remembering correctly. That you asked all the pertinent questions, not just focusing narrowly, as you tend to do."

"*I* focus narrowly. Ha! You've got some nerve. You went in there only wanting to hear one thing."

"Yeah—the truth."

"They already told the truth. Now, thanks to you, Ashley is done talking. And I'm sure I'll be hearing the same from Tug."

"What do you mean?"

"I mean she's clammed up. After your little investigation, pretending I sent you, she no longer trusts me with any information. She thinks I gave her up and told you what we discussed in confidence."

"But you didn't."

"I know that, but she doesn't." He gave her a sideways glance as they turned down the McKennas' drive. "How'd you know about their story anyway?"

"I poked around."

"If you've corrupted this investigation in any way . . ."

"Oh, calm down. I just bought Tug a couple drinks. He sang like a sparrow."

"Well, that's just great. I hope you're pleased with yourself."

"Pleased? My brother is in jail for a crime he didn't commit. *Pleased* is the last word I'd use to describe me."

"Well, that makes two of us."

"I don't know what you are getting so riled up about. You already have Ashley's statement. What more do you need?"

"You have no clue how a police investigation works, do you?"

"Ah, here's the part where you tell me what a stupid, naïve kid I am."

"I've never called you stupid."

"So just naïve? Yeah, that's much better."

"I don't think you're stupid or naïve."

"You certainly don't think I'm competent."

"That's not true either."

"No?"

"No," he said as he pulled to a stop in front of her house.

"Then what do you think about me?" She stared at him so earnestly, with so much raw emotion welling in her eyes, he was nearly tempted to tell her how he truly felt. That she was wonderful, beautiful, and brave. But he could never tell her that because her rejection would be unbearable.

"See." Her jaw set in a stubborn line. "You can't even answer because you still think I'm just some incompetent kid."

"Piper, I . . ."

"Forget it." She opened the door.

There was so much he wanted to say, so much he yearned to tell her, but he couldn't. "Piper . . ."

"What?" She turned, her voice trembling.

"I need you . . ." *So badly it hurts.* His throat constricted.

"You need me . . . ?" She angled to face him.

"I need you . . ." He swallowed as a second pair of headlights turned down the drive. Denny. He sighed. "To stay out of my investigation."

"Got it." She slammed the door, and it reverberated through his soul.

16

Landon pulled down his stone driveway, his heart in pieces. His headlights swept across his deck illuminating a solitary figure. *Becky Malone.*

She sat on his lone rocking chair, her bare legs crossed. Was she crazy? It was ten below. She stood at his approach and bent to retrieve something. Straightening, she dangled a six-pack in her right hand.

With a sigh he climbed from his truck.

Inside the house, Harvey bellowed at his approach.

"Still," he commanded, and the dog silenced.

Becky lifted her chin with that assessing gaze of hers. "Hey, stranger."

He took in her attire—yellow down jacket, mukluks, and jean miniskirt. She was nothing if not unique. "Cold?"

"Freezing. Guess you best let me in."

"That's not a good idea." It was a downright awful idea.

"Stop being such a stickler and let me in." She reached for the door handle, and he covered her hand with his.

"Mmm," she purred, "you're warm."

"Look, I'm sorry if I gave you the wrong impression the other night, but—"

"Again with the buts." She smiled. "Don't you want to have a little fun?"

"I'm afraid not." He didn't want to hurt her feelings, but he had to be clear.

"Fine." She pouted. "Then can I at least use your can before I go? I've been waiting awhile."

"Sure. Just make it quick." He wanted her gone as quickly as possible.

"No problem. I don't need to hang around where I'm not wanted when there are plenty of places I am."

He felt bad at the slight quiver in her jaw. He really hadn't meant to hurt her feelings. He just needed to give it to her straight. Nothing would happen between them.

He opened the door, and Harvey greeted them with a look of disapproval.

"So this is home." She pulled a half-empty bottle of rum from her jacket pocket before shedding her coat.

Great. She wasn't in any condition to be driving. "Why don't I make you a cup of coffee while you use the facilities?"

She gave a saucy salute. "Whatever you say, Officer." She glanced around. "Nice place you've got here."

Piper's doing. She'd insisted on adding some life to the place. The leaf-patterned curtains and matching throw pillows, the candles lining the mantel, and the pictures on the wall were all her additions. "Bathroom is second door on your right." He pointed.

"Gotcha." Becky slunk down the hall, the scent of rum trailing after her.

He started on her coffee, popping a filter in and grabbing the bag of coffee grounds.

"Nice bed," she called, her voice soft and sultry.

He paused midscoop. "I said the *second* door, Becky."

"Second, third, what does it matter? Come join me."

He knew he should never have let her in. Quickly finishing the coffee prep, he started the maker and headed down the hall. Harvey grumbled as he passed.

Rounding the corner, he found Becky stretched out on his bed, her mukluks tossed aside. Her skirt and top, what little there was to them, remained.

114

"Nice sheets." She trailed her hand across the surface. "Let's put them to good use."

"Becky, I—"

"Need a little convincing?" She got to her feet and prowled toward him, unbuttoning his shirt as she drew close. Her lithe fingers danced down his chest, and then she kissed him. The overpowering taste of rum assaulted his mouth.

Bracing his hands on her upper arms, he gently but firmly pushed her back. "This *isn't* going to happen."

Harvey barked as headlights bounced across the window-panes.

Landon glanced at the clock. *One o'clock? Who on earth?*

"Probably got the wrong drive," Becky said, trying to close the space between them.

A car door shut.

"I'll check it out while you get put back together." He extricated himself from the room and headed for the front door. He placed his right hand on his gun as he swung the door open with his left.

His breath caught. "Piper. W-w-w-what are you doing here? Is something wrong?"

"I know you think I messed your case all up, but I've got something to tell you about a new lead." She pushed past him into the house and wrinkled her nose. "Do I smell coffee?"

He was thankful that's all she smelled. "This isn't a good time."

"Why?" Her wide brown eyes searched him and her cheeks flushed. "Sorry. Did I wake you?"

He followed her embarrassed gaze down his bare chest. He turned with a start and refastened himself. Becky had quick fingers.

"Landon?" Becky's voice held a new level of seductiveness. "Aren't you coming back to bed?"

His muscles stiffened as confusion flitted across Piper's angelic face. Her eyes narrowed. "Do you have . . . ?" She stepped toward the hall. "Is somebody here?"

Adrenaline surged through his limbs, and he lunged to intercept her, but he was too late.

Piper froze, her gaze fixed on Becky.

"Well, who have we here?" Becky's voice was sweet, but there was venom lurking in every word. She leaned against the doorjamb, not bothering to cover up.

"Piper." He reached for her, but she pulled away. "I . . ." How did he explain?

Her eyes radiated an agonizing disappointment. "Sorry I bothered you." Turning, she bolted for the door.

He raced after her. "It's not what you think," he said, catching up with her in the drive.

She spun around so fast she nearly bowled him over. "Just tell me one thing . . . Is *she* the reason you've been so distracted lately?"

"What?"

"You haven't been yourself in months. You're grumpier than usual, distant, and *now* . . ." Her eyes full of fire fixed on Becky standing in the doorway.

"This has nothing to do with that."

"*This?*" Her jaw stiffened. Were those tears shining in her eyes?

"Piper." He clasped her hand. She was so cold.

She yanked it back. "To think I defended you to Denny. . . ."

"Denny? What does he have to do with any of this?"

"He said you were fooling around with Becky Malone, and I told him no way." She let out a sickened sigh. "I'm such a fool."

"You're not a fool."

"The evidence would suggest otherwise." She climbed in her Jeep and slid the key in the ignition as snow fluttered down.

17

Unable to sleep, Piper pulled a plate from the dishwasher and shoved it onto the shelf. Adrenaline still surged through her limbs. *Becky Malone and Landon?* It was all wrong. This wasn't Landon. Not *her* Landon.

She lifted another plate and clanged it on top of the other.

Landon was so rigid, so by the book. She bit her lip. Maybe Denny was right. Maybe she didn't know Landon as well as she thought, and the idea left her feeling horribly off-kilter.

She tossed the last of the plates on the stack.

"Do you know what time it is?" Kayden asked, entering the kitchen, half asleep and in her pj's. "Who ticked you off?"

Piper reached for a glass.

Kayden halted her. "Let me get that."

"Fine." Piper stepped back with a huff.

"So, who's got you this riled up?"

Piper sank against the counter. "Landon."

"Well, there's a shock." Kayden smiled.

"Actually it is." She wasn't sure which had been a bigger shock, Reef falsely accused of murder or finding Becky at Landon's.

"Reef's case?" Kayden asked as she gently placed the glass in the cupboard.

"No. Not exactly." Though Becky could explain Landon's distraction—his standoffishness.

"Then what?"

She hated to even say it, but if she didn't talk to somebody, she feared the weight bearing down on her chest would crush her. "I went to tell him something I found out, and . . ."

"He wasn't happy about it?"

"I didn't even get the chance to tell him. I was too, too shocked." Pain quickened in her chest, as it had when she'd spotted Becky.

Kayden shut the empty dishwasher. "By what?"

"By who, actually."

Kayden's dark brows furrowed.

"Becky Malone."

"At Landon's?" Kayden nearly laughed.

Piper nodded.

Kayden's mouth slackened. "Was she . . . ? Were they . . . ?"

"It sure looked like it."

"I don't believe it." Kayden leaned against the counter beside her.

Neither did she. Landon had always been so upstanding and uptight. Seeing him like that, with his shirt open, his hard stomach . . .

"What did you say?" Kayden asked, hopping up on the counter, her long legs dangling.

"I don't even remember." Her heart had thumped so hard, shock ringing in her ears, the memory seemed far off and distant—not something she'd personally experienced.

"Yeah, I really don't believe he's sleeping with her, but they could be an item. . . . I wonder if Cole knows." Kayden popped a pistachio in her mouth from the bowl Piper had left on the counter.

She hadn't even thought of that. Denny knew. How many others?

No wonder Landon thought her naïve. And no wonder Landon had balked at her matchmaking attempts for him and Nancy Bowen, if he preferred women like Becky Malone.

The thought alone strangled her. She felt sick in the pit of her stomach—that horrible homesick feeling that gnawed at her gut and made her feel lost. "How could he . . . ? Becky Malone? What would make him choose her?"

"Yeah. She doesn't really seem like the relationship type."

Relationship. How long had it been going on? Was Becky the reason he'd been pulling away from her? Would he pull even further away now that she knew about them?

Her throat tightened. She couldn't lose Landon.

Kayden narrowed her eyes. "Why are you taking this so personally?"

"I'm not." She started wiping the counter.

"Yes you are."

"Well . . . sleeping with someone outside of marriage is wrong."

"Of course it is. Completely wrong. . . . Piper, I'm pretty sure you misunderstood what was going on, but even if they are, I don't feel personally betrayed by Landon." Kayden hopped down from the counter. "You obviously do." She grabbed another pistachio. "The question you need to ask yourself is why."

⚭

Landon stood outside of Piper's house, leaning against the giant spruce beside her window. He'd seen Becky safely home and found himself drawn here, longing to climb the spruce's sturdy branches to Piper's window overhead, longing to wake her and explain. Even if Piper never viewed him as anything more than a friend, he needed her to know he hadn't slept with Becky.

He needed to tell Piper how he felt so she'd understand his "distance and distraction" had nothing to do with Becky Malone and everything to do with her. But the thought of Piper looking him in the eye, telling him she could never love him like *that,* tore the breath from his lungs. He just wasn't strong enough.

Cole and Piper said Jesus was the source of their strength. Pastor Braden spoke often about finding strength in weakness, but he didn't know. . . .

He scuffed the snow with his boot.

He'd prayed before, and his worst fears had come true. How

would this be any different? What was the point in praying if God chose not to fix the hurtful things in life?

Piper would say God was there through it all, that God had a plan and purpose, but that purpose was often hard to see.

"Now faith is being sure of what we hope for and certain *of what we do not see."*

Cole had shared that verse with the teens in his youth group not long ago. Hebrews, if he remembered right.

Taking one last glance at Piper's dark window, he turned and headed for home.

Could God really fill the hole eating away inside of him? Could He give him the strength he needed?

He gazed up at the night sky.

If you're really there, like Cole and Piper say, could you show me?

Just like on the job, he needed evidence. Blind faith wasn't an option.

18

Gage cut through the water, his fervent paddling propelling the kayak across the chilly predawn bay. No sooner had he returned to his sister's place last night than Darcy had shown up holding the signed nondisclosure agreement. While he wanted nothing to do with her, his family wasn't ready to proceed without her help. Not unless he produced another reporter. As far as he was concerned, swapping her for another reporter was simply swapping trouble for trouble.

Darcy was bright and quick, and if harnessed for their purposes, she could probably be of great help. With the paper work signed, she couldn't legally print a word about him and Meredith, but that provided little comfort. Meredith had talked to Darcy about them, and Darcy wasn't the sort to leave things be. She was too much like his sisters in that way. Always digging. Always curious.

The sun crested over the mountains, rising in the sky, its radiant beams swathing the deep blue waters. Gage increased his pace, letting the heat spread through his arms with each stroke. He'd let Darcy work the case, but he'd be right at her side, making sure she held to her end of the agreement.

∞

Piper approached the upper ski lift at Kaner Mountain Resort exactly at noon, as instructed. Kaner Resort sat directly across the mountain from Yancey on the north and otherwise barren side of Tariuk Island. Only those interested in more extreme trails made the potentially hazardous drive. The road, rather than cutting through the treacherous mountain pass, wound around the outer edge of Tariuk Island and consisted of remote stretches prone to ice and avalanches.

The resort consisted of a rustic lodge, a few groomed trails, and an open wilderness ripe for heli-skiing. Kayden ran many of Last Frontier Adventures's heli-skiing excursions out of Kaner.

"Single rider?" the lift operator called.

Piper raised her hand.

"Move forward," he instructed.

She shuffled her snowboard the few remaining feet to the open slot on the line and pushed forward as the chair swung behind her and the other single rider.

Once they lifted off, Megan Whitaker smiled and ran a hand through her shoulder-length blond hair. "Well done," she said, pulling the safety bar down in front of them.

"Thanks, but I'm not really sure why we had to be so secretive."

"After the flack Ashley got for talking to that cop?" Megan slid her pink fleece headband over her ears. "No way do I want to be known as a snitch."

"Don't people want Karli's killer to be found?"

"Most believe he already has been."

"They really believe Reef killed her?" Didn't they know her brother at all?

"Not all of us," Megan said, "and that is why I agreed to meet you."

"Thank you so much." She'd been so ecstatic with the possibility of a new lead that she'd rushed straight to tell Landon. Finding him with Becky had squelched her excitement but not her desire to find the truth.

"No problem," Megan said. "But you've only got a couple minutes before we reach the top, so I'd get to it if I were you."

"Right." She refocused her thoughts. "I know the evidence doesn't look good for Reef, but I also know my brother, and he couldn't have killed Karli. Is there anyone else you can think of who might have wanted to harm her, someone capable of such a thing?"

Megan smiled, and her striking blue eyes twinkled. "You obviously didn't know Karli."

"No, why?"

"I'm surprised Reef didn't tell you."

"Tell me what?" They'd been too upset to discuss anything other than how they were going to get his name cleared.

"Karli wasn't well liked."

"By who?"

"Just about everyone."

"Why?"

"Karli was . . . a world unto herself. She liked to drink, party, sleep around—and didn't much care who with."

"Meaning guys that were already taken?"

"Exactly."

"So that's why the ladies didn't like her, but what about the guys?"

"Karli tended to stir up trouble wherever she went. Probably why she moved around so much."

"But you roomed with her."

"No one else would take her."

"That was nice of you."

Megan shrugged. "Karli knew my cousin Tess. She said there was a kinder side to Karli, so I took her at her word."

"And was your cousin right?"

"It's hard to say. Karli and I had only been at the lodge a couple days when . . ." Megan swallowed. "Well, you know."

"You mentioned last night that you might know where Karli was living prior to the circuit."

"Yeah, she and Tess were bunkmates."

"You know where?"

"In British Columbia—a couple different places. I think they were at Wolf Creek Lodge a while back, and Tess is working there again."

"Is Karli from Canada?"

"Originally?" Megan shrugged. "No idea. Karli kept to herself."

"You said your cousin knew Karli better than most?"

"Yeah, but that's not saying much. Karli was really guarded."

"Any idea why?"

"No, I couldn't tell if she was just abrasive or if she was . . ."

"What?" Piper prodded.

The lift reached the end, and they both scooted off.

Megan waited until a pair of skiers exited the lift behind them and skied away before speaking. "It probably sounds melodramatic, especially considering the circumstances, but Tess told me she thought Karli was scared."

"Of what?"

Megan paused while another group skied off the lift.

"Tess said it was like Karli was always looking over her shoulder. She moved around a lot. Never stayed long in any one place." Megan's gaze darted to the lift. "Look, I better go."

"Who are you worried about seeing us together?"

"Anyone from the circuit." She slid her goggles in place. "You've got to understand, the extreme sports circuit is a tight-knit community. We keep things 'in house,' if you know what I mean."

"What kind of things?"

"Whatever happens off the slopes stays private."

"And a lot of that private stuff involved Karli?"

Megan nodded.

"Any of it cause for murder?"

Megan shrugged as she pushed off. "Depends on what you've got to lose."

∞

Piper took a sip of hot chocolate before pulling out of the Kaner Resort parking lot. As nervous as Megan had been about meeting, in the end she'd been helpful. Tess was her first strong lead. Now Piper just had to track her down.

She placed her drink in the cup holder and turned right onto Highway 11—the only road connecting Yancey to the north side of the island. It was only a two-hour ride back to town, but with the excitement of a true lead coursing through her, it'd probably seem a lifetime.

The road was quiet today, most skiers still on the mountain. But she had no time for boarding, no time for fun. Not while Reef was rotting in jail.

She couldn't wait to reach home and tell everyone about her discovery, though she'd let Cole pass the news on to Landon. She couldn't face him, not yet, not with the images of last night still seared in her brain. What would she say? What *could* she say? She still didn't fully understand the overpowering emotions reeling through her, and until she did, she didn't trust herself to be in his presence—not until her heart settled and her mind kicked back in.

She popped in Kutless's latest CD, praying her thoughts would focus on God and not on a shirtless Landon.

∾

Of course she couldn't leave well enough alone. The sheriff was fully convinced Reef was guilty, even the detective was looking in the wrong direction, but no, *she* had to keep poking her inquisitive nose where it didn't belong. He needed to put a stop to that. Needed to dissuade her from proceeding further, before something led her to them.

He spotted her Jeep a hundred yards ahead on the highway. He'd stayed far behind until they were well into the wilderness, assuring no one would see. He accelerated, drawing closer, until he could see her eyes widen in the rearview mirror and then he struck.

19

Landon answered his cell as soon as Cole's name flashed on the screen. "Hey, Cole."

"Piper's been in an accident."

"What?"

"I'll explain when you get to the hospital."

Minutes later Landon entered the hospital, the pounding of his heart echoing in his ears, drowning out all other sound. He rushed past nurses, his vision narrowing with the halls.

The triage bays were just ahead. He spotted Kayden's silhouette through the glass and banked right.

Someone spoke as he pushed his way through a cluster of medical personnel, but the words sounded like mush.

His heart in his throat, he stepped into the bay.

Piper sat on the gurney—alert and arguing. A few minor scrapes and bandages covered her arms, neck, and face, but nothing horrible.

Sweet relief flooded him, the built-up adrenaline burning through his limbs as it dissipated.

Gage squeezed his shoulder. "Hey, man."

"She's okay?"

"I'm fine. I just wish everyone would stop fussing." She tugged at the snowflake-print hospital gown, trying to get it to shift with her.

"You got run off the road," Cole said, standing guard at the right side of her bed. "Of course we're going to fuss."

"What?" Shock reverberated through Landon.

"It happened so fast. All I know is one minute this SUV is on my tail and the next I'm being pulled from my Jeep at the bottom of the gorge by the paramedics."

"And the other driver?"

"Gone," Cole said.

"Meaning . . . ?"

"The creep hit her, knocked her car off the road, and fled."

Landon's jaw tightened. No one local would hit Piper and flee the scene. "Did you get a good look at the vehicle?"

Piper shook her head. "It was a black or at least a dark color SUV, but like I said, it all happened so fast."

"I'll call the highway patrol and see what I can find out."

Cole nodded his appreciation. "It happened on the north side of Highway 11."

Landon's eyes narrowed on Piper. "What were you doing on the north side of Highway 11?" Also known as Avalanche Alley.

"Coming back from boarding."

"Who was with you?" He could ask them what happened.

"Just me."

"You went boarding . . . by yourself?" Piper rarely went anywhere by herself. She was too social. So opposite him.

"Yeah. I went to the slopes by myself."

Something wasn't right. She was answering too specifically, and was that a hint of a smirk on her lips? "What's going on, Pipsqueak?"

"I thought we agreed you'd stop calling me that." She linked her arms across her chest and winced at the pressure she'd put on the IV needle still in her arm. She shifted gingerly.

"You asked. I never agreed." He turned to Cole. "You know what she was doing out there?"

Cole's gaze dropped to the ground.

"Wait a minute. Does this have something to do with Karli's case?"

Piper cocked her head. "Perhaps."

He stepped closer, coming up on the left side of her bed. "What did you do?"

"Asked a couple questions about Karli."

"Piper, you've got to stop. Let me do my job."

"How does it hurt if I help?"

"You're in a hospital bed!"

Her eyes widened. "You think this has something to do with my asking questions about Karli?"

Only Piper would be excited about the possibility someone was trying to silence her. "It's too early to say."

"But you think it's a possibility?"

"It's possible," he said reluctantly, knowing it would only spur her on when she should be resting, should be staying safe.

"Which means Karli's killer is still out there." Delight danced across her battered face.

"Or someone has something to hide."

"Like the fact he killed Karli."

"Or the fact he had an affair with Karli."

"Masterson." She sat up straighter. "You think Masterson killed her?"

"How did you know about Masterson? Never mind," he quickly said before she could answer. The less he knew about her prior antics, the better. All that mattered was that she stop—*now*. Before anything else happened to her. "I'm not suggesting Masterson killed her . . ." Though the thought had crossed his mind. "I'm saying someone could want you to stop poking around so you don't uncover something they've worked hard to hide. It may have nothing to do with Karli's murder and everything to do with protecting his or her reputation."

"How could my finding out where Karli worked involve anything detrimental to someone's reputation?"

"You know where Karli worked?" They believed somewhere in Western Canada, though the lady was proving extremely difficult to track.

She smiled. "See, I'm being of help already."

"At what cost? You could have been killed."

"Please." She exhaled. "I've taken harder knocks climbing."

"At least when you're climbing no one is trying to kill you."

"Maybe not rock climbing, but sometimes I think the ice has a mind of its own." She looked at Kayden. "Remember that time in Ecuador?"

"Piper!" Landon felt at his wits' end. "Let's stay on task."

"Fine. I was pointing out how I've helped *you* by getting a lead on where Karli has been living and working when not on the circuit."

How could he go from being terrified of losing the girl to wanting to throttle her in a matter of minutes? "And where was that?"

"I met with one of the competitors—Megan Whitaker. That's what I came to your cabin to tell you last night—that I'd arranged a meeting."

He stiffened, fearful she'd bring up Becky. They needed to talk, to clear the air, but not here, with her entire family present—and not when she'd nearly been killed. To his surprise, she simply continued on.

"It turns out that Karli bunked with her cousin in British Columbia. The cousin, Tess, is currently employed at Wolf Creek Lodge about an hour outside Kamloops. I plan on starting there."

"Meaning?"

"I'm going to British Columbia."

A mix of concern and frustration heated his cheeks. "Oh no you aren't."

"Yes I am."

Landon swung his head in Cole's direction. "A little help?"

Cole cleared his throat. "Piper, it's not safe for you to go tracking down a murder victim's life in a foreign country."

"It's Canada, Cole, not the Middle East. I've traveled plenty, and more importantly, I don't require permission from either of you."

The woman liked to drive him mad—that's all there was

to it. "I've got to get back to the station. We can continue this conversation later."

"Oh joy," she said, with obvious sarcasm that had to make Kayden proud.

Without another word, Landon signaled Cole to follow and stepped into the hall.

Cole was clearly worried. "Do you really think someone was trying to shut Piper up?"

"They should have known that would be an impossible task." He sighed. "Sorry. Not funny under the circumstances. I've got too much nervous energy."

"It looks like you haven't slept in days."

Landon ran a hand through his hair. "Too much to do. Look . . ." He pulled Cole out of Piper's line of sight. "I'm going to call the highway patrol and learn what happened out there. In the meantime, promise me, one of you will stay with her at all times."

"You think she's still in danger?"

"I don't know, but I'm not willing to take any chances." Not with the woman he loved.

20

Landon left the hospital with a hundred thoughts dancing through his mind. Was Reef the killer or was the killer still on the loose? Was Piper's accident a random act of road rage, or was it linked to Karli's murder? And if it was linked, what had Piper learned that set off the driver of the other vehicle? Or was it simply the fact that she was digging around?

More importantly, how could he keep going as is when he knew Piper wouldn't stop pressing until she got herself killed? How could he possibly protect her when he didn't know where she was half the time? He knew as well as Piper's siblings that their protests were falling on deaf ears; as soon as Piper was discharged she'd be on a plane to British Columbia. He knew what he had to do. She'd left him no choice.

The drive to the station took under three minutes, not allowing him much time to plan, but he'd reached a decision.

Twenty minutes later, his ears still ringing from Slidell's rant, Landon crossed the front porch to Cole's door, bracing against the bitter winds. The temperature had dropped another ten degrees below zero. He was thankful the paramedics had reached Piper quickly. It would have taken no time for her to freeze to death. He looked across to her and Kayden's house. She was either really lucky or extremely blessed. God seemed to be whispering the second in his ear. He'd called out to God, and God had answered. Question was, how would he respond?

Cole answered before he knocked.

"We need to talk."

"Come in." Cole led the way into his family room, where Kayden, Jake, and Bailey sat.

"I'm glad you're all here." He slipped off his hat and gloves and set them on the stone mantel to warm.

"Any news from the highway patrol?" Bailey asked.

"Yes. It definitely wasn't an accident. Whoever hit Piper did it intentionally. There were no skid marks; the driver of the other vehicle didn't so much as tap his brake. Just sideswiped her off the road and kept on going." The image brought an even deeper chill to his bones.

"Why Piper?" Bailey asked. "Why not Megan too? Both had the same conversation."

"That's the critical question. I'm heading back to the hospital to get more info out of Piper."

"And then you'll talk to Megan?" Jake asked.

"If I can locate her."

Kayden frowned. "What do you mean?"

"She's gone."

"Gone? The championship hasn't even started yet."

"Regardless, she's gone. Pulled out of the competition, checked out of the lodge, and left."

"Why? You think she heard what happened to Piper and got scared?"

"News travels fast in Yancey, so it wouldn't surprise me at all. She probably feared she'd be next."

"Have you told Slidell?" Cole asked. "Surely he's got to question Reef's role in Karli's death now."

Landon swallowed. Slidell was as convinced of Reef's guilt as ever, which had made his decision even easier to make. "There's something else I need to tell you."

"Okay," Cole said, apprehension lingering in his tone.

"I've handed Karli's case over to Slidell."

"You did what?"

"I gave Slidell Karli's case, and—"

"And you might as well just sentence Reef." Kayden stood, pacing. "You know Slidell is gunning for reelection."

"I know, but—"

"Then how could you—"

"Let me explain."

∞

Landon poked his head around the doorframe of Piper's hospital room.

She was flipping channels on the TV while Gage reclined in the chair, his feet propped on the edge of Piper's bed, a comic book in hand.

"Iron Man?"

Piper's hand stilled on the remote.

"Captain America." Gage smiled. He stood and tucked the book under his arm. "If you're going to be here for a few, I'm going to grab some grub."

"Sure. I'm not going anywhere." He looked at Piper as Gage exited the room, realizing it was the first time they'd been alone since that night at his house. He slid his hands in his pockets. "How are you feeling?"

"Anxious to get out of here." She smoothed her hair back.

She looked better, more alert, even somewhat rested, but now that his initial overwhelming relief for her safety had settled, he took on the extent of her wounds. Nothing life threatening, but they were far more significant than he'd first realized. Bandages covered generous portions of her arms and face. A strand of hair was stuck in the adhesive on her right cheekbone.

"You've got . . ." He stepped toward her.

Her hand flew to her face, and she winced as it made contact.

"Let me." He leaned across her. "You've just got some hair stuck in this bandage." He gently tugged her hair as she fidgeted. "Hold still."

She frowned but did so.

Her hair felt soft and silky between his fingers. Gently peeling back the corner of the wrapping, he extracted the strands and slipped them behind her ear before refastening the bandage. "There. All better."

She grasped his hand, not letting go. Heat shot through him. "Things aren't better."

He looked her in the eye, taking in the full depth of emotion shining back at him. "I know, and I'm sorry." So, so sorry.

"Then find Karli's killer."

He slid his hand into his pocket as she released it, wanting to preserve the warmth of her touch for as long as possible. "I took a look at your report."

"My report?"

"From the accident, though I don't know why we all keep calling it that. It wasn't an accident."

A glimmer of hope brightened her brown eyes. "It wasn't?"

"No." He sank into the chair beside her bed. "Whoever drove you off that road did so intentionally. What I've got to figure out is why."

"Because of Karli. Because of questions I was asking."

"What kind of questions?"

"About her life, her past . . ."

"I'm going to need you to be more specific."

"Okay."

He listened as she relayed her and Megan's conversation in its entirety.

"Sounds like Karli had a lot going on. There could definitely be a lead in there."

"Exactly what I thought."

He shifted, unsure how she'd take what he was about to say. Would she thank him, blast him, or not care either way? "I've given Slidell my leave-of-absence notice."

"You what?" Confusion flitted across her beautiful face.

"Slidell is hindering me from doing my job, and you guys are my family, and I'm going to—" Horror radiated through him as Piper lunged for him with open arms.

He leapt to his feet, catching her midair.

Her arms wrapped snugly around him. "Thank you."

"You're going to hurt yourself." He placed her back in bed. "You're still hooked to the IV for goodness' sake."

"None of that matters."

"Your health and safety matter." More than anything.

"So where are you going to start?"

He arched a brow.

"On proving Reef's innocence?"

His heart lodged in his throat. "I . . ."

Her eyes narrowed. "You believe he's innocent. That's why you left, right?"

"I left so I could work the case with a clear conscience."

Her brows pinched together. "So, this is about your conscience? Not about proving Reef's innocence?"

This is about protecting you. "I'm going to find the truth whatever it takes."

"But you still believe that truth might mean Reef's guilt?"

"I'm looking for the truth without bias." The evidence still didn't look good for Reef, but he was beginning to believe the kid might actually be innocent. He wouldn't tell Piper, not yet, not until he was certain. "I'm heading to British Columbia to retrace Karli's steps. I'll start with Wolf Creek Lodge and hopefully Megan's cousin Tess."

"I'm going with you."

"No you're not. You are staying right here, where your brothers can keep an eye on you." He knew it was foolhardy to argue, but he had to try, had to make her see the danger she was in.

"I'm an adult. Contrary to what you and Cole seem to think, I don't need a baby-sitter."

"No, but you do need someone looking out for you—especially now."

"I can take care of myself."

He glanced at her injuries. "Clearly."

Her jaw stiffened. "I got the information, didn't I?"

"At what cost? You could have been killed." Didn't she understand that? They'd all come way too close to losing her today. He couldn't imagine a world without Piper, nor would he want to.

He tried to ignore the hum of the air-filtration system, the slow rhythmic drip of the IV, both painful reminders of where they were. Of how close she'd come to being seriously injured.

"But I wasn't," she said, her voice gaining strength.

"This time." He prayed there'd never be a next time. "You've got to be smarter about these things, safer."

"Great. Another lecture."

Heat coursed through his veins, but he maintained an even tone. Yelling would only shut her down, and he needed her to hear him. "If you'd actually listen, I'd stop giving them." He studied the tightness in her face, the stiffness in her body. He hadn't meant to upset her; he'd meant to help. His shoulders slackened. "You don't understand." He swallowed. "You don't know what I thought when Cole called. When he said you'd been in an accident. How I . . ."

"How you . . . ?" she asked softly.

For a moment he thought of telling her *everything*. How fiercely he loved her. How the thought of life without her was a bleak suffering he feared he'd never be able to endure.

The door creaked behind him.

"Special delivery for Miss Piper McKenna." Denny entered with a large bouquet of colorful balloons dancing about his head.

"Denny." Piper's gaze flashed from Denny to him and back again.

Landon stood. "I'll leave you two alone."

"But we weren't done talking," she said.

"It'll wait." He ducked out of the door before she could argue.

136

21

Landon hefted his duffel bag higher on his shoulder as he made his way through Vancouver International. He'd left before Piper could be discharged, providing her zero opportunity to join him. She'd be mad when she learned he'd left without her, and he had no doubt that, if he wasn't fast enough, she'd be showing up as soon as she was able. He would speak with Tess and a handful of Karli's co-workers and then head back to Yancey before Piper had the chance to leave the hospital. It wasn't necessary for him to learn everything about Karli's life; he simply needed to dip into it and determine if anything warranted further scrutiny.

He stifled a yawn, battling the weariness clawing at him, knowing the harder part of the journey lay ahead. A small six-seater was about to replace the roomy commercial jet he'd taken from Anchorage to Vancouver.

He didn't dislike smaller aircraft, having flown on the McKennas' floatplane since he was a teen, but this particular small craft would be flying him deep into British Columbia's rugged wilderness, where rough terrain and dangerous air currents held the potential for a deadly mix.

Reaching the end of the corridor, he pushed open the exterior door, and a swirl of snow gusted in at his feet. Peering through the snow-riddled darkness, he spotted his plane waiting amidst the thickening flakes, the floodlights illuminating the pearly metal against the black backdrop of the night's sky. *Great.*

"Hold the door," a female voice called. An entirely too familiar female voice. It couldn't be. He'd left her at the hospital last night. Surely they hadn't discharged her so quickly. He turned to find Piper loaded down with an oversized duffel and several smaller bags, hurrying toward him.

"You've got to be kidding."

"What?" She shrugged, the bags slipping down her arms. "I wanted to be prepared."

"Not that. What are you doing here? You're supposed to be in the hospital."

"They discharged me."

"And, of course, you played no part in making that happen?" She was impossible.

"The point is," she said, ignoring the question, "I'm free to travel."

"Congratulations." He gripped her by the shoulders and spun her around. "Ticket counter is that way. I'm sure they can get you back to Yancey soon."

"I'm going with you." She wriggled from his hold.

"No you aren't. You're in no shape to be traveling." All of the bandages on her face except the rectangular one above her right eyebrow were gone, but bruises and scratches remained.

"I beg your pardon?"

It was nearly impossible to tell an adventure athlete she actually required time to recuperate. "I'm worried about you."

"That's sweet . . . but unnecessary. I'm fine. Now let's scoot before our plane does."

He blocked the exit door. "Piper, you shouldn't be here. Go back to Yancey. Let me do my job." He'd never be able to concentrate with her along.

She cocked her head in that way that meant trouble was coming. "We both know I'm going—either with you, where you can keep an overprotective eye on me, or on my own. Which do you prefer?"

What he preferred was to yank her into his arms and kiss her senseless.

"Landon?"

"You're impossible." He groaned, pushing open the door.

Blustery wind swirled in as she slipped past him.

"You won't even know I'm there." She hurried across the snow-swept tarmac and handed her bags to the waiting attendant.

"Like that's possible." He sighed and climbed the metal steps into the Cessna, thrilled with and utterly terrified of being alone with Piper for a few days.

She chose the first set of seats and plopped in the window one. "Can I help it if I'm memorable?"

"That's one word for you."

"And you have a better one?"

"Dogged? Stubborn?"

"Very funny. What about you?"

Landon slid into his seat as three passengers shuffled past. "What about me?"

"If we're pointing out flaws . . ."

"Then you should be at a loss for words."

"That's hysterical."

"That you'd ever be silent? I know, but I continue to hope." He winked playfully.

"You *hope*. Now that's hysterical. You are the most—" She stopped short, her gaze shifting to the pilot, who was watching them with keen interest.

He was young for a pilot—thirty at most. A smile curled on his lips. "Are you two always like this?"

Landon sighed. "Yes."

"No," Piper corrected.

The pilot chuckled. "Must make for some passionate nights."

Piper's cheeks flushed, and her eyes darted to the rest of the passengers, their attention also focused on them. "We're not . . ." Her slender finger swished between the two of them. "I'm not . . ."

Landon leaned forward, taking pity on her. "It's not like that, man."

"So the lady is single?" He looked at Piper, broadening his smile.

"Well, yes," she sputtered.

"No," Landon said, giving his most definitive don't-even-think-about-it glare.

The pilot held up his hands and turned back to his controls.

"Now who's being impossible?" she muttered with a sigh.

Landon pulled a file from his bag. "You can thank me later."

Piper flipped open her magazine. "Ignoring you now."

He chuckled beneath his breath. She could try, but as easily as she got under his skin, he got under hers. If only everything he felt for her was mutual.

∞

He sat back with a smug smile and settled in for the flight. He'd walked right past them en route to his seat, and neither had batted an eye. He'd followed Miss McKenna, and she'd in turn led him to Detective Grainger. While the good detective's departure from Reef's case boded well for him—the sheriff had already pronounced the man guilty—the detective's little side trip with Piper set him on edge.

There was too much for them to learn, for them to uncover, but it was well hidden. It had taken him a long time to track Karli, and he was excellent at his job. Hadn't lost a target yet. But they were bright and posed a greater threat together than separately. He'd tail them, and if they got too close, he'd see their investigation ended permanently. But no sense jumping the gun—leaving two bodies and opening a world of speculation. No. He'd bide his time and if the situation required, the rugged Canadian wilderness would provide ample opportunities for "accidents."

22

Piper followed Landon to the ski instructor's desk for what would be the third attempt to locate Megan's cousin Tess. So far either no one at Wolf Creek Lodge knew the lady or no one was talking. Piper, of course, suspected the latter. Everyone became evasive the minute it was clear they were looking for someone.

"Ready for a lesson?" the cheerful gal behind the counter asked. She was young, late teens or early twenties, slim, tall, and blond. She smiled at Landon in a way that made Piper uneasy. What was with these women? First Becky Malone and now this gal, ogling him.

Sure Landon was handsome. He had deep blue eyes, chiseled cheekbones, and a strong jaw. And he was muscular, not in the WWE bulging way that she found a bit much, but in the fit, masculine manner that emphasized his rugged build and strength. He was manly, whereas Denny was refined. Landon was definitely rough around the edges, but she had to admit there was something very enticing about the fresh outdoorsy scent of his aftershave and the five-o'clock shadow that covered his neck before the day was out.

"Nope, sorry," the lady was saying.

Piper straightened, heat rushing her cheeks. She prayed Landon hadn't seen her staring at him. She blamed lack of sleep and high altitude for the stupid quickening of her heart.

"Anyone else you can think of who might know her?" Landon continued to press.

Piper reined her attention back to the situation at hand.

The cheerful, flirting girl had pulled back at Landon's questioning, just as the others had. "Like I said . . ." She handed Karli's photo back. "I don't know her or Tess."

Landon shoved the photograph back in the envelope. "Thanks anyway."

Piper leaned in to Landon as they stepped away. "What now?"

"Maybe the lift operators will be more accommodating."

They stepped outside, and snow shifted beneath their boots as they approached the first lift.

Piper eyed the operator. College-age guy—bleached blond hair fringing his shoulders, the chill of winter on his cracked lips. She rested a hand on Landon's arm. "Why don't you let me give him a try?"

Landon extended his arm. "Be my guest."

Giving her hair a quick tousle and her lips a fresh swipe of lip gloss, she approached the young man, praying for any smidge of information that might be of help to them.

She smiled as she approached him. "Hey."

He glanced from his monotonous task and returned the smile.

"I'm Piper."

"Zack."

She waited until he signaled the next group of boarders onto the open chair.

"Nice to meet you." She shimmied closer, catching sight of Landon's smirk as she did so.

"Pleasure's all mine." Zack winked. "Looks like you took a gnarly spill."

Piper brushed the hair back from her bruised face. "Not enough to keep me grounded."

He smiled, clearly impressed.

"You look like someone who knows the ins and outs of this place."

142

"Grew up on the mountain," he said proudly. "You looking for the best run, babe?"

"Always, but that's not why I'm here."

His brow hiked up as his grin grew. "Oh, really?" He signaled the next set of riders forward.

"I'm looking for a friend."

"Is that right?" He stepped closer. "Well, I happen to get compliments on just how good a friend I am."

She forced back a chuckle. The guy was a player through and through. "I'll bet you are, but I'm looking for my friend Tess."

"Oh yeah?" His gaze shifted to the right, to a group of women seated by the fire pit. "How do you know Tess?" He was clearly testing her. One of the women had to be Tess.

"I don't know her yet. Her cousin Megan told me to look her up next time I was here."

"So why'd you say you were a friend of Tess's?"

"Well, I guess I misspoke. I should have said friend of Tess's cousin."

"Right." Zack's smile faded, and his gaze shifted back to the lift. "Well, I haven't seen Tess since last season."

Last season. At least someone had acknowledged the fact that she'd worked there.

"Sorry I couldn't help." He shrugged.

Oh, but you have. "Well, thanks anyway."

"Anytime, darling."

"That looked like an interesting conversation." Landon smirked as she walked back to his side. "Did he tell you where we could find Tess?"

"In a manner of speaking."

"And?"

"We've just got to sit back and watch."

"Watch what?"

Piper hopped up on the fence rail, which was positioned out of sight of the lift, but with a direct line of sight to the fire pit. "Which of those girls Zack talks to." She pointed to the group gathered around the fire.

Landon didn't question her any further, just took a seat beside her on the rail.

"No." She tugged his arm, pulling him down to his feet and then toward her. "Stand here." She positioned him in front of her. "It'll help shield me and blend us in better." She lifted her chin, indicating the various couples canoodling around them.

Landon followed her gaze, and then his eyes locked on hers.

Her gaze focused on his mouth—his bottom lip fuller than the top. Perfect for . . .

He tapped her knee. "You still with me?"

"Yeah." She cleared her throat, embarrassment flushing her cheeks. She gazed over at the fire pit and then to the lift. Zack was gone. She gaped back at the pit. Had anyone left? Six girls. There had been seven. She quickly scanned the remaining faces, trying to picture the one that left. *How could I be so stupid?* All she had to do was watch, but she'd let Landon get in her head, let her thoughts run away again, and now she'd probably messed up their only chance at finding Tess.

Landon frowned. "What's wrong?"

"She's gone." Zack was quick.

"Who? Tess?" Landon spun around.

"There were seven women. Now there are only six, and Zack is gone. He must have warned her and they both left while I was distracted."

His brows arched. "Distracted by what?"

"Never mind. It's not important."

To her surprise, instead of reaming her out, which she actually deserved, Landon simply grabbed her hand and tugged her off the rail. "I'll go this way. You go that way. They couldn't have gotten far. It's only been a couple minutes. His hair should stand out."

Landon released her hand and headed toward the lodge. Piper headed in the opposite direction, toward the base of the slopes.

She scanned the crowd, searching for Zack's bleached blond hair as daylight quickly faded to night. Too many people were gathering, ready to return to the lodge after a day on the slopes.

Lifting on tiptoes, she peered toward the fringes and spotted what she thought might be the back of Zack's head about thirty feet ahead.

She started pushing her way through the quickly amassing throng. "Sorry, excuse me," she called as she passed.

Her view obscured by the wealth of bodies, she kept pushing forward and rising up intermittently to catch another glimpse of Zack's blond tresses. He entered the rental shop, and she ducked in after him. It took her eyes a moment to adjust to the interior lighting.

Lockers lined the walls, and a bevy of skis and boards lined the return counter, and at the far end Zack strode toward the rear door.

She moved toward him, skirting discarded ski boots, hopping over duffels littering the floor.

"Hey, watch it," someone yelled.

She turned. "Sorry." Her feet slipped out from under her and she landed—her head, back, and behind colliding with the concrete floor. Pain ricocheted through her.

"You okay?" A man appeared overhead, concern marring his brow.

"Whoa. That was a gnarly tumble." A ski instructor in a red jacket bent beside her.

"I'm fine." She stood and her head spun. She had to get out that door and find Zack before it was too late.

"You sure you're all right?" the man asked.

"I'm fine." She moved forward, ignoring the pain racking through her head as she darted for the door. Swinging it open, she rushed back into the cold. The wind splashed her face with renewed alertness. She was opposite the lodge entrance. Outside lights were flicking on, illuminating the freshly falling snow.

Her gaze darted to the ground. Fresh footprints led toward the lodge. Hoping she was headed the right direction, she followed, her pulse quickening. The prints quickly disappeared into the hard-packed snow surrounding the lodge deck.

She entered through the side door and found herself at the

end of a long hall. Racing down it, her head spun faster and faster until the wildlife-print wallpaper seemed to pop out at dizzying speed.

Rounding the corner, she slammed into a body—hard and unforgiving. Jolted back, she struggled to keep her footing.

"Whoa, there." A hand reached out and steadied her.

"Zack?" she said, looking up in a haze. Had she actually found him?

"Are you following me?"

"No. Yes. I mean . . ." She scanned the hall, hoping to see Tess, but it was just the two of them. "I just wanted to tell you, if you should run into Tess . . ." What would assure Tess that she was friend not foe?

"Yeah?"

"I'm trying to help a friend of hers."

"How's that?"

"I'm trying to find her killer."

∞

Landon found Piper in the lobby, her back to the fire, her gaze fastened to the Christmas tree.

Of course she'd be staring. All the ornaments were woodland animals, including miniature stuffed moose wearing tiny snowflake-print scarves.

He slumped down beside her on the brown leather sofa. "No luck?"

"I found him."

Landon straightened. Then why did she look so disappointed? "And Tess?"

She shook her head. "But I got a message to her, I think. I told Zack that Megan sent me and that we were after Karli Davis's killer."

"You think it will help?"

"I pray so." Piper gingerly rubbed her temple.

"You okay?"

She shrugged. "Just slipped."

146

"Are you hurt?" It seemed a stupid question with her bumps and bruises, but he meant any new injuries.

"Just sore."

"What'd you hit?"

"Pretty much my entire backside. At least it gave folks a good laugh." She smiled. "Not too often do you see a person's feet go flying above their head."

Concern welled inside him. "Let me check you out."

"I'm fine."

"I'll be the judge of that." He took her hand and led her back to her room—directly across the hall from his. He'd been waiting for her to say something about finding Becky at his house that night, but she hadn't. Not a word on the flight. Not even on the hour-long drive to the lodge. Nothing. They'd checked in last night, he'd seen her safely to her room, and today had been filled with searching. He needed to say something, needed her to know he hadn't slept with Becky, but the timing didn't feel right. Things were going well. They were talking, laughing even. He had her all to himself, at least for a couple days, and he didn't want to ruin it by bringing up Becky. There'd be time to talk on their return trip to Yancey. For now, he just wanted to enjoy her company. Enjoy having her to himself, even if she'd never be *his*.

"I'm telling you, I'm fine," she protested as they stepped into her room and closed the door behind them.

"Humor me."

"Fine." She sank onto the green-and-burgundy tweed sofa.

He started with testing her for a concussion and then did a thorough assessment of her bumps and bruises. "Well, other than the goose egg forming on your noggin"—he touched it gently and she winced—"I think you'll be okay."

"Like I said, nothing a long soak in the tub can't cure." She pulled off her boots and stood, stretching.

There was nothing overtly sensual about her actions, but the notion of Piper in the tub was . . . His mouth went dry.

"I . . . um . . . should go." He scrambled to his feet, knocking over the first-aid kit in the process. He dropped to his knees to retrieve it. Piper did the same, her face mere inches from his. He quickly grabbed every item he could, tossing them back into the plastic container without any thought or regard. His hand landed on the roll of gauze the same time hers did. Her delicate fingers hovered over his. He yanked his hand back as heat rushed over his limbs.

Standing, he tucked the kit under his arm. "I'll go so you can . . . you know."

"Okay." She wrinkled her nose in that adorable way that caused her dimples to form. She stepped in the bathroom, and the water ran.

"Just call me when you're done . . . dressed . . . ready," he mumbled, sounding like a complete idiot.

She stepped back out of the bathroom, still fully dressed. "Are you okay?"

"Of course. Why wouldn't I be?" He loosened his collar. What did she have the heat set at in here?

"You are acting all fumbly."

He wasn't even going to ask what *fumbly* meant. He opened the door and tapped the lock. "Bolt this after me."

A sweet, seductive scent emanated from the bathroom as steam filled the air.

His throat tightened. "Bubble bath?"

"Yeah. What a great lodge, huh?"

"Yeah, great." Now she'd smell even more incredible the next time he saw her. "I should . . ." He turned and yanked the door shut behind him. He waited for the lock to click in place before heading for a shower of his own—a very long, extremely cold one.

23

Piper shook her head as she stepped to her duffel to grab a fresh set of clothes. At least Landon appeared to be as distracted as she was, though she doubted it was for the same reason. Landon didn't think about her the way she'd been thinking about him.

She grabbed her toiletry bag and headed for the bath. Setting it on the sink, she rummaged until she found a clip. She pulled her hair up and inspected the scrapes on her face. She trailed her finger over the scab on her cheekbone, remembering the tenderness of Landon's touch, the warmth of his skin against . . .

Thinking she'd heard a faint sound, she shut the water off and listened.

A soft rap on the door.

"Coming." She opened it expecting to see Landon. "What did you forget?"

Not Landon. Rather it was a woman similar in age to her but with Megan Whitaker's striking blue eyes.

"Tess?"

"Can I come in?" She was the same height and build as Megan but with short dark hair.

"Of course."

Tess glanced up and down the hall before entering.

"I'm so glad you came. You're a hard person to find."

"The junior suite," Tess said, glancing around. "Nice. I've never been in one. The employees get cabins in the woods."

"That sounds nice."

"They're okay." Tess shrugged. "But I wouldn't mind a touch of the finer things." She trailed a finger along the outer corner of Piper's fluffy white duvet.

"What happened to your face? Boarding crash?"

"Actually, car crash."

Tess scrunched her face. "Ouch."

"It looks worse than it is. Would you like to sit?" She gestured to the small sitting area that consisted of a sofa, two upholstered chairs, and a rustic wooden coffee table.

Tess plopped onto the burgundy chair. "Zack said Megan sent you."

"Yeah. She thought you might be able to help us learn more about Karli."

"Karli's dead," Tess said without batting an eye, but there was clearly sadness brimming inside.

"I'm very sorry."

"Megan said they've got Reef in jail for it."

"You know Reef?"

"Everyone on the circuit knows each other."

"You're on the circuit too?"

"Was. Had to take this season off for injury."

Piper looked her over, seeing no sign of injury.

Tess lifted her right leg. "Broke my ankle and shattered my calf bone. Cast came off months ago, but I'm still not ready for competition."

"I'm sorry." No wonder she was hurting. A serious injury and the death of a friend so close together.

"It's healing well. I'm back on the slopes, just in no condition to compete. Guess we can't all be like Karli."

Piper frowned. "Meaning what?"

"That came out wrong." Tess shook her head. "I still can't believe Karli's gone."

"When did you learn?"

"Megan left me a message. Told me about Karli. Said Reef's sister was trying to prove his innocence."

Thank you, Megan.

"That was the first message."

"First?"

"Yeah. Couple days later, she left me another message. She sounded really freaked out. Said she was taking some time off and for me to be careful."

"She say why?"

"No. That's why I wasn't too keen on strangers asking about me, especially when you didn't come alone."

Landon. "He's my friend. He's helping me."

Tess pulled out a cigarette and lighter. "You mind?"

Piper shook her head. Actually she did, but she wasn't going to say anything that might send Tess away, not after finally locating her.

"I know it's a bad habit." Tess took a drag, her bright pink lipstick leaving a ring on the butt.

"Just don't see many athletes that smoke."

"I hadn't in years. Not since college, but the injury kind of knocked me back. Not Karli, though."

"What kind of injury did Karli have?"

"Torn ACL."

"Ouch." Piper had seen it sideline lots of athletes. "How'd it happen?"

"She took a bad fall the last competition of the season. It was her first run, the slopes were icy, Karli was pushing it harder than she should have and ended up in the local hospital having ACL surgery."

"This was the end of *last* season?"

"Yeah—April."

"That's a fast recovery."

"No one could believe she was back so quick."

"And I get the impression not everyone was happy about it?"

Tess released a puff of smoke. "Not the gal she bumped."

"Bumped?" Piper restrained her urge to bat the smoke away. She couldn't afford to do anything that Tess might perceive as an insult. Tess's information could very well mean the difference between her brother's freedom and a life behind bars.

"There are only so many spots on the circuit, and the competition to get in is fierce. When Karli returned, lowest on the team got bumped."

"And who was that?"

"Gal by the name of Samantha Mann."

"How'd Samantha take the news?"

"How do you think? Doubt she'd trade places with Karli now, though." Tess snorted before taking another puff.

"It really is amazing Karli could compete so soon after her accident."

"Karli had her faults—a whole laundry list of them—but she was a stellar athlete."

"What else can you tell me about her?"

"What do you want to know?"

Piper stifled the urge to cough. "Was this the last place Karli worked before she returned to competition?"

"Nah-uh. In March we moved to Vailmont Village, but after Karli's injury she went to Glacier Peak for physical therapy. And after my injury I went there too."

Piper committed the names to memory, knowing Tess was way too squirrelly for her to be writing anything down. "So if Karli left anything personal behind, it would be at Glacier Peak?"

"Yeah, probably in the staff storage lockers."

Having the locations down, Piper shifted to the heart of the matter. "Megan said Karli seemed scared, like she was always looking over her shoulder. What was that about?"

"Don't know. Tried asking her once, but Karli had this way. If you ever tried to get personal, she'd switch subjects or simply ignore the question."

"You ever get past that wall?"

"A couple times." Tess nibbled her thumbnail. "During PT."

The phone rang.

Tess's gaze shifted to it.

"It can wait," Piper said, trying to keep the flow going. "You were saying . . ."

Tess started back in after the ringing stopped. "Therapy for an athlete is intense. All your hopes are resting on the fact it'll work, that you'll make it work, because if it doesn't, you're done."

Piper knew how hard it'd been on her brother. "My oldest brother, Cole, suffered an injury that ended his skiing career."

"That stinks. Did he survive it?"

Piper knew she wasn't talking physical life or death but rather his way of life. Many athletes sidelined by injury never fully recovered. "He found a new calling, a passion he loves even more—diving."

"That's cool." Tess flicked her ashes into the glass Piper set in front of her. "Don't know if I could have hacked it. I'm already dying, having to take this season off. I can't imagine what it'd be like if I knew I'd never make it back."

"And Karli?"

"Wouldn't have made it. She lived for competition. It's why she fought so hard to recover so fast, not that the other competitors were thrilled."

"Why do you say that?" She'd already heard it from others, but she wanted Tess's opinion.

"No one liked Karli much."

"That's what I've been hearing. What's your take on the reason?"

The phone rang again, and Tess's gaze shifted back to it.

"Whoever it is can call back," Piper said. She wouldn't risk losing Tess to a phone call. "So why didn't people like Karli?"

"Because she didn't play by the rules."

"How so?"

"She drank a lot, partied a lot, sometimes right before a competition—and half the time she'd still kill the other competitors. She slept with whomever she wanted to, regardless of their relationship status. She could be crass, and it seemed she loved nothing better than getting a rise out of someone."

"But Megan and you seemed to view her differently, or at least looked past all of that."

Tess stabbed her cigarette out, much to Piper's relief, and then sat back, linking her arms. "There was more to Karli. She made it difficult to see, but if you looked closely and spent more than a few hours around her, it was there."

"Like what?"

"Determination, dedication, a surprising vulnerability."

"Vulnerable how?"

"We got along well enough to bunk together. Most of the other girls wanted nothing to do with her. But it wasn't until we went through PT together that I got a glimpse beneath Karli's tough exterior."

Piper inched forward. "And?"

"I think underneath it all she was scared."

"Of what?"

"Of who she was."

A knock rattled the door. "It's me," Landon called.

"It's just my friend. Do you mind if he comes in?"

"You're sure he's okay?"

"Positive."

"All right, then." Tess shrugged, her tense shoulders contrasting sharply with the carefree gesture.

"Piper." Landon banged. "Open up."

"Settle down. I'm coming." She unlocked the bolt, turned the knob, and Landon rushed in.

"Why didn't you answer your phone?"

"Because I have company."

Landon looked past her. "Tess?"

"Yes," Piper said. "Tess has been kind enough to answer some questions about Karli."

"Landon Grainger," he said, stepping forward and extending his hand. "Thanks for your help. Sorry about barging in like that."

"It's cool."

"Mind if I join you?"

"No." Tess smiled for the first time since arriving. "Have a seat." She patted the one beside her.

"Before you came *barging in*, Tess was telling me about how she sensed Karli was afraid."

"I barged in because you didn't answer your phone."

"I had company. Besides, what if I'd been in the bath?"

"That's why I gave you a warning call."

"Warning call?"

"Yeah. I let it ring a couple times, hang up, give you time to jump out of the tub, and then call back."

"Why would you assume I'd jump out of the tub?"

"Because we're on a case, and it was me calling."

"So you assume I'd jump for you?"

Tess's gaze darted between them. "Are you two an item?"

"Us?" Heat skipped to Piper's cheeks.

"We're friends," Landon said, as he had so many times before, but this time it left Piper feeling empty.

She sank back on the couch, wondering what was wrong with her and when this uncomfortable stage would pass.

"Oh." Tess smiled again. "Well, I was telling your *friend* here that Karli was a really private person, but pain can be a great motivator. In Karli's case, her accident and subsequent PT chipped away some of her armor. After a really powerful PT session, she let it slip that she wasn't using her real name."

"Karli or Davis?" he asked.

"The whole thing."

Piper scooted forward. Now they were getting somewhere. "What was her real name?"

"I don't know. She never said."

"Did she say why she changed her name?"

"She claims she didn't, said it was changed for her."

"By whom?"

"No clue. You guys got anything to drink?"

"No, but I could run to the vending machine and grab a soda," Piper offered.

"Mountain Dew."

"You got it." Piper opened the door and glanced back at Landon. "Be right back."

He nodded.

∞

The door swung shut, and Tess leaned forward, resting her arms on her legs. "Look, your friend is super sweet and all, but I think you're the one who should hear this."

"I'm all ears." He tried to ignore Tess's proximity, not wanting to do anything she might see as a put-off.

"I think Karli was running from her past."

"What kind of past?"

"I don't know. The way she was always looking over her shoulder, never wanting to stay in one place too long, never getting close to anyone." Tess nibbled her thumbnail. "My guess . . . she was running from an abusive husband."

"Karli ever give any hint she'd been married?"

Tess slumped back. "No, but like I said, she wasn't a sharer."

He'd offended her. He needed to remedy that fast. "It's a great possibility."

She brightened. "You think?"

"Absolutely." It was definitely a possibility, and even if the abusive husband idea didn't prove to be true, the information Tess had provided was golden.

"I think he rode a motorcycle."

"Who? The husband?"

"Yeah."

"How come?"

"Karli was terrified of the sound of motorcycles. Whenever one was around she got all tense and irritable."

"Interesting."

Tess smiled.

The door opened, and Piper walked in, three cans of soda and a handful of snacks in her arms. She handed Tess the Mountain Dew. "I thought you might be hungry too. The vending machine didn't have the best selection." She dumped the snacks on the coffee table.

Tess shuffled through the pile and finally settled on a Snickers bar. "Thanks."

"No problem." Piper tossed Landon a Sprite.

"Thanks."

"So what did I miss?"

Tess exchanged a look with Landon. "Just chitchat."

Piper opened the bag of mini pretzels. "Cool."

Tess stood. "I've gotta go."

"So soon?" Piper stood too.

"Yeah."

"But I still have a lot of questions."

"I've told you all I know."

"Anybody else you can think of we should talk to? Maybe your and Karli's physical therapist."

"No." Tess grabbed her bag. "She's out of this."

Piper trailed her to the door. "What do you mean?"

"I mean she can't tell you anything I haven't, so leave her be."

"What about the people Karli worked with at Vailmont or Glacier?"

"You can try, but I doubt anyone's going to talk to you."

"Because we're asking about Karli?"

"Because you're going about this all wrong."

Piper frowned. "What do you mean?"

"The boarding community is tight. We take care of our own and don't care much for outsiders. The deeper you go in British Columbia territory, the tighter it gets. You two start asking questions and you'll get nowhere."

"Could you make introductions for us?"

"Nah, I don't want to get any more involved." She ducked her head and glanced at Landon. "Sorry."

"Well, what do you suggest?"

"If you decide to go to another lodge, try to blend in."

"How?"

"Act like you're there for lessons. Say you're friends of Karli's.

That she recommended the lodge to you a while back and you're just checking it out. Spend time around the instructors—show interest in boarding, let them feel comfortable around you before you start asking questions. Make it feel like a casual conversation rather than an interrogation."

"Great advice," Landon said. "Can we talk to you again?" It'd be good to talk with her one more time. See if anything jarred her memory after a good night's sleep.

"Can't. I'm leaving."

Landon looked at Piper and then back to Tess. "Really? How soon?"

Tess clutched the doorknob. "Now."

24

"This is so exciting," Piper whispered behind Landon as they crouched outside Tess's cabin door.

He clicked the lock open. With one more glance around to be certain no one had seen them, he slid into the cabin Karli and Tess had shared.

"Tess said it's been months since Karli last lived here," Piper whispered, stepping inside the dark cabin behind him. "That if Karli had left anything, it'd most likely be in the storage lockers at Glacier Peak."

"It's still worth checking out while we're here. Tess said no one has used Karli's room since she left. Let's check the whole cabin—look for anything Karli might have left behind."

Piper nodded enthusiastically and clicked on her small flashlight, illuminating a huge grin.

He shook his head as she disappeared down the dark hallway. No wonder he worried about her. What other woman got excited about breaking and entering?

He turned the knob on the door closest him and stepped into the bedroom. A few posters of snowboarders and several wilderness scenes hung on the paneled walls. A desk and matching dresser, reminiscent of assigned dorm furniture, lined the opposite wall.

He scanned the shelves and furniture tops. Nothing personal in nature. A single bed with bare mattress sat against the far wall.

Karli's room. He rested the flashlight on top of the dresser and started opening drawers from the bottom up. The first three were empty, the fourth held a few items of clothing—some socks, a couple thermal tops, and a pair of snow pants. He sifted through them, hoping for any hidden items but came up empty-handed. He moved to the desk and found even less—a couple pens, a blank notebook, and a pair of sunglasses.

He dropped to his knees and examined the underside of the desk, the dresser, and finally the bed.

"You find anything?" Piper asked.

His breath hitched momentarily. The girl was like a ninja. She was the only person he never heard coming. "Nope." He got to his feet, dusting off his jeans. "How about you?"

"Tess's room is full of stuff, but this"—she held up a planner—"looked most promis—"

The cabin door creaked.

Landon steadied Piper with his hand.

"I'm telling you I saw a light flash in this window," a woman said.

"Sure you did."

Landon quietly pulled the bedroom door shut.

"I know what I saw."

"Fine, we'll check it out, but I still say you're being paranoid."

The lights clicked on in the front room.

Landon indicated the window, and Piper moved quickly for it.

"I'm not the only paranoid one," the woman said, their voices drawing nearer.

Piper lifted the sash.

"What's that supposed to mean?" the man asked, their voices just outside the door.

"Duh. Tess. She bolted after those two started poking around."

Landon shoved Piper out the window and then dove out after her as the bedroom light flicked on.

Piper grunted as he landed on top of her.

"The window's open. Who's paranoid now?" The woman's voice grew perilously close.

Landon rolled Piper with him flush against the cabin wall, hoping his dark jacket and the bushes would camouflage them.

"Maybe Tess left it open," the man said.

"Yeah right."

Landon ducked and held his breath as the man poked his head out the window.

"You see anything?" the woman asked.

"No." The window shut.

With an exhale, Landon rolled off Piper. "I'm sorry. You okay?"

She sat up slowly, and he studied her in the soft glow emanating from the window. He brushed the hair from her face, fearful he'd added to the hard knocks she'd encountered in the last few days. His hand stilled, cradling her soft skin in the curve of his palm.

She blinked.

"Are you hurt?" His throat was dry.

She shook her head.

The light clicked off, shrouding them in darkness, and a minute later the front door opened.

Landon once again pulled Piper to him as he flattened against the cabin wall. He could feel her heart thudding against his chest, skittering rapidly, like his.

"I'm telling you, something's not right," the woman said.

"What do you want me to do?"

"I don't know, but we need to keep an eye on those two."

"The ones poking around about Tess?"

"And Karli."

Their voices faded, and Landon reluctantly released his hold on Piper. He stood and helped her to her feet. "You sure you're okay?"

A grin spread across her full lips. "I'm great."

"Huh?"

"That was *so* much fun."

"Fun?" The girl really was crazy.

"Oh, come on." She brushed the snow from her pants. "You can't tell me that didn't feel exhilarating."

Every nerve ending in his body was on fire. *Exhilaration* didn't come close.

∞

Piper yanked the gloves from her hands and tossed them on the hotel-room coffee table. Her mind was racing as quickly as her heart. No wonder Landon enjoyed police work so much. The thrill of tracking down leads. . . . It was addictive. "Why do you think Tess reacted so strongly when we asked about speaking with her physical therapist?"

"I don't know." Landon slipped his jacket over the chair. "It seemed like she was trying to protect her."

"From what?" she asked as Landon knelt in front of the hearth.

"I don't know."

"Well, hopefully this"—Piper held up the planner as she plopped on the couch—"will help us find her."

Landon arranged the kindling and stacked a couple logs over it. "We should give room service a call and get some food sent up. I have a feeling it's going to be a long night."

"Good idea." She smiled, loving the thought of the night ahead—her and Landon before a roaring fire, working together to solve a crime. Just the two of them. She wondered if that was about to end, and if Becky . . .

She cut off the thought. *Don't go there. Keep your focus on the case.*

Landon struck a match and held the flame to the kindling, letting it catch fire before tossing the match in. He left his boots by the hearth and strode back to her. "You really thrive on this, don't you?"

"Working a case with you? Yes, very much."

A smile tugged at the corner of his mouth as he sat beside her. "What?"

"I'm just trying to decide if that's a good or bad thing."

25

Landon sat on the floor, his back propped against the couch, notes spread out on the carpet around him. He tried to ignore Piper's close proximity as she leaned forward from her seat on the sofa, her head hovering a hairsbreadth from his shoulder as she studied the planner in his hand. He breathed in the soft floral scent of her hair, marveled at the silkiness of her skin as her hand brushed his.

"We're getting closer." Her breath rippled gooseflesh along his neck.

"W . . ." He cleared his throat. "What?"

"Tess's shorthand." She reclined back on the sofa and crossed her legs beneath her.

"Right. Shorthand." He cleared his throat. Tess's planner was no more than a series of gridded sheets and lined pages. No months, no headings, and nothing that seemed to indicate a set calendar year had been observed. It was like she'd used up the original planning tools, torn them out, and replaced them with the extra note and grid pages as fill-ins, using a crazy organizational system of initials and numbers. What it resulted in was a nightmare to try and decipher.

Loathing the sudden distance between them, Landon stood and moved to sit beside her on the couch.

"Could you stoke the fire?" she asked before he sat.

He looked back at the dying embers. He hadn't even noticed.

"Sure." He handed her the planner and bypassed the discarded room service tray. He'd set it out in the hall when he left for the night . . . or the morning was more likely. But he wasn't complaining. It meant more time with Piper.

He bent by the hearth and stoked the fire back to life before adding another log.

"Look at this entry—JP I 2.4 23. I think JP is a person's initials," she said, and he could almost hear the wheels spinning.

Landon sat next to her and studied the entry. "Or a place."

"Okay, but the next set must be dates."

"Looks that way. Perhaps a date and then a time?" But what kind of time was 23? Unless it was military time, 2300. Or was it Tess's shorthand version of 2:30?

"So taking into account the approximate date of Tess's injury, the initials TN that repeat regularly on the dates that follow are probably related to her physical therapy."

"And we know she was living up at Glacier Peak at the time."

"So we should be looking at physical therapists in the area with the initials TN."

Landon grabbed his laptop and started searching. In under an hour, they located Wellspring Physical Therapy in Invermere, British Columbia—only a half hour from Glacier Peak resort. The lead therapist's name was Taylor Nash.

Piper reached for her cell.

"What are you doing?"

"Calling Taylor Nash."

"It's after midnight."

"Right. I forgot."

"We'll call first thing in the morning."

"Okay." She tapped her pencil against the planner in rapid succession.

"Morning will be here before you know it."

She nodded.

"I should go so you can get some rest."

"Yeah, right. We both know I'm too pumped to sleep."

"So you want to keep going?"

"Of course." She lifted the planner. "Since we know the letters represent initials . . ."

"We don't *know*."

"Fine. We're following a hunch they are."

"We're following what makes the most sense. Hence, logic."

"Call it whatever you will, but going with that theory, it appears there is only one reference to Karli back while they were doing physical therapy."

"If K represents Karli." A lot of names started with K, as did a lot of places.

"Well, let's just assume for the moment it does. The numbers that follow are different. They are too long for a date or a phone number. . . ."

"Unless there is an extension involved."

"Extension. Very smart."

"Only if it's right."

She nudged him with her shoulder. "Learn to take a compliment."

"Fine. It's brilliant, but in reality those numbers could be anything."

"Ignoring your pessimism. Now, what about the *S. Bridge*?"

This entry they assumed referred to Karli was the only entry that included more than initials and numbers.

"A place, maybe." She tapped the pencil against her full bottom lip.

"Oddly, it sounds familiar."

"It does?"

"Yeah, but I don't know why." Was it a place he'd been or a person he'd met? The familiarity was there but little else.

"Maybe we should get out an atlas and start looking for bridge names that start with S. Do you think we should start here or in Alaska?"

"I'd start closest to her home."

"So British Columbia?"

"Assuming that was Karli's actual home. All we know for certain is that she'd been living in this area a couple years." The deeper they dug into Karli Davis's life, the more of a ghost she became. No one but Tess seemed to know anything of significance about her, and even what Tess knew was sketchy.

"Why do you think she was going by an alias?"

"We don't know that she was." He draped his arm across the sofa's back.

Piper frowned. "But Tess said . . ."

"What Karli told her."

"Exactly."

"You're assuming Karli was telling the truth."

Piper's eyes narrowed. "You think she lied?"

"It doesn't seem like Karli had the best moral standards."

"Because she slept around?"

"For one."

"Interesting you should say that." She shifted to face him better.

"Why's that?"

"I'm just curious . . . Do you think sleeping with someone outside of marriage is wrong, or is it because Karli had multiple partners, some married, that offends you?"

"I'm just saying I don't think what we've learned of Karli shows her actions to be of the highest character."

"Agreed, but you haven't answered my question."

"I thought we were talking about Karli."

"We were." She scooted closer. "But now I'm asking you. Where do you stand on sex outside of marriage?"

"I think people should wait until they are married."

"Really?" She cocked her head.

"Why do you sound so surprised?" The words left his mouth before the cause of her question dawned. *Becky.* How could he have been so dense?

"I've heard you tell the teens in Cole's youth group how important it is to wait, but then . . ." She blinked and looked away, staring into the fire's renewed flames.

His throat tightened. "Then?"

The words choked in her throat. "You were with *her.*"

166

His heart squeezed at the ache in Piper's voice. "Piper, I promise you, nothing happened."

"What's your definition of *nothing?*"

Leave it to Piper to cut to the chase. "Nothing means *nothing.* Becky came over wanting something to happen. She tried to make it happen, which is what you saw, but nothing did. After you left, I drove her home and haven't spoken to her since."

His words didn't bring the relief he'd hoped to see on her beautiful face.

"Why was she there in the first place?"

"She just showed up. She was waiting on my front porch when I got home."

"Because of your night together at Hawkings?"

He winced at the hurt on her face. "I don't know what Denny told you, but we didn't have a night together at Hawkings."

"So you weren't there?"

How he wished he could say he wasn't. "I was."

"On the job?" Hope clung to her words.

He ached to avoid the truth, but he couldn't lie to her. "I'm afraid not."

"Then, why? To meet her?"

"No." He gathered his courage. "I went in for a drink."

"Oh." Her forehead creased. "I didn't realize you did that."

"I don't." Or at least he hadn't in a very long time. Not since the last time he'd tried to forget.

"Then . . . why?"

"It's a long story."

She glanced about the quiet room. "I'm not going anywhere."

He prayed that was true. "It's late." And there was no way to honestly have this conversation with Piper without telling her how he felt. Coward that he was, he wasn't ready to face that rejection yet. Besides, he didn't want her to feel horribly awkward. They still had several days of investigation before them, and he didn't want her feeling uncomfortable because her brother's best friend had fallen hopelessly in love with her. "We should get some sleep."

Taking the planner, he stood, and she followed him to the door, looking less than pleased with his abrupt end to their conversation. "What's our next step?"

"Our next step?"

"Yeah. What's the plan for tomorrow?"

"Right, tomorrow."

Her eyes narrowed. "What did you think I meant?"

"Nothing. So tomorrow . . ."

She cocked her head as he scrambled to focus. "You okay?"

"Fine." He cleared his throat. "I just think we've gotten as far as we can here."

She took a step closer, effectively pinning him between her and the door. "How far did you hope to get?"

His mouth went dry. Surely she didn't mean . . .

"On Karli's case."

"Right. Karli's case. I . . . um . . ." The door felt heavy at his back, the knob cold against his palm. His mind was playing dangerous tricks on him. Piper was asking about the case, not flirting with him.

"You . . . ?"

"Think we should move forward."

She smiled sleepily. "Moving forward sounds interesting."

"To Vailmont," he said a bit too loudly.

Her smile widened. "To Vailmont."

He nodded. "I think we've learned all we can about Karli here." He shook his head, trying to rein in his wandering imagination. "I think our next move should be to Vailmont, since Tess thinks Samantha Mann is still working there. And we can try to confirm the identity of Karli and Tess's PT before heading to Glacier Peak."

She stifled a yawn. "Sounds good."

He lingered, knowing he needed to go but loath to do so. She was right there, barely a foot from him. If he simply reached out, he could pull her into his arms and . . .

And what?

She was talking about the case. It was only his stupid mind

racing in a different direction—the dangerous direction of *them*.

She lifted on her tiptoes. "Is there something else?"

"No." He shook his head. "Nothing." Nothing she'd want to hear.

"Then I guess I'll see you in the morning."

"Right. See you in the morning."

26

Landon flipped over, scrunching the pillow beneath him, his senses tingling with anticipation. *Unfounded anticipation.*

His brain was playing cruel tricks on him, making him believe that Piper had actually been flirting with him, that she could actually feel the same way. He rolled over and chucked the pillow across the room. Trying to sleep was useless; his brain was rattling a million miles an hour in a direction he couldn't go. He reached over and clicked on the lamp. *Might as well put this energy to good use.* He grabbed Tess's planner and his notebook off the nightstand, propped his back against the headboard, and got to work.

Shortly before dawn, the reason for the familiarity of *S. Bridge* finally clicked. He knew a U.S. Marshal by that name, Scott Bridge. The man had mentored Landon's college roommate Luke his first year in the Marshals Service and had helped Luke bounce back when he lost his first witness. More than likely Tess's reference was to an entirely different S. Bridge. And perhaps the notation was for a location, as they'd originally thought and not for a person, but his gut said to make the call. He pulled out his cell and scrolled through his contacts until Luke's name and number appeared.

Landon found Piper in the lodge restaurant, a plate of half-eaten pancakes before her.

"No good?" He gestured to the plate, trying to keep the conversation on a safe topic.

"They were fine. Have you eaten yet?"

"No. I'll grab something before we head out." He snatched the laminated menu and scanned it, his eyes skimming the words but his mind not registering them. Piper was all he could think about. What they'd said, hadn't said . . . almost said.

He hated the awkwardness. He yearned for the comfort and ease that used to exist between them but knew it would never return. They'd be forced to move forward, one way or another.

But for now they had a case to crack. He flipped the menu over, still not registering a single word. "Did you get ahold of Taylor Nash?"

"No, but I left a message. The receptionist wasn't helpful at all."

"What do you mean?"

Piper stabbed at her pancakes. "She wouldn't confirm that Karli or Tess were patients."

"That's not surprising."

"Well, there is no sense driving all the way to Invermere until we know we've got the right TN. At least not until we're finished at Vailmont and are on our way to Glacier Peak."

"Which will be soon enough."

She exhaled. "I just want to know we are on the right track."

"I know." He resisted the urge to reach for her hand.

"At least I got ahold of Gage."

He set the menu aside. He'd just order coffee and toast. "And?"

"I asked him and Darcy to check into Karli's employment records with the circuit. Gage said they'd pay Masterson a visit today. Hopefully there's something in Karli's file that will lead us to her true identity."

"If she really was using an assumed name."

"You still think Karli was lying to Tess?"

"I don't know what to think at this point." *Or feel.*

"So we should pursue every angle."

"Exactly. Which is why I placed a call to a friend, Luke, with the Marshals Service."

"Marshals Service? Why would they . . . ?" Her forehead creased and then her eyes widened. "You think Karli was in Witness Protection?" she said entirely too loudly.

"Shh." He glanced around to see if anyone had heard and decided not to mention the potential lead via Scott Bridges until they were on their way to Vailmont. He didn't want her excited response broadcasting their lead to the whole lodge.

On second thought . . . maybe he'd wait until his hunch was confirmed. He didn't want her getting her hopes up, only for them to be dashed.

"Sorry." She leaned in, excitement dancing in her eyes. "What did you learn?"

"Nothing yet. Luke's going to look into it and call me back. Probably a long shot, but . . ."

She smiled. "You followed your gut."

"And it'll probably lead nowhere."

"Or it may be the key to it all."

∾

Piper followed Landon into Vailmont Village. It was more luxurious than Wolf Creek. Signs highlighting their various spa treatments filled the lobby—the airy space an unusual mix of chandeliers and exposed wooden beams. A silver Christmas tree adorned only with burgundy velvet bows glistened in the center of the spacious lobby.

She felt absolutely ridiculous after her pathetic attempt at flirting last night. No wonder Landon looked so uncomfortable. Poor guy had probably been desperate to flee, and yet . . . he'd seemed reluctant to leave.

She snagged a brochure from the metal stand to her right and leafed through it. She needed to focus on the case, on proving her brother's innocence, and let her stupid fantasies of Landon go, especially the absurd notion that he might actually be suffering from the same attraction.

"So how are we going to do this?" she asked as he directed her toward the lesson desk. They'd discussed the basic plan per Tess's suggestion but hadn't delved into specific details.

"We'll sign up for the next available class and then check in while we're waiting."

"No, I mean which one of us is going to be the beginner? The lesson pamphlet shows two levels." She held up the brochure. "Beginner and intermediate. I think we can cover more ground if we split up and each enroll in a different level."

"Smart thinking. I'll take the intermediate."

"I knew you'd say that."

"Great, so it's settled."

"Not so fast." She tugged him to a halt. "We're going to do this the fair way."

"Which is?"

She pulled a coin from her pocket. "Heads or tails?"

∞

Piper couldn't help but smirk as Landon shuffled his way to the beginner's lesson. For someone who'd been skiing nearly as long as he'd been walking, the only way for him to portray even a remote sense of being a novice was to put him on a snowboard. She'd been trying to get him on one for years, and now that she had, she planned to enjoy every minute of it. Perched on the top rung of the fence rail, she nearly rubbed her mittened hands together in glee.

Since her intermediate class didn't start for a half hour, she decided to sit back and enjoy the show. She'd finally get to see Landon out of his element, and his glares in her direction said he wasn't the least bit happy about it.

To make things even better, he'd been able to get in the class taught by Samantha Mann, the woman Karli had bumped from this year's competition—though the registrar had explained with a gleam in his eye that Samantha preferred to go by "Sami, with an *I*."

Piper was a bit less gleeful, however, when Sami walked out of the lodge and approached her class. She was blond, shapely, and gorgeous, and all the male students brightened at her appearance.

The longer Sami spent with Landon—helping him into his gear, showing him how to balance by placing her hands on his hips—the more annoyed Piper became.

Maybe splitting up hadn't been such a great idea after all.

Sami made a demonstration run down a portion of the bunny slope, sashaying to a stop with a pronounced wiggle of her derrière.

Oh, please. Piper shook her head.

"Alaska," Sami called. "Why don't you give it a try?"

Landon pointed to himself.

"Yes. You." She smiled.

Piper waited for a tumble, a fall, anything to echo a novice's moves, but Landon took off like a shot, whizzing past Sami before sliding to a somewhat shaky stop.

"Great job, Alaska," Sami said. "Are you sure you haven't done this before?"

"Nope. Guess you're just a great teacher."

Piper strained forward. Was he actually flirting?

"Intermediate class?" a woman asked, popping her head into Piper's line of sight. She turned to follow Piper's gaze and whistled upon spotting Landon. "Quite a view."

Heat flushed Piper's cheeks. "What? No. I wasn't . . ."

"Don't sweat it. I was watching him myself. I'm Mandy."

"Piper."

"Are you in my intermediate jam session?"

"Yeah."

"You look kind of banged up. Sure you're up for this?"

"Always."

"Cool. My kinda gal. We're starting right over there." She pointed to the group of boarders huddling by the base of lift two.

"Great." At least Mandy seemed cheerful. Maybe she'd even be willing to talk.

27

Still shocked that she'd managed to talk Gage into waiting in his Rover, Darcy approached Masterson's trailer. Ever since he'd found her talking with Meredith at the bed-and-breakfast, Gage had been at her side, "keeping an eye on her," as he phrased it. While she didn't mind his company, his intentions were clear. He was making sure she kept her focus on Reef's case and off of the relationship he'd shared with Meredith. She'd barely seen Meredith in passing since that night. Once Meredith realized she knew Gage, she'd kept her distance. Perhaps, she too feared Darcy would poke her nose where it didn't belong. As much as Darcy wanted to understand what happened between the pair, she'd given her word, and she intended to keep it.

She glanced back at Gage in the SUV, thankful he'd agreed to let her approach the man alone. Jumpy as Masterson was, he wouldn't take kindly to one of Reef's siblings trying to interrogate him, and knowing Masterson's reputation with the ladies, she'd be far more likely to get the answers Piper and Landon needed on her own.

She knocked, and a woman answered the door. Tall, slender, and brunette, the woman wore tight jeans, an equally tight red cashmere sweater, and UGG boots.

She gave Darcy the once-over. "What do you want?"

Darcy extended her hand despite the frosty welcome. "Darcy St. James."

The woman linked her arms across her chest.

Darcy tried a different approach. "I need to speak with Mr. Masterson."

"About?"

"It's a private matter."

"He's my husband, so any private matter you think you have with him is completely my business."

So this was the often spoke of, rarely seen, Theresa Masterson. Rumor was she'd been quite the ski bunny until she'd wed wealthy, ten years her senior, Rick Masterson.

"I apologize; I didn't realize. As I said, my name is Darcy St. James, and I'm investigating Karli Davis's past."

"He's got nothing to say about that tramp." Theresa started to shut the door, but Darcy caught it.

"This has nothing to do with your husband."

"But you just said . . ."

"I should have explained better. I am trying to look deeper into Karli's past before she joined the circuit. I just need a quick glance at whatever records the circuit keeps on her."

Theresa eyed her with suspicion. "What for?"

Darcy gauged the woman, assessing the best approach to get the information she required. "It seems Karli may not have been who she appeared to be."

"Can't say I'm surprised. She was nothing but trouble. I knew it the first time I saw her strutting her stuff like she owned the mountain. Girls like her are a dime a dozen, and they never amount to anything."

"Sounds like you're an astute judge of character."

"Honey, it doesn't take a genius to peg a hussy."

"Do you mind if I come in? I think you may be the first intelligent person I've spoken to."

Theresa's already rosy cheeks deepened with color. "Why not."

∽

Piper sat at a table in the lodge cafeteria, staring out the nearly wall-length window, wondering where on earth Landon was.

His class had been slated to end an hour before hers and still there was no sign of him. She hoped that he'd at least garnered some useful information, something other than Sami's sign, measurements, or favorite color.

Unfortunately, she had made the mistake of telling her instructor she was a friend of Karli's. While she had no idea how Karli had wronged the lady, the fact that she had was abundantly clear. Mandy hadn't so much as made eye contact with Piper again.

Two days in British Columbia and nothing to go on, except the possibility Karli Davis hadn't been using her real name. They needed more—something tangible, factual—to prove her brother's innocence. And she hadn't been helping matters any by allowing Landon to consume her thoughts. It was time to focus on the case. *Strictly* on the case.

A cold draft seeped through the windowpane. Piper rubbed her hands together, trying to warm them. She still had the uneasy feeling that someone was watching her. She turned and scanned the cafeteria. Everyone was occupied with their own business. Her gaze settled on a man—tall, dark hair with wisps of silver, most likely early fifties—sitting at a table at the back of the cafeteria. He was reading a book while he finished his lunch. He was oddly familiar, though she didn't know why. Had she seen him before? Perhaps on their flight into Kamloops. She'd been too distracted by her verbal jousting with Landon to pay much attention to the other passengers, but something about him—

"Hey," Landon said, and she jumped.

"Sorry." He set a steaming mug in front of her. "Thought you could use something warm."

"Thanks." She wrapped her hands around the red ceramic mug, reveling in the heat. She inhaled the sweet, comforting scent of chocolate.

Landon sank into the chair opposite her, tossing his stocking hat on the empty seat beside him. His tousled hair stood every which way, but he looked downright sexy. "No whipped cream, I'm afraid."

177

Landon. . . . *sexy*? She really was losing her mind. She lifted the mug and took a sip.

"How'd your day go?" He asked, tearing into a BBQ sandwich that smelled incredibly good.

"Not nearly as good as yours," she muttered.

He wiped BBQ sauce from his lips. "What?"

"Never mind." She was being petulant. "Did you learn anything useful?"

"Not yet, but I'm taking Sami to dinner tonight." He took another bite of his sandwich.

"Dinner?" Her throat constricted. "As in on a date?"

"Yeah, why?"

She looked down, praying he didn't sense her disappointment. "I'm just surprised."

"Surprised I got a date?"

"No."

"Then what?"

She scrambled for a feasible response, something other than the silly jealousy swimming inside her. "Just surprised at the pairing." Much as she had been of him and Becky Malone.

Landon smiled, but there was hurt hiding in it. "You mean why is a beautiful young lady going out with a—let me see if I can remember how you described me. . . . oh yeah—scruffy grump with no fashion sense."

"You're quoting me out of context." And that wasn't it at all. Well, maybe it was partially. She hadn't pictured Landon being interested in a ski bunny like Sami, but at the same time, she hadn't pictured Sami picking a man like Landon. "It's just that ski bunnies usually go for guys like"—she scanned the cafeteria—"him."

Landon turned to look at the man she'd chosen—tall, blond wavy hair, classically handsome. He turned back to face her. "Just because you always go for the Ken-doll type doesn't mean all women do."

"I don't always go for the Ken-doll type."

"Brad Williams, Trent Dixon, Denny."

"You can't count Brad Williams. He was nothing more than a high-school crush. We never dated." Which made her wonder how Landon even knew about her interest in Brad.

"Trent and Denny?" He prodded with entirely too smug a smile for her liking.

"Coincidence." She shrugged.

"Right," he drawled. "Call it what you will, but I happen to know that some women prefer a real man to a Ken doll."

"Is that right?" There was the obnoxious Landon she knew.

"Yep. And I'm more than happy to oblige Sami—in exchange for the right information, of course."

Her eyes narrowed, her pulse quickening. What was he saying, *exactly*? That the date's progression depended on the information Sami supplied? "You wouldn't seriously . . ." She hushed as a group of instructors passed by with Sami bringing up the rear.

"See you at eight, Alaska." Sami winked.

"Looking forward to it, Canada." Landon smiled.

"Oh, please." Piper expelled a belabored huff after they'd passed. "You can't seriously mean to go through with this."

"My date? Absolutely." He stood, collected his things, and bent to place a kiss on the top of her head. "Don't wait up."

28

"How'd it go with Masterson?" Kayden asked from the kitchen as Darcy settled into the oversized leather armchair that was quickly becoming her favorite spot.

Every night they met in Kayden and Piper's family room to discuss Reef's case and the day's progress. And every night a homey meal—usually soup or stew—greeted her arrival. Then they gathered around a crackling fire, the scent of evergreen hovering in the air, always a sharp contrast to the blustery wind and frigid temperatures outside.

Bailey always made sure there was a hot drink to conclude the meal—fresh-roasted coffee, hot chocolate, or cider—the rich scents filling the kitchen and spilling over throughout the house. Tonight it was mulled cider.

Having grown up in Southern California, Darcy wasn't the biggest fan of winter, despite her frequent trips to Mammoth, Tahoe, and the winter events she covered, but the cozy warmth that surrounded the McKennas' certainly made winter a little more enticing.

"Darcy?" Kayden said.

Darcy blinked. "Sorry, my mind was drifting."

Concern flickered on Bailey's lovely face. "Is everything okay?"

"Fine. My mind just wanders sometimes, but to answer Kayden's question, my visit went very well."

Cole's brows arched. "He was actually cooperative?"

"*She* was extremely cooperative."

"She?" Bailey said. "Meaning . . . ?"

Darcy smiled. "Mrs. Masterson."

"That's surprising," Kayden said, taking the only seat open on the love seat next to Jake. Even then an invisible wall seemed to separate them.

Darcy seriously wondered what Jake had done to make Kayden so suspicious. Though the more time she spent around the man, the more intrigued she grew. Perhaps when this case was over, she'd do a little poking around about Jake Westin.

"Darcy." Gage snapped a finger in front of her face.

"Sorry." She blinked.

"Are you sure you're all right?" Bailey asked with genuine concern.

"Do you need a cup of coffee, something to jolt you awake?" Gage asked.

"No. My mind is already in overdrive. I'm thinking too many things at once."

Gage kicked his feet on the ottoman and slumped back in his chair. "You need to learn to relax."

"Perhaps you're right."

"You were telling us about your conversation with Mrs. Masterson?" Jake prodded.

"Right. Mrs. Masterson. At first she was somewhat hostile, but when I explained I was looking into Karli's past and not her husband's, the floodgates opened. I've never seen so much hostility directed at one person."

"I'm guessing she knew about her husband's affair with Karli?" Cole said.

"Yes, and I have the feeling there isn't much she doesn't know about when it comes to him. Interesting thing is, she blames Karli solely for the affair, despite the fact that her husband has quite the reputation for indiscretions with the new recruits on the circuit."

"Sounds like a real winner," Kayden said dryly.

"Tell me about it." Darcy loathed men like him and pitied the poor women they preyed upon, though she hardly believed Karli fell under that category.

"You think Mrs. Masterson is aware of his affairs?" Jake asked.

What he was really trying to determine was whether or not Theresa Masterson had motive to kill Karli. Darcy weighed what she'd observed of the lady. "Theresa's definitely a shrewd woman, misplaced as some of that insight might be. I think it's a safe bet that she knows exactly what goes on within the circuit."

"Then why does she stay with him?" Kayden asked, not bothering to hide her disgust.

"Money, prestige . . . thinks he needs her. Very dysfunctional and very sad."

"So she blames the women and excuses her husband?" Kayden's irritation heightened in her voice.

"It appears that way, but she seemed to possess a particularly strong dislike for Karli."

"Why do you think that is?" Jake asked, clearly intrigued.

"At first it just seemed to be a general dislike for a woman with no morals, but on deeper inspection . . ." She smiled at Gage.

He returned the smile. "Darcy did some digging online, and it turns out that Karli has broken all three of Theresa Masterson's records. Of course she was Theresa Dunbar back when she set them."

"So Karli wasn't just having an affair with her husband; she was also breaking her records," Bailey said.

"Right."

"Did she seem mad enough to kill over it?"

"Possibly, and it appears it's definitely not beneath Theresa to harm another competitor."

Jake leaned forward. "What?"

"Back in 2001, when Theresa was at the height of her career, she had some serious competition in an up-and-coming boarder named Kendra Morris. Kendra totally stomped Theresa in qualifying, and everyone assumed she'd blow her out of the competition, but the next day Kendra's equipment malfunctioned during her run. She lost control, flew off course, and sustained some serious injuries. She's lucky to have survived at all."

"And you think Theresa had a role in that?" Cole asked.

"That was the rumor."

"Any proof?" Jake asked.

"No, but two years later a similar thing happened with another up-and-coming boarder named Jessica Clarkson. She hammered Theresa in qualifying, but the day of the competition she came down with a horrid case of food poisoning."

"The timing is questionable, but food poisoning happens."

"Yes, but I dug a little deeper, and Jessica ate in the lodge with her entire team, and she was the only one who got sick."

"Was there an investigation?" Jake asked.

"In the first incident, the coaches inspected Kendra Morris's equipment and said the malfunction could have easily occurred with wear and tear. All inquiry stopped there. For the second incident, Jessica complained, but not much happened. It's extremely hard to prove food poisoning when you're dealing with a cafeteria that's serving a hundred athletes three times a day."

"And it's a big leap from food poisoning to murder," Jake said. "But it would probably be prudent to dig a little deeper into Theresa Masterson's whereabouts the night of Karli's murder."

"I agree," Darcy said. "I asked Theresa where she was when she learned about Karli's murder, trying to fish without making her suspicious."

"Good plan," Jake said.

"Thanks. Theresa claims she was staying at some sort of spa on Kodiak Island and didn't learn of Karli's death until she arrived in Yancey the following day."

"Convenient. She say how she traveled here?"

"Took the ferry from Kodiak."

"That's easy enough to confirm," Kayden said.

"And easy enough to fake," Jake added.

Kayden turned on him, her dark brown eyes narrowing. "How could you fake arriving on a ferry?"

"Oh, I'm sure she came in on the ferry," Jake said. "The pertinent question is whether it was her first trip in."

"How would you come up with something like that?" Kayden shook her head. "It's like how a criminal would think."

"Kayden, you've got to stop," Cole said, his tone wavering between annoyance and pleading. "This isn't helping anyone. We need to be sticking together, not trying to tear the family further apart."

"Jake is not family."

Jake winced at Kayden's painful words. "I'm not a criminal."

"And we're just supposed to take your word?"

"Have I ever given you reason to doubt my word?"

She swallowed, giving no response.

"We need to focus, for Reef's sake," Cole said, taking advantage of the momentary silence.

"I'll see what I can dig up on Mrs. Masterson's travel schedule," Darcy said, trying to be helpful, trying to calm the tension growing in the room.

"We should visit that spa in Kodiak," Gage said. "Confirm her whereabouts. Kayden, you want to fly us there?"

"You're going to fly? *With me?*" Kayden's eyes widened.

"Yes."

She smiled. "Sweet."

Darcy glanced to Bailey. "Is there something I should know?"

"Don't worry. Kayden's a great pilot." Bailey leaned over and lowered her voice. "Gage just isn't fond of heights."

"Really?" She looked at Gage. He was actually afraid of something? *Remarkable.*

"Did you get a look at Karli's paper work?" Cole asked.

"Oh, right." She'd gotten sidetracked talking about Theresa. She pulled a folded slip of paper from her pocket. "I made copies at the library and made a few calls."

"And?"

"It all lines up, but . . ."

"But?" Jake prodded.

Darcy shrugged. "It just didn't feel right."

"What do you mean?"

"I don't know. I can't put a finger on it; it just felt forced. All the particulars were there—date of birth . . . social security number—but nothing else. No living family. Last known address was a P.O. box. It was all very clinical."

"Anything on Karli's parents?" Bailey asked.

Darcy read from the paper. "Thomas and Rebecca Davis. Both deceased."

"Are their dates of birth and death listed?"

"No." Which she found odd. "Just their names."

"You talk to Landon about this yet?" Jake asked.

"Gage and I got off the phone with Piper right before we arrived here. We couldn't speak with Landon; Piper said he was on a date."

"A date?" Kayden said, disbelief ringing in her tone.

"Something about trying to get information. Piper didn't sound the least bit happy about it."

"I bet she didn't," Kayden said with a knowing smile.

29

Piper took another glance through the peephole. Nearly midnight and still no sign of Landon. What was taking him so long, and worse yet, what had he and Sami been doing all this time?

She walked to the bed and lay down. Why was his date with Sami bothering her so? Why his time with Becky Malone—whatever that might have been?

Her feelings for Landon were definitely changing, but she had zero clue how to proceed. She didn't understand the depth of her feelings, let alone what she wanted to happen. She just knew that she wanted Landon back with her *now*.

A knock roused her, and she groggily moved to her feet.

Relief swelled at the sight of Landon through the peephole. *Finally*.

Unlocking the chain, she pulled open the door.

"Morning, sleepyhead." He stepped past her into the room. "I brought donuts and coffee."

"Morning? What time is it?" She stared at the clock—8:00.

Landon yanked open the drapes, and sunlight flooded the room.

"I must have fallen asleep." She rubbed her eyes and then narrowed them. He looked awfully chipper.

"You didn't answer your phone, *again*." He fished a donut from the brown paper bag and bit into it.

"I didn't hear it. When did you get back?"

"From what?"

"Your date."

"Let's just say it was late." He plopped on the bed and pulled a second donut from the bag.

"What happened?" She couldn't not ask.

Landon licked some icing from his thumb. "Now, Piper, you know a gentleman never dates and tells."

Uncertainty rippled through her. "You didn't . . . ?" Had something happened? Had he and Sami . . . ?

"Didn't what?"

Man, he was grinning like a Cheshire cat. "Never mind." She moved to the bathroom and shut the door.

"Where are you going?" His footsteps padded across the carpet. "Don't you want to know what I learned?"

That depended. Was it about Sami or the case?

"I don't think Sami had any role in Karli's death."

"Oh really?" Just how had he come to that conclusion?

"Sami was bummed she got cut from the circuit, but she seems way too laid-back to strike out in violence."

"And that was the extent of what you learned?" He was out all night and the only thing he got was being convinced *by Sami* that she wasn't angry enough to kill Karli?

"No. There's something else. Unless Karli was a bride at sixteen, the abusive-husband theory is out."

Piper opened the door. Maybe they were getting somewhere now. "Why sixteen?"

"Sami says Karli lied about her age so she could join the circuit at seventeen. She convinced Masterson she was eighteen, because she didn't have parental consent."

Piper stepped past him into the sitting area of her room. "Because?"

"Her parents were deceased."

Just as Gage had said over the phone last night—her parents were listed as deceased on her circuit paper work.

"How did Sami know Karli lied about her age? That doesn't sound like something Karli would share."

"Sami said the first season Karli joined the circuit she won the title. A couple years later Sami heard Karli boasting about being the youngest to ever win it, but someone else had won the title at eighteen a few years earlier. Sami called Karli on it, and since, at that time, Karli was of age and couldn't be kicked off the circuit, she told Sami she'd lied initially about her age and that she had only been seventeen when she won the title, thus making her the youngest to win it."

"That's good, but certainly not staying-out-all-night good."

"Wow. This is really getting to you, isn't it?"

Much deeper than she'd imagined. The thought of him and Sami—the thought of him and any woman—suddenly choked her. "I don't know what you're talking about."

"Sure you do. You're upset I went on a date with Sami."

"Hardly." She took a seat on the sofa, trying to ignore the uncertainty crushing down on her. She needed to pull it together. Needed to sort through her feelings for Landon and figure out exactly *why* she was feeling them. Was it because he'd been so distant lately? Was it jealousy or something infinitely more profound? Deep down she knew the answer; she just wasn't ready to deal with the ramifications of it.

"So what is it?" he continued. "The fact that I went on a date, or the fact that it was with Sami?" He studied her. "That's it."

"What?"

"You don't like that my date was with Sami." He rubbed his chin. "Interesting."

She needed to shift the focus off her and quick. "*Interesting* is the last word I'd use to describe you."

"Now you're getting catty." His grin grew, irking her all the more. "You're really fired up over this."

She couldn't let him see the truth. Not yet. Not until she figured it out. "I'm fired up about the fact that you were out all night pretending to investigate while I was doing the real work." She stood and headed back for the bathroom, but he blocked her path. He had the most annoying habit of doing that.

"No," he said.

"No?"

"No." He waggled his finger. "That's not why you're upset."

She linked her arms across her chest. "Then tell me, Sherlock, why am I upset?"

"Because my date was with someone you didn't handpick for me."

"That's ridiculous." She tried to pass, but he met her step for step, continuing to block her way.

"Is it?"

"Yes."

"Let's take a look at the facts. You're constantly trying to set me up, complaining I have no life outside of work, but when I actually go on a date, you're ticked."

"I was trying to be a friend, trying to set you up with a good woman like Nancy Bowen, not some ski bunny like Sami or someone like Becky Malone." Though even the thought of Landon with Nancy upset her now.

"So it's fine if I date someone you approve of, someone safe. Is that it?"

"No."

"You know, for someone who is always complaining about how I interfere in your love life, sure seems like you're doing the exact same in mine."

She was. But were they doing it for the same reasons? Did the thought of her and Denny being together choke the breath from his lungs? Had he spent nights awake, praying her date would end early, praying nothing would happen to pull her from his life?

She gaped at him in shock. Did she dare hope that all his brutish protests over her dates with Denny had been out of love?

30

Piper held her mug under the coffee dispenser. Unable to continue her conversation with Landon, she'd excused herself for a shower and told him she'd meet him in the lobby in an hour.

Finishing in half that time, she'd meandered to the cafeteria for breakfast.

Her head was spinning, her thoughts racing, and she needed . . . *I have no idea what I need.* Uncertainty rippled through her. To top it off, they hadn't obtained anything concrete on Karli. Just suspicions and guesses. And they still hadn't received a response from Taylor Nash. They were leaving for Glacier Peak in a half hour and they *would* be making a stop at Wellspring Therapy with or without an invitation. She only prayed they had the right TN.

"You're Landon's girlfriend. Right?"

Piper looked up to find Sami standing in line beside her. "Friend. We're just friends." Surely he'd made that clear during *their* date.

"Uh-huh." Sami slid her bagel into the toaster oven. "No one is buying that, so you might as well drop the act."

Piper grabbed a muffin and set it on her tray. "I don't know what you're talking about."

"Sure you do. No sense denying it. Landon spilled the beans."

"He what?"

"He tried denying it, but come on, it's so obvious. You two are totally into each other."

"Me and Landon?" She forced a laugh.

"Ah, honey, you can't really be that clueless." Sami took her bagel, plopped it on her tray, and headed toward the cashier.

Piper followed Sami. First the lady went on a date with Landon, and now she was insulting *her*? "I'm far from clueless." Though she didn't exactly feel as *in the know* as she was accustomed to.

Sami handed her employee's card to the cashier. "Don't get your knickers in a bunch." She took her card back and proceeded to the turnstile.

Piper paid and stepped after her.

Sami looked up as she sat down at a table overlooking the base of the mountain. "All I meant was, when it comes to Landon you obviously don't see what the rest of us do."

Was she trying to suggest that *she* knew Landon better? "And what, pray tell, is that?"

"That he is a catch and that he only has eyes for *you*."

Piper's knees wobbled. "For me?"

Sami gestured to the open seat across from her. "You were practically all he talked about last night."

Piper sat. "Really?"

"Yeah."

"But Landon and I aren't—"

"Then you should be."

"You don't understand. Landon is . . ." How could she sum up everything Landon was to her in a handful of words? "He's . . ."

"Handsome, intelligent, passionate," Sami supplied.

Piper smiled. "I'll give you the first two, but *passionate*?" The very idea of Landon being passionate . . . Memories flooded her mind. . . .

The way he'd cradled her after the shooting, the fire in his eyes when he pressed her up against his wall while trying to drive home a point. Had she missed it all these years? Landon in his driveway after she'd found Becky Malone at his place. The haggard hunger in his eyes, the despair as she drove away—it was the fiercest emotion she'd ever witnessed in him.

"You still with me?" Sami said, waving a hand in front of Piper's face.

"Yeah, sorry, I was just . . ."

"Don't sweat it." Sami shook her orange juice carton before opening it. "Landon said you are headed up to Glacier Peak resort."

"Yeah, Tess said that's the last place Karli worked."

"Sounds about right."

Piper tried to focus on Karli, on the case—hard as it was to drag her thoughts from Landon and from what Sami had just shared. "Did you know her well? Karli?"

"Yes and no." Sami shrugged. "The gal had a lot of baggage. Sometimes I even felt halfway sorry for her. Other times . . ." Sami slid a straw in her juice. "Guess it doesn't matter now."

"Landon said Karli told you she was younger than she let on."

"Yeah."

"And you believed her?"

"Karli rarely said anything truthful, so on the few occasions she did, it stood out."

"Anything else that stood out to you as truthful?"

"I don't know . . . Something about her mom dying too young." Sami took a sip of her juice.

"Karli ever mention having another name?"

"Landon asked me the same thing, but no, I don't remember her ever going by anything other than Karli."

"She ever have family visit her, friends?"

"No. She was one of the few willing to work over Christmas. Never talked about her family, her home . . ." Sami cocked her head.

"What?"

"Well, there was this one time we were talking about the best boarders, and she was adamant that surfers made the best boarders."

"Not much surfing around here."

"You've got a few crazies that hit calving glaciers over in Alaska, but I got the feeling she'd grown up surfing."

"She ever say where?"

"Nope, and I didn't ask. Didn't really care."

"It seems barely anybody cared about Karli." It was sad.

"She did it to herself."

"Sounds like she was really lost." *And alone.*

"Yeah, but the thing about Karli is, I'm pretty sure she liked being that way."

∞

Piper waited outside the lodge entrance as Landon loaded their bags into the back of their rental car. The exterior of the burgundy 4Runner had seen better days, but the luxurious tan leather interior remained in nearly prime condition.

She watched the faint orangish hue of sun slipping through the cloud cover pick up the russet highlights of Landon's hair. How had she missed the allure of his rugged handsomeness all these years?

"You ready?" He held her door open.

She nodded and settled in.

Landon climbed in on his side and started the engine. "So what did you mean about the *real work* you did on the investigation last night?"

She put on her seat belt and clicked it in place. "It means I made some calls."

"Learn anything new?"

"Actually, yes." She relayed what Gage and Darcy had told her about Theresa Masterson.

"When are they checking into Theresa's alibi?"

"They're flying to Kodiak today."

"Anything else? Did they find anything suspicious in Karli's records?"

"Not exactly."

"Meaning . . . ?"

"Darcy said everything fit, but it felt fixed or clinical somehow."

"If Karli was with Witness Protection, I'd expect as much."

"About that . . ." She shifted to face him better. "If Sami was right and Karli joined the circuit at seventeen, there's no way that Witness Protection would allow her to do that."

"Maybe she left."

"Left Witness Protection?"

"It happens, more often than you think. It's not an easy road to travel, leaving everyone you love, maintaining stringent guidelines, never getting close to anyone."

"But wouldn't Karli's parents have stopped her?" She remembered Cole's insistence that Reef not join the circuit until he'd finished high school and turned eighteen. Reef left the morning of his eighteenth birthday and had barely been home since. She'd really hoped that maybe this time he'd stay, but that had been before Karli's death.

"Sami said Karli told her that her folks were deceased before she joined the circuit. Remember?"

"That's right. Sami also said Karli mentioned something about her mom dying too young."

Landon's hand gripped the wheel. "You and Sami spoke?"

She nodded.

"When?" He was trying to act casual, but his discomfort was painfully apparent.

"This morning. In the cafeteria."

"How'd that come about?"

"She was behind me in line at the breakfast buffet." She narrowed her eyes. Had he really confided in Sami about his feelings for *her*? "Why do you ask?"

"Just curious." He tapped the wheel. "What'd you two talk about?"

"Mostly Karli."

He glanced over at her. "Mostly?"

She ignored his question, tossing one his way instead. "How about you?"

"How about me . . . what?"

"What did you and Sami talk about? Anything *besides* Karli?"

He swallowed, his Adam's apple dipping in his throat. "This and that."

"Like what?"

"Look at that." He pointed to the dash clock. "Eight o'clock already. Nash's practice is open. I better try her again before her day gets going." He grabbed his cell before Piper could argue.

Interesting. First fumbly, and now jittery. Maybe Sami had told the truth. Maybe she wasn't the only one whose feelings had changed. The possibility warmed her immensely.

∾

"Wellspring Physical Therapy," a woman answered.

"Oh, hi," Landon stumbled, his mind still racing. What had Sami told Piper? "May I speak with Taylor Nash?"

"Are you a client of Ms. Nash's?"

"No."

"Then may I ask what this is in reference to?"

"I'm calling about a client of Ms. Nash's. Karli Davis. I've left several messages."

"Just a moment."

An instrumental version of "Silent Night" played.

The other end clicked on. "You've got some nerve calling back here."

"I'm sorry. I think there's been some mistake."

"Breaking into my office was illegal, not a mistake."

"Your office was broken into?"

"Don't play coy with me. I know you did it. What, you didn't get what you were looking for from the file you stole, so now you plan to badger me some more. Is that it?"

"Ms. Nash, there's been a mistake. This is Deputy Sheriff Landon Grainger, and I'm investigating Karli Davis's murder."

"Murder?" A lengthy pause ensued.

"Ms. Nash?"

"Karli's"—her voice cracked—"dead?"

"Yes, ma'am. I'm afraid so."

"This can't be happening."

"What can't?"

"Look, I'm not comfortable discussing this without being

certain of who you are. What city's sheriff department did you say you are with?"

"I didn't say, but Yancey, Alaska."

"All right, I'll tell you what I'll do. I'll look up the number for the Yancey sheriff station, and if everything checks out and you are who you say you are, then we can talk."

Smart lady. "I'm not in Yancey. I'm here in British Columbia investigating Karli's case."

"Okay, give me a number where I can reach you. If everything is as you say it is, you can come into my office and we can speak in person."

"Thank you."

"I'll be in touch." The line went dead.

"What was that all about?" Piper asked.

"Seems Ms. Nash's office was broken into and Karli's file stolen."

"She say when?"

"No, but by the freshness of her anger, I'd say it was recently."

"That can't be a coincidence."

"Sure doesn't seem that way." But it was too early to make a judgment. He needed all the facts. No sense getting excited about something that may have no bearing on Karli's murder or Reef's innocence.

Less than an hour later, his cell rang.

31

The ride from Vailmont to Invermere, where Wellspring Physical Therapy was located, took roughly four hours. They arrived during the practice's lunch hour, when it closed its doors to the public. Landon figured it couldn't have worked out better. They wouldn't be distracted by clients and could have Taylor Nash's sole attention. She met them at the clinic's double glass doors and waited until Landon showed his badge and license before unlocking the doors and inviting them in. She was tall, slender, late thirties, perhaps, and wore rimless glasses. She appeared both shrewd and somewhat frightened.

"I thought we'd speak in my office." She led the way.

Her office was small, but open and airy. Everything was light in color—neutral cream carpet, muted lemon walls, white modern furniture. And it was immaculate. The citrus scent of Pledge hung in the air along with a hint of the more abrasive scent of Lysol. Bright paintings of vivid flowers hung beside a handful of diplomas on the far wall.

Taylor sat behind her desk. "Please have a seat."

Landon pulled out a chair for Piper.

"Thanks." She smiled up at him as she sat.

He nodded, trying to ignore the joy her smile filled him with. He sank into the chair beside her, praying for the resolve to keep his attention focused on the case at hand.

Truth be told, he'd been doing an awful lot of praying lately.

It was weird how easy the transformation came. After his dad's betrayal, Landon had refused to pray, but now, after crying out to God, or rather grunting at Him, God had filled him with the urge to pray. He was in way over his head and he knew it.

Piper's discomfort about his date with Sami felt good. It was petty, but having the tables turned for once filled him with a strange confidence. Maybe she did feel something beyond friendship for him. The way she looked at him. The way she pressed him about his conversation with Sami. He glanced over and caught her staring again. Did she know how he felt?

Piper blinked, her gaze shifting back to Taylor Nash. "Thanks so much for seeing us."

"You're welcome." Taylor's blond hair was pulled back in a low ponytail that she slipped over her shoulder to rest behind her back. "I spoke with your Sheriff Slidell." She directed her statement at Landon. "He said you've taken a leave of absence."

"It was the only way I could come to British Columbia to investigate."

She crossed her long legs beneath the glass-topped desk. "Care to explain?"

He relayed the pertinent events and explained what they'd learned through their investigation, hoping Taylor would reciprocate. "And that brings us to you," he said as she rhythmically tapped her pen atop an unused legal pad. "This morning you mentioned a break-in."

With an exhale, Taylor set the pen aside. "A few weeks back a man called asking questions about Karli."

"Did this man provide his name?"

"He claimed he was Karli's father, but I knew it was a lie." She studied Piper, clearly checking out her injuries.

"How did you know it was a lie?"

"Because Karli's parents are deceased."

"You're certain?"

"That's what Karli told me." Taylor stiffened slightly. "Shouldn't you know that?"

"We are aware of her parents' deaths, but we are trying to

discover what others know about Karli without revealing what we have learned. Does that make sense?"

"I suppose." She lifted her pen again, this time sliding it up and down through her fingers. "What happened to you?" she finally asked Piper.

"Car accident."

"Any neck stiffness?"

"No."

"Be sure to keep an eye on it. It can take days, even weeks for symptoms to appear."

Piper nodded. "Okay."

"Too many people ignore a sore neck, not realizing the damage has been done."

"Thanks. I'll keep a good eye on it."

"You're welcome." Taylor shifted her gaze back to Landon. He took it as his cue to proceed. "Did Karli ever mention what happened to her parents?"

"No, but I asked about them. Karli had OI."

"OI?" he asked.

"Osteogenesis imperfecta. It's a genetic connective tissue disorder. It was very mild in Karli but present all the same."

"Did Karli say which parent she inherited it from?"

"No, and she seemed very upset whenever I brought it up. Understandable enough, as it ends many athletic careers."

"I'm not familiar with OI," Piper said. "Could you explain?"

"Typically the patient's bones facture easily, they experience joint laxity or loose joints, along with muscle weakness, early onset of hearing loss, and sclera, which is when the whites of the eyes have a purple or gray tint. Her surgeon discovered it while repairing Karli's ACL."

"You said Karli's case was mild?" Piper asked.

"She only experienced loose joints and the early onset of hearing loss. Fortunately we were able to help her combat the wear of loose joints through therapy. At least while she was here."

"Which was how long?"

"Two days after her surgery until a few weeks ago."

"Why did she stop coming?"

"She rejoined the circuit, which I warned her was too soon, but she didn't listen."

"What happened with the man who claimed to be Karli's father?" Landon asked, returning them to the phone call they'd gotten sidetracked from. "Did you confront him about your belief that he was lying?"

"Absolutely."

"And?" Piper asked, inching forward on her seat.

"He insisted he was her father and said that Karli was confused about her past."

Piper's brows pinched together. "Confused?"

"He didn't elaborate, simply left a contact number he asked me to pass on to Karli."

"And did you?"

"Yes. I thought she should know someone had called claiming to be her father. And I was rather intrigued myself. I've never had a patient quite like Karli—so . . . private."

"How did Karli react when you contacted her?" He could only imagine the shock the news gave Karli.

"Not well." Taylor sighed, pushing her rimless glasses back up the bridge of her slender nose. "She vehemently reasserted that her father was deceased and ended the call rather abruptly. It was the last time I ever heard from her."

"Were you supposed to see her again?"

"Yes. She had a follow-up scheduled . . . maybe a couple weeks ago, but she never showed. I tried contacting her, but the number I had was no longer in use."

"Do you still have that number?" He could run a records search on it.

"Her file's gone, but I might still have it in the computer database."

"You said her file went missing after the break-in?"

"Yes."

"Any other files missing?" he asked.

"No. That's how I knew it was him."

"The man who claimed to be Karli's father?" Piper asked, excitement raising her pitch.

"And her doctor."

"What?"

"A few days after the call from her supposed father, I got a call from a man claiming to be Karli's primary care doctor."

"Did he have the same voice?" Piper asked. "Is that how you knew it was the same person?"

"No. The voice was different. I think he tried masking it, but there were similar inflections, similar pauses in his speech. I could just tell it was him."

"You sound very certain," Landon said, phrasing it as a statement rather than questioning her judgment.

"I am, and not just because I recognized his speech patterns, but for the simple fact that Karli didn't have a primary care doctor."

"Really?" Piper scooted forward until she was practically tottering on the edge of her seat. Landon prayed this would all lead somewhere, prayed Piper wouldn't have to be disappointed again.

"You're sure of that?" he asked, not wanting to take any detail for granted, not wanting to assume the information was correct without pursuing it to its core.

"I'm positive. Karli was of the mind-set that she was healthy and didn't need a doctor."

"But she needed her surgeon," Piper said.

"Yes, if she ever wanted to compete again. I'm convinced that's the only reason she went to see the surgeon, and the same reason she came to Wellspring. Competing seemed to be all Karli had."

"Did the man claiming to be her doctor leave a contact number?"

"He didn't get a chance. I hung up on him."

Landon cringed. If only she'd played it smoothly—taken his number, led him on until the authorities could track him down.

"That was the last you heard from him?" Piper asked.

"Yes."

"And the break-in?" Landon asked.

"Occurred only days later."

"Tell me what happened."

Taylor explained the event, from receiving the initial call from her alarm company, to her arrival at the scene and filing the police report, to finally completing a full walk-through for the insurance company.

"And the only thing missing was Karli's file?"

"That is correct. That's how I knew it was him."

"So all of your data on Karli is gone?" Piper asked, her voice dropping.

"I didn't say that." Taylor smiled, turning her computer monitor toward them. "We are in the process of going paper-less. My administrative assistant, Natalie, has been working painstakingly these past months to transfer all of my files to the computer."

"Had she transferred Karli's files before the break-in?"

"She was in the process. I checked before you arrived, and it appears we have approximately half of what Karli's file contained." Taylor typed in the necessary codes to access the database and retrieved what remained of Karli's records.

Landon scanned the information, struggling to ignore Piper's close proximity—the way her fingers rested so close to his on the desk.

"Karli Michelle Davis," he said. They'd never heard her middle name before.

"That's new." Piper smiled.

Taylor's perfectly groomed brows arched. "Her name?"

"Her middle name," Landon said. "Although we've recently learned that *Karli Davis* may have been an alias."

"An alias? Was Karli in some kind of trouble with the law?"

"Not that we know of."

Taylor shook her head. "I don't understand."

"She may have had the alias as a way to protect herself."

"From what?"

"That's what we're trying to discover."

Taylor sat back. "How bizarre."

"I take it she never mentioned anything about that to you."

"Absolutely not."

"Look at this." Piper tugged his arm and pointed to the screen. "Down here in the Financial Responsibility section."

Landon trailed his gaze down to the line she was pointing at, and his eyes widened. "Karli listed Rick Masterson as the responsible party on her account?"

Taylor swiveled the screen back to face her and double-checked the information. "That is correct."

"Why would she put Masterson?" Piper asked.

"I don't know why she listed him," Taylor said, "but according to our records, he paid for her therapy in full."

Landon's mouth went dry at the revelation. "I think we're going to need to ask Darcy and Gage to pay Masterson another visit."

A knock rapped on the open office door.

Taylor looked up. "Oh, Tim, come in." She turned back to Piper and Landon. "This is Tim Donovan. He also worked with Karli, did most of the hands-on therapy. I thought it might be beneficial if you spoke with him as well."

"That'd be great. Thanks," Landon said.

"Why don't we speak in my office?"

"Sure." Landon stood and followed Piper as she followed Tim.

"Thanks for speaking with us."

"No problem. Anything to help catch Karli's killer. Please have a seat." Tim indicated two wheeled chairs at the foot of an examination table. "Sorry my office isn't more glamorous."

They were seated in a large room filled with exercise equipment—treadmills, recumbent bikes, enormous nylon balls, and free weights. Along the back wall was a series of examination bays, each with a paper-draped table and a curtain that could be pulled around for privacy. Tim's desk consisted of a rolling cart with a laptop and a stack of files on the lower tray.

Landon waited until Piper was seated before taking the second of the chairs.

"Where would you like to start?" Tim asked.

"Taylor said you did most of the hands-on work with Karli," Piper said.

"Yes, Taylor likes to meet with and assess each new client, and then she typically turns them over to one of us to do the week-to-week therapy."

"How long did you work with Karli?"

"Four intense months . . . all down the drain." He shook his head. "I can't believe she's dead."

"Did she talk much while she was here?" Landon asked.

"Yeah, she talked, but not about anything in particular."

That sounded familiar.

"Tess said Karli opened up to her a few times while they were in rehab."

"That's not uncommon. Therapy can be intense for someone in Karli's and Tess's situation—fighting for what they love, what they live for. It's hard work, and everything important to them is riding on it. It can be frustrating retraining muscles that used to respond so well, working past the pain. It touches the core of a person, causes them to reassess."

Landon tried to keep his skepticism at bay. He didn't doubt that physical therapy was hard work, but Tim's description seemed a little too emotion-based for his taste. "Is that what you think happened to Karli—she was reassessing?"

"Karli was a fighter. That lady possessed a strength I've rarely seen. I don't know if she reassessed anything, but she was bound and determined to compete again, and from what I heard she nailed it."

"Sounds like you were proud of her," Piper said.

"I'm always proud of my patients. But Karli, I admired."

"Because she was a fighter?"

"Yeah, not just in therapy, but in life."

"Why do you say that?"

"My job is people. Diagnosing their hurts and figuring out how they tick. I harness that knowledge to develop a plan that'll get them healed."

"So you figured Karli out?" Landon said, growing more skeptical of Tim's approach.

"She was a tough one, probably the toughest I've seen, but deep down she was a hurting kid alone in the world."

"You're quite the philosopher," Landon said dryly.

Tim shrugged, not at all fazed by Landon's skepticism. "Call them like I see them."

"And did Karli confirm your diagnoses?" Piper asked with a smile.

Figures Piper would buy into this guy's touchy-feely approach.

"Like Tess told you, a few facts surfaced."

"Such as?"

"Karli's love for her mother. She felt that loss deeply."

"What about her father?"

"It was like he never existed."

Anger and heat coursed through his veins as he stood outside Wellspring Therapy. No doubt that good-for-nothing therapist was filling their ears full of his attempts to track Karli down. Fortunately, she had no idea who he was. But now the nosy girl and her detective friend knew someone else had been after Karli. They were discovering more than he'd anticipated. He'd wait a bit longer to see where they headed next—perhaps they'd still lead him to it. The cost-benefit ratio stayed his hand a little while longer. He wouldn't kill them until he was certain he wouldn't benefit from their continued digging, until he was certain they wouldn't lead him to the location. If they got closer to the truth, closer to *them,* the balance would shift and he'd be forced to act.

32

Gage strapped into the Cessna, feeling the urge to pray for the first time in years, but he knew it'd be useless. God didn't exist, and if He did, he wanted no part of Him. Anyone who let an innocent child die wasn't worthy of worship.

"You gonna make it?" Kayden asked with a cheeky smile. "Your knuckles are looking a bit white there."

Gage looked down at his fingers gripped tightly on the seat arm. He released it and shook out his fingers. "Just go."

"As you wish."

"Brat." He glanced over at Darcy, who was watching the two of them with keen interest. "Are your siblings as obnoxious as mine?"

"My brother had his moments."

"Had? He finally outgrew it?" he said loudly enough for Kayden to hear over the propeller, though he wasn't one to throw stones when it came to playful immaturity—he was the master.

"He died three years ago," Darcy said.

"I'm sorry, I didn't . . ."

"You didn't know."

"What happened?"

"Complications from his Down's syndrome."

"That's awful." Even more proof that there wasn't a God.

"Peter was a blessing while we had him. A real light in darkness."

206

Blessing? The poor kid had Down's, and then it killed him. "It had to be hard, seeing him suffer."

"It was, but God was kind. Peter went quickly once the complications started."

"Kind? That's the last thing I'd say about a God like that."

Her brows perked. "A God like what?"

"A God," he said, using air quotes, "who would create a child with Down's syndrome in the first place."

"Are you saying it would have been better if Peter had never been born?"

"No. Of course not." He hadn't meant . . .

"Then, what exactly are you saying?"

"I'm saying if there is a God, it would be cruel of him to create a child that would have to struggle his whole life."

"Yes, Peter struggled, but he also was one of the best, most amazing human beings I've ever had the privilege of knowing."

"I didn't mean to imply he wasn't." That was the last thing he meant.

"Peter was kind and selfless and had a childlike faith that blew me away."

"Faith in God?" She had to be kidding.

"Faith in his Creator and Sustainer."

"Sustainer? You just said Peter died three years ago."

"God chose to take Peter home, but that doesn't mean He stopped sustaining him. He will be sustaining him for eternity."

"I understand your need to think that . . ."

"Obviously you don't."

"I understand loss." And all the torturous pain associated with it.

"That may be, but you clearly don't understand God."

"It's kind of impossible to understand someone who doesn't exist."

"Why do you think God doesn't exist?"

"Because it's obvious."

She leaned toward him. "Enlighten me."

"There is way too much suffering and purposeless pain in the world for there to be a God."

"Why do you assume painful circumstances are without purpose?"

"What purpose was there in Peter's suffering? In your suffering his loss?"

"There are some things we can't comprehend fully this side of heaven."

"I've heard that kind of rationalization before." He snorted.

"Because it's true."

"No, it's because when someone dies senselessly there's nothing else to say."

"No one dies senselessly."

"My son did."

Darcy waited until Gage went to use the restroom before turning to Kayden.

"I feel like such a heel," she said as they waited for his return.

"You couldn't have known."

"How long ago?"

"Almost ten years."

"Wow. He was young."

"Meredith got pregnant halfway through their senior year."

Meredith. Well, that explained their bitter connection.

"They were planning to marry and move to Anchorage after the baby was born. Meredith was going to attend college while Gage went to culinary school in the evenings. They had it all worked out. All these dreams and plans."

"What happened? I mean, how . . . ?"

"Their son was born prematurely and died two days after birth. Everything fell apart. Meredith decided she wanted to go on as planned, just without Gage."

Darcy swallowed, watching Gage stride back across the concourse toward them, her heart breaking. "How awful."

"He hasn't been the same since." Kayden tossed her empty

soda can in the trash. "I just thought you should know, so you'd understand why he said those things. He wasn't trying to be insensitive or cruel."

"I understand."

"He's a good man. He's just lost and hurting."

∞

Piper adjusted the heat, warming her hands in front of the vent as Landon paced outside their rental vehicle—still parked in Wellspring's lot. His friend with the Marshals had called, and they had been talking a half hour. Piper didn't think she could contain her anxiety. What was Luke telling him? Had Karli been part of the Witness Protection Program? Was that why she was dead . . . because of her past?

Finally Landon climbed back in the 4Runner. Cupping his hands, he blew on them.

She directed the heat vents in his direction. "Well?"

He smiled. "Karli was definitely part of Witness Protection."

Relief flooded her. This was it—the key to solving Karli's murder. The key to finding Karli's killer and proving Reef's innocence—she just knew it. "That's wonderful. What was her real name? Why was she in the program? What happened to her parents?"

"There's a slight complication."

Her chest tightened. "What kind of complication?"

∞

Gage led the way up the Kodiak Inn steps with Darcy on his heels. She'd been awfully quiet since their arrival, ever since he'd left her and Kayden alone.

It was clear his sister had taken the opportunity to enlighten Darcy fully about his past. Usually Piper was the blabbermouth, but leave it to Kayden to take on the role in their sister's absence.

The way Darcy looked at him now, with careful compassion, grated on his nerves. His life and *his* son were none of her business.

He paused at the door, turning to face her. "I know Kayden blabbed."

"She just—"

He held up a hand to silence her. "Let me stop you right there. I don't care why she felt the need to share my personal business. The point is, it's my business. *Mine*. And I won't be answering any of your burning questions. Got it?"

"Got it."

"And I don't want you pestering my family either. I know someone like you may find this hard to accept, but there are things in this world that are private, and they deserve to remain that way."

"I totally agree."

"Ha!" She was a piece of work. The least she could do was admit it.

"You think you've got me pegged, but you don't know anything about me."

"I know what I need to."

She linked her arms across her chest and cocked her head in the superior way that got under his skin. "And what exactly is that?"

"Getting the story always comes first. It's what drives you, and because of that you will always choose your career over people." Just as Meredith had.

"If that were the case, you'd already be reading about you and Meredith in the paper."

"So what, I'm supposed to thank you for not publishing my business?"

"I'm simply saying you're wrong about me, and if you'd actually get off your high horse for a millisecond, maybe you'd see that." She stomped past him into the inn.

He grunted. She'd better be phenomenal at her job for him to put up with the aggravation she was causing him.

∞

Gage placed an order at the coffee shop around the corner from the Kodiak Inn. Darcy had continued her conversation with the inn owner long after they'd learned what they needed to—that Theresa Masterson had a rock-solid alibi for the night of Karli's murder. He'd taken the opportunity to politely excuse himself and told Darcy to meet him at the café when she was done. He needed time to clear his head. To get away from Darcy's emotion-filled gaze. At least she was no longer looking at him with pity. After their argument, she'd quickly shifted back to indignation, and that suited him just fine.

"Winter Wonderland" played over the shop's speakers; silver garland lined the glass door, and paper snowflakes dangled on shiny silver pipe cleaners from the dropped ceiling.

He sat on a stool while the gal behind the counter worked on his order. Darcy assured him she'd only be a minute, but he knew better. Getting Darcy away from a source was like taking a pacifier away from a sleepy toddler.

His cell rang. He looked at the number and smiled. "Hey, kiddo. How's it going?"

"We're making progress," Piper said. "How about you?"

"Darcy and I just finished checking out Theresa Masterson's alibi."

"And?"

"Large peppermint mocha," the gal behind the counter called out.

"Hang on a sec, sis." He set his phone down and moved for his order. He thanked the lady and slipped a tip into the jar.

Setting his drink on the table, he retrieved his phone. "You still there?"

"Yeah, I'm here. You were saying something about Theresa's alibi?"

"Yeah. We confirmed she was a guest at the Kodiak Inn the night of Karli's murder, and the owner herself vouched for Theresa's presence the whole night."

"Guess we can't argue with that."

"You don't sound too upset."

"Because I think we found something even better."

"Oh yeah?" It was about time one of them had good news.

"Yeah, but we're going to need your and Darcy's help."

"Name it."

∽

Darcy entered the coffee shop, found Gage at the far table, and moved toward him. He looked her way and smiled. She nearly stopped short. She turned to make sure he was in fact smiling at her and was pleased to find no one standing behind her.

It was the first time he actually looked happy to see her, and while it surprised her to no end, what surprised her more was that it warmed her from tip to toes.

"Make any more progress?" he asked as she took a seat.

"Just being thorough." Why was he smiling so brightly, almost grinning? "What's up?"

"Piper just called."

She prayed it was good news for the McKennas—after all they'd been through, they needed some good news. "And . . . ?"

"Landon just heard back from his friend, Luke, with the U.S. Marshals, and Karli Davis was definitely part of the Witness Protection Program."

She nearly reached over and hugged him. This was huge. "That's awesome."

"Yes and no."

"What do you mean?"

"Luke was able to confirm that Karli was part of the program and that she withdrew of her own accord five years ago, but that's it. Her file was sealed."

"Is that normal?"

"Luke says who a person was before Witness Protection is usually only known to their handler. Karli's name shows in the database for the years that she was part of the program, but all other personal information remains between her and her handler."

"Did Luke contact her handler?"

"He's trying to track him down, but the guy retired shortly after Karli left the program. Sort of went off grid. He gave her a new contact person at Witness Protection should she ever desire to reenter the program—a guy named Scott Bridge. He's a good friend of Luke's, so the two of them were able to bypass a few hurdles, but to find out Karli's original identity, we're going to need to find Karli's handler."

"Did they give you the handler's name?"

"Henry Mars. Last known address was in Homer, Alaska."

"Think Kayden will mind flying us over to Homer?"

"Not for a break this big."

33

Landon disappeared into the gas station as large flakes began to fall. Piper slipped her cell back in her bag, confident Gage and Darcy would be able to track Henry Mars down. The answer to Karli's murder rested with him, she was sure of it. What she was far less certain of were her emotions. She felt like a preteen dealing with her first crush. Sami's words at breakfast, and Landon's obvious discomfort with the topic, caused hope to well inside her—perhaps Landon felt the same way about her.

She loved Landon—had loved him ever since her family had informally adopted him so many years ago. But what she felt now was love of a different kind. The thrill of butterflies caused by the right guy, *the* guy, fluttered inside her. At her age, it was ridiculous. That it was Landon was even more ridiculous, and yet . . . somehow it felt perfectly right.

He returned to the car and handed her a Styrofoam cup. "Tea."

"Thanks." She let the warmth infuse her fingers. "Serious temperature drop."

He started the ignition and cranked the heat to high. "We are heading north."

"True."

"You all right?" His voice was deep, and concern clung to it.

"Yeah, why?"

"I can see the wheels spinning."

She sighed. "They never stop." Or at least they hadn't since they'd left Yancey.

"Want to tell me what's moving them this time?"

She bit her bottom lip. "I'm not sure."

"Not sure what's moving them or not sure you want to tell me?"

"The latter."

He swallowed. "I don't want to push you."

"That'd be a first."

The sharp contrast of the frigid outside temperature with the warmth inside fogged up the 4Runner's windows, sealing them off from the rest of the world.

"It's just I feel . . ."

"Unsettled?" he ventured.

"Yeah . . ."

"About the case?"

She nodded. *But there's more, so much more.*

He shifted closer. "Anything else?"

She swallowed. "Like?" She leaned toward him, needing to be close, needing to feel him next to her, yearning for him to say something, *anything* that might explain how he felt about her.

He scooted closer still, the warm cedar scent of his aftershave comforting and entrancing. "Something Sami said?"

She nodded, leaning in until his face was a breath from hers.

"I was afraid of that."

"Why?"

"Because . . ."

"Because you don't really feel that way or because you didn't want me to know?"

He held her gaze, passion brimming in his eyes. Passion for *her*. "The latter."

Emotion rushed over her, and she leaned forward, pressing her lips to his. It was stupid and impulsive and she never should have, but . . .

He didn't pull back.

His lips were softer than she'd imagined—slow and hesitant

at first, but then with a groan he deepened the kiss. His strong hands reached up to cup her face with surprising tenderness.

∞

Piper entered Glacier Peak resort in a trance, not recalling how they'd made it there. The only thought in her head was the memory of their kiss. Her and Landon's kiss. It seemed surreal, and yet it had been more real than anything she'd ever felt before.

"Checking in?" the man behind the counter asked.

"Yes," Landon said.

At least one of them was able to form words.

"We'll need two rooms—preferably near each other."

"I'll see what I can do." The man began typing, his fingers flying over the keyboard as he spoke. "How long will you be our guests?"

Landon shrugged. "A few days."

"Wonderful. Can I ask how you heard about us?"

"Our friend Karli Davis recommended we visit."

"Oh . . ." The man looked up, his expression unreadable. "You're friends of Karli's?"

"Yes." She'd finally managed to form a syllable.

"That's strange."

"Why? Because she didn't have a lot of friends?" Piper said, adding a smile. Trying to prove to the man that they knew something about Karli.

"Yeah, you obviously knew her well." He smiled. "But no, I meant you're the third and fourth friends of Karli's I've talked to at this counter in less than a month. For Karli, that's really strange."

"Oh." Piper tried to curb her excitement. "Any chance you remember their names? We might know them too."

"Nah." The guy shook his head. "Just some dudes."

"Were they young? Old? Short? Tall?"

"The first dude was Karli's age, my height, dark hair, but the second guy was a bit too old for her, if you ask me, and not really Karli's type."

"How old are we talking?" Landon asked.

"Late forties, early fifties. Karli wasn't exactly picky about age, but he definitely seemed more elderly, if you know what I mean."

"He stay long?" Landon asked.

"Nah. Left as soon as he learned Karli had."

"You tell him where she was going?" Piper asked.

"How could I? None of us knew where she was headed. We didn't even know she was leaving. Just took off one day."

"That sounds like Karli." Piper smiled.

"You didn't know she was headed back to competition?" Landon asked.

"No. We were all shocked to see her name on the lineup." His gaze shifted to the door. "Hey, Todd," he greeted a man entering the lobby. "These guys are friends of Karli's."

Todd's approach slowed, and he gave them a quick once-over before lifting his chin in greeting. "How's it going?"

"Can't complain," Landon said.

Todd directed his attention to Piper, a smile curling on his lips. "You hitting the slopes? You look like a diehard boarder, and we've got some killer virgin powder."

"Definitely," she said.

"Cool." He winked. "See *you* out there."

∾

Piper unlocked the door to her room, and Landon carried her bags inside. Glacier Peak was a stark contrast to the last two lodges they'd stayed at. Still luxurious, he didn't really consider it a resort. The grounds consisted of the main building, where they were staying, and a series of cabins for both guests and staff. There were no groomed slopes or chair lifts. If guests wanted to ski or board, they did so via helicopters. One hundred fifty acres of untamed wilderness surrounded the lodge grounds—fresh, untouched powder just waiting to be shredded.

"Should we sign up for tomorrow's excursion?" she asked as he set her bags down.

"Definitely." He swallowed, wondering how long the pleasantries would last. They'd kissed. He and Piper had actually *kissed*. And all he wanted was to kiss her again and again. But what was she thinking, feeling? He prayed not regret.

"Sounds good." She unzipped her duffel and pulled a sweater from it.

The room, while well appointed with a large canopy bed and stone fireplace, held a damp chill. "Are you cold?"

"Just a little." She rubbed her arms. "I'll bump up the thermostat."

"I'll make you a fire before I go."

"Thanks."

"No problem." He bent in front of the hearth and got to work. "Looks like you have a new admirer," he said as he laid a log on the grate.

"Who? Todd?"

"I saw the way he gawked at you." Like all men gawked at her. She was exquisite.

"Did you also see the way he faltered at the mention of Karli's name?"

Landon slipped in some of the kindling provided and reached for the box of matches. "You think they were involved?"

"Maybe. I'll see what I can get out of him tomorrow. Sounds like he'll be part of the excursion."

Landon pulled a long match out of the box and struck it on the side. It lit and he carefully caught the kindling on fire. "We'll both go." He stood and set the box on the mantel, then moved back toward her.

"I might get more out of him on my own."

"I know, but . . ."

"But what?"

The fire sparked to life behind him, the flame spreading from the kindling to the wood. Heat spread across his back.

"I've had an uneasy feeling ever since we left Yancey."

"You, relying on instinct?" She laughed. "We must really be in trouble."

If he didn't get out, they would be. His restraint was rapidly deteriorating. All he could focus on were her lips—sweet and full and . . .

He rubbed the back of his neck. "I should go."

"Shouldn't we talk first?"

Talking wasn't what worried him. If he didn't leave soon, he'd be kissing her all over again. "We should talk in the morning. After we've both had a good night's sleep." After he'd taken a *very* cold shower.

"You're going to get all logical about this, aren't you?" She sank on the edge of the bed.

He tried not to picture laying her back on it, her lush brown hair fanning through his fingers. . . . *Logical* was the last thing he felt at that moment. He cleared his throat. "It's important to apply logic to an otherwise impulsive decision."

She swallowed. "Are you saying what you told Sami about me was impulsive?"

"Yes." He should have never admitted his feelings for Piper to Sami.

Hurt creased her brow. "So you didn't mean it?"

Of course he meant it. Meant every word of it. "That's not what I'm saying."

"So what *are* you saying?"

"I'm saying we need to think clearly." He closed his eyes and tried to focus. "We are spending a lot of time together in close quarters. Danger is involved, and . . ."

"You think it's not real."

He prayed more than anything it was. He just didn't want Piper to regret anything. To get caught up in the emotion of it all and then realize it was a mistake. That *he* was a mistake. "I'm just saying—"

"Never mind." She stood and moved to the door. "You're probably right. You should go."

He nodded and left, heartbreaking pain raking through him with each agonizing step away from her.

34

"Everybody on?" Todd asked.

"I count six," the pilot said.

"Six it is. We're ready."

The propeller started with a *whoosh*, and Piper sat back for the helicopter ride. Her heart burning in her chest, she longed for Landon to say something . . . *anything* to break this silence between them. She'd asked him to leave last night because she couldn't take him reasoning their kiss away so quickly. The taste of him had still lingered on her lips while he tried to convince her it wasn't real, that their feelings were due to circumstances. While their close quarters amplified things, the feelings had been simmering beneath the surface since last summer. They'd finally broken through, and circumstances or not, they'd need to face them.

"We're close," the pilot said.

"Go ahead and gear up," Todd instructed.

Piper stomped into her bindings and locked them.

"It's blustery out there today," Todd said. "Make sure you cover up."

She zipped her jacket over her fleece and yanked on her gloves, praying the excursion would provide a much-needed adrenaline release.

Todd bent over, resting a hand on her shoulder. "You ready for the ride of your life?"

She looked at Landon, finally catching his gaze. Their eyes held, and she couldn't help but wonder if they were on the precipice of something great or about to take a terrible fall.

"Two minutes," Todd said. "We'll do two teams out there. Piper, your friend, and me, drop one. Kurt"—he lifted his chin toward the other instructor—"you and your party take drop two. We'll rendezvous at base one for lunch at eleven hundred hours."

Kurt nodded, and they all prepared for the copter door to open.

"Ready to roll," the pilot said.

"All right." Kurt rubbed his hands. "Fresh powder just waiting for us. Doesn't get much better than this."

"Remember, be kind to the mountain, and hopefully she'll be kind to you." Todd signaled for Landon to jump first. He moved into place and the bitter winter wind swirled in as the door opened to the elements. "You're clear."

Landon glanced back once at her and jumped.

Todd signaled her to move into place. "We give him thirty for clearance and you're up."

Adrenaline coursed through her as she stared out over the vast snow-covered wilderness. Pristine canvas waiting to be carved. Kurt was right. It didn't get much better than this. She needed this distraction, this release.

"You're clear," Todd said.

With a grin, she jumped. Joy surged as she plunged toward the virgin snow. The tension melted from her body, replaced by the addictive rush of adventure.

She hit the powder, thick and fresh, cushioned her impact. She glided over the pristine snow and a few yards ahead spotted Landon waiting for her. As she approached, she pulled a one-eighty across his path.

"Show off." He laughed, the heavy weight of seriousness appearing to ease some.

He pulled in front of her, bending his knees as he swooshed around the natural moguls, kicking a spray of powder up in his wake.

"Not bad, old man." She grinned, speeding past.

"Who are you calling old?" He shot past her again and flew off the precipice. He tucked effortlessly into a flip, his skis perfectly crossed.

Her breath hitched until he landed, smoothly pulling out and swishing to a stop.

She hovered at the edge. "Impressive."

"Let's see what you got."

"You might want to move back. I go big."

He smiled, and she turned to make her run. Taking a deep breath, she cleared her mind and focused only on the jump ahead. With a push, she dropped into it and pulled a three-sixty as she soared over the cliff.

She righted and landed, boarding to Landon's side.

He clapped. "Not bad for a rookie."

"Rookie? Ha! I just schooled you."

"Not bad, you two," Todd called down from the overhang. "I can see we're going to have some fun today."

It'd be a lot more fun if it were just her and Landon.

∞

"So you're a friend of Karli's?" Todd asked, squatting beside Piper as they broke for lunch. They all sat on the canvas chairs the support crew had brought along with their lunch to the appointed rendezvous spot.

Landon gave her space to converse with Todd but was keeping a close eye on them from his vantage point by a copse of snow-covered trees.

She wiped peanut butter from her lip. "Yep. I'm a friend of Karli's." She was growing more attached to the deceased woman with each passing day, feeling deeply for the loss of life and for the struggles Karli had endured—many self-inflicted, it seemed.

Todd retrieved his sack lunch from the cooler and settled into the chair beside her. "So how'd you know Karli?"

"We met about a year back."

"Where at?" Todd popped his soda open.

"On the slopes."

"You two hang out a lot?" He bit into his sandwich.

"I wouldn't say a lot, but we had some mutual friends."

"Like who?"

"Megan Whitaker and Tess Girard."

"Tess is a cool chick. How about you?" He fingered her hair, which had to be flat and snow-flaked. "Piper, isn't it?"

Okay, maybe Landon was right and Todd was a player. While she normally wouldn't give a player the time of day, she needed whatever information she could get. *For Reef.* "That's right." She smiled up at him.

"Are you a cool chick?" he asked, his voice deepening.

She fought the urge to hurl. "I like to think so."

"Cool like Karli?" He winked.

She forced herself to maintain her smile. "I think we all fall short of Karli's level of coolness."

He chuckled. "So we're having a party tonight at my place. Just the crew and a few guests of our choosing."

"Sounds like fun."

"So you'll come?"

"Sure. What time?"

"Ten. Just leave your friend behind."

"My friend?"

"The guy you came with. I'm assuming you two aren't an item?"

"No." How could they be if Landon wouldn't open up to her?

"Cool. So leave him behind."

Landon would never go for it. "How come?"

"Guy-to-chick ratio. Need to keep it even. That's not a problem, is it? Because if you'd rather hang with him . . ."

"No, it's not that. He's just protective."

Todd wrapped his heavy arm around her shoulder. "Tell him not to worry. I'll take good care of you."

Yeah, that'll help.

"No way!" Landon roared.

She hadn't expected anything less. "But it may be our only chance to get information."

"We'll find another way." He paced the length of his room, his shoulders rigid.

"Come on . . ." she said, remaining on the couch, refusing to give in to his hurried stride. "You know this will give you the perfect opportunity to get in to the staff storage area. Todd said nearly all the staff is coming, plus a lot of the guests. Besides, they'll be drinking."

He halted briefly at the mention of alcohol. "Yet another reason I don't want you going in there alone."

"I understand, but the employees are way more likely to talk freely with a few drinks in them."

"They are way more likely to do a lot of things with alcohol in them—none of which I'm okay with. You don't know these people."

"I'll take my phone and text you at the first sign of any trouble."

"Cell service is sketchy at best up here."

"Todd's cabin is less than a hundred feet from the lodge. I can come back if anything feels wrong."

"That's not good enough."

"Well, it's going to have to be." She was going. It would give Landon time to find Karli's locker and could be what they finally needed to break the case open. She got to her feet and headed for the door, praying she'd reach it before he could stop her. "We have to do whatever it takes to help Reef."

He clasped hold of her arm. "Not whatever."

She ignored the intensity in his eyes. "You know what I mean."

"But those guys don't."

"I can handle them, and you know we need this."

"No lead is worth risking your safety."

"It's just a party, Landon. There will be tons of people. I'll be okay, I promise." She wasn't giving him a choice, and the resignation in his gaze said he knew it.

35

Darcy approached the small mobile home on the outskirts of Homer. Three wooden steps led up to the door. She glanced back at Gage, and he lifted his chin, prodding her on.

Taking a deep breath, she rapped on the storm door, praying they'd finally found Henry Mars. The low murmur of a TV hummed in the background. Steeling her courage, she knocked again, louder this time. The murmuring ceased, and a moment later the door cracked.

"What do you want?"

"Mr. Mars?" She tried to peek in the crack. Light emanated from it, but she could make out little else.

"Who wants to know?"

"My name is Darcy St. James, and this is—"

"Gage McKenna." He stepped beside her on the wooden stoop and extended a hand.

The slit in the door didn't widen. "What do you want?"

"We're here about Karli Davis."

"Never heard of her." He shut the door.

Darcy knocked again.

No answer.

She had to break through to him. They needed answers only he held. "Karli's dead," she said, loud enough for him to hear through the door.

The door swung open, and Darcy held up the article covering

Karli's murder from the *Tribune*. The man stepped back and ushered them in. His living quarters were reminiscent of her grandmother's. Floral wallpaper in shades of rose, blue, and mauve covered the top half of the wall while wood paneling covered the bottom. Blue shag carpet blanketed the floor, and a TV teetering on a rickety table flickered without sound.

Henry Mars lifted the remote and clicked the TV off. Turning to face them, his shoulders bowed. "How?"

Gage cleared his throat. "Her throat was slit."

Henry winced. "And the killer?"

"That's who we're after."

"You two?" Humor danced across his weary features. At least he was too polite to laugh outright.

"We're just helping track down leads. A law-enforcement officer is hunting the killer."

"Does he have any decent leads?"

"That's where we're hoping you'd come in."

Henry said nothing, just stared at the lifeless TV.

"So how long were you with the Marshals Service?"

"Thirty-two years."

"Wow. That's impressive."

"Or crazy." Henry slid into his easy rocker. "All depends how you look at it."

"And you worked with Karli?"

"From the time they joined the program until the day she walked away."

"They?" Darcy asked.

Henry looked at them as if trying to decide whether to tell them what he knew, and then he shrugged. "Karli and her mom, Regina."

"Why'd they join?"

"No choice." He set his mug down on a doily.

Darcy wondered if there was a Mrs. Mars and, if not, where all the feminine touches had come from.

"No," Henry said wistfully, "I suppose that's not correct. Regina made a choice. A very brave choice to enter the program."

"Would you tell me about her?" Darcy asked, picking up on the tenderness in Mars's tone whenever he spoke of Regina.

"Regina?" Henry gazed off in the distance. "Her real name was Michelle Evans, and her daughter was named Angela."

Darcy looked at Gage with unbridled excitement. Piper had told them that Karli had filled out papers, listing Michelle as her middle name. Guess she wanted to keep her mom with her in some small way.

"Michelle's husband, Bryan, was with the Mongols."

"The outlaw motorcycle gang?" Gage asked.

Henry Mars nodded. "Michelle had firsthand evidence of their corruption. She brought it to us in exchange for protection for her and Angela."

The repercussions of that ricocheted through Darcy. "You weren't kidding when you said Michelle was brave."

"Her testimony helped put a handful of very powerful criminals, including her husband, in jail."

"How old was Karli"—Darcy shook her head—"I mean Angela, when she and Michelle entered Witness Protection?"

"Calling her Karli is fine. That's what you knew her as, just as I knew Michelle as Regina. So she'll always be Regina to me. It's easier to latch on to one name and stick with it. Karli was born Angela Evans, and then she became Suzanne Wilson and her mom Regina Wilson when they entered the program. After Regina was killed, Angela aka Suzanne became Tori Anderson, and finally after leaving Witness Protection she took the name of Karli Davis."

"That must have been hard, always losing her identity."

"Life in Witness Protection certainly isn't easy. And to answer your original question, Karli was six when she and her mom entered Witness Protection."

"Did Karli know? I mean, did she fully understand the situation at any point?"

"Her mom told her that bad people had killed her dad and that they were after them. Regina wanted Karli's dad to be dead to her. She felt it was way better than the alternative of Karli learning that truth."

"It's better to think your father is dead?" Gage asked.

"Better than realizing he's a hardened criminal? Yes," Henry said unequivocally. "Regina did what she did to protect her daughter. Besides, if Karli knew her dad was still alive, there was always the chance that she'd try and contact him."

"Did Karli ever learn the truth?"

"I don't know, but she didn't learn it from her mom. Regina went to her death protecting her child."

"When did Regina die?"

"They got her five years ago."

"Got her?"

"The Mongols tracked her down and killed her."

"But not Karli?"

"No. Karli survived because she wasn't where she was supposed to be."

"Where was she?"

"She'd snuck out to meet a friend."

"How did Karli react when she discovered her mom was dead?"

"How do you think?" A mixture of heartache and guilt weighed down Henry's features. "We told her that the men after them had found them and that we had to move her somewhere safe."

"How'd she deal with it all?"

"Not well. Her mom was everything to her. She blamed us. Blamed me."

"For not protecting her mom?" Darcy asked.

"Regina and I . . . we grew close over the years. Karli held me personally responsible for her death. She wanted nothing to do with me after her mom's death, so I placed her with another handler. A female who posed as Karli's aunt, but Karli was angry and restless and . . ." He shook his head, sadness welling in his gray eyes. "She took off first chance she got. I'd track her down, bring her back in, and she'd just bolt again."

"And go where?"

"Anywhere she could. The last time was to join the circuit. I tried to warn her it was too dangerous, that if she was good she'd be in the public spotlight, but there was no reasoning with Karli. She said hiding hadn't done her mother any good, besides she'd only been a child when they'd entered the program. She doubted anyone would recognize her, even if she made the news, but I knew better. I've been dreading this day ever since."

"So you believe her past finally caught up with her?"

His forehead creased, his salt-and-pepper brows bunching. "You don't?"

"That's why we're here. Who do you think killed Karli? Surely not her own father?" Darcy couldn't even fathom such a thing.

"They say Bryan came out of prison a different man, but the Mongols have codes of loyalty that I'll never understand. Still, I wouldn't peg Bryan for the hit. My bet would be someone else in the gang. Someone more detached. You've got to remember Regina's evidence put a handful of men behind bars, each with an axe to grind."

"There were some gouges on Karli's leg," Gage said, pulling the crime scene photo from the file. He handed it to Henry. "Any chance that's a Mongol symbol or insignia?"

Henry pulled his glasses from his sweater pocket and slipped them on. He took a moment to carefully study the photograph. "Not as is, but it appears to be unfinished."

"That was the medical examiner's opinion as well."

"If finished, could it be a Mongol symbol?" Darcy asked.

"Not a symbol, but maybe their initials. Could be the start to an M."

Darcy smiled. Now they were getting somewhere. She couldn't wait to call Landon and Piper and share the good news.

36

Landon watched from the shadows, impervious to the storm raging around him. He didn't trust a single man at Todd's party, but short of holding Piper against her will, there had been no stopping her. Now he waited for her to come safely back to him.

He observed several more women arrive at the party and felt slightly better about having to leave his sentry spot, however short his absence might be. As much as it pained him to leave, Piper was right. Todd's party provided the perfect opportunity to search for Karli's storage locker. It was late; most guests were in bed, and the majority of the staff were at the party. Only a newbie manned the front desk, with a couple of maintenance guys on call if anything cropped up.

The gal at the desk didn't even notice as he entered the *Staff Only* stairwell and proceeded down to the lowest level of the lodge.

The floor was dark, save for a few lit *Exit* signs. The metal doors along the corridor were solid, giving him no idea of what each room contained. He started with the first door on his right, found it locked, proceeded to the next, and found it locked as well.

Having to pick every lock just to see what every room held was going to take a lot more time than he'd hoped. He prayed Piper was being wise and that she kept her promise to call at the first sign of trouble.

A frustrating hour later, Landon popped the lock on the last door along the right-hand side of the corridor. He clicked the light on and smiled at the row of orange lockers and storage cages before him.

Considering what they'd learned thus far about Karli, he doubted she'd leave anything personal behind, at least nothing that identified the contents as belonging to her. Her years in Witness Protection had surely drilled that into her. But Tess had assured him that while traveling the circuit, the athletes were forced to pack light, so the bulk of their belongings remained wherever they called home. For Karli, Glacier Peak had been that place, at least the most recent one, temporary as it may have been.

❈

Todd, wearing a lopsided Santa hat, draped an arm over Piper's shoulder in the close quarters of his cabin's front room. "How you doing, babe? Having fun yet?"

Bored to tears. Drinking parties were about as far from her idea of a good time as a lobotomy, but with nearly everyone who'd worked with Karli present, she couldn't ask for a better opportunity to get some answers, so she forced a smile. "Doing great."

"Let me get you something to drink."

"I'm good, but thanks."

"Not a drinker?"

"Not really." She waited for his displeasure as was often the case with guys like him, but Todd surprised her.

"How about a soda, then?"

"That would be great." Even though it was eighteen below outside, Todd's cabin was roasting with everyone jam-packed inside.

"You got it." Todd winked. "I'll be right back." He quickly disappeared through the crowd that had taken over his front room. Music blared over the stereo, but with the high-pitched buzz of the crowd, she couldn't make out any of the lyrics, could only feel the bass vibrating the walls of the tiny cabin.

Piper found an open spot along the wall and leaned against it, skimming the crowd, trying to determine who to chat with next.

∽

Landon slammed the door of Karli's locker. Just as he'd feared. Some clothes, bedding, but nothing helpful. He propped his arm against her locker. The girl was nearly impossible to track down.

Even her personal effects taken into evidence from the crime scene back in Yancey had contained nothing identifying. Had she never taken pictures? Never applied for a driver's license? Never written anything of significance down? It was like she was a ghost.

Tess had been so sure that anything Karli wanted saved would be stored here.

Tess.

Landon exhaled, scanning the rest of the lockers and smiled. *Of course.*

∽

Piper finished her soda and moved to set it on the table beside her. It took her a couple tries before she managed to set it upright. The room was sweltering. She felt dizzy and drowsy, much as she had after getting her wisdom teeth pulled.

"Hey, babe. You want another drink?" Todd asked. "Maybe something stronger this time." He chuckled.

She shook her head, and the room spun.

"Whoa! Looks like you could use some fresh air." He wrapped an arm around her waist. "Come with me. I'll take good care of you."

She leaned into him as he pushed through the crowd, the air cooling as they moved farther from the noise.

Todd opened a door, and darkness surrounded them.

"Are we outside?" It still felt too warm and the air too thick. She tried to take a step but wobbled.

"I gotcha." Todd lifted her into his arms and carried her a few steps before laying her down.

The surface moved wavelike beneath her, and her stomach mimicked the motion.

Something was wrong—*very, very* wrong. "Landon?"

"Shh." Todd clicked on a lamp beside them. "My name is the only one you'll be calling out soon."

Panic swarmed in her belly, and her vision narrowed, but not before she realized where she was.

Todd stepped to the bedroom door and locked it.

Struggling to lift her arm, she forced her nearly limp hand to her pocket and pressed the first button on her cell phone she came in contact with.

∞

Rage tore through Landon as he barged through Todd's front door screaming Piper's name. Everyone gaped as he shoved them aside. Where *was* she? How could he have left her, even for a second? "Where is she?" he roared.

"Duuude." One of the partygoers grabbed his arm. "Chill out."

Landon pulled his gun from his holster and aimed it at the man's face. "Where are Piper and Todd?"

The music screeched to a halt, and the chatter morphed into gasps.

The man tilted his head toward the back hall.

His heart in his throat, Landon raced down the corridor. A light shone beneath the door at the end of the hall. Kicking the door in, he found Todd on top of Piper.

Fury pulsating through his veins, he ripped Todd away. He shoved him against the wall and pressed his gun to Todd's temple. "If you hurt her in any way, I swear I'll pull this trigger right now."

"Nothing happened." Todd's voice cracked. "We didn't do anything yet."

"You mean you didn't do anything *to* her yet?"

"No, man, I swear."

Landon looked at Piper practically unconscious on Todd's bed. Her sweater had been pulled off, but the rest of her clothes remained intact.

He handcuffed Todd to the bedpost.

"What's going on in . . . ?" One of the female ski instructors stopped short at the door, her horrified gaze shifting to Todd.

Landon draped Piper's sweater over her and scooped her into his arms. "It's okay, baby, I've got you now."

The recently awoken lodge manager burst into the room, his gaze flashing from Todd to Piper to Landon. "The authorities are on their way."

❧

Landon thanked the paramedics for seeing to Piper in her room. Though the threat had been real, Todd hadn't hurt her, and they agreed that what she needed was rest and she would find that much easier in the comfy hotel bed rather than a hospital one.

Locking the door after everyone, Landon turned to Piper. How could she ever forgive him for not being there, when he'd never forgive himself?

He knelt at her bedside, brushing the damp hair from her face. "I should have never left you."

"Don't," she said weakly. "Don't blame yourself for Todd's actions. He's to blame. Not you."

"But I shouldn't have let you go."

She pressed her slender fingers to his lips to shush him. "You couldn't have stopped me."

"Then I should have gone with you."

"Then we wouldn't have gotten anywhere."

"But you would have been safe. That's all that matters." *That's all that's ever mattered.*

"I'm safe now because of you." She cupped his cheek with her clammy palm.

"Because Cole called me." *Thank God for that.*

Her brow creased. "Cole?"

"You must have hit his speed-dial number. He saw it was you calling and heard Todd . . ." Landon clinched his fists. "He heard Todd talking trash and knew something was very wrong. When you didn't respond, he called me and . . ."

"And you rescued me." She caressed his cheek and he leaned in to her touch. How could she forgive so readily? "I'm just sorry I ruined our cover."

"Piper." He exhaled. How could she be worried about that after what had almost happened? "You haven't ruined anything."

"Please. Everyone here knows who we are, and after seeing Todd hauled off in handcuffs, I doubt they'll be willing to talk to us about anything."

"It doesn't matter."

"How can you say that?"

"Because it doesn't. *You* are all that matters."

She swallowed. "But Reef—"

"Will be very happy to learn that we've discovered Karli's true identity."

Her eyes widened with hope. "Gage and Darcy found Karli's handler?"

"They called while the paramedics were examining you. They found Henry Mars."

A small, soft smile crept across her pale lips. "And . . . ?"

Indescribable peace filled him at the sight of her smile. "Looks like we're flying to Cali."

∞

He tossed the makeshift paramedic outfit on the bed. The detective had been too distraught to realize his hadn't matched the others. The short time in their room confirmed they didn't have it, but they were heading for California in the morning. They'd discovered the truth of Karli's identity.

∞

Landon sat in the chair facing Piper's bed, thankful she'd finally fallen asleep. She needed her rest. It wouldn't be long before he'd be forced to wake her for their flight, but he was thankful they'd be leaving this lodge and all its ugliness behind.

Why did Piper have to experience such ugliness, and how could she stay so upbeat throughout it all? If anyone deserved happiness, it was her. He wanted so much for her, and none of it was in his power to give or even control, try as he might. What was it going to take to protect her?

Something outside of himself.

Some*one* outside of himself.

He dropped to his knees.

For her he'd humble himself fully. No more halfway. No more testing. God had spared Piper tonight. God had been with him since that night he stood outside her window. He'd revealed himself just as Landon had asked, only in a way Landon never expected—deep in his heart, in his soul. He couldn't deny His presence any longer. It was time to surrender.

I know you've been with me ever since I called out to you that night, and I know I need to surrender it all to you—my resentment and bitterness over my dad, the foolish belief that I can do it on my own, that I'm somehow in control. I need you, and I'm finally willing to admit it.

He looked at Piper asleep on the bed.

These past weeks you've shown me my frailty—in excruciating depth. Thank you for not letting Todd . . .

The words choked up in him, and he let his soul do the talking.

Please, Father, I'm on my knees, begging you to come fully into my life. Help me become the man Piper and you deserve me to be.

37

Piper settled into the window seat beside Landon for the first leg of their journey to California. He was thankful the color had finally returned to her cheeks and that her wounds were finally starting to heal and fade.

It was a good thing he still believed in the power of the law or he'd have applied his own justice on Todd. The image of finding him about to . . . Landon squeezed his eyes shut. It was seared into his mind.

"I don't think I've ever been happier to leave a place," Piper said, staring out the tiny window at the tarmac below.

He gripped her hand. "You and me both."

"Maybe the feeling of someone following us will finally abate. I think it was starting to get to me."

"What do you mean?"

"I kept thinking I saw the same man."

"Where?"

"On the plane, in the Vailmont cafeteria, with the paramedics last night."

Landon stiffened. "What?"

"I'm sure it wasn't him."

"What did this man look like?"

"I don't think it was the same man all three times. I noticed a man reading at a table across the lodge cafeteria, so his face was angled down. But there was something familiar about him—I thought maybe I'd seen him on the plane."

"And he was in your room last night?"

"I thought one of the paramedics looked like him, but I wasn't thinking or seeing very clearly after Todd . . ."

He clutched her hand tighter. "I'm so sorry you had to go through that."

"I know. I am too, but there were blessings in it," she said softly.

He swallowed. Did she know the extent of the blessings? That he'd been saved because of it. It still amazed him how God could turn a horrible situation into something good. Despite the circumstances, he felt lighter, like a weight he wasn't meant to carry had finally been lifted off.

Thank you, Jesus.

Maybe now he could truly look to the future. A future that he prayed included Piper at his side.

She shifted next him, lifting the packet of Karli's belongings he'd retrieved from Tess's locker. "We finally got a glimpse inside of Karli's life."

"A very small glimpse." A couple photographs and a newspaper clipping about an upcoming sports competition, but it was something.

"We know what her mom looked like and we know that Karli kept personal items that I'm sure Witness Protection had taught her not to." Piper spread the items out on the tray table before her.

"Karli hardly seemed like one to obey the rules."

"It's understandable, though. She wanted to keep someone she loved close. I could never leave my family behind, even if all that remained of them was a photograph."

That's all that remained of his father—one photograph of them fishing when Landon was five. He'd planned to throw it away with all the rest, but something had stayed his hand. He hadn't looked at it in years. It was in his old pencil box along with the few Cub Scout patches he'd earned and a couple hockey trading cards his dad had given him. He'd convinced himself he'd kept them because they were worth a lot of money, but deep down he knew better. He'd been unable to sever all memories of his childhood, despite the hurt.

Somewhere deep inside a part of him still clung to the image of the dad he'd loved, still clung to the lie because the truth was too painful. His heart went out to Karli, for the struggle warring inside her until the day she died. He'd never met her, and yet he knew her. Understood the part of her that wanted to put as much distance as possible between her and her past, yet still clung to a shadow of what it had been.

Recent memories filled his mind. The clawing lure of alcohol.

Please, Father, never let me return to that—to running from the pain instead of facing it. I pray you'll be my strength and provision from now on.

"Hey, check this out." Piper handed him the newspaper copy refolded to showcase the article on the back of the competition piece.

"'Bryan Evans released from prison after fifteen years.' It's dated seven months ago."

"Karli must have figured out the truth about her dad." Piper's eyes widened. "You don't think Karli contacted him?"

"It could explain how the Mongols found her after so many years."

"That would be horrible. I couldn't imagine her own father, despite his crimes, would have any part in his daughter's death."

He prayed no father could, but he'd witnessed just the opposite in several cases over the years. It was gut wrenching and flat-out evil.

Piper set the clipping aside and lifted the small stack of photos. She flipped through them, pausing on a fairly recent picture of Karli and a young man. "Who do you think the guy is?" She handed Landon the snapshot.

Landon studied the man—tall, curly dark hair, blue eyes. He and Karli were both wearing boarding jackets and snow pants. It was clear by the angle of the photograph that they'd taken it of themselves. "From what we know of Karli, my guess would be a temporary boyfriend. Possibly the man the guy running the desk at Glacier Peak described as visiting Karli—tall, dark hair . . ."

"It's hard to believe Karli would keep a picture of someone temporary. His is the only photograph outside of the ones of Karli with her mom. He had to mean something to her, had to have a stronger connection."

"I suppose we could ask Reef and some of Karli's competitors if they recognize the guy when we get back to Yancey. See if they knew him. Maybe he'd been part of the circuit at some point."

"I pray there are no more lingering questions by the time we reach Yancey, that we will have found Karli's killer and have the evidence to prove it."

Landon smiled softly, genuinely. "I pray that too."

∞

California sunshine filled the cabin of the 747 as they touched down at LAX. Piper reveled in the warmth and the feel of Landon's arm resting against hers.

He shut his phone and slid it into his pocket. "Gage says they'll be waiting for us at baggage claim."

"I'm glad he and Darcy decided to meet us. We'll be able to cover more ground this way."

"And with Darcy's local ties, she'll no doubt be able to dig deeper than we could."

Landon still hadn't brought up the subject of their kiss, but she had no doubt his feelings for her ran deep. She'd seen it written on his face when he rescued her from Todd, etched on every line of his face while he knelt by her bedside.

So much was stirring inside her, it was dizzying. Her love for Landon was changing, growing, deepening. When the case was over and her brother's innocence was proven, she and Landon had a lot to discuss. When they were back in Yancey, out of close quarters and danger, then she'd approach him. Surely he wouldn't deny his feelings.

She smiled at the tender, protective touch of his hand resting against the small of her back as they disembarked and proceeded down the gangplank—the way a smile cracked on his lips when he caught her smiling. It was hard to believe it was Landon, and yet somehow it'd *always* been him.

But she was getting way ahead of herself again.

"Baggage claim is down one level," he said as they passed beneath the overhead sign. A foot from the escalator, he halted.

"What's wrong?"

The crowd divided around them as they obstructed the path.

"Nothing."

"Then why are we stopping?"

"Never mind. It can wait." He grabbed her hand and took a step, only to stop again. "No it can't."

"What's going on?"

"You know how you always give me a hard time about being so logical?"

"Yeah."

"For once I don't want to be logical."

"Okay . . ." Her heart skittered in her chest; her pulse quickened.

Landon dropped his carryon and lowered his mouth to hers. Warmth surged through her as his strong arms engulfed her. His kiss was hungrier this time—passionate, and a bliss she'd never experienced welled up inside her.

He pulled back, and her head spun.

He collected his bag, clasped her hand, and stepped toward the escalator.

"Wait . . . what just . . ." she mumbled as they walked. "Shouldn't we talk?"

He smiled. "Definitely."

"Now?" she asked as they stepped onto the escalator.

"Gage is waiting." He pointed to her brother standing just beyond the escalator's base.

"But I, but we . . ."

"Piper," Bailey called and rushed forward, wrapping her in a warm embrace. Cole, Gage, and Jake quickly followed.

"Jake." Piper tugged his shirt collar. "I can't believe they got you out of Yancey."

"We didn't give him a choice," Cole said. He reached for Piper's carryon and flung the strap over his shoulder.

Jake slid his hands in his jean pockets. "Reef is more important than my dislike of travel."

"I'm glad." It was good to have him here. To see him included.

Cole tugged Piper to himself. "Not as glad as I am that you're here. That you're safe."

"You have Landon to thank for that. If he hadn't been there . . ."

Landon shook his head. "I never should have left you in the first place."

"Don't start with that again."

"You were there when it counted." Gage clapped Landon on the shoulder.

"Seriously," Cole said, his somber expression matching his tone and words, "we are so grateful you were there."

Tears welled in Bailey's eyes as she draped an arm across Piper's shoulders. "You must have been so frightened. We've been praying for you."

Piper bit her bottom lip. "It was scary, but Landon was there for me." Her gaze lifted to meet his. "He's always there for me."

They were in the middle of an airport filled with thousands of people, but she saw only him and he was looking only at her. She reveled in the thought of what the future could bring and considered sitting her family down in the middle of baggage claim so she could tell them—

A siren announced the arrival of their flight's luggage.

"Let's grab your bags." Gage headed for the turnstile. "We have lots to do."

∞

With luggage in hand, Landon followed Gage through the sliding airport doors to the rental car line. Palm trees draped with twinkly Christmas lights bordered the road.

Seventy-two degrees felt like a scorcher after five days spent at nearly twenty below. Shrugging off his jacket, Landon draped it across his arm, noticing Piper was doing the same. Seeing Christmas decorations in such warm weather seemed surreal.

Gage scanned the cars until he spotted Darcy waving from a white van about eight vehicles ahead. "This way."

"We've already checked into the hotel," Cole said, falling in step beside Landon. "We thought we'd head back there, grab some dinner, get a good night's rest, and head out first thing in the morning."

"Uh-huh." Landon nodded, hearing Cole and not hearing him at the same time, his gaze fixed on Piper.

"You okay, man?" Cole asked, waving a hand in front of his face.

Landon cleared his throat, dragging his gaze away from the woman he loved. "Yeah."

The woman he loved. It was hard to believe and yet it made so much sense. All those years of protecting her had been out of so much more than duty to his best friend. It'd been out of love. Yearning to guard and shield her purity for the right man—who, if things turned out the way he hoped, would be him.

"It's good to be together again," Cole said.

Landon nodded, wondering if Cole would feel the same way if he had witnessed what had taken place atop the escalator mere minutes before. He still couldn't believe it himself. The feel of Piper's silky skin still danced across his fingertips. He was completely at her mercy, at God's mercy. It was a scary sensation surrendering everything. He had nothing, and everything, to lose.

It had taken him so long to throw himself at God's feet; he'd had to nearly touch rock bottom before he lifted his voice for help. But he wouldn't have traded it for anything. A day ago he'd been totally self-dependent and miserable. Today he was totally at God's mercy, and joy filled his heart, despite the unknown road that lay ahead. He felt as if he could breathe again, for the first time in years.

As Cole took the driver's seat, with Bailey in the seat next to him, Landon settled himself beside Piper in the rear of the van, needing to be close to her.

Darcy swiveled in the middle seat to address everyone at once. "I thought we could cover the most ground if we divide and conquer. After speaking with Henry Mars, it seems we need to speak with John Terry—the man doing time for the murder of Karli's mother. The lead detective on his case is working homicide out of the 9th Precinct in Long Beach and we have the names of Terry's closest associates."

"And Karli's dad," Piper cut in. "I want to speak with him."

"He was hard to find, but we finally got an address for him from his parole officer. He's up in Huntington Beach. Turns out he was released from prison . . ." Darcy shuffled through her papers, looking for a date.

"Seven months ago," Piper supplied. "Landon found a newspaper clipping about his release in Karli's belongings."

"So she knew her who father was?" Bailey said. "Knew he wasn't dead, as she'd been led to believe?"

Landon exhaled. "It appears that way."

Bailey shook her head. "Not that I had stellar parents, by any means, but I can't imagine the devastation of learning that one of my parents was a criminal."

Landon watched Cole reach out and squeeze Bailey's shoulder—his silent signal to stop that line of conversation. But she clearly didn't understand why, as evidenced by the confusion marring her brow.

"What? We all believe Reef isn't guilty," she said.

So she doesn't know. Cole had continued to protect *his* dirty secret.

Cole looked at him in the rearview mirror, his eyes full of apology.

While Landon appreciated the sentiment, there was no apology needed. He just prayed the conversation went no further. If Piper didn't know yet, and he truly believed she didn't, he had no desire for her to find out this way. He wanted to be the one to tell her. She needed to know before things went any further between them. Needed to know the truth about who he was.

As if on cue, her inquisitive gaze shifted to him, and he saw the question burning in her big brown eyes.

"Am I missing something?" Darcy asked before Piper could.

Great. Landon groaned. Leave it to the reporter to press.

"Now don't go worrying that pretty little head of yours," Gage said, tugging Darcy's blond ponytail. "We've got work to do."

Darcy squinted. "I'm not sure if I should consider the fact you called me pretty a compliment, or the fact that you're clearly patronizing me an insult."

"I'll let you decide." Gage winked as he snatched the file from her hand. "So how do we want to split up the to-do list?"

"We thought Bailey, Jake, and I would start working on the list of associates," Cole said. "Most are still living right in Long Beach. Henry Mars said their main hangout was a place called Frank's Bar and Grill. Most likely still is."

"Landon and I can speak with the detective and then Karli's dad," Piper said.

"I guess that leaves us John Terry," Gage said to Darcy.

"I think that's best," Cole said. "I definitely don't want any of the ladies going anywhere without one of us men."

"I'd say that was sexist." Bailey jabbed Cole playfully with her finger. "But given the circumstances and the people we are dealing with, I think you're right."

"You're all witnesses." Cole puffed out his chest. "She finally admitted I was right."

Bailey smirked. "Bound to happen sooner or later."

"Well, I can think of at least one other time when I was very, very right." He lifted her hand and kissed the engagement ring on her finger.

Bailey smiled up at him, her love radiating in her eyes.

Landon wondered if Piper would ever look at him like that, and suddenly nothing seemed more important. But the timing couldn't have been more wrong. They had a job to do. Waiting until it was over before he pursued what was developing between them was the right thing to do, torturous as it might prove to be.

38

Bailey stepped out of the bathroom, rubbing lotion on her hands and arms. "Do you want any?" She offered the trial-size bottle to Piper. "It smells wonderful."

Piper set her Bible on the nightstand. "Sure." Bailey was right; it smelled like a meadow after a soft spring rain. "Oooh, it does smell good."

"One of the perks of staying in a nice hotel." Bailey pulled back the covers on her bed. "I'm glad we get to be bunkmates."

"Me too." It'd be nice to have another female around. Piper was so used to living with Kayden that staying alone in hotel rooms for the past week had felt strange.

Bailey crawled into bed, rustled under the covers, and then rolled on her side to face Piper. "How are you *really* doing?"

Piper adored Bailey, loved how she always went straight to the heart of the matter, but in a tender, loving way. "I don't know. I feel . . . confused."

"About what's happened?"

If only Bailey knew the full magnitude of what she'd experienced over the last few days, the past few weeks. Of it all, the situation with Landon had her most perplexed. And that seemed wrong. Her brother was in jail, and she was giddy over a man. And not just any man—the man who'd put her brother in jail in the first place. But he'd only been doing his job, and he'd actually put that job aside to help her track down Karli's real killer. That was something she'd never thought she'd see—Landon putting *her* before his job.

"Piper, you still with me?" Bailey asked.

"I'm sorry. My head is all over the place."

"Should we pray for clarity?"

"Clarity would be a very good thing—and discernment."

"Okay." Bailey closed her eyes and prayed aloud, her love for Piper, Reef, and their entire family so abundantly clear. Piper prayed that God would show her the next step and walk with her down the unfamiliar path that loomed ahead.

∞

Landon sprawled on one of the beds in the hotel room.

Cole tossed him the Nerf football Gage had brought along.

Gage. Landon sighed, tossing the ball at him. The man didn't know how to sit still. It was a wonder he managed to sleep. Though it was abundantly clear that part of Gage's need for constant motion was due to the fact he'd rather keep moving than think deeply *about anything.* Of course, Landon was hardly one to judge. He'd been running from reality, from the woman he loved, from his own emotions, and worse yet from God for years.

"You and Darcy seem to be getting along *a lot* better," Jake said as Gage tossed the ball to him.

Gage stretched out on the couch. "I know what you are implying, and you're way off base."

Jake shot the football straight back at him. "And what am I implying?"

"That there's something going on between me and Darcy."

Landon nearly choked. "You and the reporter?" He would have never guessed that one, but he was obviously an idiot when it came to relationships.

"There is no me and the reporter." Gage rocketed the ball at Jake. "The woman drives me nuts."

"Isn't that kind of the point?" Cole chuckled.

"Not in that way," Gage bit out.

"Okay . . . whatever you say." Cole grinned.

Gage released a long sigh and pinned his exasperated gaze on Jake. "Thanks, man."

Jake chuckled. "Just trying to keep the conversation lively."

"Let's give someone else a turn. Landon . . ." Gage tossed him the ball. "What about you?"

Panic seared through him, and he jolted upright, his shoulders bumping against the wooden headboard with a thud. "What about me?"

Gage grinned. "Looks like I hit a sore spot."

"I don't know what you're talking about." Landon forced his tone to remain light and relaxed, even if he couldn't force his actions to do so.

"You're awfully jumpy over there," Jake remarked with a critical eye. "Maybe Gage is on to something."

"Gage is just trying to divert attention."

Gage swung his legs over, pulling to a seated position, his bare feet planted on the patterned carpet. "And it looks like I succeeded. So . . . who is she?" He rubbed his hands together.

He was about to say no one, but Piper was hardly no one. She was everything. "You're grasping at straws."

Cole's assessing gaze raked over him, and Landon purposely avoided eye contact. He couldn't look his best friend in the eye and lie. Considering Cole's astute judge of character, it wouldn't take him long to put the pieces together.

Gage smirked. "Thinking about her?"

"I'm thinking it's been a long day and I'm ready for bed."

∞

"So what was that all about last night?" Cole asked Landon over eggs at the breakfast buffet line.

Landon slid two slices of French toast onto his plate. "Gage was just trying to divert attention."

"And you?"

"Didn't feel like being the scapegoat."

Cole's eyes narrowed. "So there is someone?"

Landon forced himself not to look at Piper. It'd be a dead giveaway. "Maybe." Who knew a simple word could hold so much hope?

Cole poured himself a glass of orange juice. "That's great, man. Who is she?"

"Who is who?" Piper asked, slipping between them to grab a bundle of silverware.

"Landon's new gal."

Her hand stilled midreach. "What?"

"Rumor is Landon has a woman in his life—someone he's keeping secret."

Landon swallowed. "I didn't say . . . Gage was just . . ." Beads of perspiration broke on his skin. He didn't want Piper to think he was assuming anything.

"Gage?"

"Gage was razzing Landon last night." Cole topped his plate with bacon.

"About . . . ?" She tucked the silverware bundle in her pocket and stepped back a bit.

"About the possibility of Landon having it bad for some mystery woman." Cole chuckled.

"Is that right?" she smiled.

Mortification held Landon rooted in place. "I . . . they . . ."

"Are you guys planning to eat or just stare at your plates?" Gage asked as he loaded his plate with seconds. "Already taste-tested it all, and it's good, if that's what you're worried about."

"He taste-tested all of mine too," Darcy said blithely. She grabbed a mug and headed for the coffeepots.

"You can thank me later." Gage winked before directing his attention back at Piper. "Go eat. Darcy says we're leaving in ten."

"Right." With a smirk on her face, Piper headed for the table.

"Seriously, man," Cole said. "Who's the lucky lady?"

Landon swallowed, wondering if Cole would think her so lucky when he figured out it was *his* sister Landon had fallen in love with.

"Naturally Landon will be point person," Cole said as they stood around their rental cars in the hotel parking lot. "Check in with him if you aren't going back to the hotel by ten. Any major developments, call immediately."

Darcy and Gage took the white rental van they'd all ridden in from the airport, and Cole, Bailey, and Jake took the burgundy SUV, leaving Landon and Piper with the tan sedan.

"Should be about a half-hour drive, depending on traffic." There. He'd spoken. His words had formed, and he hadn't made a complete idiot of himself . . . *yet*. He waited, nearly holding his breath, for her response.

"So tell me about the mystery woman."

There was the Piper he knew. Never shy.

"Gage was trying to divert attention off him and Darcy."

"Gage and Darcy?" Her eyes widened.

Landon shrugged.

"I can't believe I completely missed that."

"You've had a lot going on. And we've been away."

"So are Gage and Darcy an item?"

"I don't know, but that's what Jake seems to think."

"Jake's got a good eye for what's going on around him."

Which worried him. Jake, out of all of them, would be the first to recognize the change happening between him and Piper.

"Speaking of what's going on . . . The mystery woman . . . ?"

He looked over at her, totally at her mercy. She held the power to make him the happiest man alive or to break him beyond repair. He exhaled. "You."

She turned her head so he couldn't see her expression. "I see."

"But it's not like it sounded," he blurted out. He wasn't assuming . . . that is, he didn't expect . . .

"How did it sound?"

"Like I was suggesting that you and I"—he cleared his throat—"that we were *already* together."

250

"I see. So the kiss in the airport, the kiss back in Canada, those were . . . ?"

"Completely out of line on my part."

"Because you acted on your feelings?"

"Yes." He should have waited. Should have told her how he felt first. Should have—

"And that's bad?" she said, cutting into his thoughts.

"What?"

"Having feelings?"

"No, of course not. It's just . . . feelings make things complicated."

39

Complicated. She didn't know what she'd expected Landon to say, what she'd hoped he'd say, but calling whatever was going on between them *complicated* wasn't it.

Frustration and confusion surged within her as she followed Landon into the 9th Precinct. It felt odd wearing a T-shirt and summer skirt in December, but it was already getting warm. Fortunately Bailey had the foresight to bring along some of Piper's warm-weather clothes. Bailey was so thoughtful that way. She and Cole were so perfect together. Unlike her and . . .

She looked up at Landon. What were they? She'd thought after the kiss—after *both* kisses—that things were on track for them, but obviously he wasn't sure. Wasn't he feeling even a fraction of the heat and emotion coursing through her?

"We're here to see Detective Williams," Landon said to the officer working the front desk.

"Is he expecting you?"

"Yes. I spoke with him this morning." Landon pulled his badge. "Deputy Landon Grainger."

"Take a seat. I'll let him know you're here."

"Appreciate it." Landon guided Piper over to the row of metal chairs lining the battered green wall.

"I'll stand, thanks." She was too restless to sit. Her entire being yearned for something she'd never expected, with a man she feared might not fully step up to the plate.

She took a deep breath of the sweet California air wafting through the open precinct door. Perhaps she was being too hard on him. It had to be awkward—his best friend's baby sister and all. But he'd clearly managed to push past that twice, kissing her with a passion she had no idea existed inside him. Wasn't she worth pushing past the awkwardness to actually declare how he felt, not just show it in a kiss?

A horrible thought crossed her mind. Maybe that's where the trouble lay. Maybe he didn't know how he really felt. Maybe he regretted his rash actions and didn't know how to tell her he'd made a mistake. She swallowed the pain that possibility invoked.

Sunshine spilled through the doorway into the drab stone building, and she gravitated toward it, stepping onto the tiles flooded with sunlight, letting the warmth envelop her.

A few weeks ago the very idea of Landon acting rashly would have been absurd. Now everything she thought she knew of Landon was shifting. Saying it was unsettling didn't come close. Next to God, he'd been her main anchor for so long. She'd never even realized how important his steadfastness had become, how dependent she truly was on him. He was her voice of reason, annoying as it was at times. He was her protector, her friend. *And now . . . ?*

"Deputy Grainger." A man in his fifties greeted them. His gray hair was slicked back, his moustache a matching shade. "I'm Detective Paul Robertson. Call me Paul."

"Paul." Landon shook the man's hand. "Landon Grainger, and this is Piper McKenna. She's . . ."

"I'm helping him with the case." She extended her hand.

Robertson's grip was firm and he studied her face, but apparently was too polite to comment on the lingering bruises. "Nice to meet you." He turned to Landon. "You said on the phone that you're looking into Michelle Evans's murder?"

"Actually we're looking into the death of her daughter, last known as Karli Davis."

Pain, but not surprise, shot across the detective's brow. "Yeah. I heard about that. Why don't we step into my office?"

Robertson led the way past a roomful of detectives and desks into a crammed nine-by-nine office with a picture window facing the room from which they'd just come. Stacks of paper work littered his desk, and the scent of cheese curls littered the air. A trumpet sat propped against a bookcase on the front wall.

"You play?" she asked.

"I try."

"My brother Gage plays too. Got hooked on it listening to our dad's old Jackie Gleason records."

"No kidding. I love those old jazz albums."

"Most people only know Jackie as the actor."

"Half the kids today don't know him, period."

"I suppose not. It's a shame. You can learn a lot from those who've gone before."

He smiled, the gesture lightening his years in a single motion. "Why don't you take a seat and tell me how I can help."

As they sat, Landon began, "We know Karli Davis, aka Angela Evans, and her mother were part of Witness Protection. We know Karli's mom was killed by John Terry. What we're trying to determine is who killed Karli."

"I heard they already have someone behind bars."

Piper swallowed. "Yes, my brother."

Detective Robertson straightened.

"We believe they've got the wrong man," Landon said.

"Because he's related to her?"

"Because someone was after Karli before she died, someone other than Reef McKenna."

"Well, I'll tell you what I know, but I'm not sure how much help it'll be."

"Any insight you can give us into the Mongols and Karli's link to them would be helpful."

"I pulled Michelle's case file after you called." He slid it to Landon.

Piper leaned over to get a better look as Landon skimmed through it. It was hard to believe less than twelve hours ago his lips had been pressed to hers, that his strong arms had been wrapped around her. What she wouldn't give to go back to that moment when everything seemed so clear, so right.

"I was working vice here in Long Beach when Michelle turned on Bryan and his crew and went into Witness Protection. When we got word from the Marshals that Michelle had been killed in Government Camp, Oregon, we offered our services to the police in that neck of the woods. They were very cooperative and let us spearhead the case, since we'd been following the Mongols for more than a decade at that point."

Landon glanced up from the case file. "It looks like the evidence against Mr. Terry was quite compelling."

"He got sloppy, and we got lucky."

"How do you mean?"

"Most times these guys go in at night and kill the victim without any witnesses around. They make it quick and clean, while still leaving a powerful message."

"What kind of message?" Piper asked.

"If you rat on the brotherhood, you'll pay with your life."

"Meaning sliced tongues, guts spilled out . . ." Landon said.

"Exactly."

Piper stiffened. "That's horrible."

"That's organized crime. Makes no difference whether it's Mafia, drug cartels, or outlaw motorcycle gangs. They all have rules—you break them, and you'll be punished."

"And Michelle broke the rules by turning State's evidence on her hubby."

"And a handful of his brothers, all senior-ranking officers in the Mongols' outfit."

"All of them went to jail?"

"Yes, and all are out now, except two." Robertson slid over their rap sheets.

"We found an article that indicated Karli's father was released this past summer," Piper said.

"Correct."

"You don't think her own father . . . ?" The thought was too horrid.

"What you've got to ask yourselves," Robertson said, "is how much effort the Mongols are going to be willing to go through to try and kill Karli again. When they killed Michelle, the house was rigged to explode. Karli would have simply been collateral damage if she'd been home. Going after her a second time as a specific target, not just collateral damage, is an entirely different matter. And I am not certain what their motive would be."

"And why wasn't Karli home?" Piper asked just to be sure they'd gotten their facts straight, that Karli had snuck out to meet some friends.

"Karli went to meet Erik."

Piper leaned forward. "Erik?"

"Karli's handler, Henry Mars, grabbed Karli as soon as she showed back up at what remained of her house and moved her immediately. As soon as I got the call, I hopped a plane to Government Camp and worked the case. It's a small community and it didn't take long interviewing folks to learn that Karli spent the majority of her time with one boy in particular, Erik Johnson. His picture's in the case file."

Landon flipped to the photos, scanning them quickly. "These are of Karli and her mom. And they look like surveillance photos."

"That's exactly what they are. I told you John Terry got sloppy. Not only did a neighbor remember seeing a gas company worker poking around the outside of Karli and Michelle's place earlier that day, she was able to give us a good description. Cracked the case wide open. We narrowed in on Terry right away.

"The fool must have thought he was untouchable, because he hadn't even bothered to dispose of any of the evidence, including the surveillance photos he'd taken of Karli and Michelle prior to the hit." Robertson leaned across the desk and pointed at a dark-haired young man in the background of the first photograph. "There and . . ." He flipped to the next photograph of Karli outside of school with the same young man walking a few feet behind her. "There."

"I recognize him," Piper said.

Both Robertson's and Landon's gazes shot to her.

"You do?" Landon asked.

"I'm pretty sure he's the guy from the picture you found in Karli's belongings. He's got the same dark, curly hair."

"Could be. He looks a good five or six years older."

"Which would fit the time gap."

"You think she kept in touch with him after her handler moved her?" Robertson asked.

It certainly wouldn't surprise her, not with what they'd learned about Karli's inclination to break rules.

"Looks that way," Landon said.

Robertson rubbed his palms together. "It's hard to believe it took them five years to track her down."

Landon slumped back with a sigh. "Yeah, it is."

She knew that sigh, and it wasn't good. "What?"

"I'm just thinking . . . why *did* it take them so long? Tracking her down should have been easy. It looks like she kept in contact with someone she shouldn't have, she joined a high-profile extreme sports circuit, pulled herself out of Witness Protection and—"

"She did what?" Robertson nearly choked.

"You didn't know?" Landon asked.

"I'd never worked with Henry Mars before. We were only brought together because of Michelle's case. After Terry was convicted, we had no reason to stay in contact."

Piper fastened her gaze on Landon. "I don't understand where you're going with this." Was he starting to doubt that Mongols were responsible for Karli's murder?

"I'm just spitballing. Karli kept in touch with someone from her past; she pulled herself out of Witness Protection and joined a fairly public sport." He shook his head. "And why track her for five years when she wasn't even the one who broke the code in the first place?"

Was he trying to throw away all their hard work? "Maybe they couldn't track her. We know Karli moved an awful lot. Maybe someone just happened to spot her at an event."

"I doubt any California Mongols have been attending extreme snowboarding in Canada and Alaska."

"Okay, maybe they spotted her on ESPN's coverage of an event."

"Maybe, but the question still is, why would they go after her?"

"To tie up loose ends."

Robertson broke in. "If they killed her, it would have been for some twisted form of vengeance. If you still consider this lead worth following, I suggest you look at the guys recently released from prison, including Karli's dad, though I'm not seeing that one."

"Because she was his child?" Piper asked.

"Because he claims to have found God in the joint."

∞

"What was that back there?" Piper asked Landon as they exited the station.

"I was just thinking out loud."

"Thinking Reef's guilty?"

"I didn't say that." He unlocked the car and held her door open for her.

She climbed inside. "If you no longer think the Mongols killed her, who else is there?"

Landon rested his arm on the roof of the car, leaning in to converse with her. His fine muscular form blocked the sun from her face. How could someone she was so attracted to make her so mad?

"Part of working a case is looking at all the threads—logically. I'm just not sure how logical it is that a gang member wanted Karli dead so badly that he spent five years tracking her down when she wasn't even the one who testified."

"Maybe it was a kid or a brother of one of the guys Michelle's testimony helped put away."

"Maybe. We've got a copy of the case file. We'll go consider family and friends of each of the guys Michelle's testimony put away. I'll call Cole and tell him to key in on that when he questions the associates. In the meantime, Detective Robertson said he'd see what his insiders are reporting. If a Mongol took out somebody, word will have spread."

"He's got cops inside the gang?"

"I doubt it. The only law-enforcement officer to successfully get inside the Mongols was William Queen back in the late nineties. But I'm sure there are men and women from vice on the fringes, planted in Mongol hangouts, bars . . . that sort of thing." He strode around the car and climbed in on the driver's side.

Piper shifted to face him better. "I can't imagine how it would feel being surrounded by such darkness all the time."

"Someone's got to do it."

"Is that how you feel? That you have to do your job?"

"Somebody needs to."

"Because?"

"Because justice is important. Because there are consequences for breaking the law and for hurting others."

He spoke with such passion, such conviction, that Piper again began to see deeper inside the heart of the man she'd unwittingly come to love. As much as she didn't want to hear what he was saying, the same doubts about the Mongols having killed Karli were beginning to creep into her heart. But they couldn't walk away now, couldn't give up hope that for some reason a Mongol had sought Karli out after so many years and exacted revenge. Otherwise they were back at square one, and Reef's trial date was steadfastly marching nearer.

40

Darcy's heart fluttered as they waited for John Terry to appear. Though glass would separate them, she hated the thought of being so close to a cold-blooded killer.

A buzz sounded, and Terry entered, his orange jumpsuit the only color in the otherwise bland room. The officer led him to the seat opposite the glass and Terry plunked down with a slightly curious glance. His eyes raked over Darcy, and he smiled in a way that made her skin crawl. She was so thankful Gage was right behind her. She leaned forward and picked up the phone on her side of the partition, and Terry did the same.

He whistled. "Too bad this ain't a conjugal visit, because you are fine."

"Mr. Terry, I'm—"

"Nah." He waggled a finger. "We ain't going to go there. It's John. Call me John."

"Okay, John."

"And you are?"

She swallowed, the thought of giving this creep any personal information about her making her hesitate, but in the end she complied and prayed he'd do so as well. "Darcy."

"Now I like the sound of that." He leaned forward, only the glass partition separating his face from hers. "What is it you want from me?"

"I want to talk about Michelle Evans."

"That's easy." He slumped back with a shrug. "She's dead."

"You killed her?"

"I'm not in here for the three square a day."

"And Michelle's daughter? You kill her too?"

He chuckled. "You obviously haven't done your homework. The kid wasn't home when the house blew."

"I know that. Angela Evans, aka Suzanne Wilson, aka Karli Davis, was recently murdered in Yancey, Alaska."

"Is that right?" He smiled, no surprise on his face at the news.

"I have a feeling you already knew that."

"What's it to you if I did?"

"Because it could be evidence of your role in her death."

He laughed. "How do you figure that? If you haven't noticed, I'm not in the position to be killing anyone outside these walls."

"But you could have ordered the hit."

"Why would I bother? I killed the rat—her stupid kid meant nothing to me."

"You'd planned to kill her back in Oregon, but she escaped."

"She didn't escape. She just wasn't home when the bomb went off, and it was no sweat off my skin. Like I said, I got the rat."

"So the fact that Karli's dead means nothing to you?"

"No different than any other dead broad."

"If you had nothing to do with her death, how'd you hear about it?"

"I got the message last night that a group was down from Alaska poking around about Michelle and her brat."

"And you're claiming that's the first you heard of Karli's death?"

"I ain't claiming. I'm telling you, that's the first I heard the kid was dead."

"Karli—her name was Karli Davis," Darcy corrected, annoyed at his derogatory tone when he said *the kid*.

"Whatever. I never knew her name. Just knew she was Michelle and Bryan's kid. The fact is, she's dead and I had nothing to do with it."

"What about the rest of the Mongols? Anyone else want to see Karli pay for what her mom did?"

"Look, this is getting old and you ain't listening. If we'd wanted her dead, she would have been dead five years ago, just like her momma. We sure wouldn't have waited all these years to hunt her down."

"Maybe you couldn't find her until now."

He burst out laughing. "Couldn't find her." He shook his head. "You really don't get it, do you? We can find anybody, anywhere, anytime."

"Sounds like a lot of talk."

"Oh yeah?"

"Yeah."

"You and your crew"—he looked at Gage with contempt—"are staying at the Marina Del Ray Hotel."

She ignored the trepidation shooting along her spine. "That's not hard to find out."

"All right. How's this? You're sleeping all by your lonesome in room 203. The other two foxes are in 204. The dude behind you is staying in room 206 with his brother. And the deputy and the other guy are in 205." Terry's smug grin widened. "It's clear you're way out of your league, darlin'. I suggest you head back to Mammoth and the snow reports."

Gage leaned across Darcy, staring Terry straight in the eye. "You or your goons come near her, and I'll . . ."

"You'll what?"

"Do whatever is needed to keep her safe."

"Trust me, if we were after her, that would hardly be enough."

"Is that a threat?"

"Mongols don't make threats. We act."

"Like you did with Michelle?"

"Exactly."

"And now with Karli?" Darcy said.

"Darlin', I'm only going to say this one more time. Mongols had nothing to do with the death of Michelle's kid. If we'd wanted her dead, she would have been the day after her momma."

❈

"What do you think?" Darcy asked as they stepped back into the sunshine. She'd never been quite so thankful for fresh air.

Gage pulled out his phone. "Time to change hotels."

"You really think it'll make any difference?"

"Probably not. But I'll tell you one thing—they try and come after us, we'll be ready for them."

"You really think you, Landon, Jake, and Cole can hold off an army of Mongols?"

"They never send in an army to do their dirty work, just a handful of guys."

"Armed and dangerous ones."

"We protect our own."

She knew he would do anything in his power to protect her and his family, and his strength comforted her, despite the fear.

❈

"Kayden?" Piper pressed her cell closer against her ear.

"Yeah. Where are you?"

"In the car, driving up to Huntington Beach to speak with Karli's father."

"Any progress?" Hope, usually foreign to Kayden, lingered in her tone.

Piper couldn't share the disappointment she'd just experienced, couldn't share Landon's doubts, even if they were reasonable and made more sense than she dared admit. Not with him sitting right beside her. "We're still hard at it."

"Oh."

"What's wrong?"

"I hate to tell you this, but I thought you guys needed to know that Judge Morrell rejected Harland's request for an extension."

"What?"

"I know. I couldn't believe it."

Landon looked over at her, worry heavy on his face.

Piper fought back a sob. "It's so unfair. Didn't Harland

explain the extenuating circumstances, all the new evidence that's been uncovered?"

"Yes, and Judge Morrell said he may present any of those facts in Reef's defense during the trial. But since there is no clear evidence that Reef is innocent or that the Mongol club or any of its individual members killed Karli, she refused to approve a trial delay."

"But it's taking time to find that evidence. That's exactly why Harland is asking for the extension." After all the progress she'd thought they'd made, it suddenly seemed like it was all crumbling.

"Meredith argued that you were all on some wild-goose chase that could go on indefinitely. Unless something other than supposition and conjecture is discovered, the trial begins as scheduled."

Piper hung up, tears stinging her eyes.

"The extension was denied?" Landon asked softly.

She nodded.

"I'm sorry."

"You don't even think the Mongols did it," she lashed out, knowing it was wrong and completely undeserved. It wasn't Landon's fault. She just wished, just hoped, that he would stick by her regardless of what logic said. That he'd put her before logic, ridiculous and unfair as that was.

"I didn't say that."

"I can see the change in you. You no longer think Karli was killed because of her past."

"I still think it's possible . . ."

"But not likely."

He didn't answer. He didn't have to.

"Then what are we even doing here?"

"Trying to find Karli's killer."

"If you don't think the Mongols did it, then who?" She prayed he had come up with another suspect, anyone other than Reef. That they hadn't circled back to the start.

He exhaled. "I have no idea."

She bit her lip, trying to cut off the tears.

He clasped her hand. "I'm not saying we should quit investigating the Mongols and their link to Karli, but . . ."

"One talk with Detective Robertson and you're ready to believe *their* innocence."

"I highly doubt any of them are innocent. But of Karli's murder, I'm not so sure they're guilty."

"What was it that changed your mind so quickly?" She was a fool for asking; she knew exactly what had done it. It was the same things that had cast a shadow of doubt in her own mind of the Mongols' involvement, though she wouldn't admit it yet. She couldn't. Not when doing so would mean all their hard work had been in vain and Reef would once again become the only viable suspect.

"Looking at it logically—the timeline, the fact Karli played no role in what they saw as Michelle's betrayal. . . . When it comes down to it, I've got a bad feeling it's not going to pan out, but I hope I'm wrong."

"You've got a feeling? Well, that's a first." She tried to lighten her swiftly declining hope with a forced laugh.

He glanced over at her with a weak smile. "Seems you've unleashed all sorts of feelings in me."

41

Landon worked to keep his voice even, to not react to the news on the other end of the line as Piper climbed back in the car with a bag of food. She had barely eaten breakfast and he refused to let her skip lunch, so they'd stopped for fast food on their drive to Huntington Beach.

"Did you hear what I said?" Gage asked on the other end of the line. "I think we should switch hotels."

"I agree. Someone working there must have ties to them."

"Okay, so when we all get back, we'll move."

Piper handed him his soda.

Landon nodded his thanks. "Wait on that," he said.

"On what?" Gage asked. "Moving?"

"Returning." He was thankful Piper was intent on doling out their order. He prayed she wasn't paying close attention. He didn't want her to worry.

"Oh, so don't head back to the hotel," Gage said.

"Right. Not until we're all there."

"Gotcha. We're heading to talk to John Terry's wife now."

"How did it go with Terry?"

"He says the Mongols had nothing to do with Karli's death."

"Do you believe him?"

"I don't want to."

"I know the feeling."

"Who was that?" Piper asked as soon as he hung up with

266

Gage. She popped a fry in her mouth, and the delicious scent of peanut oil and warm potatoes filled the car.

"Gage."

"How did it go? Did they get to speak with Terry?"

"Yeah. They are headed over to talk with his wife now."

"What did Terry say?"

"Claimed he and the Mongols had no involvement."

"Of course he did." She slid a straw into her lemonade. "Why did you say 'Not until we are all there'?"

Of course she'd been listening. She always listened. Though it was curious, she hadn't asked whether Gage believed Terry or not. "Just that we can all discuss everything we've learned in detail tonight when we're all together."

"Good idea." She bit into her burger. "Mmm."

He chuckled. "Good?"

"Delicious."

He smiled, thankful to see her appetite had returned. Ever since Todd had slipped her the Rohypnol, her desire for food had been meager, which was very unlike Piper. For such a slight thing, she normally maintained a hearty appetite.

"What?" she asked, mayo glistening on her lip.

Lips he ached to kiss. But he couldn't take that liberty again, no matter how strong the urge, not until he'd laid it all on the table. And now was not the time. He'd waited this long to tell her he loved her—he could restrain himself a few more days, couldn't he?

"Why are you staring at me?"

"Sorry. Just starving."

"Eat your burger."

"Right." He loosened the wrapping, not at all hungry in that way.

∞

Bryan Evans's address led them to a tiny bungalow on Oceanside in Huntington Beach. It wasn't fancy, but the view was stunning. The blue house with white shutters sat relatively silent at their approach; only the soft melody of a wind chime and the rhythmic pounding of the surf could be heard. A Harley sat out front.

Piper looked at it. "I'd say we're in the right place." Now Karli's fear of motorcycles made sense. Every time she'd heard the distinct sound, she must have feared they'd found her.

"Old habits die hard," Landon said, rapping on the door.

No answer.

"He said he'd be here." Piper peered in the front window. The interior was neat—white wicker furniture, a handful of hanging plants, a small decorated palm tree in place of a traditional fir—but no sign of Bryan Evans.

"Let's try around back."

A narrow stone path led around to the rear. The gate unlocked, they entered through, passing a weather-beaten deck and on to the beach.

A man sat at the water's edge, his surfboard propped upright in the sand beside him. A golden retriever frolicked in the waves before him.

Piper looked to Landon and he shrugged.

Taking off their shoes, they crossed the warm sand. It was finer than that of Yancey's shores—fewer rocks and a lighter shade of caramel, but Piper preferred Yancey, all the same. It was home. It was where she belonged.

"Mr. Evans," Landon called over the crashing waves. "Bryan Evans?"

The man turned. He had dirty blond hair, the length a tad longer than was typical for his age. His skin was tan and weathered. A smattering of wrinkles fringed his eyes, eyes the same ocean blue as they'd seen in pictures of Karli.

"We spoke earlier," Landon said, approaching with hand extended.

"Right, the cop." Bryan got to his feet and shook Landon's hand.

"Deputy Grainger," Landon said. "This is Piper McKenna."

Bryan moved to shake her hand but stopped short. "McKenna?

As in Reef McKenna?" His perplexed gaze shifted from her to Landon.

"He's my brother," she said, knowing it was always best to be upfront with people.

"That explains why you're searching for another killer."

"Evidence suggests someone else was after Karli," Landon said, surprising her.

Bryan rested his hands on his hips. "And you believe it was a Mongol?"

"That's what we'd like your opinion on."

"My opinion? Well, I'll be glad to give it to you. It's the least I can do for my baby girl, but I don't know how helpful it'll prove to be."

"We appreciate any insight you can give."

"Insight?" A sad smile crossed Bryan's face. "It's been a long time since anyone was interested in my insight." He grabbed his board. "Let's go talk on the deck."

"Great."

Bryan turned and whistled.

The retriever's head shot up.

"Come on, Max."

The dog bounded over.

"Nice place you got here," Landon commented as they made the short walk across the beach to the deck.

"One of the families at my church owns it. They're renting it to me at a really fair price while I get back on my feet."

"That's very generous of them."

"To rent to a convict?"

"Yes."

Bryan chuckled. "At least you're honest." He propped his board against the deck railing and took a seat at the old wooden picnic table, gesturing for Landon and Piper to do the same. "What do you want to know?"

"Do you think your daughter was murdered by a Mongol?" Piper asked.

"I've been told it wasn't a Mongol's deed."

"And you think they'd tell you the truth?"

"They were my brothers for thirty years. If they took out my kid, yeah I think they'd have the decency to tell me."

Decency seemed a strange word for it.

"Are you still part of the Mongols?"

"Not actively."

"Meaning?" Landon prodded.

"Meaning, I'm going a different direction with my life."

Landon's eyes narrowed. "And they just let you walk away?"

"Things are straight between us."

"Why leave?" Piper asked. "What changed your mind?"

"I found God. Or rather I should say He found me."

"And now?"

"I'm trying to live for Him."

"Your parole officer said you volunteer a lot with the troubled youth of the area."

"If I can steer even one away from the rotten choices I made and toward God, I'll be thrilled."

"What about your daughter?" Landon asked. "You ever try to contact her, to steer her away from poor choices after Michelle was killed?"

Bryan shook his head. "I had no idea where she was, and I figured she was better off without me after all these years."

"Did you know about the hit beforehand?"

"I knew they were going to go after Michelle for what she'd done."

Landon shifted, resting his arm on the table. "I imagine you were pretty upset with her yourself."

"Disappointed's more like it. It was a stupid move. She put our kid's life in danger, got herself killed."

"Why do you think she did it?" Piper asked.

Bryan swallowed, pain etched across his sun-weathered face. "It was my fault. I wasn't upfront with her when we hooked up. We were married and she was pregnant with Angie before she figured it out."

"That you were in the Mongols?"

"What the Mongols were all about, and the fact that I was deeply involved in their criminal activities."

"How did she find out?"

"Micki—that's what I called Michelle." Bryan squeezed his eyes shut for a moment as pain flickered across his face. He opened his eyes, and the wrinkles around them appeared deeper, graver. Perhaps he truly was sorry for what had happened, for his role in it all. "Micki was a bookkeeper for some lawyer downtown. Not long after Angie was born, she decided she wanted to be home more with the kid, so I arranged for her to work the books for the club."

"The Mongols?"

"Our chapter's at first, and then our region's. Didn't take long for her to figure it out."

"Figure what out, exactly?" Piper asked.

"It was all there in the ledger—all the money that changed hands from arms sales, drugs, prostitution. It was the last one that really got to Micki. Some of the girls were young, and having a daughter made Micki extra sensitive to the situation.

"One afternoon things came to a head. Micki was working in the back office when this hooker brings her money to Nick— he was in charge of the girls. Anyway, Nick says the hooker is short. He figures she's holding out. He's high at the time, which doesn't help, and things escalate. He punches her. She throws back. The hooker ends up dead."

"And Michelle witnessed this?"

"Yeah, I was in the back unloading some new inventory. I heard a scream and caught Micki as she came busting out the rear door."

"What happened then?"

"I took her home, settled her down. At least I thought I had, but Micki, she couldn't let things lie. I guess she called that lawyer she'd worked for and he put her in touch with the Feds. I came home from work the next day and they were gone."

"Michelle and your daughter?"

Bryan nodded, his face tightening.

"Did you know she'd gone to the Feds?"

"I was hoping she'd just run, but when the Feds busted in not long after, I knew she'd talked."

"And you knew she'd be killed for it?"

He nodded once, his jaw growing rigid.

"You do anything to try and stop them?" Piper asked, indignant.

"You can't stop vengeance."

"And your daughter?" Didn't he even care?

"I asked them to spare her. Said she was only a kid, that she hadn't done anything."

"You asked Terry?"

"No. I had no idea who they'd send. Those orders come from higher up."

"So you spoke to someone higher up?"

He nodded.

"And?"

"He said he'd take it under consideration."

"Did you warn the police it was coming?" Piper asked.

Bryan released a bitter laugh. "They knew it was coming. Every marshal on every case knows it. That's why they attempt protective custody."

"Statistically the marshals have a one hundred percent success rate when those in the program follow the rules."

"Tell that to my wife."

Interesting that he still referred to Michelle as his wife.

"What happened to your wife was extremely unfortunate and a rare exception," Landon said. "But for all we know, she might have let one of the rules slip."

Bryan lifted his chin. "Keep telling yourself that."

"When Michelle was killed and your daughter survived, did you think they'd still go after her?" Piper asked, trying to keep the conversation on topic.

Bryan rubbed his hands on his thighs. "I hoped not. I hoped killing Micki would be enough."

"And after five years went by, did you believe your daughter was safe?"

"Yeah, I figured they'd laid the matter to rest with Micki's death."

"And now? Now that your daughter's been murdered?"

Bryan pinched the bridge of his nose, his agony evident.

"Do you think they killed her?" Piper asked him outright.

Bryan swallowed, his throat muscles flexing with the movement. "No."

"How can you sound so certain?"

"They told me about Micki after the deed was done; they would have told me about Angie too."

"Even now that you are no longer active?"

"I told you we're square. A brother still tells his brother when one of his own is taken. Angie was dead and some outsiders were poking around. I called an old friend and asked for it straight. The Mongols didn't kill Angie. Someone else took my baby's life." He coughed back tears. "They say she was killed up in Alaska?"

"In Yancey, our hometown."

"Was she buried, given a proper funeral?"

"She's still in the morgue."

"I'm going to call my parole officer. Tell him I need to go lay my baby girl to rest. I didn't do right by her in life. I need to at least do right by her in death."

"Would you do it differently if given the chance?" Piper asked. Bryan seemed genuinely grieved by his daughter's death, but she couldn't decide if he was actually contrite over his past actions.

"If I could go back, I'd live my whole life differently. And maybe I'd still have my wife and child." He rubbed his bristled chin with a shaky hand. "You have no idea what it's like knowing the woman you love is dead because of you. That your child is on the run because of you. If Micki had just come to me instead of going to the Feds . . ."

"What would you have done?"

"I don't know. I'd like to think I would have done the right thing—gotten us all out of there. But in all honesty, I probably would have continued to drag them right down with me." He rubbed his brow.

"She was beautiful, you know. A surfer. She taught me how to ride a board, and I taught her how to ride a hog. I can still see her when I look at the waves, gliding over the top of them on her board, Angie no higher than my knees, perched on the board in front of Micki—both of them smiling."

"That's a good memory," Piper said, reaching out to clasp his hand.

He swallowed, biting back tears and regret. "That's all I've got left of them, and no one to blame but myself."

A few minutes later, as they reversed out of Bryan Evans's drive, Piper said, "He seemed genuinely remorseful."

"I usually say once a criminal, always a criminal, but for once I agree. He seems like a changed man."

"God can change even the hardest of hearts." Only He could.

"The trouble is determining when God has really changed someone and when they're just using their supposed newfound religion as an excuse to get your forgiveness." Landon banked right onto the small neighborhood road.

"What do you mean?"

He tapped the wheel. "Just that a lot of people claim they are reformed when they get out of jail; many claim they've found God, but a liar knows what to say to try and manipulate you."

What was he talking about? And why such intensity over a stranger? "Manipulate you into what?"

"Forgiving them. Starting over with them. Expecting you to trust them again."

"How is Bryan trying to do any of that?"

"I'm not talking about Bryan."

"Then who?"

Landon exhaled. "My father."

42

Piper shifted restlessly as they followed Coastal Highway back down to Long Beach. While a handful of the houses they passed were decorated for Christmas, it was the boats that were truly decked out—ribbons, garland, lights. They definitely gave her something to stare at during the awkward ride. She was dying to ask, dying to know, but for once she knew she needed to wait for him to share.

He, unfortunately for her curiosity, kept the topics of conversation to the scenery and the weather—that is, when he bothered to speak at all. Mostly he'd remained silent since flooring her with the statement about his father, and she'd been scrambling to put the pieces together ever since.

Landon's parents had divorced right around the time Landon started high school. His dad was quickly out of the picture. His mom remarried and moved to Florida with her new husband, and Landon had come to live with her family.

She'd been sheltered often as a child, coddled as the baby of the family, but surely she would have known if Landon's dad was a criminal.

Landon looked over at her with a sigh when they finally pulled into the hotel parking lot an hour and a half later. "I know it must be killing you, so go ahead and ask."

"Is that why Cole was shushing Bailey on the ride to the hotel from the airport? About having a criminal in the family?"

Landon nodded as he cut the ignition.

"Bailey doesn't know?"

"No—at least not then. Cole may have explained by now."

"How is it possible that I didn't know?" She shifted to face him, propping her back against the car door. "You lived with us."

He shifted as well, draping one arm over the steering wheel as he reclined. "Your folks were so kind. They never brought it up. When I first moved in, you asked where my parents were. You were curious even then. But your folks simply said—"

"That your parents had chosen other places, but that we had chosen you." She smiled at the memory.

"Everyone in town was used to Dad being gone. He traveled a lot for work and he'd been in Fairbanks for nine months, working a temporary reassignment, when everything happened. He was arrested and tried up there. Mom acted like they'd simply split up and told everyone Dad was remaining permanently in Fairbanks. She never talked about what he'd done. But there were those who knew, of course. Thelma Jenkins, for one."

"Is that why your mom left Yancey?"

"She wanted a fresh start with Phil."

"And your dad?"

"Served twelve years for fraud and embezzlement up in Fairbanks. And you want to know the crazy part?"

"If you want to tell me."

"My dad swore he was innocent from the time they arrested him, all through the trial, and even after he was behind bars. And I believed him. It's why I decided to become a cop, so I could rework his case and prove his innocence."

"Is that why you joined the force in Fairbanks? So you could be close to your dad?"

He nodded.

"And did you rework his case?"

"I did and . . ." He looked down. "Turns out he was guilty after all."

"Oh, Landon." She rested her hand on his, her heart going out to him. "I'm so sorry."

"So was I. I went to see him, confronted him with what I found, and you know what he said?"

She shook her head.

"'You got me.' No explanation, no remorse. Just 'You got me.'"

Her hand closed over his.

"Of course he changed his tune a few years ago—claimed he found God. But I don't know if it's true or just another one of his lies." Shame filled him. "So now you know the truth. I'm the son of a thief and a liar, and I was foolish enough to believe in him."

"It's not foolishness to have faith in those you love."

"Even if they aren't worthy of your faith?"

All of Landon's comments about those closest to a person having the ability to harm them the most suddenly made perfect sense. He knew the disappointment and disillusionment firsthand. He'd lived through the betrayal of someone he loved letting him down in the worst possible way, of someone he loved injuring him.

It all made so much sense—Landon's rigid adherence to the law and his reluctance to go by his gut rather than hard evidence. He'd done that once and it had backfired. He was bearing the burden of his father's guilt, carrying the shame of a crime he didn't commit. "Your father's mistakes and failures are his own. They aren't yours. You," she said, sliding close, "are worthy of the faith I have."

"How can you be so sure?"

"Because . . ." She ran her hand through his hair, settling her palm on the nape of his neck. "I know you, and . . ." She leaned in to him.

"And?" He swallowed.

"You're the man I love."

"Piper." Her name came out a breathy choke as his lips descended on hers.

A heavy rap sounded on the windshield.

Piper started, and Landon jolted upright.

She looked out the window and winced. "Cole."

Landon exhaled, exchanging a knowing glance with her that said he was about as thrilled to see her brother as she was.

She smoothed her hair as Landon opened the car door.

"What is going on here?" Cole didn't bother suppressing his outrage.

"I . . . we . . ." Landon stumbled.

"We," Piper said, clasping Landon's hand, "have to figure that out together before we can explain it to you."

Cole's brows shot up. "It? Are you two . . . ?"

"Are those two what?" Gage asked, walking up beside Cole.

"Nothing." Piper sighed.

"I'd hardly say kissing is nothing."

"Kissing?" Gage's voice dropped. "These two? You've got to be kidding!"

Cole's grim expression was answer enough.

"Pipsqueak and Landon?" Gage choked out.

"Don't call me that, Horatio."

Gage held up a stern finger. "There's no need to go there."

"Horatio?" Darcy said, joining their little party in the parking lot, along with Bailey and Jake.

"Great." Landon offered a sarcastic smile. "We're all here."

Piper held Cole's gaze, imploring him to realize this wasn't the time for discussion.

"What's going on?" Bailey asked at Cole's distressed expression.

"Something about someone named Horatio." Darcy shrugged.

A smile broke on Bailey's lips as her gaze flitted to Gage.

"You told her?" Gage's voice upped a pitch.

"It may have slipped out in conversation," Cole said sheepishly.

"Wait . . ." Darcy's gaze swung to Gage. "You're Horatio?"

"It is the middle name my mother gave me. I had no choice in the matter."

"Oh." Darcy pursed her lips, her cheeks reddening in an obvious attempt not to laugh. "That is unfortunate."

"Our mother gave us middle names after all her favorite literary characters. At least they weren't our first."

"Oh, so Horatio Hornblower."

Gage grimaced. "Just Horatio, thank you."

"And the rest of yours?" Her brightened gaze shifted to Cole next.

"His is Huckleberry," Gage blurted out.

"Thanks, bro," Cole said with zero enthusiasm.

"No problem." Gage smirked. "Piper's is Lucy."

"Lucy?" Darcy frowned.

"From The Chronicles of Narnia. They were my mother's favorite books as a child," Piper explained. "I rather fancy mine."

"Of course, because you got a normal name," Gage groaned.

"And Reef's?" Darcy asked.

"Sherlock," Piper supplied.

"And Kayden's?" Jake asked.

"Beatrice," Piper said, trying to contain a laugh of her own. "From *Much Ado About Nothing*. But if you tell her I was the one that blabbed, I'll kill you."

Jake held up his hands, amusement dancing across his handsome face. "Got it." He rocked back on his heels. "Kayden Beatrice McKenna." Clearly he realized the ammo he'd just been given.

"Now that we've had our fun," Gage said, "let's get back to the matter at hand."

"Right," Cole said, gazing at Piper.

Piper held her breath. There was no reason to have this discussion in front of everyone before she and Landon had even discussed what was happening amongst themselves. She was an adult, and Cole was treating her like a child. She braced herself to take on her brother as Landon stepped forward to protect her.

"The matter at hand is that we need to change locations," Cole said. "It's no longer safe at this hotel."

"What?" she asked, thankful he'd shifted the conversation but surprised at the direction it'd taken. Had something happened?

"Are you sure that's the most *pressing* matter?" Gage asked, tilting his head in Piper's direction.

"What's most important right now," Cole said, "is our safety."

SHATTERED

"Right," Gage said, his demeanor shifting to a more serious one. "Since the Mongols know exactly where we are staying, down to the room numbers, we need to move."

"How is that possible?" Piper asked.

Gage looked at Landon. "Didn't you tell her? Or were you too busy with *other* things?"

"I didn't want her to worry." He looked apologetically at Piper. "I was going to tell you as soon as we got back."

"Okay, so where do we go now?" Darcy asked.

"We find another hotel a good distance from here," Cole said.

"Do you really think that'll help?" Gage asked.

"It's our only option," Landon said grimly. "At least until our investigation here is concluded."

280

43

The ride to their new hotel in Santa Barbara was gorgeous and agonizing at the same time. Having pared down to two rental cars, Jake joined Piper and Landon for the journey, giving them no time alone to discuss what had just happened.

After hearing the words he'd never dreamed possible from Piper—that she loved him—Landon couldn't believe he had to wait to tell her he loved her too. Couldn't hold her hand or caress her face. Not without Jake seeing.

And what he and Piper needed to share was very, very private. Once they agreed where they were at, then they could share the good news. If it *was* good news. But what else could it be? She loved him—that's all that mattered. Right?

"How did it go with Karli's dad?" Jake asked.

"I don't believe he had any part in her death," Landon said.

"He seemed truly changed," Piper added. "Sorrowful over his past and his choices."

Jake leaned forward, resting his hands on the back of their seats. "Regret is all well and good, but it doesn't bring back the dead."

Landon glanced at Jake in the rearview mirror. It was the most profound and personal statement he'd ever heard him make.

Jake straightened at Landon's appraisal. "So . . ." He tapped the seat back. "Does he believe the Mongols are responsible for Karli's death?"

Landon looked back at the road. "No."

"I was afraid you were going to say that."

"Why?" Piper asked.

"Gage and Darcy got similar feedback. And us too."

"What do you mean?" she asked.

"Everyone we spoke to said there was no use in killing Karli. Michelle was the problem and she'd been dealt with."

Just as Detective Robertson had said.

"How do we know the Mongols aren't lying to us?" Desperation clawed at Piper's voice. If the Mongols didn't kill Karli, they were back at the start.

"We don't," Jake said. "At least not until their alibi checks out."

"Don't you mean alibis? Surely they don't all have the same one?"

"They're claiming they do."

She shook her head. "No. They can't seriously be each other's alibi."

"They aren't."

"Then who are they claiming is?" Landon asked.

"The Long Beach Police Department."

Piper swung around. "What?"

"They claim they were all arrested that night for a brawl they had with a rival gang. Spent the night in lockup at the 16th Precinct."

"Have you verified?" Landon asked, his worried gaze flashing to Piper.

"Darcy's running it down now. We should hear back tonight."

"I'll put in a call to Detective Robertson over at the 9th. Ask him to follow up on it as well."

"And if their alibi holds?" Piper asked.

"I'm sorry, darling," Jake said, "but it'll mean we're at a dead end."

∽

The Oceanview Inn sat perched at the edge of Requino Canyon, nestled idyllically between the Pacific Ocean and the

Santa Ynez Mountains. White fences, freshly painted, lined the winding drive leading to the Spanish Ranchero style inn. If the Mongols decided to come after them, Landon wanted to see them coming, and that meant getting out of the city and finding a good vantage point. It'd taken a little searching on the Internet, but Oceanview Inn appeared to be the perfect hiding spot. All their investigative work complete, they could spend the night away from it all while they awaited word on the Mongols' supposed alibi.

Landon couldn't help noticing the group's atypical silence as they followed their host to their rooms.

"It's gorgeous," Bailey said as Patti Miller, co-owner of the inn, opened the girls' cottage. Set about a hundred yards from the main building, the cottage offered the added layer of seclusion Landon was looking for.

They followed Patty inside. A living room, open kitchen, bath, and two bedrooms—all with whitewashed paneling and thick Berber carpet. A small Christmas tree sat atop the island separating the kitchen from the main room. Its ornaments were a collection of seashells and miniature horseshoes. It was certainly unique.

Cole set Bailey's and Piper's bags in the first bedroom, while Gage set Darcy's in the second.

"There are extra linens and towels in the armoire." Patti pointed to the antique piece at the end of the hall.

"Thank you," Bailey said.

Piper had remained surprisingly silent since they'd departed Los Angeles. Jake's presence had kept them from talking about their relationship, but even so, it was clear Piper had other things on her mind. Landon was convinced the Mongols had not been involved in Karli's murder, but he couldn't blame Piper for holding on. Without the Mongols, they had nothing.

"I'll show the men to their place," Patti said. "You ladies holler if you need anything. Supper is served at six on the patio."

After another round of thank-yous, Patti led the men to their cottage and left with the same reminder about supper.

"I think I'll grab a shower," Jake said, excusing himself.

"I'm going to take a walk." Gage grabbed a water bottle and ducked out the door.

Great. Just him and Cole.

Cole didn't waste any time. "What's going on?"

"I love your sister," Landon said, surprised at his own boldness.

"*Love,* love her?" Cole nearly stumbled.

"I'm afraid so."

"And does she love you too?"

"I think so." She'd said it, but he couldn't say anything about that—not until he heard the answer to the question burning in his mind.

"You *think* so?"

"We were about to discuss it when you arrived." It seemed a nicer way to say *barged in.*

"Sorry about that. She's my baby sister. She's my responsibility. I know she views that as an intrusion."

"I think she views it as none of us treating her like the adult she is."

Cole rubbed the back of his neck. "You're probably right."

"I'm just as guilty of it."

Cole swallowed. "So when did all this happen?"

"For me, it started last summer. Seeing Piper nearly die made me realize how much she meant to me."

"Then why Becky Malone?"

Landon exhaled. "You heard about that?" Had he also heard that *nothing* happened? If not, he needed to set that record straight.

"Kayden mentioned it and the drinking."

Landon nodded, shame suffocating him. "Kayden knows too?"

Cole shook his head. "After Piper saw you, she told Kayden. Kayden didn't know what was going on but told me. Figured you might need a friend. You headed out before I could ask about it."

"You're always there for me."

"That's right."

"It isn't like last time."

"No?"

"No. It was a small blip, comparatively."

Cole slid his hands in his pocket. "So you're excusing it?"

"No. Quite the opposite." Landon needed to lay it all on the line. "When I realized how I felt about Piper and that she'd probably never reciprocate those feelings, I fell back into old patterns. I turned to the wrong places for comfort." He sat beside his friend on the sofa, his friend who had rescued him from the pit both times before. "I know now that's not where the answers are to be found."

"Oh?"

"I asked Jesus into my life."

Cole's eyes widened, more in happiness than surprise. "You did?"

Landon nodded, looking down, still ashamed of how weak he'd been, how dependent on wicked things when he'd thought he was being so strong.

Cole clasped his shoulder. "That's great, man. I've been praying for you."

"I know you have, and I can't thank you enough."

"Have you told Piper?"

"Not outright."

Cole looked at him, confused.

"We haven't had time to really talk."

"But you've had time to kiss."

Landon exhaled. "There's that . . ."

"What are your intentions?"

"I love her."

"I got that part. What I want to know is what you intend to do about it?"

"I want to be with her, if she'll have me."

"As in . . . ?"

"Marry her." He hadn't fully grasped it until he'd just said it. Piper wasn't someone he'd date. She was the woman he'd marry.

"Marry?" Cole said.

Landon nodded.

"You know I think the world of you . . ."

"But . . ."

"This is my baby sister, Landon. Marriage is huge. You need to be sure you are in the right place, that the urge to self-destruct when things go bad isn't your default setting anymore, that God is the one steering your life. As a friend, I'm asking you to take time to be certain before you make the next step."

Hours later, Landon lay in bed, Cole's words still ringing in his ears.

Please, Father, help me to honor Cole's wishes. Help me to honor yours.

Taking things slow felt like the worst possible idea. All he wanted to do was rush to Piper, pull her in his arms, and tell her he loved her too. But Piper deserved the best. His best. If taking time, as Cole suggested, ensured she received the best, then he'd gladly endure the torture waiting would inflict.

Please, Father, I want to do this right.

44

Landon's heart dropped when he got the news over the phone the next morning. "And you're certain?"

"Positive," Detective Robertson said, confirming his worst suspicions. "I wish I had different news for you."

"Thanks, Detective."

"I hate to see that sweet gal's face when you break the news."

It would break her heart.

"Well?" Piper said, anxiously beside him.

Landon set his cell aside and looked into his family's faces with trepidation. "I'm sorry."

"Their alibi checked out?" Jake said.

"I'm afraid so. Everyone in question spent the night of Karli's murder in lockup. There is no way any of them could have killed her."

Piper deflated before him.

Cole wrapped his arms around her before Landon could. "I'm so sorry, kid."

Shell-shocked, Landon watched as one by one they all faced the inevitable.

"I'll call Kayden," Bailey said. "She'll want to know."

"Should I contact the airline?" Gage asked. "Secure our flight home?"

"No," Piper said, pulling back. "We aren't done."

"Piper, they didn't do it. The Mongols aren't responsible for Karli's death," Gage said.

"There's nothing more we can do here," Cole said softly.

"Maybe not here, but . . . somewhere."

"Where, Piper?" Cole asked. "We have nothing else to go on."

Landon prayed for guidance, for wisdom. How could he help Piper face reality—they were at a dead end—without crushing her?

"There's got to be something else. Somebody we are overlooking." Piper pulled out their copy of the case file.

"We looked at every logical Mongol connection," Darcy said.

"Then we look at someone outside the Mongols." Piper spread the photos out before her.

Landon sat down beside her. "What are you thinking? Someone else from Karli's past?"

"I don't know. Maybe."

"We ran through all the ties to Karli's past," Darcy said, kindly but matter-of-factly.

"Not all of them." Piper held up the photo of Karli and Erik Johnson.

"The boyfriend?"

"He's the only person from her past who Karli kept in touch with."

"You think he killed her?" Jake asked.

"Not necessarily. Karli clearly trusted him, allowed herself to be vulnerable by continuing her relationship with him. So maybe he was the one person she was willing to confide in."

"You think she told him why she was scared? Who she thought was after her?" Darcy asked.

"I pray so."

Darcy grabbed her laptop. "I'll track him down."

"I'll help," Jake offered.

Two hours later, Jake entered the room, nearly out of breath. "We found him."

Landon watched as hope welled inside Piper.

"Erik Johnson works as a computer engineer at BioTech Pharmaceuticals in Portland, Oregon."

Landon squeezed her shoulder. "Looks like we're headed for Portland."

Cole stood. "Do you need our help? Should we come with you?"

Landon looked at Piper. "I think we've got this."

She nodded.

❧

Portland was a mixture of rain and mist. The drive from the airport to BioTech Pharmaceuticals took them along the expressway and around the edges of the city.

"How you holding up?" Landon asked.

"I'll let you know after we talk with Erik."

He prayed Erik would be helpful, that if nothing else, he'd point them in a new direction.

BioTech loomed on the horizon—a gray glass building, against the drab winter sky.

They entered through the front doors only to face a nearly immediate halt at a security station eerily similar to the airport security they'd faced only hours ago on their departure from California. Three rows of conveyor belts leading into a metal detector lined the pathway to the interior of the building.

"Do you have an appointment?" the armed security officer asked Landon.

"No." Landon pulled out his badge. "But we need to speak with Erik Johnson."

"May I?" The security officer extended his hand for Landon's badge.

"Sure." Landon handed it over.

"Wait here."

As if they had any option.

"Get a load of this place," he whispered to Piper.

"I know. What did you say they do here again?"

"Darcy said something about pharmaceuticals and biomedical advancements."

"Must be pretty important."

"Or highly valuable."

A few minutes later, the guard returned. "Come with me."

He led them through security and had their belongings scanned before allowing them to proceed. "You'll need to leave your weapon with us," the guard said.

Landon's hand closed over the handle. "I don't release my weapon."

"Then you won't be coming in."

Piper looked up at him. She needed this, needed to follow the last lead before them, no matter how thin.

He exhaled. "All right." He handed his gun over, and they proceeded.

The guard swiped his security card at each door they encountered. A series of offices lined the sterile halls, and the final door led them into a gigantic workspace—easily four times the size of the McKennas' garage at their shop back home. White-fogged plastic covered the metal walls and divided the various cubicles within the large space. Each employee wore a white lab coat, their attention completely immersed in their work. Not a single person glanced up at them as they passed.

The guard stopped at the third cubicle on the left. "This was Mr. Johnson's work station. Mr. Thompson will be with you shortly."

"*Was* his work station?" Piper asked, but the guard was already halfway back to the door. She looked at Landon. "This place gives me the creeps."

"Yeah," he said, looking around. "It's definitely strange."

After a several-minute wait, a man in his late forties strode into the cubicle and returned Landon's badge. "Deputy Grainger, is it?"

"Yes."

"I'm Ed Thompson, president of operations here at BioTech."

"Quite the operation you've got here."

"We are the leading supplier of insulin in the world. Ten thousand vials a day."

"So all the security is to protect the insulin?" Landon asked, skeptical.

"No. It's to protect our innovations."

"Innovations?" Piper asked.

"Here at BioTech, pharmaceuticals constitute only a fraction of our work. Our main focus is on biotechnology, as the name implies."

"What type of biotechnology?"

"It's complicated, but we develop solutions to revolutionize the pharmaceutical industry. For example, Mr. Johnson worked in our package development."

"Worked?" Piper asked. "You're the second person to refer to Erik in the past tense. Does he no longer work here?"

"I'm afraid Erik Johnson was killed in a car accident a few weeks ago."

Landon steadied Piper as she digested the news.

"He's dead?" she said, her voice cracking.

"I'm afraid so. Were you friends of his?"

"No." Landon shook his head. "We are investigating the death of a friend of Erik's. We were hoping Erik might be of some help in tracking her killer."

"Oh, that's terrible."

"Yes, it is." Landon looked around at the workers still studiously keeping their attention on their work. "Would it be possible to speak with some of Erik's colleagues?"

"What for?"

"Perhaps they can help answer some questions."

"I highly doubt it. Erik was only with us a short time and we discourage interoffice friendships."

"Why is that?" Piper asked.

"We find they distract the focus from the work."

"I see," Landon said. "So that's a no?"

"I'm afraid so." He waved two fingers, and the security guard stepped into the cubicle. "Mr. Nelson will escort you back out. Sorry you had to travel all this way for bad news."

"Not as sorry as we are," Piper said.

As they followed the guard out, Landon whispered, "Do you get the feeling he can't wait to get us out of here?"

"Yeah, I wonder why that is?"

They exited the first set of double doors and began the long trek down the windowless hallway.

"Not the cheeriest place to work," she commented.

The guard just kept walking, not bothering to respond.

Another hallway and another set of doors found them back at Security. Landon's gun was returned and they were outside within twenty minutes of entering.

"That was bizarre," Piper said.

"The timing of Erik's and Karli's deaths so close to each other is also bizarre."

"You think there was foul play involved?"

"I don't know, but I think we should see if we can get a look at Erik's accident report."

A woman crossing the parking lot cleared her throat, drawing Landon's attention.

She was headed in their direction with her gaze fastened on them. She dropped her purse and the contents spilled out across the asphalt.

Landon stepped to help her, bending to lend a hand.

Instead of thanking him, she slid him a folded piece of paper. "Don't look at it now."

"Who are you?"

"A friend of Erik's."

"You work at BioTech?"

"No time for questions. They're watching."

Landon wasn't surprised; he'd already spotted the cameras attached to a number of light poles in the parking lot.

"It's Erik's parents' address. You need to pay them a visit," she said hurriedly as she shoved her things back in her bag and stood.

"Wait . . ."

"I'll meet you there later." She rushed past him and Piper, and headed for a car.

"What was all that about?" Piper asked.

"We have a new lead." He smiled.

✵

Now they'd gone too far, hit too close. His ear still rang from the boss's rant. It was time to take action. He pulled out of BioTech's lot, knowing exactly where they were headed, and it played perfectly into his hands. Perfectly into the trap he'd set for them.

45

The small ski village of Government Camp sat nestled at the southern end of Mt. Hood Village, about an hour's drive southeast of Portland. With a population of fewer than three hundred, it was no wonder Erik and Karli had bonded. Two teenagers in a town with nothing to do but ski or board must have had a lot of time to get acquainted.

"Make a right on Winters Crest," Piper said.

Landon did as instructed.

"Twelve hundred Winters Crest," Piper said, pointing at the brick rancher with red shutters. "This must be the place."

"What are we going to say to them?" Piper asked as Landon opened her car door.

"You, without words?" He chuckled, trying to lighten the mood. "That's a first."

"Very funny. Seriously, what are we going to say? Hi, Mr. and Mrs. Johnson. We think your son's accident maybe wasn't an accident."

"The woman in the parking lot said she'd meet us here at some point. We'll just wing it until she gets here."

"You wing something?" Piper smiled. "That's a first."

"I've been winging quite a few things these days." He winked, fighting the urge to pull her into his arms.

The front door opened, and a man stepped onto the porch. "Can I help you folks?" He was in his early sixties and looked to

294

have stepped straight out of an L.L.Bean catalog. Plaid flannel top, tan Dockers-style pants, and leather loafers.

Piper smiled. "I sure hope so."

The man's countenance brightened as she approached.

"I'm Piper McKenna, and this is Deputy Landon Grainger."

The man's brow pinched. "Deputy?"

Landon picked up the conversation. "Yes, sir, we're down here from Alaska, investigating a woman's murder."

"Oh?"

"We believe she knew your son, Erik. We heard about his accident. Please accept our condolences."

The man nodded, his eyes downcast. "Thank you."

Landon cleared his throat and continued. "We were hoping we could chat with you."

"Don't see why not. You two might as well come in out of the cold. The wife's just put on a pot of hot cider. I'll tell her to grab two more mugs."

"That's very kind. Thank you," Piper said, following the man inside.

"I'm Stanley Johnson, by the way."

"Pleased to meet you, Mr. Johnson."

He led them into the front room. A shiny black baby grand piano, with a series of photographs in gold frames arranged on top, sat in front of the large bay window. Pictures of Erik—as a child, in his early teens, and in his graduation cap and gown. His parents looked old enough to be his grandparents, though.

Piper examined each. "Your son was very handsome."

"Bright too. Graduated top of his class at the University of Oregon. Not too bad for a ski-village kid."

"Was he your only child?" she asked, praying her question wasn't too forward.

Stanley nodded. "Gladys and I weren't able to have kids. We tried for years but finally settled on adoption. Erik was the pride and joy of our lives."

"I thought I heard voices." A woman entered the room. Her gray hair was swept up in a bun. She wore a soft pink blouse, tan corduroy skirt, and flowered apron. "Who do we have here?"

"This is Piper McKenna and Deputy . . . ?"

"Grainger," Landon supplied.

"Deputy?" the woman said.

"They are down from Alaska, investigating some poor woman's murder."

"How unfortunate. Is it someone we knew?"

"I'm not sure, but she knew your son."

"Erik?"

"Yes, ma'am," Landon said. "She lived in Government Camp a short time, many years ago. Karli Davis."

"I'm afraid I don't know a Karli Davis."

Right. What name had Karli gone by then? "My apologies. I believe she went by Suzanne Wilson while she lived here."

"That one." Mrs. Johnson waggled her finger.

"You remember her?"

"How could I not? First woman to break my Erik's heart."

"Do you mind if we ask you a few questions about their relationship?"

"You can ask, but it wasn't much of a relationship." She stepped to the piano, clasping one of Erik's pictures in her hand.

"Do you remember when Erik and Karli—I'm sorry, I mean Suzanne—met?"

The woman nodded. "On the bus to Sandy."

"Sandy?" Landon asked.

"If you live on the mountain, you go to high school in Sandy, Oregon. Erik and Suzanne became friends on the bus. It's an hour ride each way with stops, which leaves a lot of time to get to know someone. If you're willing to let someone know you, that is."

"Gladys," Stanley said, moving to stand by his wife's side.

"You're talking about Suzanne?" Landon asked, finding it difficult to not call her Karli. He'd never met her while she lived, and yet she would always be Karli Davis in his mind.

"That girl, I felt sorry for her. Seemed pretty unhappy."

"Did you know she was in Witness Protection?"

"Not until her mother's death." Gladys's hands twisted in her apron. "I'll never forget that night. The explosion rocked the mountain."

"It's a wonder we didn't have an avalanche," Stanley said.

"Is that when Erik found out who Suzanne really was?"

"A few days after," Gladys said. "There was an article in the paper about her mother, about the whole story. Erik was stunned in a way, but he said things suddenly made sense."

"About Suzanne?"

Gladys nodded.

"We know that your son and she remained in contact." Piper handed Gladys the picture of Karli and Erik at Glacier Peak. "She'd been going by Karli Davis since she left Government Camp."

Gladys clasped the picture and sat down on the sofa. "This must have been taken the last time he saw her."

"Do you remember when that was?"

"Right before his accident. Erik went to see her. I don't know why." Gladys looked down, knotting the handkerchief in her hand. "I thought Erik was finally moving on. Dating a nice woman from work."

"We were told interoffice relationships were frowned upon at BioTech," Landon said.

"That sounds like something one of them would say."

"One of whom?"

"Those dictators at BioTech. I don't know why Erik stayed. They were control freaks. He and Elaine started dating and were told to break it off or look for new jobs."

"Did they break it off?" Piper asked.

"No. They just kept quiet about it at the office. They both had too much invested in their research to just walk away from BioTech. They planned to finish the projects they were working on and then look for other employment."

"Do you know what Erik was working on?" Landon asked.

Gladys shook her head. "I never understood Erik's projects."

"Why don't you come with me," Stanley said. They followed

him through the house and out back to a work shed. Looking around to make sure they were alone, Stanley unlocked the door and instructed them to step inside.

"Ham radio?" Landon asked, taking in the equipment.

"It's how Erik got started."

Piper frowned. "I don't understand. I thought Erik worked in the pharmaceutical industry."

"He was a scientist at BioTech, but not in pharmaceuticals. He was part of their innovation and advancements team."

"Which means?"

"It's a fancy catchall title for the various projects they did. Erik worked with RFID technology."

"Radio frequency?"

"Microchips," Stanley said.

"What does microchip technology have to do with the pharmaceutical industry?" Piper asked.

"Why don't we step inside and I'll explain," a feminine voice said.

They turned to find the woman from the parking lot.

"Elaine." Stanley hugged the woman.

"Mr. Johnson, it's good to see you again."

"Stanley, please. Does Gladys know you're here?"

"No, I spotted you out back when I pulled up, so I headed out here first."

"She'll be so pleased to see you."

❧

Landon sat back, trying to take in the information Elaine was sharing. "Let me see if I can wrap my mind around what you are saying. . . . Erik was working on the RFID containers that the insulin is stored in?"

"Correct." Elaine nodded.

"But he thought something was wrong?"

"Right. He came to me, concerned that the transmitters were compromising the integrity of the medicine."

"Compromising how?"

Elaine explained the entire process, and Landon struggled to keep up when she went into elaborate technical detail, but he grasped the big picture. BioTech's advancement of encasing insulin in traceable containers was negatively altering the medicine because of the heat the transmitters emitted.

"Did Erik share his concerns with anybody?" Landon asked.

"Of course. Erik immediately took his concerns to Ed Thompson."

"President of Operations at BioTech?" That figured. No wonder Ed Thompson had been eager to get them out of there.

"That's him," Elaine said, not bothering to hide her distaste for the man.

"And what was Mr. Thompson's response?" Though Landon could already guess.

"He thanked Erik for his hard work and said he'd pass the information along to the right people."

"But you don't think he did?"

"Neither did Erik. Production continued as usual. Erik questioned him and was told it had been handled. Thompson told him he needed to focus on his work."

"And to stop asking questions?" Piper said.

"Exactly."

Landon exhaled. "But he didn't?" *Good man.*

"Not Erik. He continued to research it, and when he learned that a dozen people who had taken BioTech's insulin had died, he knew he had to do something."

Piper's eyes widened. "They died from the insulin?"

"It couldn't be proven, not from the outside, but questions were being asked. And those are only the few cases Erik was able to confirm. I fear there are many more out there."

"Did Erik go to anyone else?"

"Yeah. Somebody at the FDA."

"Do you remember his name?"

"No. Erik said the less I knew the better. The man told Erik they couldn't do anything without some kind of proof, something more definitive than Erik's hunch."

"Twelve deaths weren't enough?" Piper asked, her tone indignant.

"I guess not, not when the victims were elderly and had diabetes."

"So what did Erik do?" A man like Elaine was describing wouldn't just quit. Not when he knew more lives were at stake.

"Up until his death Erik was working to compile the proof, his studies, the data, but it wasn't a quick process. You've got to understand; we are kept under a microscope. There are security precautions, no equipment allowed in or out of the lab, no laptops. Everything is searched upon arrival and departure. Erik couldn't simply print out his findings and walk out the door with them."

"Could he have e-mailed them to somebody?" Piper asked.

"All computers are monitored."

"Then how did Erik conduct his research?" Landon asked. Surely he was watched at the lab.

"At first only at the lab, but after taking his findings to Mr. Thompson and seeing how that ended, he started working on his own at his apartment, trying to piece the research together as best he could."

"So we should access his home computer." Hope filled Landon that they'd finally have access to some solid evidence—though he had no idea how all they were learning linked to Karli.

"I'm afraid not." Elaine's dark braid tumbled over her shoulder, and she slipped it back into place, tightening the rubber band at the base in the process. "The last day Erik came to work . . ." She swallowed. "The last day I saw him he told me he was going to take a few days and pay a visit to Phyllis Wheeler's family."

"Who is Phyllis Wheeler?"

"Phyllis Wheeler was the most recent victim of BioTech's tainted insulin. As I said earlier, the deaths were always viewed as being caused by natural complications of the disease, but Erik knew better. His investigation led him to believe he could prove their deaths weren't natural if he could get ahold of one of the vials Mrs. Wheeler was using. Neither of us had access to the filled vials—only sample casings—and it takes time for the contamination to occur. Erik needed a vial that had shipped at least two weeks prior for it to show evidence of contamination.

"Erik spoke with Phyllis's husband by phone, hoping to convince him to let him examine one of the unused vials or even better still to have an autopsy performed on Mrs. Wheeler. He was convinced the tainted insulin would leave a trace if properly looked for, but Mr. Wheeler was too distraught over the death of his wife to listen. Erik planned to visit him in person. He called me after leaving the office that day to say his apartment had been ransacked. His computers, his hard drives, everything was stolen. He tried to contact the man he'd spoken with at the FDA, but was told he no longer worked there. Erik started to get paranoid."

"What do you mean paranoid?"

"He thought someone from BioTech had gotten to the FDA contact."

"Did Erik have proof of that?"

"Not that I know of. I think it was just a hunch. Erik said something about BioTech's reach being longer than he realized."

"So who does Erik believe broke into his place? Someone from BioTech?"

"Yes."

"Did the police look at BioTech?" Surely suspicions had to be raised.

"No. Whoever did it made it look like a regular robbery. They trashed the place and took anything of value."

"But you think it was them?" Landon asked, totally in agreement based on what he'd heard.

"I *know* it was."

"And Erik's accident?" Piper asked, inching closer to Elaine.

Elaine wiped the tears slipping down her cheeks. "Was no accident."

"You believe they killed him to silence him," Piper said softly, resting a hand on Elaine's arm.

Always trying to comfort. Her love inspired him.

"I think there was more to it," Elaine said, sniffling. "After Erik left for Canada, I saw Grant Nelson, head of security, searching Erik's work station."

Landon tilted his head. "Looking for what?"

"My guess, a microchip. Or the evidence that Erik had been building one."

"A microchip?"

"A microchip could store all of Erik's data. It's small enough to hide from the eye and, if made with the right materials, undetectable by the security detectors," Elaine explained. "We only design them at BioTech; we don't manufacture them. But Grant pulled items from Erik's trash that suggested Erik had been assembling one there."

"So if Erik had the proof he needed, why did he go to see Mr. Wheeler?"

"Scientific data is one thing; tangible evidence from a victim of the tainted insulin is another. He felt he needed concrete proof before anyone would believe him, and he wasn't sure whom to trust."

"Wait a minute," Piper said. "Did you say Erik went to Canada? His accident was in Canada?"

Elaine nodded. "The Wheelers lived in Vancouver."

"So he died in Vancouver?"

"No." Elaine shook her head. "That's the part I don't understand. Erik left to go speak with the Wheelers in Vancouver, but at the time of his death three days later, Erik still hadn't arrived at the Wheelers'. He died outside of Nicola, two hours north of Vancouver. And the really weird thing is he was driving *southbound* on Route 5 at the time of his accident—completely opposite of where he should have been."

But precisely en route from Glacier Peak resort, where Erik's folks said he'd been visiting Karli.

46

Snow rained down as they pulled out of the Johnsons' drive. It was eerie how quickly the blizzard had begun, eerier how Mr. Johnson had anticipated its imminent arrival.

"Where do we go from here?" Piper asked.

Landon considered their options. "We need to figure out if that microchip still exists. I think Erik might have given it to Karli for safekeeping. Why else would he travel to see her right before his death? And that would explain why someone was after Karli."

"The older man that paid a visit to Glacier Peak?" Piper said.

Landon nodded. "I bet he's the man who called Wellspring claiming to be Karli's father and then her doctor and who broke into the clinic to steal her file."

"Do you think he retrieved the chip when he killed Karli? Maybe we're already too late. Maybe we have been this entire time."

"I don't think so."

"Why not?"

"There were marks on Karli." He swallowed. "What I'm now betting were torture marks."

"You think the killer was trying to get the microchip's location out of her?"

"Yes, but Reef interrupted him before he could finish. He couldn't leave a witness, so he killed Karli and hid until he could escape."

"And then what?"

"I think he assumed Karli had passed the chip to Reef." Landon's breath caught as the pieces fell into place and he realized the danger Piper had been in from the start. "It explains the sense you had that someone was in your house the night of Karli's murder."

"He thinks we have it?"

"Or that you're trying to find it."

"Do you think he's still following us?"

"I'm afraid so."

"It's sweet, really."

"What?" He gaped at her.

"No. Not that the killer is following us. I was thinking about Karli and Erik. It's sweet that after all those years he knew he could trust her to keep his secret safe. To protect the microchip until he had the physical evidence he needed to make his case."

"He knew she was an expert at hiding, and with her living only hours from the Wheelers' it would have been an easy drop-off."

"I wonder what went through her mind when Erik didn't return. When she realized they'd gotten to him? Poor thing. She sure had more than her fair share of heartache in this life."

The sheer rock wall of the canyon loomed large on their right, heavy snow blanketing it. The wind swirled tufts of snow through the pass in front of them. Landon gripped the wheel more securely. Ice, no doubt, was hiding beneath the freshly falling snow.

Something clicked beneath them. It was faint, but Landon heard it all the same.

"What was that?" Piper asked.

Reaching under his seat, he felt a device taped to the underside of his seat.

"What's wrong?" she asked.

"We've got to get out."

"What?"

He slowed as best he could without fishtailing them, opened the driver's side door and yanked Piper. "Now!"

Landon's left shoulder collided with the snow-packed surface, pain burning through his socket. Piper landed beside him with a grunt, her slender form jolted by the unforgiving surface. An explosion shook the earth as they tumbled over the embankment's edge, the ground slipping away from them. Snow and debris clouded his field of vision; jagged rocks battered his body as gravity propelled him downhill. He slammed into a steadfast object that ripped the air from his lungs.

A copse of trees had broken his fall, nearly breaking his back in the process. Piper hit moments after him, a cry escaping her lips. Fighting the sharp pain in his chest, he forced himself to roll onto his side so he could check on her.

"You okay?"

Snow and pine needles clung to her hair. Blood trickled from her forehead. "I'll be all right." She propped herself gingerly onto her elbows. "Was that a—"

"Car bomb."

"When?"

"Probably planted it while we were . . ." His words dropped off as his eyes focused on the mountain towering above. *Dear God.*

"What's wrong?"

A billowing wave of snow roared toward them.

"Avalanche!" he hollered.

Horror filled Piper's eyes as she caught sight of the wall of snow charging at them. It was too late to move out of its path.

"Grab hold of the tree. Don't let go. Shield your face." He wrapped her arms around the trunk, praying it was sturdy enough to not get yanked up with the debris. Wrapping his arms around her, he too grabbed hold of the tree, shielding her with his body "As soon as it slows, cup a hand over your face and stretch your other arm up as high as it can—"

The deluge swallowed his words, crashing over them, white engulfing his vision. A never-ending torrent of snow roared past them, moving at what had to be sixty miles an hour. His arms burned as he held to the tree, struggling against the surmounting pull of the avalanche.

Sound faded and white turned to black.

～∞～

He smiled with satisfaction as the explosion shook the mountain. He'd left Government Camp as they left the house, sped to get through the pass well ahead of them, knowing the explosions would seal off the pass. He had no desire to get stuck in the poor excuse for a town, not for the time it would take to clear the road. The chip's whereabouts still remained a mystery, and that bothered him, but the threat had been dealt with. Surely no one remained to trace it back to them. Mr. Thompson owed him an apology.

47

The roaring finally stopped, and all was silent—deathly silent. Piper continued to thrash her head and body until the snow settled, praying she'd created enough room to form an air pocket and allow movement. Her right hand was cold; she prayed that meant she'd cracked the surface, but then again, all of her was cold. She was buried in snow and ice. Too frightened to open her eyes because of what she might find, she prayed.

Please, Father, help us to survive this. Help them to find us quickly.

Opening her eyes, she found herself wrapped in a cocoon of white, but relief filled her at the faint light seeping in around her hand. She'd broken the surface. *Praise God.* That opening greatly increased their chances of survival.

She could feel the warmth of Landon's body behind her. She'd felt the strength of his muscles straining against the avalanche as it bowled over them. Now he was still—*too still.*

She wiggled her head around in the space she'd created and found him unconscious. She pressed against him, trying to rouse him within the tiny confines. No movement. No response. Her heart sank.

She wiggled her hand as far above the surface as she could, trying desperately to draw attention to their location. Using her free arm, she began digging, tunneling, fighting to reach the surface, the motion of her arms mimicking a swim stroke.

Faint light filled the cavity. She prayed the snow falling in was from the sky and not from the accumulation burying her again. Trying not to push too hard against Landon, she braced the soles of her boots against the trunk and used the traction to help propel her upward.

She broke the surface to snow swirling around her, white engulfing her. The blizzard had fully moved in. She squeezed her eyes shut, knowing it would hamper search and rescue. She fished her cell from her pocket, only to find it crushed.

Lying flat on her stomach, she dug to free Landon. His left hand sticking above the surface helped direct her efforts. Ignoring her numb hands, she dug, praying she wouldn't be too late. After the fifteen-minute mark Landon's chances of surviving being buried in snow dropped to twenty percent.

Ignoring the pins and needles stinging her fingers and hands, she kept digging until she'd cleared his head.

She cupped his face in her hands. "Landon." She rubbed his cheeks, the blistering wind burning hers. "Landon, can you hear me?"

No response.

Clearing the powder down past his shoulders, she sat on the snow behind him, a leg draped on either side, her boots once again braced against the tree trunk. She looped her arms underneath his shoulders for leverage and, pressing hard against the tree, lurched back. The snow shifted beneath her, terrifying her that it would all give way, but it didn't. She tried again and this time managed to raise Landon's torso above the snow line. Heaving and pulling, she finally pulled him onto the surface. She located his cell, only to find it dead. She fought the desperation threatening to close in on her.

The snow was so thick and dense, she couldn't see past her hand. She screamed at the top of her lungs. Surely someone heard the explosion. Surely someone would know they needed help.

Tying her yellow jacket to the tree, she moved a few feet in a straight line from Landon in the direction she believed the road to be. They couldn't have fallen that far. If she could make it to the road, they'd be much more likely to find help. *If the road even still exists.* An avalanche of that magnitude probably buried the entire pass. Another step and she lost sight of her jacket. The heavy snowfall, mixed with thirty-mile-an-hour winds and the avalanche's destruction, obscured everything. She had to go back to Landon—quickly, before her footprints disappeared. If she didn't, she risked losing him in only a matter of feet.

Making it back, she found a thin layer of snow already covering him. They needed to find shelter of some kind, because the harsh reality was they might not be found until the blizzard passed, and there was no way they'd survive out in the elements.

She tried rousing Landon, but to no avail. How could she move him? She couldn't carry him, needed a way to pull him. Removing her jacket from the tree, she secured a sleeve around Landon's right leg, finding his left swollen. She prayed it wasn't broken, but now wasn't the time for assessment. They needed to find shelter before night crept in and the temperatures dropped even further. She pulled off Landon's outermost layer, his shell jacket, and secured it to his left ankle below the swelling. She gripped the loose sleeves from both jackets over her shoulders and used them as a harness to pull him across the snow.

Watching the ground at her feet for any protruding objects that could injure him, she moved downhill. It would conserve energy, and with the pass buried, it would probably be their only way out. She'd search for a stream, even if it was frozen, as it might lead them to a waterside cave, or if they were extremely fortunate, they might come across an avalanche shelter or ranger's station.

Darkness soon swallowed what faint light there'd been. Landon moaned, his eyes flickering open intermittently, but she was never able to rouse him fully. Wind burned her cheeks, her lips. She stuck out her tongue, hoping the melting snow would ease her dry throat, but it only chilled her deeper. Pins and needles danced in her feet, so painfully she wanted to pray for it to stop, but she knew when it did, it would mean frost-bite. She'd already lost all feeling in her fingers; she didn't even know how she still managed to grip the jacket sleeves. Bleakness threatened to seep in with the cold, but she refused to give in to despair. When nothing else could shelter them, God would.

48

Landon woke to the crackle of burning wood. Warmth radiated along his right side and pain along his left. He opened his eyes. Shadows danced along the ceiling—a rough-hewn wooden ceiling. Where was he?

He shifted, and pain racked his body. He groaned.

"You're awake. Oh, thank God." Piper knelt by his side.

He smiled, the simple movement excruciating. "Where are we?" His mouth was so dry that his lips cracked with the motion.

"An avalanche shelter."

"Avalanche?" The horrid memory flooded back. "Are you okay? Are you safe?" He shifted to sit, and pain knocked him back down.

"I'm fine." She placed a cool rag on his head. "You're the one who needs tending."

"My left side . . ."

"Your leg's swollen but thankfully not broken. Your ribs, I'm not so sure about."

Why weren't they at a hospital? Why had the rescue team opted to take them to a shelter instead? "Where is the rescue team?"

"They haven't found us yet."

"Haven't found us? Then how did we get here?" Had he managed to walk somehow and not remembered?

"I got us here."

311

"You?"

She smiled, holding a cup to his lips. "You don't have to sound so surprised."

He took a sip of the cold water; it felt gloriously soothing along his parched throat. "How did you manage that?"

"I fashioned a sling of sorts."

"A sling?" How could someone as slight as Piper bear his weight for who knows how far?

"I dragged you like a sled."

"That probably explains the aches and pains." He chuckled, regretting it the moment the stabbing pain returned to his side.

"I'm sorry, I didn't know how else to move you."

He covered her hand with his. "I'm joking. You saved my life—both our lives."

"So far . . ."

"You got us shelter, fire, water. You're amazing."

"You've got a fever." She brushed his hair from his face. "I crushed some Tylenol into your water, but I couldn't get you to swallow it. There were no antibiotics or stronger pain-killers in the first-aid kit."

"I'm fine."

"You're just saying that."

He clasped her hand tighter. "I'm alive because of you."

She nodded, biting her bottom lip.

He reached up and cupped her face. "Your family will fly to the rescue as soon as they hear we're out here. Cole won't stop until they find us."

"If he even knows where to look."

"If he can't find us, Jake will. I've never seen anybody track like Jake can."

"The blizzard hasn't let up."

"Give it a day."

"It's been two."

"Two?" He'd been out for two days? Piper had to face everything alone for *two* days.

She nodded.

312

"I'm so sorry that you've had to face the last two days alone."

"I wasn't alone. God never forsakes us, and I had you."

"Unconscious."

"I'd take you unconscious any day rather than face a single day without you." She leaned into his hand.

"I love you, Piper."

"I know you do."

"No." Ignoring the pain, he pulled to a seated position. "I *love you*, love you."

"Like Cole loves Bailey?"

"More, if it's possible." He loved her so fiercely, so deeply.

"When did you know?"

"It hit me last summer."

"Hit you?" She intertwined her fingers with his.

"Like a freight train. All of a sudden I realized how deeply I felt about you." He stroked her hair, relishing the silkiness. "That I loved you. But looking back . . ."

She leaned into him. "It was there all along?"

"Yeah. In some way, buried deep down, I think it was always there." It had just taken the events of last summer for him to realize it, for him to fully grasp the depth of his love for her.

She kissed his fingertips, and heat flared through him.

"I feel the same way. I always knew you were *my* Landon. I just never realized what that meant."

He cupped her face. "Sure you still want me? Busted ribs and all?"

Her hand tightened on his. "Always."

∞

Landon finished the soup Piper had found stocked in the pantry and set the bowl aside.

"Okay." She rubbed her hands together. "Now take off your shirt."

He coughed. "What?"

"We need to take your shirt off so I can check you out."

A smile tugged at his lips. "You want to check me out?"

313

Color flushed her cheeks. "You know what I mean. I need to check your injuries."

"Oh well, can't blame a guy for trying."

"No." She pursed her lips. "I suppose I can't. Now, take off that shirt so I can check your ribs."

"I'm sure it's nothing. They're just sore."

"I'll be the judge of that." She bent beside him, helping him lift his shirt over his head.

Piper sucked in her breath.

"What are the chances that was a 'Wow, you are so sexy' gasp rather than an 'It looks really bad' one?" He glanced down. Black-and-white splotches marred his left side.

She bit her bottom lip and then smiled sweetly, though concern still brimmed in her brown eyes. "It's a combination of both, I'm afraid."

He took a ragged breath as her fingers touched his bruised rib cage.

Her fingers felt cool, but her touch was warm. He winced as she pressed harder.

She frowned. "Just as I suspected . . . I think you've got a couple broken ribs. Try to take a deep breath."

He inhaled.

"No trouble getting air?"

"No." He grimaced.

"Painful?"

"It's nothing," he lied, not wanting to worry her. She was amazing and brave, and he felt horrible that she'd had to endure the past two days alone.

"Try it one more time, and this time let me listen."

She wanted to be sure a broken rib hadn't punctured his lung.

She moved behind him and trailed her fingers over the scar at the apex of his right shoulder blade. "I've never asked how you got this."

Her touch felt so incredibly good—her fingers cool against his fevered skin, but she was inciting warmth all the same.

"Gunshot."

"You were shot? How did I not know that?"

"It was my first week on the force up in Fairbanks. Fresh out of the Academy. I walked straight into the middle of a drug deal by accident."

"How does that happen by *accident*?"

"I was in this pizza joint. I placed my order and went to use their restroom while I waited. Two kids were in the middle of a deal. One was high. He took one look at the uniform, panicked, and shot. Luckily I got a shot off too or he might have finished me off."

"Did Cole keep that from me too, to protect me?"

"No. I never told Cole. I didn't want any of you to worry or fuss."

"Like I am now?"

"Please don't worry. I'll be fine."

"I meant how I'm *fuss*ing over you."

"Trust me," he clasped her hand over his shoulder, pulling her against his bare skin. "I *love* how you're fussing over me."

49

"It's suicide to go out in this," Bob McAllister, the head of Oregon State Search and Rescue, said as Cole loaded supplies into his rental SUV.

"Our sister and my best friend are out there," Cole said.

Search-and-rescue efforts to find Piper and Landon had been stopped before they'd even begun. Word of the avalanche reached the highway patrol within minutes of occurrence, but the news that the pass was completely buried came only minutes later. Before a search-and-rescue campaign could be launched, it was shut down until the blizzard passed. McAllister refused to add to the casualty count by sending rescuers into a deadly environment.

But Cole and his family could not wait out the storm while Landon and Piper perished in it.

"We'll abide by every safety precaution available," he said to the man still standing behind him, arms crossed, feet in the military "at ease" position. "Use guide ropes, beacons, stay in constant radio contact."

McAllister looked him straight in the eye. "The overriding safety precaution to obey is the search-and-rescue commander's call. *No go* means no go."

As dive rescue captain and commander of Yancey's search-and-rescue squad, Cole knew that only too well. He'd had to make that call numerous times over the years. It was never easy, but the lives and safety of his team came first.

But this was different. He wasn't the captain of an official rescue team. He was a brother trying to rescue his sister and best friend. If he died trying, so be it.

He had peace. He knew Christ had died for his sins and he'd gladly accepted the free and glorious gift of eternal life with Him. He didn't fear death; rather, he feared losing those he loved.

"I'd rather die trying to rescue them than condemn them to death."

"You and I both know the odds are high that they're already dead." The statistics weren't pretty. The odds of rescuing someone buried by an avalanche dropped below one percent after forty-five minutes. It had been *days.*

Cole cinched his radio in place. "We know the risks." Having worked search and rescue for years, Gage, Kayden, and Jake knew them all too well. "And we're going. But I appreciate your warning."

The big guy relented. "At least take the snowmobiles."

"You sure? There's a high chance they won't make it back."

Bob handed Cole the keys. "I'll take that risk. I just can't in good conscience send my people in."

Cole shook his hand. "I understand."

Their vehicle fully stocked and loaded, and the snowmobiles secure on the trailer, Cole pulled out of the station. Jake sat in the front passenger seat while Kayden and Gage sat in the rear. He'd done his best to dissuade Kayden from coming, but she'd have none of it. She was searching for Piper with or without him, which left him no choice.

The blizzard had lost its edge but hadn't ceased. Snow still fell at the rate of two inches per hour, continuing to obscure their line of sight, and twenty-mile-an-hour winds continued to erase any trace Piper and Landon might have left behind.

"We'll get as close to the pass as we can," Cole said.

Jake spread the topographical map out across the dash. "Bob said this quadrant would be our best starting point. From there I think we should head south along this riverbed. The avalanche would have pushed anything in its path down this steep embankment."

"I don't mean to be pessimistic," Kayden said. "I'm bent on searching, but without some sort of sign, we could be searching right over top of them and never know they're buried a few feet below."

Cole knew it was true. "Then we need to pray for a sign."

50

Piper lay curled up before the fire, the glow of the flames dancing along her pale skin. Her head rested against Landon's shoulder. He threaded his fingers gently through her silky hair, trying to soothe her as she stirred restlessly in her sleep.

She'd done an excellent job rationing the wood and other supplies she'd found in the avalanche shelter, but the grim reality was they were running out. Should they attempt to hike out in a blizzard without equipment or wait to be rescued, knowing that it could be days, possibly weeks before they were discovered?

Father. He inhaled, thankful for the breath that filled his lungs. *Please let this blizzard pass. I know Cole . . . if he has any idea we're out here, he'll be searching. Gage, Kayden, and Jake too. Please protect them and lead them to us.*

He smoothed the hair from Piper's brow.

Please keep her safe.

∽

"Up ahead." Jake pointed, his extended arm barely visible in the falling snow.

Cole squinted. A faint light flickered in the increasing darkness. Trudging through the snow by instinct alone and with no strength of his own, he pushed forward until he saw the shape of a cabin. He radioed Gage and Kayden. "We've found a shelter. It looks like someone is inside."

Please, Father, let it be them. Let them be safe.

"Is it them?" Hope and anguish danced in Kayden's voice.

"Give us a minute."

He peered in the slit of the window that remained visible over the snow line. Even with a candle's waning flame lighting the interior it was too dim to tell who was inside.

"I found the door," Jake called.

Cole moved toward Jake's voice and found him already shoveling. He joined him, warmth surging through his limbs from the exertion. Within minutes, they had the rough-hewn wooden door clear, and with a kick, Jake knocked it open. Swinging inward on its hinges, the door banged against something. His heart in his throat, Cole stepped inside.

"Here," a weak voice said.

Pulling his flashlight, Cole scanned the room.

Landon and Piper huddled before an empty fireplace.

Relief swelled in Cole's heart as at the same time concern racked his body. "We got them." He surged forward, kneeling beside them.

"Piper," Landon said, his voice barely audible. "They're here. They found us."

She opened her dark-rimmed eyes. "Cole?"

"I'm here, honey. We've got you."

Landon woke to white-starched walls and the smell of antiseptic.

Every inch of him hurt.

"Well, hello there, sunshine. I'll let them know you're awake."

Landon rolled his head to the side to find Jake with a cup of coffee in one hand and a newspaper clasped in the other.

"Piper?" he asked, his throat still miserably dry.

Jake smiled and set his paper aside. "She's fine. She's in the next room. I'll go get her."

"No. Don't trouble her."

"Trouble her? Please. Wild horses couldn't keep her away. She's been bugging me nonstop to see if you're awake."

"She's okay?"

"Right as rain." Jake smiled.

Landon squeezed his eyes shut. *Thank you, Lord.*

Jake's boots echoed along the linoleum flooring. A door creaked. He heard Jake's muffled voice and then a shriek of delight.

"Piper, wait!" Cole called.

Piper rounded the corner, her hair flying behind her, and an enormous smile on her face. "You're awake." She lunged for him, nearly tackling him in the bed. Cole, Gage, Bailey, Kayden, and Darcy entered after her.

"Piper, you're going to injure him all over again," Cole protested.

He'd take the severest of injuries just to feel her near.

"I'm sorry." She pulled back. "Am I hurting you?"

"Not even close." He tugged her back to him. "Jake said you're okay?" He scanned her face and found the cut on her forehead was scabbing over nicely.

"I'm fine. How are you?"

"A little sore, but I'll live, thanks to you."

"Good. Now how are we going to prove BioTech's guilt?"

"Piper," they all said in unison.

Landon chuckled and then regretted it. He clapped his hand over his ribs.

"I was right, by the way," she said, sitting up beside him. "Two broken ribs."

"Great."

"But the fever finally broke and the swelling in your leg is going down." Piper kissed his brow, and warmth filled him again. "So what is our next step?"

"You have no next step," he said. "We'll let the authorities handle it."

She sat back. "You've got to be kidding."

"Hardly. You just survived a car bomb and subsequent avalanche. No way I'm letting you back in the line of fire."

She patted his face. "You're adorable."

He clasped her hand. "I'm not joking."

"I know, and that's what I love about you."

Gage's brows shot up, and his gaze shifted to Cole.

"That's a discussion for another day." Cole sighed. "When
Piper told us what happened, we contacted the Portland police."

"And?"

"We spoke with a detective. He said they'd look into it, but
without any proof . . ."

"I figured."

"So what are we going to do?" Piper said.

"The way I see it," Jake said, sitting forward, "you've got a
couple options. Without the microchip and without Erik as a
witness . . ."

"Elaine," Landon said. "She was heading for Portland a few
minutes after us."

Piper looked down.

"They got to Elaine too?"

"Brakes went out on her car. She careened straight into the
mountainside," Cole said.

"Let me guess, her car exploded upon impact."

"Yeah." Cole nodded.

"Any evidence of an incendiary device?"

"Police are still sorting through the ashes."

"So that leaves us with no witnesses and no hard evidence."

"Jake"—Piper turned to him—"you were explaining our
options."

"Why are you asking him?" Kayden said. "Landon's the law
official."

"Yes, but Jake obviously has a plan."

"Which no one else finds strange? I mean how does he know
so much about criminals?"

"Not this again," Cole said. "Jake's just trying to help."

322

Kayden slumped on the edge of the bed. "I can't believe I'm the only one who finds it strange . . . or who cares."

"Jake," Piper said, "please continue."

Jake nodded, his wounded gaze shifting off Kayden and back to Piper. "As I see it you have three avenues. You can try and find the microchip."

"Definitely possible," Piper said.

"You can attempt to figure out what was on it and re-create the information . . ."

"Not possible," Landon said. They didn't have the scientific ability or access to the data Erik had gathered.

"Or option three." Jake leaned forward, resting his hands on his knees. "We catch the guy Ed Thompson hired to kill you and get him to turn on Thompson."

"How exactly would we do that?" Cole asked.

"I'm sure he's heard by now that his attempt on our lives failed. I just make myself a target while the rest of you set a trap," Landon said.

"I'm the one he wants," Piper said.

Landon shook his head. "No way."

"I'm the one he tried to run off the road in Yancey. For some reason he is focusing on me."

"She's right." Jake stood. "I know you're all going to disagree, and with good reason, but Piper does make a far easier target."

Landon knew it was true, but it meant endangering the woman he loved yet again.

"Why don't we just locate the microchip?" Darcy asked.

"We'll start searching," Landon explained, "but we don't know for certain that Karli passed it on to Reef. And even if we find it, nothing on it would prove that Ed Thompson had Erik and Karli killed. It only proves the insulin was tainted. If we want Karli's and Erik's killer . . ."

"And Elaine's," Piper added.

"And nearly both of yours," Darcy said.

" . . . then we need to catch him ourselves." Landon looked

around the room. "Somehow we need to get him to show himself."

"He obviously wants the microchip," Piper said. "If we find it, he'll come after us."

"She's right," Landon said.

"So, what? We find the microchip and lure the killer in?" Darcy asked.

Cole cleared his throat. "That sounds incredibly dangerous."

"But necessary." Landon looked at Piper and sighed. How was he going to keep her out of danger?

51

They returned to Yancey, began their search for the microchip, and made sure the killer knew they weren't backing down. Piper was right; even if they located the microchip, they still needed the killer to prove Thompson was behind the murders. Otherwise, it was simply conjecture. Sound conjecture, but conjecture all the same. They needed tangible evidence, and so far they had none—no helpful trace evidence or fingerprints from the crime-scene, no physical description other than the basic appearance of the man Piper had seen: tall, slender, with dark hair. If they were going to catch the killer, they needed to draw him in.

Piper played her role perfectly, calling BioTech, threatening Ed Thompson, letting him know they were on to him and that they'd be painfully vocal about it. Meanwhile they tediously searched through Reef's belongings, trying to locate the microchip.

It pained Landon every second of every day waiting for the killer to appear, knowing he would, but also believing they had no choice. They'd set up an elaborate surveillance system at Yancey's port and marinas, calling in every law-enforcement favor Landon had garnered over the years. They'd left Slidell out of it—though he wouldn't intentionally ruin their plan, they couldn't trust him not to muck it up.

If an outsider stepped foot in Yancey, they'd know it. The trick was determining if he was the killer.

Two days after they returned to Yancey, Gage burst into Last Frontier Adventures's storage garage, where they'd set up temporary headquarters out of sight of any onlookers. "Jake just called. He thinks we have a winner."

Landon stood. "Where?"

"A man just checked into Trailside Lodge. According to Bev he's been there once before."

Landon straightened.

"The same week Karli was murdered." Gage smiled.

"His name?"

"That's the thing. Bev says he went by Mr. Smith the first time and Mr. Sanders this time. She asked him about it, but he told her she was mistaken."

"Any chance she is?"

"Not Bev. She's got a knack for faces and names."

"Is Jake keeping an eye on him?"

"Yeah, but from a good distance. He doesn't want to risk scaring him off. So far Mr. Sanders hasn't left his room."

"We need to discover his real identity. Did Jake get a picture?"

"Not at the lodge, but since you have a team photographing every nonlocal that steps off the ferry, we can take Bev's description and hopefully find a match. Jake said he'll text the description and you can get online and compare it to the images they're downloading from the ferry station."

"Great. Once we have a match, or at least a few options, I'll send the photos over to Piper and Reef and see if either one recognizes him. It's possible seeing the photo might jog Piper's memory of whoever ran her off the road. Or if we are really lucky, Reef might remember seeing him around the circuit events. The killer had to be tracking Karli for some time to be able to strike at the opportune moment."

"We might be even more fortunate than that," Gage said.

Landon arched a brow.

"Seems dear old Bev is a CSI fan. When the guy signed in under a different name, it piqued her interest. Soon as he headed for the elevator, she slipped the guest ledger pen into a plastic bag and insisted Andy run it straight to the lab."

"Awesome. I'll make sure they run it for prints ASAP. In the meantime, let's not let Mr. Sanders out of our sight."

❧

"And you're certain you've seen him before?" Landon asked as Reef studied the photograph a second time.

"Yeah, I figured he was part of the event staff."

"Why?"

"He wore a yellow jacket."

"And?"

"Midnight Sun staffers wear yellow jackets."

"Is there any kind of insignia or writing on these staff jackets?"

"Yeah, there is a falcon on the front chest, right side."

Landon leaned forward, resting his hands on his knees as he sat beside Reef on his cell cot. "This is extremely important. I want you to take all the time you need and really think about it, but do you remember if his jacket had the event insignia on it?"

Reef sat back, closing his eyes, and inhaled. "He had something on it, but I can't say for sure if it was the event symbol or just something that looked similar."

"Okay."

Reef opened his eyes. "Does that help?"

"Absolutely. I'll have Jake speak with Rick Masterson and see if he recognizes the man. He may have taken a temporary job with the circuit or maybe just the local event to gain better access to Karli." Landon put the photograph down. "And you're certain Karli never passed anything to you?" They'd been over this so many times that he almost felt foolish asking, but sometimes repeated questioning jarred something loose and an answer came.

"Man, I've been racking my brain, but no, Karli never gave me anything."

"It would have been small, no bigger than the head of a pin." They'd searched the contents of Reef's and Karli's hotel rooms, Piper and Kayden's house, even Reef's belongings locked in evidence, but no microchip.

"I'm sorry, man. You don't know how badly I wish I knew where that thing is."

"I think I have a pretty good idea." Without Erik's evidence compiled on the chip, no testimony, not even Elaine's, had she lived, would have been the rock-solid proof they needed. Where was it? "What about Karli?"

"What about her?"

"You knew her."

"About as well as anyone could, but obviously not that well. I had no idea she'd been in Witness Protection, no idea what she was going through." Regret was clear on his face.

"Where would Karli stash something of value?"

"I don't know." Reef slumped back, thinking. "Could be anywhere in the lodge."

"Think something more personal. Something Karli was attached to . . ."

Reef laughed. "Her equipment."

"What?" Landon turned.

"Sorry. That wasn't funny. It's just Karli had zero attachment to people, but her equipment . . . You touched it, you died."

"Thank you, Reef."

"Huh?"

Landon strode out of the station, dialing Piper. She was at the lodge, insistent the chip had to be there somewhere. She picked up on the second ring.

"Hey, sweetheart."

"Hey there." He could hear the smile in her voice, and it warmed his heart.

"I need you to do something."

"Okay."

"But you can't go alone. Jim's still over there, right?"

"Yeah."

"Okay, so take him with you and go check Karli's equipment."

"Her equipment? Why didn't we think of that before?"

∽

Piper hurried around to Trailside's storage shed, where she'd been told all unclaimed gear left after the competition ended was being housed. Deputy Jim Vaughn waited outside as she ducked into the cold metal building. Flipping the fluorescent lights on, she strode down the first aisle. Reef had provided a description of Karli's equipment. She was looking for a red Burton board with *Rebel* scrolled in Gothic calligraphy across the bottom. The shed was filled with junk that had accumulated over the decades, so it took several aisles of searching to locate it, but she did.

She bent to examine the bindings, the various intricate grooves and spots where a rhinestone could have been replaced with a microchip. *Nothing*. She grabbed Karli's boots, examining the outside and then running her hand along the black furry interior. Her hand stilled along the bottom of Karli's left boot. It took a minute, but Piper tore the lining out and found a small metal chip glued to the surface. *Bingo!*

She wrapped the chip in a scrap of the boot's lining and pulled out her phone to call Landon. "I got it! We'll meet you in the lodge—at the front desk."

∽

He'd known it would be the girl that found it. And the smug smile on her face was proof that she had. But there were too many people around the shed. He'd wait until the deputy escorted her back into the lodge, and then he'd strike. It'd be messier than he preferred, but they'd left him no choice.

∽

Piper stepped into the lodge through the rear door. She hadn't taken but a few steps when she heard a *thwack* behind her. She turned to find Jim slumping to his knees. She bent to help him and something whizzed overhead, shattering the glass of the door. *He's here.* She ducked, dropping to the ground as Jim's blood seeped into the carpet.

"Piper," Landon rushed down the hall from the opposite end.

"Get down," she hollered.

An arm reached out and grabbed Landon, pulling him into the adjacent hall.

"Landon." She scrambled to her feet. Stumbling, she stopped short at the corner. Taking a deep breath, she peered around, and her hope died.

A man held a gun pressed to Landon's temple, his other arm tight against Landon's chest.

"Go back!" Landon screamed.

"Toss me the chip," the man hollered.

Her eyes narrowed. It was the man from the cafeteria, from the plane, from her room at the lodge.

"Now!" he roared.

She pulled the lining-wrapped chip from her pocket.

"Don't do it. He'll just kill us both," Landon said.

"Shut up," the man hissed.

Footsteps thudded down the hall. Help was coming.

The man shook his head, kicked the emergency exit door open behind him, sounding the alarm, and yanked Landon outside.

"He's got Landon." Piper stuffed the chip back in her pocket and tore after them, as voices rang from behind.

"Piper, stop!" Cole hollered.

She shoved the door open, and sunshine blinded her momentarily. Squinting, she searched the trees, the grounds. People stood stunned and staring. A snowmobile started on the north side of the woods. "He's taking off." She bounded through the snow, only to be caught short by a hand.

She turned to find Cole, his deep breaths a white vapor in the frigid air. "You're going to get yourself killed."

"He's got Landon."

"And the chip?"

"I have it." She pulled it from her pocket, amazed something so little could cause so much devastation.

"Then you have the bargaining power."

"So . . . what? You're suggesting we just sit back and wait for him to contact us?" She didn't give him a chance to answer. "No way. Bev and Andy have snowmobiles. I need to go after him."

"Then you need Jake. We both know no one can track like him."

52

Cold seeped through Piper's gloves despite the fleece lining. They'd been tracking Landon and his captor for hours. They'd found the snowmobile with an empty tank of gas at the base of the thickly wooded forest. He'd chosen his route well. Even though they had extra containers of gas, their snowmobiles couldn't fit through the tangled roots and narrow passages this section of evergreens afforded.

Jake remained stubbornly silent on the skirmish that must have ensued before Landon and the man entered the woods. Blood and haphazard tracks said it all. Landon was hurt, but two sets of footprints remained, filling Piper with an unsettling mix of hope and dread.

"We wasted too much time," she said, trudging through the dense undergrowth barring their way. They'd given them nearly a half-hour head start while coordinating and supplying their search party.

"We had no choice," Cole reminded her. "We're better prepared. He's out here without supplies, which means we have the upper hand."

She yanked her foot out of the tangle of roots and vines ensnaring it. It sure didn't feel like they had the upper hand. But they knew this mountain far better than he did—and he was outnumbered. They'd catch him. She only prayed they wouldn't be too late.

Piper hovered over Jake as he bent to examine the fading tracks. The snow had started an hour back, thickening in intensity over the past ten minutes. Even an expert tracker like Jake was having difficulty finding what remained of their imprints.

"We're going to lose them," she said, her chest tightening.

"Then we vary our approach." Jake stood, eyeing the landscape. "He's going to move for shelter in this storm."

Landon could tell the man where to find shelter, but would he? Would he think it best to let the man wear down in the elements or lead him to shelter so they'd be easier to locate?

"From here there are three options," Jake said. "The ranger station at Ford's Pass, the observation tower on Northface, or the emergency shelter by the spring."

"The station is best supplied," Cole said.

"But the tower has the best vantage point," Piper said. He knew they were tracking him. He'd want to see them coming.

"If they're holed up in there, he'll see us coming even in this storm," Jake said.

"I know, but I'm betting that's where they'll be."

Cole shook his head. "Landon wouldn't lead him there."

"He might not have had to," Jake said.

"What do you mean?"

"The man has shown some clear knowledge of the area in the path they've taken."

"You think he planned for this contingency?" Piper asked.

Jake shook his head. "I don't know that I'd go that far, but he knew the most remote area to run you off of Highway 11. It wouldn't surprise me if he'd studied the terrain or at least had the resources available to him."

"But if he doesn't have a plan, Landon would surely take him to the ranger station," Piper said. It was not only the best supplied, but the most frequented.

"So which do we head for?" Cole asked.

"All of them," she said.

"What?"

"We have to split up and check all three."

Cole shook his head. "No. That's too risky."

"We don't have a choice. If we choose the wrong one, we risk losing him completely."

"She's right," Jake said.

"Fine, so how should we split up?"

"I'll go with Piper to the observation tower," Gage volunteered. "Kayden, you and Jake head for the emergency shelter. Cole, you take the ranger station."

"Fine. We check in every fifteen minutes," Cole said, holding up his radio. "Any trouble, light a flare."

Kayden sighed. "I doubt it'll do much good in this storm."

"You'd be surprised the punch they hold," Jake said.

Cole clasped a hand on Piper's shoulder. "Be safe. You won't do Landon any good if you're hurt."

She nodded. All that mattered was saving him.

She and Gage headed north, into the wind, the shelter of the trees thinning and the cold sweeping more heavily down on them.

Gage's radio crackled. He signaled Piper to stop.

"Gage, it's Darcy. Can you hear me?"

Gage held it to his ear, cupping his hand over it. "Yeah, Darcy, I got you."

"We got a hit off the fingerprints."

Finally. Piper exhaled. Some good news.

"His real name is Carl Anderson, but he's got a handful of aliases."

"I'm guessing he has a record."

"Yeah, several aggravated assault charges in various states up until a year ago, and then he kind of dropped off the grid. His last-known address is in Portland. We forwarded the information to a Portland detective named James Reno who'd worked a couple of Anderson's assault cases. He's heading out to Anderson's last-known address now and running everything he can find under Anderson's aliases."

"That's great news. Thanks, Darcy."

"Still haven't found them?"

"Not yet, but we're closing in, I think. Piper and I are headed for the observation tower."

"Be careful. Weather service says this storm is picking up speed."

"Roger that." Gage slipped his radio back into his jacket and smiled at Piper. "We've got him."

"We've got his name but not him." She resumed her pace, trudging through the thickening snow as best she could, trying not to think about the cold seeping into her bones or what Carl Anderson might be doing to Landon.

53

How had he known about the observation tower? Landon struggled to loosen his bonds. His head still swam from the knock he'd taken to the back of the head as soon as they'd entered the shelter. A fire blazed in the metal stove, illuminating the small space.

The man sat on the lone cot, working on some sort of device. "They'll be coming soon."

"Who?"

"Don't play dumb with me, Detective. We both know they've been tracking us all day. They'll be here soon, but I'll already be gone."

Landon narrowed his eyes. "Where do you plan to go in this storm?"

"Never you mind about that."

"They'll track you wherever you go."

"Not if they're dead." The man stood, the device clutched in his hand. He set it on the small table and flipped a switch, testing it. A red light blinked.

Landon's eyes widened. He was going to blow the tower.

"Don't worry." The man flipped the switch back. "I won't detonate it until I'm sure they're here rescuing you. Quite poetic, don't you think?" He stepped to the window to watch for his prey. "People think men in my line of work are just hired thugs, but I assure you I am far superior to my brothers in arms."

"Your brothers?"

"Fellow assassins," he explained. "You see, Detective," he continued, "I put a lot of research into my work. For example, I know that Michelle Evans was killed by a natural gas explosion."

"There was nothing *natural* about her death. Mongols assassinated her."

"As I will you all, removing every loose end, including that infernal chip, ending this little saga with a salute to the past."

"Are you suggesting you had something to do with Michelle Evans's death?"

"Of course not. I'm simply paying homage to the event. Michelle took information that didn't belong to her and paid with her life. Her choice to take Karli on the run eventually led Karli to Erik, who in turn gave her something that didn't belong to her, and she paid with her life too."

The man was even more unhinged than Landon had realized. He struggled to release his bonds. He had to get free, had to protect Piper and her family from this madman.

∞

Piper lay beside Gage on the boulder, staring up at the tower with floodlights lit.

"He's going to see us coming."

"Unfortunately, there's only one way up." Gage slid back down to the boulder's base.

She scooted beside him. "Not necessarily."

Gage's eyes widened. "It's too dangerous."

"Not any more than walking into his crosshairs."

"Northface is dangerous enough to climb during good weather. With the snow and ice, no way."

"I'm not asking permission." She stood and moved around the wide rock base to the rear of the eighty-foot wall forming the back of the tower's base.

"At least give the others a chance to get here."

As soon as they'd seen the tower was occupied, they'd radioed the others, who had then redirected their course and alerted the authorities.

"There isn't time."

Gage's footfalls crunched on the snow behind her.

Her heart racing in her chest and adrenaline coursing through her veins, she labored her way to the base of the rock wall. She dropped her backpack and fished out the rope.

"You don't even have the proper equipment." Gage set his pack beside hers. "What if I—"

"Gage, how long has it been since you've climbed? It has to be me." She fished through the gear bag they'd snagged from her Jeep before setting off after Anderson. "I have rope, and . . . there are carabineers in here somewhere."

"Harness?"

"Give me the rope from your pack." She held out her hand.

"Swiss seat?" he asked, handing it over.

"Not comfortable, but tied correctly, just as safe as the store-bought ones." She repeated their father's mantra, thankful he'd put so much time into teaching them wilderness survival as kids. She began fashioning the homemade harness.

"And what am I supposed to do? Just sit here and watch you climb to danger?"

Taking one end of the rope, she wrapped it around the back of her waist, keeping the center point at her hip. "Belay me; wait for others and for my signal."

"Signal?" he said as she fashioned an overhand knot at her navel.

She pulled tight and looped the other end of the rope back around her waist. "I haven't figured it out yet, but it'll come to me."

"Somehow that isn't comforting."

She pulled the rope ends between her legs and tucked them under the rope at her waist, tying a half hitch on each side. "Sorry, bro. Gotta go by instinct on this one." She squatted to set the knots, then stood and encircled her waist with the remaining rope ends, finishing with a square knot.

"Piper." He placed a hand on her shoulder as she locked in. "You're going on the assumption the climbers before you left sturdy pins in place. Assumptions can be deadly."

"I know, but I've got to do this." She'd free-climbed Northface last summer and remembered seeing anchors along the way. In the snow and ice, free-climbing was too dangerous; she'd at least try and anchor in as best she could. Besides, if their places were reversed and it was her up in that tower, nothing would stop Landon from coming for her.

She scaled the wall as silently as she could, praying Anderson was too focused on watching the south approach to even think about them approaching from the rear.

Wind lashed at her face, her exposed fingers numbing quickly. She couldn't climb well with regular gloves and her ice-climbing ones hadn't been in her Jeep. Strengthening her resolve and keeping Landon's charming smile at the forefront of her mind, she pressed on. She also prayed Cole didn't cause too much ruckus when he arrived and discovered what she'd done, prayed she'd already be in position and have her signal ready.

What signal? What plan? She was running out of time to solidify both. She only knew she had to keep moving.

<hr/>

He paced the room, his gaze ever watchful on the detective. Heat spread through his limbs with each step. Something was wrong. They were taking too long. He stared back out the window. Not a shadow. Not a hint of movement. What were they up to?

He needed to spot them well in advance, so he had time to escape. With a rock wall behind, there was only one way in or out. He paused. The research he'd done on the McKenna family, on Piper in particular, flooded his mind. "Your girlfriend is quite the rock climber, isn't she?" he said, striding to the rear of the tower.

The detective struggled harder behind him, but he had more pressing matters.

Piper cleared the wall and climbed onto the platform on which the observation station sat. Untying the lead rope from her harness, she secured it to the tower's metal rigging. Taking a deep breath, she crept around the corner toward the door. It swung open with such force it knocked her from her feet. Her head hit the floor with a crack. She stared up blearily at Carl Anderson bent over her.

"Hello, darling. So nice of you to join us." Grabbing her right leg, he yanked her inside, her back and head thumping over the metal door plate along the way. She squirmed against his grip. "A lively one you are, but not for—" His words stopped short. He stared at her and toppled on top of her.

She wrestled under his weight.

"Piper," Landon hollered.

Anderson slid off her and slumped to the ground beside her.

Landon bent down, a wood plank still gripped tight in his hand. "Are you all right?"

"I was supposed to be asking you that."

Landon retrieved Anderson's gun and tossed the plank aside. "You have a radio?" he asked as he helped her sit up.

She nodded.

"Let the others know Anderson's unconscious and we're waiting for them." He winced as he pulled her to her feet.

"What's wrong?"

"Nothing." He coughed. "Just a catch in my back."

"Are you sure?"

He brushed the hair from her face and cupped her cheek. "I'm positive." Another dry cough racked him.

"Landon?"

"Really, I'm fine. How far out are the others?"

"Climbing the stairs now," Cole relayed over the radio.

54

Landon ignored the stabbing pain in his chest as he opened the interrogation room door.

Slidell yanked him back. "Seriously, Landon. We can handle the questioning. Go get checked out. You look like death warmed over."

"Thanks, but I'll be fine."

"Do I have to order you out of here?"

"I'm doing this." He would see this through to the end.

Slidell held up his hands. "Fine. Be my guest, though I doubt you'll get anything out of him."

"We'll see about that." Landon entered the interrogation room with a confident swagger, knowing he had to go in strong to get what was needed out of Anderson.

Anderson smirked. "You'll get nothing out of me. I have access to the best lawyers money can buy."

"That's good. You're going to need them because we've got you on three counts of murder, two counts of attempted murder, assault, battery, and more than likely . . . tax evasion. You get the picture."

"You've got nothing."

"That's where you're wrong, Mr. Anderson. We've got your storage facility."

Anderson's face paled.

"Yep. Portland Detective, James Reno, called less than an

hour ago. Sounds like you two go way back. And I've got to tell you, he left the best message I've ever had waiting for me. I obviously don't need to list the evidence available to them in said storage facility, as it all belongs to you, but suffice it to say, we've got ironclad proof of the premeditated murders of Erik Johnson and Karli Davis. We have proof of your payments from Ed Thompson—which the Feds have frozen, by the way, pending the outcome of this investigation. And to top it off, you gunned down a police officer and abducted another. Shall I go on?"

Anderson's jaw stiffened. "What do you want?"

"Ed Thompson. You give us him and testify about his role in all of this, and the D.A. has agreed to take the death penalty off the table." Landon stood. "Do we have a deal?"

"I want it in writing, from the D.A."

"You got it."

Landon couldn't wait to tell Piper. They'd gotten them both. He exited the room and tried not to gloat at Slidell, who'd been listening on the other side of the glass.

"You want me to get the D.A. on the phone?" Tom asked.

Landon started to nod, and the room spun.

"Landon?" Tom's brow pinched.

His vision narrowed, darkening.

"You okay?" Tom said. "You're looking kind of—"

❧

Piper rocked back and forth in the ER waiting room. She glanced up at the clock. Landon had been in surgery for what seemed an eternity.

Kayden rubbed her back—physical touch a rarity for her sister. "He's going to be fine."

"How do you know?"

Kayden bit her lip.

"Doctors repair punctured lungs all the time," Gage said, trying to be helpful.

"And people die from them all the time. I should have known. I should have insisted . . ."

"He wouldn't have listened," Cole said, crouching down in front of her. "And we both know it."

"Cole's right," Gage said. "Landon's as stubborn as the day is long—just like you."

"I got you some tea," Bailey said, handing her the Styrofoam cup.

"Thanks." Now if she could just stop shaking long enough to take a sip.

"Can I get you anything else?" Bailey asked, concern evident on her sweet face. "Something to eat, maybe? It's been way too long."

"I couldn't eat if I tried." Not with her stomach knotted the way it was.

Cole exhaled, his worry palpable.

"Why don't we pray?" Bailey said, pulling a chair up to them, starting the beginning of a circle.

Cole clasped Bailey's hand. "That's a great idea."

Darcy dragged a chair over to join them. "Wherever two or three gather . . ." she said, reminding them of the Lord's promise in Matthew. She glanced at Gage. "Everyone is welcome."

"I'm good here, thanks." Gage leaned with his back against the wall.

Which just left Jake. To Piper's utter surprise, he joined them, and her heart welled with the simple gesture. Jake had always been silent when they shared family prayers, and somehow uncomfortable with the topic of faith in God, but he'd never expressed disbelief. She'd come to think Jake believed but that something held him back from embracing God. She hadn't been able to peg exactly what that was—his aversion to something external or his own internal struggle. She guessed the latter. But the fact that he cared so much about her family, and especially Landon, that he was willing to put that aside and join them in prayer spoke volumes to her heart.

She closed her eyes, her loved ones gathered around her, and pleaded with the Lord to heal the man she loved.

Landon woke, feeling as if the wind had been knocked out of him with a two-by-four. He swallowed, but his mouth produced no saliva. Opening his eyes, he found a dropped stippled ceiling above. Trailing his gaze down, he found lime-green walls. *The hospital.* He winced. Last thing he remembered was Tom Murphy asking if he was all right. Apparently, he'd been worse off than he'd imagined.

His gaze shifted to Piper asleep in the chair, curled up like a kitten, her legs draped partially over the arm, her head dropped back at what looked like a painful angle.

He chuckled, regretting it as pain shot through his side.

"What's so funny?" Piper asked in a sleepy voice.

Gage strode into the room. "He's awake," he called over his shoulder. "How you doing, man?"

Cole, Bailey, Jake, Kayden, and Darcy filed in after him.

"Doc Stevens said you nearly lost a lung." Gage swiped a fry from the lunch tray on Landon's table.

"Guess Someone was looking out for me." He held Piper's loving gaze.

"Right," Gage said, his doubt abundantly apparent.

It was okay. A few weeks ago, Landon had been in the same place. If God could reach him, He'd work His way into Gage's heart too.

Cole slipped his hands into his pockets as he approached the bed. "You tell him, Pipsqueak?"

"Exactly how old do I have to be before you all stop calling me that?"

Gage shrugged. "A hundred and one."

"Very funny."

"Did you tell him?" Kayden prodded.

"Tell me what?"

"Tom Murphy dropped by the hospital while you were in surgery. . . ."

"And?"

"And Anderson signed the confession."

"He gave us Thompson and agreed to testify?"

344

Cole jumped in. "Tom said that detective in Portland . . ."

"Detective Reno," Piper supplied.

"Right," Cole continued. "Tom said he spoke with Detective Reno and they were already preparing to arrest Thompson."

"Preparing? How long are they going to wait?"

"Well, seeing as that was two days ago . . ." Gage grinned.

He'd been out two days? That was one habit he had to break.

Piper squeezed his hand. "They arrested Thompson this morning."

"Have you told Reef?"

Reef poked his head around the doorframe with a wide smile. "They told me."

Cole strode toward Reef. "I called Harland as soon as Anderson confessed. All charges against him have been dropped."

"I owe you an enormous thanks," Reef said, extending a hand.

"It's your sister who deserves the thanks. Piper had enough faith for us all."

55

Piper entered the hospital through the side entrance that brought her more directly to the elevators and Landon's room. The doctor had said he could go home today, and she'd brought him a fresh change of clothes.

She pressed the third-floor button and waited for the doors to slide closed. Peggy Wilson, one of the nurses and a friend of her family for years, walked by the elevator and smiled broadly before the doors finally shut. A ping signaled her passing the second floor, and another ping announced her arrival on the third floor. The doors slid open, and Cole greeted her.

"I'm so glad you're here. Landon needs you." He grabbed her hand, yanking her off the elevator.

"What happened? Is something wrong?" She moved toward Landon's room.

"No." Cole tugged her back. "He's in the pre-op doctors' consultation room."

"What? Why?"

"You'll see when you get there." Cole pushed her along the corridor.

Panic flared as they rushed past the nurses' station. Everyone they passed glanced up at her, but she couldn't read their expressions. Had something gone wrong? Why the consultation room? Was Landon headed back for surgery?

They moved through the final set of double doors.

"Third door on your right," Cole said, his voice falling farther behind along with his footsteps.

Why was he slowing down? "Aren't you coming in?" she asked as she reached the door.

"No. I'm going to wait out here."

"But?"

"Go. He's waiting."

Piper entered expecting the worst and found Landon down on the floor, his knee bent, his arm draped around Harvey. Why was his dog there? She rushed toward them. Had he fallen out of the chair? "Are you okay? What happened? Why is Harvey here?"

Landon laughed.

Laughter? Was he delirious?

"I should have known you'd try and help me."

"Of course. I wouldn't leave you on the floor." She knelt beside him, giving Harvey a reassuring pat. The dog had to be worried about his master. She was terrified for him.

"Where is your doctor?"

"My doctor?"

"Yes. Aren't we supposed to be having some sort of consultation?"

"No. I just asked if I could use the room."

"To spend time with Harvey? It must be bad news if they let your dog in the hospital to see you."

He chuckled. "You're so missing the point."

"Why are you laughing? Why aren't you telling me what's happening?"

"I'm trying to," he said as she struggled to help him up. "But you kind of need to leave me on my knee for this."

"What?" She stilled, studying him.

He clasped her hand. "Take a seat."

"Okay." She rolled a chair in front of Landon and sat, confusion and worry consuming her.

"Piper, I'm fine. In fact, I'm better than fine."

"Landon, you're in the surgery consultation room. You're obviously not fine." Tears burned her eyes.

"No." He shook his head. "I should have considered how this would look." He cupped his hand over hers. "Let's start over. I'm fine. Harvey's fine. Everything is fine."

"Then why are you and Harvey in here?"

"Because we wanted some privacy. Because we have a very important question to ask you."

Piper looked at Harvey, who sat proudly at Landon's side, a bright blue bow tied around his thick neck.

"Harvey was with me at this hospital the first time I wanted to tell you I loved you, but it didn't work out."

"What? When?"

"It doesn't matter. What matters is I'm here now, and I thought Harvey should be too. I had to pull a few strings, but I was determined. Just like I'm determined to tell you how very much I love you."

"I love you too."

Landon's smile spread. "You have no idea how phenomenal that is to hear."

"Yes I do. I just heard it too."

"But I heard it from *you*."

Harvey nudged Landon's arm, licking it.

"All right, boy. He's getting impatient."

"For what?" she asked, still totally at a loss.

"For this." Landon reached around Harvey's neck and removed a slender pouch from the ribbon. Shifting again onto one knee, Landon pulled a ring from the pouch.

Piper's eyes widened as shock and comprehension jolted through her. "Is that my mother's ring?"

"When I asked Cole for your hand and he gave his blessing, he told me that all of them had agreed long ago you should be the one to wear your mother's ring when the time came. He's held on to it until now." Landon lifted the ring.

"Marr . . ." She swallowed. "You're proposing to me?" Landon wanted her to be his wife? She'd get to spend the rest of her life married to her best friend. It was too amazing to be true. She fought to keep the sobs of joy at bay—to let him speak before she burst into a blissful frenzy of emotion.

348

"I've loved you as far back as I remember. First as family, then as a dear friend, and now more deeply than I can possibly describe. I know this may seem sudden, but I've known you your whole life and I know beyond a shadow of a doubt that I want to spend the rest of my life with you. So, Piper Lucy McKenna"—he held the ring out to her—"will you make me the happiest man alive and agree to be my wife?"

Tears flooded Piper's eyes, gushing down her cheeks, making her vision so blurry she could barely see Landon's handsome face and his desperate anticipation.

Harvey licked her face, nudging her side with his cold nose.

"He thinks you're upset," Landon said, fear tugging at his tone—fear of rejection.

"I've never been happier in my life."

"Really?" Joy filled Landon's voice.

She nodded, tears streaming down her face, bouncing off her hand as she reached out for him to place the ring on her finger. "Really."

"That's a yes?"

"Yes, yes, yes!"

He slid the ring on her finger, his hand shaking the entire time, and then he sprang for her. Pulling her to him, his hands splaying through her hair, he kissed her so deeply, so passionately, she never wanted the kiss to end.

The door creaked open behind them.

"Was that a yes?" Cole asked.

Landon pulled back, tears pooling in his eyes. "She said yes."

Cole, Gage, Reef, Jake, Bailey, Darcy, and Kayden all piled in.

"You all knew?" Piper asked, bewildered.

"I thought it only right to ask Cole's blessing," Landon said, running his thumb reverently across the band on her ring finger.

"And I couldn't help it." Cole shrugged. "After Landon and I spoke, I had to tell everyone."

"What if she'd said no?" Landon asked.

"We all saw the way she looked at you," Kayden said. "No way she was saying no."

"I can't believe you all kept this from me." Piper huffed.

"Yeah, for all of three hours," Cole said.

"And you . . ." She stared down her big brother. "You let me think something horrible had happened to Landon."

"I'm sorry. He told me to."

"Way to throw an already injured man under the bus," Landon complained.

"I've seen that look." Cole indicated Piper's stare-down. "You're the one marrying her; you get to deal with her wrath from now on."

"As long as she's mine, I couldn't care less."

"Wow." Kayden leaned against the doorframe. "He's really got it bad."

Piper sat back beside Landon, clutching his hand. "No worse than I do."

"Great." Kayden rolled her eyes. "You know I've got a low tolerance for that lovey-dovey junk."

Piper smiled. "Then you might want to exit the room quickly because here comes some more." She pressed her lips to Landon's and chuckled at her sister's gagging sounds. She was going to have fun with this.

∽

Darcy watched each of the McKennas in turn thank Harland Reeves as he prepared to leave the courthouse and the town of Yancey, now that the case against Reef had officially been dropped. The McKennas would be celebrating with a big family dinner at the girls' place tonight, and they'd been kind enough to include her. She'd fallen in love with the family, and while she was thrilled Reef's innocence had been proven, she wasn't ready for her time in Yancey to end.

"How can we ever thank you?" Piper asked, wrapping the man in a hug.

"No thanks needed." He patted her back. "I'm just thankful the truth prevailed."

"Thanks in great part to Darcy." She turned and smiled at Darcy.

"My part was small. You and Landon discovered the killer."

"But your investigative work helped lead us there. You believed in my brother when few others did."

She knew Piper was speaking of Reef, but deep down Darcy believed in Gage too. He was a good man. Hurting, but good, and her heart ached for him. She turned to smile at him and found him gone. *Curious . . .*

She scanned the lobby and hall. No sign of him. And then it hit her. He'd gone to find Meredith.

She turned back to Piper. "You're very welcome. Now, if you'll excuse me. I've just got . . . something."

"Sure." Piper smiled. "Catch up with you later."

"You got it."

She headed for the counselors' lounge, knowing that's where Meredith would be.

Rounding the hall, she proceeded down the corridor to the third door on the left and paused outside as voices carried from the room.

"Don't stand here and presume to lecture me," Meredith said, her voice cold. "We both know you're not that different from me."

"I am where it counts," Kayden replied.

Kayden? Darcy opened the door, just wide enough to peek through.

"You keep telling yourself that," Meredith said, hand on her hip.

"I can't believe we used to be friends, that our family used to love you."

"And I can't believe that you've gone all mushy and sentimental like your siblings." Her disdain for the McKennas was abundantly clear.

Kayden shook her head. "I feel sorry for you, Meredith. You must lead a very lonely existence."

Before Meredith could reply, Kayden brushed past her and exited out the opposite door.

Darcy turned at the sound of footsteps behind her and saw

Jake walking away. When had Jake arrived? Had he overheard the conversation?

"What are you doing here?"

Darcy turned, startled. Had Meredith spotted her outside the door? Darcy peered through the crack to find Gage standing in front of Meredith.

"Thought I'd say good-bye," Gage said. "Since I doubted you'd bother."

Meredith slipped files into her briefcase. "Still hung up on the past, I see."

Gage stepped closer and lowered his voice, clearly longing for something that was never going to be. "It wasn't so long ago."

"That's your problem, Gage." She snapped her briefcase shut. "You allow the past to control you. You let one little setback ruin your life. It's pathetic, really."

Gage's hands balled at his sides.

Darcy fought the urge to rush in and let Meredith Blake have it. How could she be so cold? And how could someone as amazing as Gage have ever loved her?

"He wasn't a setback," Gage said, his tone turning fierce. "He was *our* son."

Meredith slid her briefcase strap over her arm. "I'm sorry you haven't been able to move on, Gage, but I have. And I *won't* be looking back." She stepped past him and straight out the opposite door without so much as a backward glance.

Shock and anger reverberated through Darcy. How unfeeling could the woman be? Not even the faintest hint of compassion for Gage or sadness over the death of their child.

She knew what she was about to do was probably a mistake, but she couldn't help herself. She slid out the exterior door and rounded the building toward the parking lot. Meredith Blake wasn't going to verbally assault Gage and simply get away with it.

Pushing herself into a jog, Darcy darted around the side of the brick building and scanned the wintery lot until she spotted Meredith trudging through the snow and ice patches toward her rental SUV.

"Meredith," she called, sprinting to catch her. "Meredith Blake." The cold air burned her lungs.

After a moment, Meredith turned, irritation swarming her pursed face. Clearly she was searching for what annoying creature was delaying her departure. She spotted Darcy and practically groaned. "Yes?"

Anger at Meredith's mistreatment of Gage was sparking a fire in her. "How can you be so unfeeling?"

"I beg your pardon?" She contemplated Darcy with all the value she'd place on a gnat.

"With Gage . . . " Darcy pointed to the building they'd just exited. "Back inside there. How could you be so cold?"

Meredith's eyes narrowed. "Are you and Gage . . . ?"

"Friends," Darcy said.

"I see. You're the reporter, right?"

"Yes."

"Or at least attempting to be one." Meredith tossed her briefcase on the passenger seat of her vehicle. "Not that it is any of your business, but just for the record, I'm not cold. I'm simply *not* sentimental."

"How can you not be sentimental about your child?"

Meredith rolled her eyes. "I am not going to stand here and explain myself to you. And I certainly am not going to apologize for who I am."

"But Gage is such a wonderful man. How could you just toss him aside?"

Meredith smiled, but there was no warmth in it. Instead it seemed to add an extra chill to the air.

Darcy rubbed her arms.

"I suppose Gage is great for a certain type of woman."

Darcy squared her shoulders. "And what kind of woman would that be?"

"Someone who is naïve and foolish enough to stand in the middle of a parking lot presuming to lecture someone they know nothing about on something they have no knowledge about."

"I know what's important."

"Of course you do, dear."

"Wow. Everything that comes out of you is ugly. Guess that makes sense if that's all that's inside."

"I've wasted enough time in this dead-end place talking to people who aren't going anywhere. And that includes you." Meredith climbed in her SUV and slammed the door.

Darcy stepped back as Meredith reversed out of the spot. "I'd rather not go anywhere than turn into a shrew like you," she yelled as Meredith drove away.

Good riddance.

Straightening her jacket, Darcy took a moment to compose herself before heading back inside. She wasn't proud of losing her cool, but she was proud she'd stood up to Meredith.

Epilogue

Careful to avoid the icy patches, Landon hobbled on crutches beside his fiancée. *My fiancée.* He didn't think he'd ever cease thanking God for her. God had blessed him abundantly, and he would be eternally grateful.

Piper helped him onto one of the metal folding chairs placed before Karli's closed coffin. He had wondered at the reasoning behind an outdoor service, but once he was snuggled with Piper under the blanket she'd brought, he approved the decision and began to study the beauty surrounding them—the evergreen tree limbs covered with snow, the freshness of the crisp air, the brilliant red of the poinsettias donning the pearly white casket. It was breathtaking, just like the woman beside him.

Karli's father, Bryan Evans, stood shivering at the foot of Karli's casket. He said he'd failed Karli in life and the least he could do was give her a proper burial.

The McKennas were in full attendance, along with Jake; Darcy St. James; the medical examiner, Booth Powell; sheriff's deputies Tom Murphy and David Thoreau, whom Landon had hope for yet; Megan Whitaker; and her cousin Tess. For a lady who tried to keep others at arm's length, Karli's life and death had had a profound impact on a number of lives.

He studied Bryan Evans, and the genuine remorse evident on the converted Mongol's sorrowful face made Landon realize true repentance could occur, even in the worst of offenders. Landon finally understood. People really could change through the transforming power of Christ. Maybe even his dad. Hope remained.

As the pastor began the graveside service, Landon clutched Piper's hand, so utterly grateful for the working of Christ in his life. The journey might not always be easy—actually, he suspected it rarely would be—but he now had confidence it would be a journey filled with purpose and at its end an eternal paradise.

∞

Gage knelt at his son's grave, clearing the tombstone of the snow and ice covering it.

Tucker McKenna
Beloved Son
Born August 9, 2002
Died August 11, 2002

"I'm sorry I haven't visited, son." Gage bit back tears. "I hope Cole and Kayden and Piper are right and you're in a much better place. That there is a heaven, and you're in it."

He looked up at the clouds, trying to picture the possibility in his mind and feeling utterly foolish, despite the childlike yearning to let his mind imagine. "I just hope . . . wherever you are"—he had to believe his son was *somewhere*—"that you're happy and that you know I love you." He clutched his chest, where his son's tattooed feet were imprinted above his heart. "I carry you with me every day. You'll never be forgotten."

A gentle hand rested on his shoulder. *Piper.*

She knelt beside him, and for once he didn't fight her tenderness but rather leaned into her, releasing the sadness he'd pent up for so very long.

After Sunday dinner with the McKennas at Cole's place, Darcy prepped herself for the good-byes. Her last meal with the family she'd come to love so dearly. She'd lingered as long as she could, staying through Karli's funeral, but now she had no excuse.

She'd watched, tears trailing down her face, as Gage knelt at his son's grave, and she wondered if she'd brought any healing or goodness to his world, or if she'd only reminded him of the pain. She prayed it was the former and would continue to pray for the man who had somehow managed to burrow into her heart, despite her utmost attempts to dislike him.

He laughed beside the fire with Cole as they joked about something. It was such a treat to see him smiling. She was glad that was the last mental picture she'd have of him. So when she prayed for him or he invaded her thoughts, as she feared he would, she could picture him full of laughter and mischief.

She hated to leave, but it was time to return home. Christmas was the day after tomorrow, and she wanted to spend it in California with her family. But leaving this family was proving much harder than she imagined.

Gage seemed to sense her preparing for departure. He looked up, and his gaze held hers. "You going?"

"Yeah. I've got an eight-o'clock flight."

"Okay, I'll walk you out."

Everyone hugged her so kindly and offered such heartfelt well-wishes, her reluctance to leave only grew.

"We'll expect you back here for both weddings," Piper said.

"Absolutely," Bailey chimed in.

Darcy smiled. "Wouldn't miss them for the world."

Gage rested a hand on her back and guided her down the hall toward Cole's front door. "So what now, Darcy St. James? What story will you be chasing after?"

"I don't know. Perhaps an exposé about Alaskan adventure outfitters."

"I hear they've got some smoking hot ones."

"I'll bet." She laughed.

"I'm just saying, if you decide to go that direction, I might be able to help you out."

"You'd do that for a leech reporter?"

"No, but I'd do it for you." He tugged the end of her ponytail. "And I wish you the very best."

She smoothed the collar of his shirt. "And I'll keep you in prayer."

"Of course you will."

"What can I say? I've been told I'm a tenacious spitfire."

"You can say that again. I've never heard anyone call Meredith a shrew before." His charming smile spread. "But it suits her perfectly."

Darcy bit her lip. "You heard that?" What else had he heard? The part where she'd called him amazing?

"Yep, you've got some pretty stout lungs in that little body."

"I'm so embarrassed." Heat rushed her cheeks.

"Don't be. I'm impressed."

"Really?"

"Absolutely. You've got, as my grandma used to say, hutzpah." Darcy smiled.

"Thanks for what you said." He brushed the bangs from her eyes. "About me."

"You heard that too?" Just as she feared.

"Yep."

She glanced down but then, gathering her courage, looked at him, into his gorgeous soulful eyes. "Well, it's the truth."

"Thank you for believing so."

"You're welcome."

He held her gaze a moment; then his charming grin returned. "So . . ." He play-punched her shoulder. "I'll see you around?"

"Wouldn't surprise me. Turns out Alaska holds a lot of possibility."

He lifted his chin. "I liked the look of California too."

"Then, I'll see you . . . one of these days."

He smiled. "One of these days."

She stepped outside, the warmth of the house quickly vanquished by the cold Alaskan air, and she wondered just how much she was leaving behind.

∞

"You're not peeking, are you?" Landon asked, his hands gripping her shoulders, guiding her along.

"You've got me blindfolded; I couldn't peek if I wanted to." She couldn't see a thing, yet she felt so safe.

"Exactly why I have you blindfolded—because otherwise you'd peek."

"That's not true." He knew her well.

"Come on, Piper; it's me. I know you."

She bit her bottom lip. "Fine. I might have peeked."

He chuckled, the sound vibrating through his throat nuzzled against her neck. He was so close and smelled so good and . . ."How much longer?"

"You're awfully impatient. I thought you loved surprises."

"I do."

"Good. Just a few more steps."

She continued to let him guide her. She could tell they were in the forest, surrounded by the scent of evergreens but not far from the shore. She could hear the lap of waves against the beach.

"Okay. I'm going to have to take your blindfold off for this part, but your Christmas present is up top."

"Okay." Curiosity flowed through her as the cloth slipped from her eyes.

A tree trunk. Not what she'd been expecting.

"Up."

She followed the line of his outstretched hand to a tree house nestled high in the branches.

She looked back at him, catching a glimpse of his cabin in the distance. "You built me a tree house?" It was so cool. Just like the one she'd had as a kid. "But when did you . . . ?"

"Your brothers helped me when you went Christmas shopping with Kayden."

"Wow. You work fast."

"We had a mission."

"You sound like Gage."

"You should have seen him. Came with every tool known to man."

"I can only imagine."

"Shall we go up? I'm sure you're dying to know what your present is."

"Huh? I thought the tree house . . ."

He smirked. "There you go thinking again."

"Ha. Ha. Very funny."

Landon grasped the rope ladder and held it steady for her. Once she was on the platform, he followed her up.

The tree house was adorable. Two large rectangular windows were cut on both the north and south sides. A roof hung overhead and a large platform deck wrapped all around. She moved to the south window and stared out at the ocean lapping against Tariuk's shore. "The view is fabulous."

"Yes it is," he said, leaning against the wall, taking in the full sight of her.

Heat rushed to her cheeks.

"But that's not your present."

"I don't understand."

"This window." He held out his hand, and she followed him to the north-facing window. "We may have to be patient."

"Okay. Patient for what?"

He shook his head. "Always so curious." He opened the wooden box built into the wall and pulled out a large comforter. "Take a seat."

She settled onto the bench. He joined her and wrapped the blanket around them.

Mmm. She could get used to this.

"Oh, I almost forgot." He reached over and retrieved a thermos. "Cocoa to keep us warm."

She nuzzled against him. "I don't think we need any help in that department."

"Patience," he murmured, more to himself than her. He poured her a cup and then wrapped his arms back around her. "Now we wait."

"For what?"

"You'll see. Keep your eye trained on that copse of trees."

She took a sip of cocoa, curious what Landon had in store, but as long as she was at his side, she didn't care.

"There," he said, straining forward.

She focused on the spot . . . on movement.

A moose entered the small clearing. Her favorite animal. She smiled.

"Wait for it," he whispered, his breath tantalizing her ear.

Two calves followed, one after another. The three animals bent, grazing on the foliage protected by the canopy of spruce from winter's harsh elements.

"How did you know they were here?"

"Harvey startled them a while back. I've kept him away from this side of the cabin, hoping they'd return. When they did, I decided to build you a viewing platform."

She gazed around. "A very elaborate viewing platform."

"Well, I wanted you to have cover, and then Cole suggested the bench, and Gage . . ."

She smiled. "I can only imagine Gage's suggestions."

Landon chuckled. "Most were outlandish, but he had one great one."

"Oh yeah?"

Landon nodded and stepped from the blanket.

She was about to protest, wanting him near, when she caught sight of the smile curling on his lips. This was going to be good.

He stopped in the center of the room and pulled a cord from overhead. The ceiling split and a flap opened out. "Sunroof." He grinned.

She stepped over to the hole. "Nice."

He pulled her back into his arms. "I figured on clear nights we could open the roof, spread out a blanket and lay here gazing up at the night's sky."

"And then?"

"And then you'll be my wife and we can . . ." He didn't finish his thoughts, just lowered his lips to hers.

Acknowledgments

Jesus, my Lord and Savior: Thank you for your abiding love and grace. I'd be lost without you. May every story be for your glory.

Mike: For always believing, for always being there, for loving me like you do.

Ty: For last-minute plotting sessions, for grammar lessons, Starbucks runs, for everything you do and are. I love you beyond measure.

Dave Long and Karen Schurrer: My amazing editorial team. I am so grateful for you both. It is a joy and an honor to team with you.

My Bethany House family: I am so blessed to be part of such a talented group of believers. Each and every one of you is a privilege to know and work with.

Dee: I thank God upon every remembrance of you, friend.

Lisa, Maria, Kristin, Donna, and Kelli: Thank you for sharing your lives with me. I am the richer for it.

The DEBS: Katie, Beth, Olivia, and Rel, I am so grateful God brought us all together to share this amazing path He's called us to. I love walking it with all of you.

Katrina Turner and Becca Addington: For your amazing support and for sharing *Submerged* with so many of your friends.

Dani Pettrey is a wife, homeschooling mom, and author. She feels blessed to write inspirational romantic suspense because it incorporates so many things she loves—the thrill of adventure, nail-biting suspense, the deepening of her characters' faith, and plenty of romance. She and her husband reside in Maryland with their two teenage daughters.

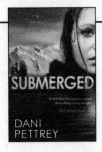
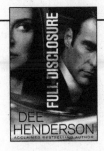